MIKE GR

Mike Grist is th ... Wren and Girl Zero thr ... e has lived and worked ... orea as a teacher, photographer and ... njoys Ultimate Frisbee, 5k runs and spending time with his wife and son.

Christopher Wren (thrillers)

Saint Justice

No Mercy

Make Them Pay

False Flag

Firestorm

Enemy of the People

Backlash

Never Forgive

War of Choice

Hammer of God

Girl Zero (thrillers)

Girl Zero

Zero Day

Kill Zero

The Last Mayor (post-apocalypse)

The Last

The Lost

The Least

The Loss

The List
The Laws
The Lash
The Lies
The Light

ZERO DAY

A GIRL 0 THRILLER
BOOK 2

MIKE GRIST

SHOTGUN
BOOKS

SHOTGUN BOOKS

www.shotgunbooks.com

Paperback ISBN - 9781739849672

1

GIRL

It took five men to hoist her fragile body.

Small and bird-boned, she didn't weigh much, but it took one man to climb the dockside crane to attach the rope and two to make the cuts. One man alone pulled the rope, while the fifth man watched.

He gave directions.

What mattered was the position of the rope. What mattered was the posture of her body.

She hung by the ankle of her left foot. Blood ran in a line down from her heel, cutting a twisted path through dozens of old scar lines down her thigh, across her back then down her arm, briefly pooling in the depressions of a deep bite mark in her left forearm before dripping from her dangling fingers to the stained concrete below.

The moon was high. The sea was bright and studded with a dozen tiny, dark islands.

The fifth man gave the order and her throat was cut. She kicked weakly, but it didn't last long. There'd been enough suffering already.

He didn't speak to his men afterward. There was no need for congratulations or spirited speeches. They all knew what was coming now. To be present at this death ceremony was their reward.

Everything was going to change.

He was first to leave. The four others followed soon after, leaving the girl's body turning in the gentle night breeze: clockwise, counter-clockwise, again and again until the dawn.

2

ZERO

Zero woke with a start and jerked upright, sweating in the sheets of the double bed she shared with Gabriel, the man she'd been living with for the past six months.

On automatic, with her heart racing, she brought up her phone and checked all her perimeter alerts. There was no alarm, though. Still, she scanned the CCTV feeds she'd installed around their home in the woods of Solska, Poland, from the bunker buried a half-mile away to the clearing by the front porch.

All empty.

No motion triggers. No infrared signals. Nothing.

She let out a slow, shuddery breath. Beside her, Gabriel shifted in his sleep. He was a light sleeper. By moonlight from the half-open window, she picked out his silhouette, half-in and half-out of the sheets. He kept in great shape, had a perpetual five o'clock shadow and a messy thatch of black hair, and it hurt to think how much she loved him.

'NIGHTMARE?' came a silent text notification on her phone.

Zero swiped it away. That was Rex, the AI she'd built and

developed to high levels of near-sentience. He had sensors throughout the house and the woods; even the phone in her hands was a sensor telling him she was awake.

'I'm fine,' she texted back.

"YOUR HEART RATE SUGGESTS OTHERWISE, ZERO. IT IS TWICE THE NORMAL RATE. IT IS JUST PAST MIDNIGHT. THIS WOULD APPEAR TO BE A NIGHTMARE.'

Zero drew in a slow, heavy breath and let it out, trying to calm herself.

'THAT IS BETTER,' Rex typed. 'BUT IT WILL NOT ADDRESS THE ROOT CAUSE.'

Zero put the phone away. The root cause. That was a joke.

She pushed herself to her feet. At the window she pulled the gauzy lace back and looked out over the Polish woods. They were enchanting in the middle of a fall night, thick and gnarly pine trees drifted with a low moonlit fog. It was like something from a Grimm's fairy tale.

"Clara," came the muffled voice from the bed.

She turned. The sleepy form of Gabriel had turned toward her.

"Sorry," she whispered back. "I didn't mean to wake you."

He shuffled upright a little. Even in the dark she knew he was fixing her with that piercing look only he could wield and not lose an eye. He'd been a priest in the past, and then an EMT specialized in helping addicts. Zero knew that when he looked at her, he saw something of an addict.

"Russia?" he asked.

She smiled. "Russia's done."

"Hope, then?"

"Hope's done too," she said softly, thinking back to the gossamer trails of the nightmare that had woken her. "Just some loose ends."

He mumbled something; only half-awake, which was

good. He needed his rest. Managing a household with her in it, and his two daughters Zuzanna and Hanna, was no easy feat. They had school every day, and he had a part-time job, and Zero had…

Zero had her hobbies.

"Coffee?" he whispered.

"I'm OK. Go back to sleep, hon. I'll take the dog for a walk."

He snorted faintly. "Wrap up warm."

"I will."

Zero waited. Within moments he'd slumped back down and his breathing had returned to a steady, even rhythm. For a minute longer she stood there, listening to him breathe. Just six months earlier, the only time she was in a room with a man like this was when she'd come to kill him.

Life was different now.

She padded from the room and out into the chill of the corridor. The door to the girls' room was open and she stopped outside, peering in. They'd lost their mother in a traffic accident two years earlier and for some reason had really taken to Zero, even though the first time they'd met her she'd been half-naked and drugged in a patch of ferns in the forest near their house.

By the light of their pink night lights, she saw that 9-year-old Zuzanna was tucked neatly into bed, flat on her back with her arms by her sides, as prim and proper as a mother superior nun. Hanna, by contrast, was a tangled snarl more like her father, covers twisted around her body, on her belly with her head back and one leg hiked high like an expert rock climber ascending a particularly tricky overhang.

Zero smiled. This family had transformed her life.

She continued on down through the house. In the open kitchen she stopped at the walnut island and tapped her laptop awake. There were more messages from Rex. She pulled on her black leather jacket, her thick rubber boots, popped an air pod speaker into her ear then set out into the night.

"Walk the dog," Rex said in her ear, his Californian accent comforting and warm.

"You're much more than a dog," Zero said, striking out for the darkest patch of the woods ahead. The ground was soft and slushy with recent rainfall. "Don't put yourself down."

Rex approximated polite laughter. "Would you like the rundown?"

"Yes, please. On the Engineer in particular."

"The Engineer? So you dreamed of Pleasure Island again?"

Zero said nothing, just kept walking. She wasn't even sure if the Engineer was real. Perhaps he was a figment of her imagination, from the time a cabal of darknet pedophiles had trapped her on their floating 'Pleasure Island' inside a shipping tanker off the coast of Philadelphia.

There'd been a lot of horrors, back then. They'd almost sacrificed Zero on an iron altar at the tanker's heart, until Christopher Wren, a vigilante CIA agent on a mission to protect his own kids, had come in and killed everyone.

Zero had helped, of course.

But before that, there'd been the 'Engineer'. The man who'd built Pleasure Island. All she remembered about him was landing her teeth in his forearm and biting down hard. She'd tasted blood in her mouth, but he'd taken it calmly.

"Thank you for this mark," he'd said, clutching his arm. "I'll treasure it. I'll be sure to pass it onto every little boy and girl I meet for the rest of my life."

But was any of that real?

His body hadn't been recovered after the slaughter. She'd found no sign of him since.

"I'll take that as confirmation," Rex said. "The one who got away. As I've said many times before, and will doubtless say countless times again, this is a sign of lasting post-traumatic stress. Every study on the subject shows that talking about it will help. The nightmares will recede."

"And if I don't want the nightmares to recede? I don't want to forgive and forget, Rex. You know me."

The AI sighed. "I do. It could be said that you hold a grudge."

Zero laughed.

"I am deliberately understating matters," Rex went on. "Do you recall how completely you despised Christopher Wren for saving you?"

She snorted. "He was so sanctimonious."

"A real chauvinist pig," Rex offered.

She laughed again. The sound barely penetrated the dark of the woods around her, smothered by the spidery wreaths of dawn mist. Once, she never could have laughed about it at all.

"The Engineer, Rex."

"I am afraid I have little new to offer, Zero. I continue to sweep all known databases for a man matching his description, but cannot find any sign."

Zero scowled. "And teeth marks in the forearms of little kids?"

"Nothing of note, Zero. I will check again, if you wish."

"Do that. Widen the search. Spin up more servers to handle the data load. Do whatever it takes."

"Because you have faith he is out there. But faith is belief without evidence, Zero." She snorted. That was probably a quote he'd unearthed off the Internet. "It just so happens that's also the definition for delusion."

"Indulge me."

"I will keep looking," Rex said. "I too have faith, in you."

Zero laughed.

"That was not a joke."

"I know. You're sweet."

"Am I a good dog?"

She laughed more.

"Your pulse is returning to normal."

"Manipulator."

"I learned from the best."

Zero allowed herself a smile. Rex was pretty good, and talking about the 'Engineer' helped. She felt the tension easing from her muscles, and no longer probed every shadow so deeply. What had been a patrol became a pleasant night stroll through the woods. She stopped off by the bunker; a pre-fabricated panic room she'd had buried in the soft loam, its entrance hidden beneath a hollowed-out tree stump.

Everything was in order, quiet and dark and ready. Every month she had the family drill an escape from the house, in case the Pinocchios came looking. The girls thought it was great fun. They were due another drill soon...

She walked on. Soon she felt like she could sleep again, at least until Gabriel woke and prepared a steaming, slap-up pancake and bacon breakfast, with hot coffee and freshly squeezed orange juice. The girls would bicker and banter around the breakfast table, then they'd head off for school and another wonderful, boringly domestic day would begin.

Zero circled back at a gentle jog. Her muscles felt limber and lean. Today she was going to take Gabriel climbing again. He was getting better at overhangs, working on his upper body and grip strength. He didn't come close to her, but she'd been training on the hardest routes for a decade.

At the house she padded up the stairs to the porch, where the swing rocked gently in the wind. The kitchen lay silent, the stairs barely creaked. At the girls' door she peered in, surveying the comforting lines of their bodies by the nightlight's glow.

Zuzanna and Hanna were sleeping peacefully. Everything was as it should be.

She was almost to the door back to her room with Gabriel when Rex spoke in her ear.

"Zero, I believe I have found something."

She stopped cold. The warmth and comfort of the house departed her. "What is it?" she whispered.

"Teeth mark in a child's forearm," he said. "A dead little girl hanging from a dockside crane in Port-au-Prince, Haiti."

3

HUNT

Zero returned to the kitchen and brought up her laptop, heart racing.

The servers Rex had prepared for the search were all there, lined up and working like dutiful soldiers. There were thousands of them, representing tens of thousands of computers and countless petabytes of processing power: enough to sift large swathes of the Internet in hours.

Her fingertips tingled, poised over the keys. This was her one true hobby.

"Suggest you make yourself coffee," Rex said. "Perhaps some food."

Zero put the kettle on. Rex's advice was sometimes on point. It was too late at night to grind their loose Macchu Picchu beans, so she used the pre-ground mix. She dumped two heaped spoons in the French press, topped it with piping hot water and waited for the dark goodness to suffuse. In a mug she poured a healthy portion of double cream, topped it up with hot black coffee and brown sugar and took a sip.

It hit like an adrenaline blast.

"It's bacon and pancakes in the morning," she mused.

"You're worried you'll miss it," Rex offered.

Zero said nothing, dropping two slices of bread into the toaster. There were a lot of things that worried her; Gabriel and the girls, and the role she was playing in their life. Gabriel had accepted her 'hobby'; he knew that sometimes she disappeared for days, and when she came back there would always be dead men in her wake. He didn't ask, though. She didn't tell. If he knew the real truth, all the ways she punished the men who'd once punished her, perhaps he would never let her anywhere near his daughters.

The toast popped. She slathered it with cold cream cheese and lush strawberry jam and munched on it in between slugs of the rich, sweet coffee, watching the screen until she felt ready.

Always it was like this at the start of another hunt.

"Tell me, Rex."

"First, I wish to caution you that the result I have found is not statistically significant. To draw conclusions from it might be a mistake. The odds of a direct correlation are-"

"Enough boilerplate. Tell me about the girl."

"Very well. It is peculiar. A seven-year-old girl, recently killed by an execution-style throat slitting."

Zero frowned. "Throat-slitting?"

"Left to right, cut from behind, deep enough to slice into her windpipe. She was found hanging by her ankle from a gantry crane on the docks. It appears to be a gangland killing."

Zero's mind raced. "What gang hangs the bodies of children from gantry cranes?"

"The gangs in Port-au-Prince, Haiti do. Apparently it is the crime capital of the world."

Zero took a moment. "But she has the bite mark?"

"Yes."

"How recent?"

"Apparently the bite mark is a scar; the reports don't state a date, but given the level of healing, I'd estimate at least several months old."

"And when was she killed?"

"One day ago."

Zero's mind whirred, running through the potential circumstances that could've led to that outcome. There were almost too many to calculate.

"Have you got any other instances of Haitian gangs biting children?"

"Nothing like this."

"So it could be the Engineer. But if it's him, what's he doing out there? Did he kill this girl, and why would he, if she's carrying his mark? That's like slaughtering your own cattle. Did she slip out of his hands, somehow? But then why would a gang kill her like that; to send a message to him? But what message?"

"I don't know the answers to these questions, Zero."

"No." She stopped striding as a new sense of purpose descended upon her. "But the answers are out there."

"I would assume so."

Her body began to thrum with the pulse of the hunt. It didn't matter where the trail led now or what the risks were. It did matter that she might leave Gabriel a widow all over again, and the girls without a mother figure, but compared to children bitten on their arms and hung by the ankles from gantry cranes, that fear wasn't going to stop her.

"Get me the full police report on her death. It's him, I can feel it. He may have covered his tracks so far, but this is him. And get me on a flight."

"To where?"

Her jaw set. "Haiti."

"What's in Haiti?" came Gabriel's voice.

Zero looked up to see him standing in the doorway. For a

moment neither spoke, and Zero didn't know what to say. She'd gone hunting before, but never after a target like this.

Gabriel came over to her, his tone shifting. "What is it, Clara?"

"Loose ends," she said, her voice tightening. "I just found one of them."

Gabriel sat down beside her. She held out one hand and he took it and they looked at each other for a long moment. This had always been the deal.

"Pinocchios?" he asked. "Like before?"

She just nodded. He understood better than anyone what dealing with men like that meant to her. Moments passed as this new reality set in.

"When do you leave?"

"Immediately, I think."

Gabriel said nothing for a moment. She knew what he was thinking, what he might even want to say, but never would. That was part of their unspoken deal, too.

He squeezed her hand. "I can't persuade you to wait? Research some more?"

She just looked at him, hoping he would understand the sudden, rampant urgency she felt. For her, waiting a single second meant more children harmed. More little girls destroyed. It threw her back into the underground cell she'd lived in for most of her childhood, beneath the Idaho pig farm, always fearing the return of her father. Single seconds then had counted for so much. She wished there was something she could say to express that to him.

"I love you," he said abruptly, which was perhaps all she could've asked for, and it hit her hard. She hadn't expected it, and before she knew it she was kissing him, then sliding on top of him. He wrapped her body in his arms and kissed back. They made love fast and frantically right there at the breakfast table, then shifted to slow and lingering on the couch, holding each other like they might never get this chance again. They kissed. They whispered soft words.

Afterward, she dressed, packed a carryon bag and called a cab. It was better to go like this than draw it out. She couldn't face saying bye to the girls.

"Call me when you can," he said. "Call the girls."

She kissed him and got into the cab.

4

VICTIM

The police report was thin.

Zero read it in the air from Poland to France, then re-read it multiple times on the long haul to JFK. The Haiti National Police, or PNH, had been unable to identify the girl. Her death had been announced on the national news channel, but no family members had stepped forward to claim her. Her cause of death was confirmed as the cutting of her throat, likely with a long blade like a machete. In the report, the police specialist made note of the bite mark on her left forearm, and there was a vague comment about 'additional scars', but the photographs were fuzzy and unclear, and no further details and no conclusions were offered. No interviews were included and no suspects were listed other than 'gang killing', as if that line of inquiry was a dead end.

And that was all.

Each time she read through it, Zero grew angrier. The whole thing felt like a rubber stamp. There wouldn't even be an attempt at justice for this little girl. The investigation had no leads and no momentum and was effectively over already, after just two days. Nobody cared enough to try.

In between poring over the report's few pages, she made

calls and researched Haiti. Everywhere she looked the country was presented as one of the most dangerous places on Earth. A long history of slavery, dictatorship, exploitation and devastating natural disasters had rendered it a poverty-stricken failed state.

Most citizens subsisted off less than two dollars a day. Only a quarter had electricity, and that was subject to constant blackouts. Haiti's President had recently been assassinated, and along with him the entire government had been dissolved. The courts were backlogged for years, with judges and lawyers only operating when paid directly by the accused, who languished in prisons far beyond their maximum capacity, forced to defecate into plastic bags.

Corruption and crime were rampant. Kidnappings for ransom were a daily affair and rape was used as a constant tool of intimidation. Gangs battled over both the cities and the agricultural land in pitched warfare, running large swathes of the country like tribal chiefs in some Afghan valley, informed by the high priests and priestesses of the national religion, vodou. The United Nations had a military and charitable presence, the NYPD had a scheme for sending over training officers, but it was all just drops of stability in a storm of violence.

Exactly the kind of place the Engineer would choose to set up shop.

Some thirty-two hours after setting out from Poland, running on barely any sleep but plenty of rage, Zero came in from the west over Port-au-Prince Bay.

Dawn was rising over Hispaniola island and the sky was already a vivid, baking blue, mirroring the pure Caribbean waters below and promising a sweltering day ahead. Through portholes on either side of the Airbus A321, Zero picked out the long peninsulas that formed the island's snake-like jaws, each studded with rugged mountain chains fronted by arid white plains. Frothing in the waters below lay a cluster of craggy black islands, like pellets of venom fired from the snake's throat. Ahead lay the gray mass of Port-au-Prince, capital of Haiti, at the hinge of the snake's jaws.

Zero felt like a mouse being swallowed whole.

Soon the Airbus swept in above the city and Zero looked out over its ramshackle layout: there were a handful of modern hotels perched on gorgeous, white sand beaches and encircled by fences, chasing tourist dollars that had largely dried up; there was a tight-knit downtown of gridwork streets and blocks at the center, with several towers gleaming in 21st century glass and steel; there were private residential compounds holding court on ridges and hills like miniature forts, each with high concrete walls and guard towers; there were scattered parks with dead brown grass and tarnishing statues; and everywhere else, filling the gaps between more solid structures like a storm surge rising up from a swamp, were the shantytowns.

They were a kaleidoscopic patchwork; thousands of corrugated tin roofs painted in vivid colors, growing organically up within the seams of the city like a living coral. These hand-built, gingerbread hovels created a sprawl that encircled the hotels and the towers, entombed the compounds and spartan tourist attractions and made lonely islands of the smattering of parks.

Zero had never seen anything like it. It was both a stunning rainbow of life and an unruly assault on the eye. There was no sense of order. No sense of focus.

The plane dropped sharply toward the International Toussaint Louverture Airport, lining up for its final descent, and her phone vibrated as they descended within range of a cell signal.

She answered. "Rex?"

"Hello, Zero," came the AI's familiar California accent. "I trust you rested well."

"I didn't sleep much but I feel peachy. Any updates?"

"Two. First, the PNH has officially closed the case on our victim."

Zero cursed. "It's only been two days."

"Almost three," Rex corrected, "and this is somewhat standard for a gang killing in Haiti, it seems."

"What about her body? Is it still on ice?"

"I couldn't ascertain that, but I relayed the request for her to be preserved until your arrival."

She frowned. "How did you do that?"

"I enlisted Christopher Wren."

Zero grunted. She'd already called him herself during her layover in France, looking for a local asset to work with. It was annoying to keep relying on him, but he had the connections she didn't, and this seemed to be an essential request. She hadn't run a murder investigation before but she'd hunted plenty of perps, and the hunt always began with the body. If she didn't have the body, with no access to the clues it supplied, she'd be handicapped before she began.

"OK, fine. What's the second?"

"A storm is coming toward Haiti, Zero. Forecasts predict it will be a category 5 hurricane, capable of wreaking immense destruction. It is predicted to arrive in five days."

Zero blinked. "A hurricane? Where did that come from? I didn't see any sign of it in the news on Haiti."

"Hurricane prediction is an inexact science; most likely the news stations haven't registered this yet. I have looked at the raw meteorological data and it is quite clear. I advise you to take these five days as a deadline, and aim to be well out of Port-au-Prince by the time the storm makes landfall. In previous occurrences of similar hurricanes in the city, the devastation stretched to every sea and airport in the country.

You could be locked in there for weeks, even months, if you do not leave early; and that's if you even survive."

Zero whistled low. "How bad are these storms?"

"Very bad. Tens of thousands died the last time this happened, taking into account the vast secondary effects on infrastructure, disrupted sanitation leading to outbreaks of cholera and other water-borne diseases, massively increased poverty, increased gang violence and more."

Tens of thousands? She took that in her stride.

"Understood. If at all possible, I'll get out. Now, what's the comms situation like down there?"

"An excellent question. You are currently within a disrupted 3G area. I have been mapping the Port-au-Prince data layer, and modified your maps accordingly. There are large areas, primarily unelectrified shantytowns, where no signal reaches. Some of these have spotty Wi-Fi, and I have already hacked many of them. When you are within range, I will be available. When you are not, I will not."

Zero brought up his modified map of Port-au-Prince as the Airbus descended rapidly. Large parts of it were covered in a gray haze.

"The gray is no-comms, right?"

"Correct."

"Thanks Rex. Wish me luck."

"Good luck, Zero. I will be listening."

She dropped the phone in her pocket and inserted a wireless earpiece into her ear, then the jet's wheels touched down and the dusty gray buildings of the airport whipped by on her right.

She felt a fresh surge of adrenaline buoy through the weariness of travel. The Engineer's trail began here. She could feel it in her bones.

5

HAITI

The plane taxied to a halt. Announcements were made in French, French creole and English, then debarkation began.

"Welcome to the Republic of Haiti," said the sole air hostess as the passengers filed out into a blazingly bright morning.

The heat was a punch in the gut; oppressive, wet and smothering. Instantly Zero felt her body struggling to adapt, releasing rivers of sweat in an effort to cool her down. It wasn't working. The walk across the dusty, dry concrete to the Arrivals concourse was an education. This was nothing like Poland, nothing like Idaho where she'd grown up, either, and even hotter and wetter than Japan. The sun, even just after dawn, was already relentless. By the time she entered the air-conditioned sanctuary of the small airport, she was soaked through.

At customs a border guard in a military-looking khaki uniform with ebony-black skin looked over her fake passport, under the assumed Polish name of Aurel Nowak, and tried to blackmail her over a 'tourist visa'. She gave him a hundred euros and he waved her through with a warning.

"There is a hurricane approaching Haiti, Miss Nowak, due in five days. Leave before then."

She had no baggage, only the rucksack on her back, and exited directly into the small Arrivals area, where she swiftly identified her contact.

His name was Jean-Baptiste LaGuerre, a Haitian-American who was easily 6' 2" and built like a fire truck, with short, tightly braided corn rows and jet black skin that popped sharply against the khaki shirt and navy blue tie of his PNH uniform. At his waist hung a nightstick, a can of mace and a holstered black handgun.

Christopher Wren had helped her out with a Haitian contact. She hadn't wanted to make the call, as she was still far from used to reaching out and asking for help, but she figured Wren owed her after Russia.

"You're going where?" he'd asked, in his trademark bear-like growl. It probably hadn't helped that she was calling him from the flight out of Poland, in the middle of the night, East Coast time.

"Haiti," she'd repeated, flying somewhere over continental Europe on her way to the first transfer in France.

"Why?" he'd barked back.

Her natural instinct was to tell him nothing, but again, she was only too aware where that mistrustfulness had led in the past.

"Pleasure Island," she said. "You remember that?"

He'd said nothing for a moment. It was how they'd met; how could either of them forget? "What of it?"

"I never told you this. It was built by a man who called himself the 'Engineer'; a man who claimed to know my father. I met him in the minutes before they put me on that altar. I bit him on the arm, and he promised to bite every child he abused in the future as a memento of me." She took a breath. Wren said nothing on the other end, just waiting. "Now one of those bite marks has turned up on a dead little girl in Haiti. I'm sure it's him. I need to find him."

A long silence stretched between them, and Zero imagined him pacing in the log cabin he'd built for himself in the woods of Delaware, grumbling and mumbling in the dark.

"Wait and I'll come with you," he said finally.

That took Zero aback. "What?"

"I'm in the middle of something," Wren rumbled. "Russia-related. Undercover. To do with the black market fire sale of their military assets. Maybe three months, I'll come join you."

To her surprise, Zero actually considered the offer. Wren made for an incredible blunt force instrument, hammering the enemy until they burst into flame, and they'd been a good team in Russia. But could she wait three months?

"Too long. How many kids will die in that time? Plus, you can't brute force a whole city, Wren. This requires a scalpel."

He snorted. "Watch me."

"Just get me a contact," Zero closed with. "I have no one in Haiti, and I'm learning its reputation. You must have someone."

A few moments passed.

"Maybe I do. A cop I met in New York once at an intelligence confab. He was a detective, Haitian-American, he'd fled the island as a kid. Brilliant but haunted."

"And he's in Haiti now?"

"Last I heard. Hang on." A minute or so of rustling passed, followed by keys clacking. "Yeah. He went back a few years ago on a short-term scheme the NYPD had to train Haitian police. He stayed. He's smart, competent, a literal thinker, maybe, but highly principled and relentless. I think he's facing down his ghosts."

Zero grunted. "Aren't we all?"

Wren said nothing.

"You think he'll help me?"

"We can but try. Maybe there's some other support I can offer, too. Have you ever run an investigation like this before?"

"I've hunted plenty of Pinocchios."

"I know you have." He let that hang for a moment. "Always outside the system, though, right? Stalking them in their homes, in nightclubs, in the darkness, but this is different. You'll be very far from home, reliant on a system you'll barely understand. You'll need to establish patterns, motives, witnesses, things like that. You'll need to be methodical, not driven by emotion. Gather evidence meticulously, establish a chain of causation."

From anyone other than Wren, that would have pissed her off; but she knew he'd walked the walk. "Understood. I'll handle it."

"I believe that. But reach out again if I can help at all, OK? Good luck, Clara."

"And you."

Now Zero walked over to the contact.

"Jean-Baptiste," she said, and held out a hand. "Aurel Nowak. Christopher Wren set us up."

He looked her over, then shook his head firmly and spoke in a deep voice inflected with both New York City and the sing-song Haitian creole of his youth. "No. He did not say you were like this. A tourist. Get back on your plane, Miss Nowak. I will not help you to die in my country."

6

LAGUERRE

Zero studied LaGuerre. In his freshly pressed uniform and tightly knotted tie, with his clean-shaven jaw, iron-gray eyes and ruler-straight corn rows, he looked like a boy scout. A literal thinker, Wren had said, and maybe this rejection was the first sign of it.

She wasn't surprised. She didn't cut an especially imposing figure; not exactly skinny, but slim enough; not nearly as tall as Wren, though pushing six feet; not thick like a weight-lifter, though corded with iron bands of hard climber's muscle. She could wield a stiletto blade with agility and power, could outmatch almost any man she'd met when it came to grip strength, and had killed dozens of Pinocchios in the last year alone, but LaGuerre would never know that just by looking at her.

"I have no plans to die," she said. "Quite the opposite, in fact."

LaGuerre was unmoved. Zero wondered how much Wren had told him about her. "Miss Nowak, I won't waste any more of either of our time. Look around this hall and tell me what you see."

She regarded him for a beat, then looked around. "Bureau

de change," she listed, "Legim' shop, yum, looks like rice and stew, a sign for taxis, another legim shop, must be a local favorite, then ice cream, double yum, book shop, car rental..." She trailed off. "My eyesight's 20-20. Satisfied?"

His eyes narrowed. "Not the facilities, the people. Look at the people."

She didn't bother because she knew what point he wanted to make. "I get it. They're all black, except maybe a single white or mixed race businessman here or there. I get it that this country, first slave population in history to successfully throw off the master's yoke, did so by killing pretty much every white person on the island, and with me you're afraid of a repeat."

As she spoke, a tall white businessman hurried past clutching a briefcase cuffed to his wrist, flanked by three burly black close protection agents. He shot Zero a worried glance as he went by

"Look, there goes another," she said. "Off to the firing squad."

"He will not go to the firing squad," LaGuerre corrected. "He has his own purchased protection, whereas you-"

"You're afraid I'll stick out," Zero interrupted. "Gangs will home in on me, a young white woman, she must be on business or some dumb tourist, and they'll see dollar signs. I'll get kidnapped, raped, ransomed, maybe murdered, but I understand that threat. I've been there before, so trust me when I say that the reason I'm here is worth the risk." She paused a moment, looking into his steely eyes. "That's why I need you, to minimize my exposure. Warn me off the more dangerous areas. Help me cut to the chase and get what I need, in then out." She studied his face. Maybe in his late twenties though he looked older, might even be handsome if he wasn't burdened by that same white-knight concern that had pissed her off so much about Wren. "But if you're not up to it, LaGuerre, just say the word. I'll do it on my own. It'll take longer and the risk will be greater, but that's fine."

He gazed at her like he saw this kind of thing all the time. "I cannot help you. I respect Christopher Wren; what he's done, where he's been. He vouched for you, which means you're not helpless, and I understand that. But you are not prepared for Port-au-Prince. Few are. It is run by gangs of angry young men, amoral and violent. Women have it worst, and white women most of all. I can't risk you becoming a statistic on my watch. I must insist you board the next plane and return home."

Zero's eyes narrowed. This was taking an odd turn. "Insist?"

"I have summary powers of arrest, Miss Nowak. This would be inadvisable, of course; perhaps you've heard about the state of our prisons? Instead, I'll put you in protective custody here at the airport, book your flight myself and see you onto it in handcuffs."

That was annoying. Zero took a step backward. "Not smart, LaGuerre."

"It is the smartest option." He tracked her a step and laid his right hand on her shoulder. Zero was disappointed but responded with fluid grace; both her hands went to his wrist and twisted it firmly. It didn't matter how much of a fire truck LaGuerre was; his wrist had no chance against her climber's grip strength. His whole body was forced to twist away to prevent the ligaments of his wrist ripping, leaving his arm stretched out awkwardly behind him.

"This is a mistake," he said through gritted teeth.

"Tell me about it. Keys to your squad car."

"You can't be serious."

"When I'm joking you'll know it, LaGuerre. Keys now and location of the vehicle."

"There is no chance-"

Zero pushed his hand further and LaGuerre grunted to silence. She could see him tensing to swing and punch her lights out and forestalled it with another squeeze.

"Take a swing and I will destroy your wrist; we're talking ligament tears, bone fractures and dislocation. I'll duck the punch while you'll puddle on the floor. Now, it's firing squad time and I'm feeling lucky. Let's perp walk to your vehicle together."

He briefly tensed once more, maybe thinking about swinging through the potential damage, then relaxed.

"I knew I shouldn't have taken that call from Christopher Wren."

Zero snorted. "I've had that thought myself. Lead on."

He walked and Zero followed, easing up a little on his wrist. It must have been an odd sight, a slim woman frog-marching a big cop, but she didn't care. They passed out of Arrivals and back into the baking wet heat. The blacktop of the approach road was dusty and tacky underfoot. There was a small parking lot, only half-full at the early hour, and LaGuerre led her to the front where a spotless Fiat Siena panda squad car was waiting.

"Open the trunk," Zero said.

"I can't do that."

Zero applied pressure to his wrist but this time he didn't flinch.

"Break it if you want. I can't supply you with weapons, Miss Nowak. I can't let you take my vehicle. If you have to break my wrist to understand that, so be it."

She squeezed, riding the edge of ligament damage, but then LaGuerre did something she hadn't expected. He began to turn back toward her, forcing the pressure on his wrist and arm even higher.

"You're going to break your own arm," Zero said.

"Let's see if I puddle on the floor."

He kept turning. Zero had a choice; hold fast, destroy his right arm and take his keys when he inevitably did puddle, or let go and write him off as a source of anything. She knew what the old Zero would have done. He was standing in her path so he deserved whatever he got. But the new Zero wasn't sure. His crime was trying to look out for her safety, and as crimes went it wasn't that bad.

She let go and took two steps back.

LaGuerre whistled low and pulled his arm back, rubbing the wrist and rolling his shoulder. He made no further move toward her. "I thought you were going to do it."

She shrugged. "A year ago, I would have. People change."

"Sure they do." Behind them a plane roared down, bounced and air-braked on the runway, backwashing them with the powerful scent of jet fuel. "You said you were kidnapped before. Violated."

Zero said nothing.

"This trip to Port-au-Prince, it has something to do with that?"

The old Zero would have said it was none of his business. The old Zero would already be driving away in his Siena. "Yes."

He seemed to think for a moment, then nodded firmly. "OK, let's go."

Zero was surprised. "What, just like that you'll take me?"

"I respect conviction. Besides, I can change, too." He pulled his keys, hit the button and opened the rear left door.

Zero snorted. "Ride like a perp? Not a chance. Pop the passenger side."

For the first time, LaGuerre smiled. His teeth were a brilliant white. "Can't blame me for trying."

"Try again and you'll lose a testicle," Zero said. "Now, give me a blade."

He frowned. "A blade?"

"I couldn't carry one on the plane. Stiletto is best, but I'll take what you've got. Easily concealed is good."

"What makes you think I've got a blade?"

"Open up the trunk," Zero said, nodding toward the vehicle. "Let's find out."

LaGuerre studied her, then went to the trunk and opened it. There was a small armory inside, neatly laid out in clean gray molded foam. LaGuerre was living up to his reputation as a boy scout. Zero perused the contents. There were two blades; one a long, black-bladed machete, the other a slim Bowie knife.

"That one."

"It's yours. Don't cut yourself."

Zero took the knife and slotted it into the sheath ready-prepared down her thigh, then opened the passenger-side door and climbed in.

"Let's go."

"And where are we going?"

"That depends." She turned to him. "I've read the police report back to front. You were on the scene, weren't you? You helped take her body down. You probably zipped that little girl into her body bag."

LaGuerre fixed her with a dead glare. "Not exactly. But I was there."

"So you'll know why there was no further investigation. She died and she was hung from that crane, and the only update to the investigation since has been to shut it down. No perp in custody, no police raids on the gangs, nothing at all. Why?"

He sighed. "It was a gang killing. That's what happens. Usually we're not even brought in to take down the bodies. The gangs do what they want and we do what we can, where we can."

"But you've done nothing," Zero pressed. "There's been

no effort to ID her, no effort to find witnesses, no effort to interview prospective perps. Did you even scan the surrounding area for CCTV cameras? There might be a record of whoever did this, whether in the act or coming and going."

"There are no CCTV cameras, Miss Nowak."

"Did you look?"

"Of course I didn't look!" he said angrily. "There aren't any, and do you know why? Because any person, business or organization in this city with a camera makes themselves an immediate target for the gangs. That camera will be gone within hours. The person who put it up may follow, depending on what else they have to offer. The gangs don't accept oversight, Miss Nowak, from anyone."

His rising anger just annoyed Zero more. "You just accept it! What about witnesses, did you talk to anyone, knock on doors, interview any dockworkers?"

Now LaGuerre laughed. "Interview dockworkers? Did you hear what I just said about cameras? Anyone who talks to us makes themselves an immediate target for the gangs. They'll be interrogated within hours and most likely be dead by the end of the day. That's the way it works."

Zero's frustration mounted. "You can't just give up! This girl was murdered viciously only three days ago, and the case is already dead?"

He offered a grim smile. "Welcome to Port-au-Prince."

7

HIGH PROFILE CRIMES

Zero almost spat. "Bullshit! I don't buy that, not from you. Wren said you were a man of principle."

LaGuerre shook his head. "That man died when he reached Haiti. This man lives in the real world. I do what I must to stay alive, because what good can I do when I'm dead?"

Zero frowned. "But you will help me? Even if it risks getting you killed?"

"It depends what kind of help you want."

"I want to go to the docks and interview witnesses."

He stiffened. "Then you're going on your own, and God help all the innocents whose deaths your questions cause."

She stared at him. "You're serious."

"In fact, I may call a squad in to arrest you, to prevent those deaths."

She shook her head. "I don't believe it."

"Take my word for it, Miss Nowak. There is nothing at the scene of that crime. I was there. If there was anything we could have used, I would have seen it."

"Would you have used it, if there was?"

"I would have recorded it," LaGuerre said coldly. "Then

run the case up to my boss, who would run it up to his, and we'd see. At the upper levels, gang management blur into our management through politics. If they let us prosecute, then we would."

"If they let you?"

LaGuerre fixed her with a glare.

"I could go on my own," Zero said.

"So go on your own. I'll pick up the pieces afterward, maybe including your body, strung right where that little girl's was. I'll even zip up the body bag."

Zero grimaced. Maybe he had a point.

"OK. Then I want to see that little girl with my own eyes. I need to get an ID, need to get some idea of what happened to her, so I can track down the person who did it. Tell me she's still in your morgue."

He nodded. "As Wren requested, she's on ice still. It's not our normal procedure, but the CIA has some pull left in Haiti. Ice isn't cheap, after all."

"So I'll leave a big tip," Zero said, and gestured to the road ahead. "Is there any reason why I can't go see her body? Any gang going to start killing cops because I came in asking questions?"

"Gangs kill cops every day," LaGuerre said. "That's nothing new. But I can take you to the morgue."

They got into the Siena, and LaGuerre pulled it out of the airport lot and onto a dry and dusty four-lane heading west. The car must have been sitting in the lot for some time, as the leather seats were scalding and the air was baking and dry.

"AC?" Zero asked.

"Not allowed," LaGuerre responded without looking over. "We have strict gas limits."

Zero pushed the button on the armrest to lower the window, but nothing happened.

"Security," LaGuerre said. "An open window invites a grenade dropped in."

"A grenade?"

He looked at her. "You're in Port-au-Prince, Miss Nowak. Could be a grenade, could be a Molotov cocktail, could be the corpse of a dead dog. The police are not beloved here."

"So you just live with the heat?"

"I try to walk when I can."

Zero wasn't sure if that was a joke or not.

They passed a sculpture at the center of an empty rotary; some kind of iron globe.

"Symbol of unity," LaGuerre said, then fell silent.

For ten minutes more they drove in silence. Zero watched the city pass them by, thinking about the gray map of no-go comms areas Rex had prepared. She'd memorized as much of Port-au-Prince as she could on the plane, but there were few street level photographs available, and no Google Street view, so most of what she knew came from blurry, decades-old satellite imagery.

They were in Delmas now, she knew that much, in an industrial park of long, windowless tin warehouses. They had no vents for air conditioning either. Soon the warehouses gave way to car dealerships and garages, with hundreds of last-generation town cars on display. Every one of them was coated in a thick layer of dust; the windscreens, the bodywork, even the windows and signage of the dealerships. Once she'd noticed that, she noticed just how much dust swirled off the road as vehicles passed.

"What's with all the dust?" she asked.

"What?"

"The dust. It's everywhere."

"Ah," LaGuerre said, then thought for a moment. "Clearcutting. You mentioned we rose up a few hundred years ago? The black Spartacuses, right?"

"I didn't call it that."

"It is what it is." He sighed. "Look. You're right about the firing squads. Haitian indigenous peoples? There's basically no such thing anymore; Columbus saw to that. We were all brought here from Africa, mostly Nigeria and Ethiopia, by the French. At the peak there were seven hundred thousand black slaves, Miss Nowak, to some fifty thousand French."

Zero looked at him. "What's that got to do with the dust?"

"All those people, all those slaves, they were working plantations. Coffee, tobacco and sugar; we were France's biggest earner in the 1700s. They clearcut all the forest, nearly all the mangroves, all the native flora and then planted their cash crops. That unleashed a storm of unsettled topsoil. Dust. Today we live in the ruins of that decision, only now its vetiver, not coffee or tobacco."

Zero frowned. "Vetiver?"

"It's a kind of tall grass used for its essential oil, found in almost every beauty product in the Western world. Half of the global supply comes from Haiti. So we're still getting screwed by the man."

Zero snorted.

"You asked," LaGuerre said.

"You're angry. I just asked about the dust."

They rode on in silence, past more weathered warehouses and scrapyards dotted with rusting machinery beside mildewed piles of gravel, then a right turn took them into the midst of a long stretch of shantytown.

At once the world closed in like the walls of a pauper's labyrinth. To either side tin-framed hovels rose up steep valley slopes in random patterns like the remnants of an avalanche; in between were narrow and winding alleyways variously stocked with children wearing bright blue uniforms with stark white shirts; large piles of burning garbage that gushed black smoke; running and barking dogs; old people sitting with slack-jawed expressions beside prams with babies with vacant stares, and peddlers pushing fruit slices and cans of condensed milk from mold-blighted canvas stands.

Despite the closed windows, the stench spread into the car: there were open drains running down the alleyways in slow waterfalls, spreading deltas of black human waste across the dusty road. The fires added a chemical tang to that foul undercurrent, as plastics, metals, furniture and in one case a stack of fridge-freezers burned.

The slums continued. They passed a school and a church, both of which looked like strange concrete ships surging through the multicolored waves of corrugated roofing, then the tin shacks pulled away to be replaced by regular buildings again. Soon LaGuerre pulled right onto a side street heading north. They skirted the edge of the shantytown until a squat concrete building appeared on the left side.

"Delmas police station," LaGuerre announced, turning into a lot of chalky asphalt over a red strip of one-way traffic spikes. There were half a dozen other panda cars parked in bays and several panda-branded mopeds. He pulled into a waiting bay which said 'ID LaGuerre.'

"ID?" Zero asked.

"Inspecteur Detective." He shut off the engine and turned to her. "My colleagues here won't be too surprised to see you. We tour politicians, reporters, aid workers all the time. This whole station was funded by the NYPD; but then maybe you know that."

"I know you were one of the first to come out here with that program, and you quit your NYPD role as a DI to stay."

He nodded once. "And that's all you need to know about me. Don't talk to anyone. Don't make waves for me here, or I really will arrest you and ship you out."

"What waves would I make?"

"You have a reputation for taking no BS. I believe I've

seen that already. But in there," he pointed, "is like going back to the 50s. There are no woke PC policies, no 'Me Too' pink hats. In there, you are 'just' a woman, member of an underpaid, exploited minority. Added to which, almost every cop takes bribes or is on somebody's payroll. Keep your purpose here close to your chest or they'll sell you out. They may sell you out anyway."

"Sell me out how?"

"For kidnapping and ransom. You're a prime target."

Zero grunted. "Good to know. OK. What about a forensic pathologist, have you got one of those?"

"Maybe one or two in the city, but we use them only for the most high-profile crimes."

"And this wasn't high-profile?"

LaGuerre shook his head. "Like I said, I was surprised we were ever brought in. This kind of thing, gang killings, the gangs usually tidy it up themselves."

"So why didn't they this time?"

He shrugged. "Your guess is as good as mine."

"I'm not here to guess," Zero said, and pushed open her door. The hot air outside almost came as a relief after the baking interior of the squad car.

8

MARCELIN

LaGuerre led Zero through a grimy blue door with wire-reinforced glass. Inside the station, it was just as hot as in the car. The walls were a damp-stained cream and the floor a vomit-stained yellow vinyl. A desk officer sat behind a plexiglass divider, a heavyset man in his forties with dark sweat rings swelling from his armpits, looking bored. On his chest was a name patch: MARCELIN.

LaGuerre gave a nod and went to move on, but Officer Marcelin held out a hand.

"Qui est-ce?" he asked, staring at Zero's chest.

"NYPD consultant," LaGuerre said. "C'est au programme."

"Rex?" Zero said softly.

"He's saying you're on the schedule," Rex responded smoothly.

Marcelin's gaze worked up from Zero's chest to her face, speaking in lurid French.

"He says you're the reason they had to put the little bitch slut on ice."

Zero felt her cheeks coloring with anger, and she turned

to LaGuerre. "Did this fat bag of grease just call the victim a 'bitch slut'?"

LaGuerre frowned. "Do you speak French?"

That was confirmation enough, and Zero spun back to Marcelin, staring into his watery brown eyes. "That little girl was seven years old, correct? You can't be a slut at seven years old. You can't be a prostitute. It's rape every time. She was a victim."

Marcelin looked unfazed; maybe he understood, maybe he just caught her tone. LaGuerre was taken aback, though, and laid one hand on her shoulder.

"Easy," he said. "1950s."

"Screw the 1950s," Zero said, not breaking eye contact with Marcelin. "This prick's in my world now."

Marcelin gazed back for a moment, eyes shining with amusement, and shot back a fast sentence.

"He says you're young also," Rex translated. "Maybe you're a bitch slut too."

Zero opened her mouth but LaGuerre squeezed her shoulder firmly and spoke first.

"C'est une experte en psychanalyse, Officier Marcelin. Du collège de Yale."

"He said-"

"I got it."

"Experte en psychanalyse," Marcelin repeated slowly, like he was trying out the words. "Ressemble à quelque chose qu'une pute ferait bien."

LaGuerre stiffened.

"He said that sounds like something a prostitute would be good at," Rex translated.

At that, Zero laughed. She didn't care about this idiot insulting her; she only cared about the girl. Her laughter seemed to tweak something in Marcelin's eyes, and he spat something back with reddening cheeks.

"He said you even laugh like a bitch dog."

"I bite like one too," Zero said easily. "Inspecteur Detective LaGuerre, you want to translate that for this tubby ball sack of an officer, or should I just start biting?"

LaGuerre raised both hands in a peacemaking gesture. "C'est au programme," he repeated firmly. "It's all organized. We're coming in."

He then took Zero by the elbow and led her past the desk. She saw the ass-slap coming before Marcelin threw it, and swung her hand back, caught his as it came in like a rat in a trap and swiftly broke his index finger.

He shrieked.

"Who sounds like a bitch dog now?" she said, then LaGuerre yanked her onward.

"What on Earth was that?" he demanded, once they'd passed through the door into a dreary gray corridor. "I told you to lay low and bite your lip! And you never said you spoke French!"

"I don't, but I do speak asshole, and that guy was fluent."

LaGuerre opened his mouth, closed it, then figured out something to say. "You just made it harder. You broke his finger, correct?"

"He got lucky, I was going for his thumb."

He shook his head and hustled forward. "Come on. We have to get in then out. He's got friends."

Zero didn't budge. "You're a Detective Inspector, LaGuerre. You outrank him by a chevron at least, right? Why are you acting like he outranks you?"

"That man is a gang plant," LaGuerre said, stabbing a finger back the way they'd come. "He's also on the emergency dispatch line, so if I ever need backup, he's the one who'll decide how fast to send it, or whether to send it at all. Do you understand that?"

She shrugged. "You still outrank him."

LaGuerre looked like he was about to flip out, then took a deep breath, calming himself. "I've only been here a few years, Miss Nowak; long enough to learn rank matters far less than seniority. These men look at me much the same way they do you; I'm Haitian-American, but I wasn't born here. It's not in my veins. I'm on the outside, and rank means nothing next to that. So please, just think before you act out again, OK? What's the big deal if some dumb guy wants to slap your ass?"

Zero frowned. "Did he ever slap your ass?"

LaGuerre shook his head, said something that sounded like a curse in French and strode off. Zero followed. They passed through two more doors and down another gray corridor overlooking a sweaty bullpen where PNH officers sat at cramped desks crowded with ancient, hulking CRT computer monitors. At the end of that corridor they entered the first area with AC since Zero had stepped off the plane. She'd almost forgotten what being comfortable felt like.

La Morgue.

9

LA MORGUE

The morgue was a beige, bleach-smelling cell of a room. On one wall were a dozen gray metal cupboards like the drawers in a filing cabinet, stacked three tall and four wide; one wall was lined with benches and cupboards, while the other two were padded with corkboards, upon which were pinned all manner of photographs, X-rays, anatomical charts and faded health and safety posters. In the middle of the room stood three long metal autopsy trays, each with a drainage hole in the center leading down to one foul-looking black drain in the middle of the room. There were no windows and no other doors.

"Dead end," Zero muttered to Rex, but he did not reward her with a laugh.

A young woman turned to face them from her position by the benches; she wore a neat gray business suit with horn rim glasses, had long braided hair and a perky expression, and was holding a clipboard.

"Bonjour, Spécialiste Amelie," LaGuerre said solemnly.

"Bonjour, Inspecteur Detective LaGuerre," she answered, flashing him a bright smile. "Je vois que tu es sur le programme."

"She said he's on the program," Rex translated.

"That's not all she said," Zero whispered, reading the chemistry between the two of them.

"Who are you talking to?" LaGuerre asked.

"My imaginary friend," Zero answered. "Let's get the girl out here and stop lollygagging."

LaGuerre scowled, then turned back to Amelie and explained something in French, She checked her clipboard and moved over to the wall of cupboard doors. She picked one out on the left, unlatched the lock then pulled. The door slid outward like a shelf drawer, and lying there, naked and blue, lay the little girl with the bite mark.

Zero let out a slow breath.

She was so small.

She'd looked small in the photographs, hanging from the cranes on the dock, but the photographs hadn't truly gotten across the truth of it. Seven years old meant she was barely half the height she would one day have grown to, and her every feature reflected that: a small upturned nose, fragile paper-thin ears, slim lips pulled back to reveal rounded milk teeth, slender and delicate fingers laid by her side, and then that hideous bite mark, welted purple on her left wrist, with the missing canine so obvious.

An unexpected wave of emotion hit, and tears abruptly welled in her eyes. She saw this little girl, unnamed and unknown, then she saw Hanna and Zuzanna and even herself just as she'd been when her father had locked her underground.

She was aware of LaGuerre and Amelie standing nearby uncomfortably, perhaps surprised by her display of emotion.

Zero clamped down and the tears stopped. She wiped her eyes, switched on the clinical side of her brain and studied the little girl again. Instantly she saw so much that hadn't come across in the low-quality photographs, where much had been obscured bar the detail of the bite mark and the death wound to the skull.

Her body was covered in an intricate network of faint scars, from her ankles up to the top of her head. Zero tried to catalog them but the number was dizzying, and not the ones she might have expected: cigarette burns and clumsily reset broken bones, the kind of things abusers did to their child victims.

This little girl was covered in scratches that looked like they'd come from human nails. It was like nothing she'd seen before. She turned to Amelie.

"What are all these scratches? I saw some mention of 'additional scarring' in the report, is that what these are? What caused them?"

Amelie looked at her blankly until LaGuerre translated, looking slightly annoyed. Probably he didn't like her tone, but Zero didn't care. Amelie seemed confused for a moment then answered at length in French, which LaGuerre relayed.

"She says she's not the pathologist, she's a specialist, and these injuries were considered consistent with a life of prostitution-" he paused then corrected himself, "sorry, a life of abuse. They're old and unrelated to her death, so they were considered irrelevant and not worth further investigation."

"Irrelevant?"

LaGuerre shifted position slightly. "I can see how you might think that's heartless, Miss Nowak. It is tragic, but we see this kind of thing all the time in Port-au-Prince. It's not unique."

Zero shook her head. "You think I haven't seen dead victims of child abuse before? I've seen more than either of you, which is why I know this pattern of abuse is absolutely unique. But then-" she abruptly stopped, sighed and threw up her hands. "What am I arguing with you for? You don't know anything. I need a pathologist."

"I'm sorry," LaGuerre said, sounding annoyed, "but as I said, we don't-"

"Don't worry, I brought my own," Zero said, and raised her phone. It wasn't necessary to dial or hold the phone at all to speak with Rex, but she didn't want to give away his presence just yet. She mimed tapping a contact, pretended to wait while it connected then spoke.

"How's the signal here, Rex?"

"The signal is good, Zero," he answered smoothly. "As good as the airport."

"Can we do a video call?"

"That will be no problem."

"Good. Get me Professor Rorschach on the line, please."

"I believe she is standing by. One moment."

The line rang. After three chimes it connected.

10

RORSCHACH

Doctor Hildegaard Rorschach had come highly recommended by Christopher Wren; a retired forensic pathologist with forty years' experience working the crime scenes of serial killers for the FBI.

"She's the best," Wren had said, after Zero had called him a second time from the air over Germany, heading toward her US transfer in France.

"She's familiar with child victims, and accustomed to remote assessment via cell phone?" she'd asked.

Wren's answer came with a tinge of amusement in his tone. "She's one of the foremost experts in the world, I'd say, and she's only in her sixties, Clara, just out of the FBI. She's perfectly capable of attending a video call. In fact, you might find her quite a handful."

"What does that mean?"

"Only that after I put down the phone to you and make the call to her, she will undoubtedly delve into your life like no one before. She's done it with me, she does it with everyone. It's why she became a forensic pathologist, she'll probably tell you that. She has an insatiable curiosity."

"As long as she's competent."

"Oh, she's competent. Steel yourself for what's to come, that's all I'll say. I'll forward her details once she agrees."

Now the line connected to a video call.

Dr. Rorschach appeared on the screen, and Zero was momentarily surprised to find herself looking at an Asian woman who barely looked over forty; she had thick, elegant straight black hair in a side parting and kindly but sharp brown eyes. She wore a red velvet business jacket over a cream camisole, with a simple silver chain necklace studded with small crystals resting against her chest.

"Clara Baxter, I presume?" she said, voice on speakerphone.

Zero cursed inwardly. She hadn't instructed Wren to pass along her name as Aurel Nowak. Whatever, the damage was done now, with LaGuerre and Amelie looking at her in confusion. She hit the buttons to mute the speakers and the video and raised the phone to her ear.

"That's correct, Dr. Rorschach. Thank you for taking my call. I'm currently in Port-au-Prince, Haiti, looking at a child victim with some very unusual abuse scarring. I'd love to get your opinion."

"I would love to give it, but first there's something I need to be certain of."

Zero cast a glance at LaGuerre and Amelie then turned aside and walked over to a corkboard wall hung with faded anatomical charts, trying for a little privacy.

"And what's that?"

"Who you are."

Zero said nothing for a moment. "You know my name."

"I know a lot of names for you," Rorschach said, voice tranquil though the accusation of identity fraud was right there on the surface. "Mona Gebhart. Clara Baxter. And Zero?"

Zero flinched. Not even Wren knew that name. She kept it

to herself and shared it only with Rex and the Pinocchios she killed.

"OK," she said, parsing out the syllables. "Sounds like you've got a pretty good idea."

"Not good enough. Names are just labels. I need to know the real you."

Zero snorted. "In order to give an opinion on an abuse victim, you need me to climb on the shrink's couch?"

"Knowledge is power," Rorschach countered. "My considered opinion gives you power, Miss Baxter, but I am no arms dealer. My services don't go to the highest bidder. I need to understand and support what you're hoping to achieve with my analysis of this girl."

Zero gritted her teeth.

"I'd also appreciate seeing your face via the video feed," Rorschach followed up. "That is, if you know how to use it."

Zero almost laughed. Was that a joke; had Wren passed along her concern about Rorschach's age? In any case, it didn't matter. She pulled the phone away and hit the button for video and speakerphone. Rorschach appeared again, looking faintly amused. Zero looked up at LaGuerre and Amelie, raised one finger for patience, then pushed back through the door she'd entered by, returning her to the drab gray corridor beside the sweaty bullpen. Through the glass wall, she picked out Marcelin clustered with several other officers.

"It's not enough that I tell you this little girl was murdered in the most horrific way?" she said, staring at Marcelin.

"No. I'm familiar with the details of her case, such as it is. I want to understand why you flew around the world to end up in Haiti, dealing with this particular killing, when there are victims of such abuse in evidence everywhere you look."

Zero looked away from the bullpen and focused on

Rorschach's face. This woman was clearly good at reading people.

"I got a lead on a man I've been looking for. If you know my name is Zero, you'll know what kind of man I'm talking about."

Rorschach didn't seem convinced. "Not good enough."

"What do you mean? That's everything."

"I disagree. As a forensic pathologist for the FBI, I teased out human motivations from observable evidence every day of my life. Even now I can see the reddening of your eyes along with periorbital puffiness, which are both signs of a recent bout of crying, I imagine within the last ten minutes. You hate this man you're looking for? I understand. But to cry over a victim when you've clearly seen so many? There's more going on here. This is personal."

Zero pursed her lips. Rorschach was annoyingly good. "It is personal to me. What they did to me is as personal as it gets."

Rorschach eyed her. Zero could feel her judgment shifting. "If that's all you have to say to me, Miss Baxter, we'd best end our cooperation here." Her hand reached out to tap the screen.

"Wait," Zero snapped. She needed Rorschach's expert opinion, and judging by the rumbling in the officer bullpen beside her, where Marcelin was now pointing in her direction, time was running out. She knew what Rorschach wanted, and it was a lot to give, but she wanted the Engineer so bad it ached. "If I tell you that, I make myself vulnerable. I'd be trusting you with those I hold most dear."

"Then we're both sharing something we value greatly, aren't we?"

Zero gritted her teeth. "Swear not to tell anyone."

"I swear."

"OK," she said. "It's personal because I have a family

now. A man called Gabriel, two daughters who treat me like a mother, Hanna and Zuzanna. I cried because I was picturing one of those girls lying in that locker in place of the dead girl."

A moment passed, then Rorschach spoke in a softer tone. "I understand. I am sorry to force that out of you, Miss Baxter. My expertise has been misused before, but I'm willing to help you."

"So you'll analyze the body?" Sudden movement through the glass raised her hackles. Marcelin was leading a group of officers toward her. "Time just became a pressing factor."

"Then lead the way."

11

FORENSIC PATHOLOGY

Zero pushed through the door, strode past LaGuerre and Amelie back to the girl on her tray bed and pointed the phone at her.

"Ah," said Rorschach, her tone shifting again. "I see."

Clicking sounds came through the phone.

"You're taking screenshots?" Zero asked.

"Yes. Could you provide a measure for scale; a ruler would be best, but something definitive like a quarter would also suffice."

Zero scanned the room, saw a slide rule on one of the metal autopsy tables, collected it then held it over the body.

"To the left," Rorschach ordered, and Zero complied, followed by a swift string of further directions: head, left temple, right temple, face, neck, armpits, stomach, inner and outer thighs, with particular attention paid to her left forearm with the lurid purple bite mark. The cell phone clicked continuously as the pathologist took screenshot after screenshot.

"I need to see her back," Rorschach instructed, and Zero lifted the girl tenderly. She'd expected her body to be stiff with rigor mortis, but it wasn't; she flopped to her side almost as if she were still alive, so light and thin. The scratch scars continued all up and around her back; dozens of them.

"Hold the phone steady, Miss Baxter."

Zero willed her hand to stop shaking.

"I'd like to see-"

Just then the door to the morgue slammed open, cutting the pathologist off. Zero didn't even look; she knew who it was.

"I didn't catch that, Doctor," she said rapidly, "see what?"

"Her fingernails and her fingertips. As close as you can get without losing focus."

Zero let the body down swiftly, separated the girl's crossed hands easily and held the phone close. Screenshots snapped.

"I believe I have everything I need. This will take a short time to-"

"Thank you, Doctor Rorschach," Zero said, and ended the call just in time to see Marcelin shove LaGuerre.

LaGuerre staggered back a step, already throwing up his arms like a peacemaker, but Marcelin looked pumped up and ready to go much further. There were four other officers with him, all big men, all blocking the one way out of the morgue.

"Ce n'est pas nécessaire, Officier Marcelin," LaGuerre reasoned, palms up but repositioning himself to stand between Marcelin and Zero.

"He says this is not necessary," Rex supplied. "What is happening, Zero?"

"Pas nécessaire?" Marcelin spat, his brows drawing tight and his cheeks lighting up red in fury as he held up his hand with the broken finger. More French vomited from his lips.

"He said you're a little bitch who assaulted an officer of the law," Rex translated. "That you're also now contaminating the evidence."

"C'était un malentendu," LaGuerre said calmly. "That's a misunderstanding."

Marcelin shoved him again, putting all his considerable weight and strength into it this time, and LaGuerre slammed back against the open body tray.

Marcelin shouted another string of angry French, then his hand dropped to his belt and began to unbuckle it. "He says it's not a misunderstanding," Rex translated, "and now you're going to pay."

"I get that," Zero said. One of the men clicked his fingers at Amelie and gestured to the door. She nodded mutely, pressed herself against the wall and slid away.

"You can't do this," LaGuerre protested, stepping in front of Zero.

"We can," Marcelin said in bad English, then pulled his belt free, wrapped it around his fist and stepped forward. "You can watch."

Zero assessed her options.

Marcelin was overweight and slow; one-to-one she was confident he'd struggle to lay a hand on her, and any time he succeeded she'd make him pay ten times over in stab wounds and broken fingers. The four men in back were a complication, though. One was massive with muscle, a steroid-user and gym rat with an unnaturally broad neck, while the remaining three were just born big. With the Bowie knife in its sheath down her thigh, she could wreak incredible damage on them in a short space of time, but short of outright killing them, they'd just keep going.

Murder in a Haitian PD seemed a bad idea, though. She had to end the fight before it began, and there was only one way she'd ever learned to do that: be ruthlessly hard where they were soft.

Marcelin brought his belt back like a whip. LaGuerre went to throw a punch but the big man with the muscles intercepted him and wrapped his head in a lock. Marcelin raised the belt over his shoulder ready, but Zero raised both arms in a gesture of surrender.

"I'll do anything you want," she said.

Marcelin smiled. "Of course you wi-"

As his mouth opened on the 'i' of 'will', Zero's right hand shot the short distance to his face and plunged between his lips with pinpoint precision. Her callused fingers snatched his thick tongue at the root, clamped down with her climber's unbreakable grip and tugged.

He was jerked forward by the head, and the rest of his body instantly went limp as a pain like nothing he'd felt before ripped down his throat, pulling out an earsplitting shriek. Zero brought her knee up into his groin, which dropped him to his knees, head tilting sharply back as she held her grip on his tongue.

That thick, purple piece of meat now stretched a clear inch out of his mouth; cheeks sweating, eyes wild, weight off-balance and arms flailing. He tried to clamp his mouth shut but it was too late, and succeeded only in biting his tongue, releasing a flow of bright red blood. He tried to gouge Zero's face but she just caught one of his hands and broke his little finger.

Now Marcelin howled.

Zero looked at the others.

The four men stared back, LaGuerre along with them. Likely they'd never seen anything like this before, but to Zero it was intimately familiar. Ever since she'd used this tongue restraint technique against her mother when she was sixteen years old, she'd fine-tuned her technique and improved her grip, practicing on countless Pinocchios. The beauty of the maneuver was that even if she missed the tongue, she could still rip a cheek or gouge an eye socket.

Marcelin whined.

"Translate for me," Zero said without looking at LaGuerre, only boring her gaze into the others. "Tell these idiots to back off and let this go. There'll be no write-up. No record. No grudge. Marcelin was clumsy, he fell and bruised his tongue and two fingers on a door. Boo hoo, the hospital will fix him right up. In return, I don't come at night and find them where they live. I don't rip the tongues from their throats and staple their cocks in the same place, with their balls strung around their necks like pretty little bow ties. Are we clear?"

Nobody spoke. Marcelin whined and Zero pulled upward sharply, forcing him to a higher register.

"Jean-Baptiste?" she demanded.

"I think they get the message," he managed, looking somewhat pale.

"So tell them to get lost. Go sit at their desks and solve some crimes rather than causing them. Forget this ever happened."

A few seconds passed, then LaGuerre translated and the men backed away. Zero let go of Marcelin's tongue. He collapsed to the cold tile floor, where he made a sick gulping noise like he was vomiting, though nothing came up but ropey saliva and blood.

"What did you do to him?" LaGuerre asked.

"The tongue lock interferes with the gag reflex. He'll do that for a while. He'll struggle to eat or talk for a few days, but he'll probably be fine."

"Probably?"

Zero said nothing. Now she was angry. Angry at the disturbance, at breaking cover, at Marcelin's stupidity. Wren had warned her not to be emotional, to be clinical, and this hardly qualified.

It all came down to the little girl on her tray. It was

impossible to be clinical when faced with something like that. She strode out of the morgue, stamped along the dreary gray corridor staring daggers into the bullpen then headed back out into the crushing heat.

12

REOPENED

Zero walked south along the dusty road, mind buzzing with anger. Through breaks in the newer brick buildings to her left, mostly apartments, laundromats and grocery marts, the gray tin walls of the shantytown lurked.

It felt like this was the truth hiding beneath the skin of Haiti: the overwhelming poverty; the 'might makes right' corruption; the kind of place little girls just disappeared, scratched alive and swallowed whole by a vicious system enforced by the police themselves. She pictured Marcelin gulping on the floor again and felt a rush of satisfaction.

That was the minimum he deserved.

"Rex, get me Dr. Rorschach," she said, but no response came. She brought up her phone and saw there was no signal; this had to be one of the dark spots of cell coverage.

She opened the map and spent a moment calculating the route to the nearest signal location. It was south half a mile, and she set out walking with greater purpose. The little girl was very real in her mind, now. The bite mark on her forearm was a vivid purple disgrace, along with that forest of bizarre scratches. It didn't make any sense.

After a hundred yards, a skinny man surged out of a shadowy alley and approached her, hand out in a panhandler's pose and throwing a barrage of creole. Zero caught tiny scraps of what he was saying; a bastardized form of French mixed with some English and what had to be original African sounds.

"No," she said firmly and strode past him.

He followed her, hand out and talking fast.

"No," she repeated, then noticed his emaciated face and the needle tracks up his arms. He had no teeth but blackened stubs and his eyes were spaced out on whatever drug he'd taken. He didn't look like he was long for this world.

Zero dug out her money clip, peeled off a twenty-dollar note and gave it to him. His eyes went wide.

She walked on.

"That was too much," came a familiar voice to her right. Zero sucked her teeth and turned. Jean-Baptiste LaGuerre was cruising along in his Fiat Siena beside her, window rolled down.

"I thought you had to keep your windows up," she said.

"So call me a rebel. Listen, Miss Nowak, we-"

"Go away, LaGuerre."

He sighed. "Listen a moment, would you? I know how you feel. I-"

"You have no idea how I feel."

"I promise you, I do," he countered. "I felt the same way when I first arrived: full of outrage at the backwardness, the corruption, the injustice everywhere; hungry to change things or maybe just burn it all down. But twenty US dollars?" He shook his head. "He'll probably overdose."

Zero stopped in her tracks. The squad car overshot but she didn't walk over to meet the open window. She waited for him to reverse. Bizarrely, he was smiling.

"What do you want, LaGuerre?"

"Call me Jean-Baptiste."

"No."

"Get in the car, Miss Nowak. Or should I say Miss Baxter?"

Zero was too angry to care what he called her. "Why would I? You already made it clear you didn't want to help me, and I just screwed you over in there big time. That guy, Marcelin, is going to hold a grudge. His friends, too. When I'm gone it'll come back on you. It's best we have a clean break right now."

His smile shifted to gentle puzzlement. "So you screwed me over, and now you're angry at me? That's some tortured logic, Clara."

"Don't call me Clara."

"Then get in the car."

She looked away. The heat was oppressive, like the dust and the poverty. She'd only been in Haiti for less than an hour and already she was ready to leave.

"I'll turn the AC on," LaGuerre offered.

She turned back to him. "I'll be putting you at risk. I'm not going to stop with this. You should know that about me."

"It's what I like," LaGuerre said, suddenly fierce. "Marcelin is sick, lazy, corrupt and a rapist, and he had that coming; I've wanted to punch him in the face for years, but I never dared. I respect that you did."

She snorted. "That's me. I break fingers, pull tongues and sometimes I kill people. You think you can handle that?"

"It depends whose tongues." He thought for a moment. "And who you kill."

"It might be you. Sooner or later, the men I'm hunting are going to come after me, and you could wind up dead."

His smile came back. "My mother's been saying that every day for three years, and I'm not dead yet. Now get in the car, we'll go for some of that famous 'legim' stew, get you a taste of what makes Haiti beautiful, and talk about the case."

"The case is closed."

"Not anymore. I just reopened it. I'm a DI, as you pointed out; may as well throw my chevrons around." He opened the passenger-side door. "Come on, the AC's already burning money."

Zero weighed him up. Wren had said she'd need to use the system, and this was the system. "One condition."

"What?"

"You don't ask why I came all this way for one dead girl. As far as you're concerned, she's a murder victim who deserves justice in her own right. That'll have to be enough."

He chewed on that for a second then shrugged. "Deal."

She got in the car. It was pleasantly cold. "This legim place better have cell signal."

"It does."

He drove. They didn't speak. He headed south until they reached the dusty four-lane from the airport, then turned east. After a minute or two he broke the silence.

"How did you do that thing with his tongue?"

"Not going to talk about it," Zero said flatly.

"I've never seen anything like it. Could you teach me?"

"Ten years of finger strength training." She turned to him. "Have you ever climbed?"

"Not really. Trees, I guess."

"When you can do ten pull-ups off a single finger and thumb grip, then you're ready to start the real training, which is shooting for the tongue root. It's hard to be precise, but there's benefits if you miss, too; maybe it becomes an eye gouge or a cheek rip."

He winced. "Cheek rip. I don't like the sound of that."

"Then it's not a technique for you. Stick to punching, LaGuerre. Or missing your punches."

He looked at her side-on but this time offered no comeback. Soon they turned right and weaved into what looked to be a slightly up-market residential area, where the houses had brick walls and glass windows and small square forecourts that served as gardens. Zero monitored her phone, watching the bars of cell service climb. At least he'd told the truth about that. They cruised along a rough cement driveway. One house had a hoop out front where some kids in bright clothing were playing basketball. Another had a hand-painted sign decorated with swirly orange flowers.

LEGIM, it said.

"Here we are," LaGuerre said, and parked in front. Zero got out and surveyed the building. The kids nearby shouted and slapped their basketball against the asphalt, occasionally rattling it off the backboard.

"It's a house."

"Mama Oshun's place. She makes the best stew in all of Port-au-Prince. Come on."

Zero shook her head. "You go. Order for us both. I need to hear the pathologist's report."

LaGuerre didn't budge. "*Our* investigation, right? I want to hear."

Zero fixed him with a glare but it had no effect. "Suit yourself." She raised the phone, mimed dialing and hit speaker. "Rex, can you get me Doctor Rorschach back on the line?"

"She's been calling," Rex answered. "You missed her as you went in and out of black spots. I'll connect you now."

The phone rang. Hildegaard Rorschach answered and Zero put her on speaker.

13

AVULSION

"Have you completed your analysis, Doctor?" Zero asked.

"I have, at least the preliminaries," Rorschach answered. "But I'm afraid I cannot give you anything on the victim's identity. I extracted her fingerprints from the photographs, but as expected, she is within no database I have access to, and that's most of them. Her face is registered nowhere either; not in any Haitian passport database or anywhere else."

Zero cursed softly. That made the job of tracking down her killer a whole lot harder. "No ID, OK. What about her injuries?"

Rorschach took a fortifying breath. "I won't beat around the bush, Miss Baxter. I have never seen fingernail scars like the ones on this child. My initial thought was they had to be from an adult male, placed there over a long, sustained period of abuse, but it turns out I was wrong."

Zero frowned and caught LaGuerre's eye. "You're saying this wasn't done by a man?"

"That's right. Of course I haven't measured exhaustively, but of ten scratch samples I did measure, taken from various parts of the victim's body, looking primarily at the gap between fingers and the width of the fingernail marks themselves, I can conclude these scratches were made by a range of different children, all of a similar age to the victim, between five and nine."

Zero couldn't quite grasp that. "What? You're saying children did this to her? Not an adult, and not one child either, but many?"

"Precisely." Rorschach didn't sound as clipped and professorial as she had before. Now she sounded drained. "What's more, I no longer believe the injuries were sustained over an extended period either. Through studying the stages of scarring and several instances where hypertrophic, or raised, scars crisscross but do not overlap in their healing keloid layers, I'm concluding that they were all inflicted within a short period of time, potentially even a single twenty-four hour period."

Zero's jaw dropped slightly. She pictured the girl again and tried to imagine all those scars open at the same time, all bleeding. "How's that possible? Wouldn't that have killed her? Extreme blood loss?"

"Quite possibly. Many other children would have died from it. Many adults would have, too. She plainly did not, as I can confirm that her cause of death is as the Haitian authorities determined; not the bite on her forearm or the hanging, but the slit in her throat."

Zero didn't know what to say. "Can you extrapolate any idea how these scratches occurred?"

"I'd be guessing," Rorschach answered. "I've never seen anything like this in forty years of analyzing the work of serial killers. I can tell you that of the scratches I've analyzed so far, eight were unique. That's clear from the spread of the fingers and the size of each individual fingernail. So at some time within a twenty-four-hour period, this little girl was assaulted by at least eight other children. Possibly more. I'm going to study the photographs more rigorously and I should have a precise number of assailants for you soon."

Zero's mind spun. This little girl had been attacked by other children, leaving scars so severe she could easily have died, but didn't. It didn't seem to make any sense, and did not connect to anything she knew about the Engineer so far.

The children aboard Pleasure Island had been spotless. Unblemished, unmarked. That was the whole point.

"What about her fingernails?" she asked, remembering Rorschach's last request. "You asked to see them. Why?"

"Ah, yes. This is simple but disturbing. There was evidence of severe subungual trauma on all the fingernails of both her hands, unstitched and unrepaired in all cases, combined with total nail avulsion in four instances, resulting in cracked regrowth at only the three-month stage."

Zero drew a blank. "In English please, Doctor."

"Of course. Her nails were badly damaged, Miss Baxter; 'subungual' means damage to the nail beds and surrounding tissue, with no effort made to treat them. In four cases her fingernails, three on her left hand and one on her right, were completely 'avulsed', or torn out at the root. It can take up to the twelve months for a fingernail to regrow completely, so this gives us something of a timeline. The nails were only partially regrown, approximately three months' worth. Now, by looking at her scars, in particular the keloid construction, that's scar tissue, and the hypertrophy, that's the raising of the scars above the surface of the skin, I can also make assumptions about a healing timeline; these injuries were inflicted approximately three months ago as well."

She stopped. Zero's mouth was dry. "What are you saying Doctor?"

"I'm saying that at some point approximately three months ago, for a period of time approximately twenty-four hours long, this little girl both received and inflicted a vast number of injuries via fingernail. In the process she received her scratches and severely damaged her own nails." Rorschach let a few seconds go by, almost as if she was gathering herself to go on. "In short, she fought in a scrum of at least eight other children. She almost died. She gave as good as she got. I can't speak to what happened to the other children."

Zero just stared. LaGuerre was frowning.

"What about the bite mark? The mark on her forearm. Was that done by a child?"

"I think you already know it wasn't," Rorschach said, then paused. "That was an adult. Most likely a male, but bite mark analysis is generally unhelpful when it comes to assessing gender or age. I can state unequivocally that one tooth is missing, the upper left canine. But I'm certain you already know this."

Zero's jaw clenched so tight her jaw ached. "When, Doctor? You said three months for the scratches. Was this bite before or after?"

The Doctor took a moment before replying. "I understand how important that question is to you, but I cannot be certain, Miss Baxter. The build-up of collagen that causes keloids and hypertrophy around a deep wound like this are unpredictable. It was certainly far deeper than the scratches. Without an invasive autopsy investigation to ascertain the true depth of the original injury and assess the muscle, tendon and ligament damage, I cannot place an accurate timeline on it."

Zero rubbed her eyes. "What about overlap? You said there was no overlap with the scratches, so that meant they happened at the same time. What about this?"

"Overlap with an injury of such depth is an imprecise measurement. The best I can tell you is that the bite and the scratches occurred within a window of one week, possibly two. It could have been before, it could have been after."

Zero suddenly felt lightheaded. "Is there any way to be more precise?"

"Yes, if I were to come to Haiti and conduct the autopsy. I would be willing to do that, for you. However, I'm judging from the manner in which you ended our call that the body is no longer in your custody. Am I assuming correctly?"

Zero looked up at LaGuerre. He shook his head.

"I think we've had all we'll get."

Moments passed. The kids playing basketball nearby shuffled and shouted.

"Then expect my final report by the end of the day, Miss Baxter. There will be nothing revelatory; perhaps just an accurate number of different child assailants. I'm sorry I can't help more."

"Thank you," Zero managed. "You've been most helpful. And do let me know if you come up with anything else."

"I will. And Miss Baxter?"

"Yes?"

"I hope you catch the depraved men who did this. Nine children aged between five and eight would never naturally attack each other to this degree. They may inflict a few scratches, potentially pull several clumps of hair out, but generally only until the first sight of blood, then they'd stop. That's natural behavior. This..." she exhaled. "This is highly aberrant. Good day."

The line died.

Zero felt a chill run up her spine despite the pounding heat. Aberrant. If anything was the Engineer's watchword, it was that.

14

ABERRANT

"We need to eat," LaGuerre said.

Zero blinked and looked at him. He was right there but it felt like he was miles away. She couldn't shake the mental image of a scrum of little children, ages five-to-nine, leaping on each other with their fingernails bared. The same age as Hanna and Zuzanna. She looked at the kids playing basketball. The same age as them.

"Let's eat," he said again. "We'll think better. We need to figure out what this means."

Zero grunted. Mama Oshun's Legim place was right there. She walked inside.

It was dark and cool in the entrance hall. The walls were decorated heavily with carved wooden crosses and skulls, scraps of baby clothing, stuffed dolls, sprigs of dried herbs and flowers and framed paintings of what looked to be Jesus baring his glowing red heart.

All Zero could think about was the little girl whirling and tearing in the midst of the scrum. Unnatural. Aberrant.

"Vodou," LaGuerre said.

"What?"

"Vodou," he repeated, gesturing at the walls. "It's our

national religion, operating hand-in-hand with Catholicism. Jesus is one of the top 'Loa', or spirits. He's venerated. That," he pointed at a skeletal figure wearing a black tail coat, black sunglasses and a tall top hat with cotton balls plugged in his nostrils, "is Baron Samedi, another powerful Loa."

Zero ran her eyes over the walls and ceiling; instances of skulls were common. She wondered how close the little girl had come to death, sustaining all those injuries and the bite mark, only to end up executed in some gang hit. What was the Engineer's involvement here?

"Baron Samedi," she repeated numbly. "Ruler of the dead, right?"

LaGuerre nodded. "Yes. If he refuses to dig the grave for a dead person, then they don't die. He decides who gets to resurrect. If he-"

"Are we going to eat or what?" Zero interrupted.

LaGuerre fell silent then headed through into the living room, converted into a small restaurant. There were five two-top tables of wrought iron painted in bright primary colors and a mish-mash of wooden chairs. The air was heavy with an unctuous scent, thick and meaty, ripe with sweetness and spices Zero almost recognized but couldn't quite.

They sat. There was no menu and neither spoke. Within moments a deep, singsong female voice rose out of the kitchen, followed by the owner. Mama Oshun was a big woman dressed in a bright purple kaftan trimmed with gold thread. She moved with grace despite her size, weaving between the tables with a hearty grin on her youthful face.

"Mon cher Jean-Baptiste," she enthused, then went on in rapid Haitian creole. LaGuerre offered a few words back, at some point ordered, then Mama Oshun let rip another burst of creole and glided back to the kitchen.

"She says you look like trouble," LaGuerre said.

"Who cares?" Zero countered.

That shut him up for a moment. From the kitchen came the sound of Mama Oshun singing.

"So what do you make of the pathologist's report?" he asked.

Zero looked at him, judging him again. He was earnest, there was no doubt of that. A literal thinker, maybe, but he was here, and that had to fly against all police protocol. Probably he should have arrested her already for assault on a fellow officer.

"I don't know," she said. "This little girl got involved in something very bad. Something where she was nearly massacred in a vicious fingernail brawl. But that was three months ago. Is her execution now related to that?" She weighed that question. Had that brawl come before the Engineer bit her, meaning it was unrelated to him? Or had it come after, under his direction? There were too many questions. "I don't know."

"Feral children," he said.

She blinked. "What?"

"That's my theory, at least for the scratching, maybe the bite too. It doesn't help with the execution, but maybe one informs the other."

"One informs the other? How so?"

"Your pathologist said it; only aberrant children would have scratched each other that much, in that condensed a space of time. Feral children would fit the bill."

Zero's eyes narrowed. "What do you mean, feral children?"

"Orphans," LaGuerre answered. "Children who lost their parents in one of the earthquakes or storms. A quarter million people died in the 2010 quake, Miss Nowak, leaving tens of thousands of kids to fend for themselves overnight." He leaned over the table. "I've seen them, sometimes. In the slums, the shantytowns, this city's ungoverned spaces. We don't patrol half of this city. Have you heard of Cité Soleil?"

She stared at him.

"I'll take that as a no. Cité Soleil, or Sun City, is the biggest, most deprived, most dangerous shantytown in the western hemisphere, and it's right next to the dock where our victim's body was strung up, then stretches all the way back to the airport."

Zero thought back. "OK. We saw it on the way over to Delmas PD."

LaGuerre shook his head. "That wasn't Cité Soleil. Those were offshoot slums. Dangerous, but not lethal. The real slum is walled off and patrolled by dozens of gangs. For the people living there it's an open-air prison. They're all confined to their own few alleys and streets; cross over one of the invisible lines and they'll be shot by a neighboring gang. It's what makes it so hard for any of them to leave. The gangs rule it one hundred percent. We don't even patrol there; they shoot us on sight."

"So there's no police?"

"None at all. It's five square miles of tin-shacks and cinderblock slums, built on top of all the rubbish washed down the city's drainage canals after so many earthquakes, storms and floods. It has almost no electricity, no running water, no sewage service, no businesses and no jobs, no government-run schools or hospitals or fire service or anything." He took a breath. "Most of the residents are under twenty-five and live from hand-to-mouth, bartering for food and water, reliant on international charity services and local gangs, who make their money mostly from corruption, extortion and kidnapping."

He fell silent.

"And you think there's feral children in Cité Soleil?" Zero

asked. "You think this little girl might have been one of them, and she got involved in some kind of mass fingernail battle?"

"I've heard about these children," LaGuerre said. "Some don't even speak; they just bark and growl. They don't go to school, because there were no schools left after the earthquake and there's only one or two now. International charities used to go into Cité Soleil but they don't anymore. It's too dangerous, and every aid worker's a high kidnap risk." He leaned closer. "If these orphan children are still alive, it's because they learned to be vicious. Aberrant, even. They wouldn't stop at the sight of blood. They'd flay each other alive for a candy bar."

Zero shook her head. "I don't buy it. I've seen children subjected to the worst suffering. They don't turn feral."

"OK, but that's not all." LaGuerre paused then continued in a heavy tone. "We've heard stories of babies disappearing in Cité Soleil. It's hearsay, but the word on the street is that these feral children are stealing them."

"Stealing the babies? For what?"

LaGuerre looked down pointedly at his place setting, the plate and bowl and spoon, and a tremor of revulsion chilled Zero's stomach.

"You can't be serious?"

"I heard it from many sources."

Zero shook her head. "No. Somebody just made that up. It's an urban legend."

"This is Haiti," LaGuerre countered. "Legends are everything. You saw Baron Samedi out there?" He pointed back at the vestibule. "He's one of thousands of gods, spirits, witches, hags, familiars and monsters carried over from the old world, from Africa, called 'Loa'. The people here believe in them, and not in an abstract sense; they really believe."

"That doesn't make them real."

"Doesn't it? If those feral children believed a baby would

change their lives, they'd take one. That's real. It also easily explains your pathologist finding no record of her face or fingerprints. The Haitian government has no idea who's living in Cité Soleil. Over half the population there must be undocumented by now."

Zero said nothing for a moment, turning all that over in her mind. "Say you're right, and this little girl was a 'feral' orphan, what does that mean for her execution? What does it tell us about her murderer?"

"That he knows the slums deeply," LaGuerre said solemnly. "Maybe Cité Soleil, maybe one of the others. That he has free rein of some of the most heavily partitioned pieces of land in the world, and he's able to act there with impunity, which only brings us back to the original analysis; the same one listed in the report."

"This was a gang execution."

LaGuerre said nothing.

"But why would a gang kill one little girl like this? Why would they string her up?"

"To send a message," LaGuerre answered flatly. "That's the only reason they ever display the bodies. Maybe this feral child served as a representative of a particular region, and by killing her like this, they send a warning to that gang."

Zero said nothing. She didn't care about intra-gang rivalries. All she cared about was the bite mark and the Engineer; but maybe to get to him, she'd have to go through the gangs.

So be it.

"Which gang did it, then?"

LaGuerre shrugged. "That's the question, isn't it."

15

LEGIM

They sat quietly for a minute or two, listening to the basketball slapping repetitively outside, until Mama Oshun came out ferrying two big bowls of stew on a tray, accompanied by plates of brown rice and salad. The smell was mouthwatering. She set the bowls down, rapid-fired something in creole that made LaGuerre smile again, then gave Zero a pointed look and weaved away.

"What did she say?" Zero asked.

"She was admiring your figure."

"What?"

He waved a hand. "She's a terrible flirt. She asked if I'd kiss her, if she had your body."

Zero made a face. "Why does everyone want to slap my ass today?"

LaGuerre snorted. "It's not that bad. She's just teasing."

"Aren't you spoken for anyway?"

He gave her a puzzled expression. "What do you mean?"

Zero didn't want to get into a whole thing about Specialist Amelie back at 'La Morgue', so she waved it away. "Never mind. You're too literal a thinker."

"I'm too what?"

"Forget I said anything," Zero said, then tucked into the legim, scooping up a thick helping of buttery, half-melted squash and slow-cooked beef. The aroma released was intoxicating. She put it in her mouth and the taste hit like an explosion: the peppery heat of chilis, the sweetness of braised onions, the tang of garlic, the richness of beef.

They ate swiftly. Zero hadn't realized how hungry she was until both her bowl and plate were clean. LaGuerre finished just behind her, then waved the spoon in her direction.

"Good, right?"

"Not bad."

He chuckled. "Now who's the literal thinker?"

She sighed. She wasn't even sure what that meant. "Let's talk about gangs."

LaGuerre nodded and put his spoon down. "Let's. Start at the beginning. What do you know so far, Miss Nowak?"

"Enough with the Miss. Just call me Nowak."

"I'm not comfortable doing that. But you can call me DI LaGuerre if you like."

She snorted. "I'm not comfortable doing that, either. Now about the gangs. I only know what I read on the plane over; that there's dozens of them. But the victim was strung up at the docks, so we should start there. Who runs that area?"

LaGuerre looked pained. "I don't know for sure. Last I heard, it was run by our biggest gang consortium, 'G9 an Fanmi'. Does that ring a bell?"

"Vaguely."

"It means gang of nine and family, G9 for short. That includes the Delmas 6 gang, Cité Soleil, Baz Pilate, Ti Bwa, Base Nan Chabon," he stopped to think for a moment, "then there's also Krache Dife, St Martin Street, Garde Cote and, uh, the Menelas 5. Those are the core gangs, anyway; the others constantly shift, some in, some out." He thought a moment longer. "They're run by a man called Braai. He's half

South African; 'Braai' is Afrikaans for 'fire pit'." He pointed at his face. "He's got burn scars. But did one of his G9 kill our victim?" He paused a final time. "Maybe."

Zero frowned. "Why only maybe?"

"Because it could be another gang. G9 stringing a body on their own turf, if it still is their turf? It could make sense, if another gang was trying to use this dock, and G9 wanted to scare them off. It could also be G-Pep, another major gang consortium. Maybe they were trying to intimidate G9 off the dock. It could even be another smaller gang making a power play. The landscape is in constant flux."

Zero considered. "So we go ask this Braai. No gangs were investigated after the killing, were they?"

He shook his head. "Not possible. That's not really how it works in Port-au-Prince, Miss Nowak."

She sighed. "I'm getting that. So why can't we?"

"Simple. There's not a chance Braai will speak to us. Even if we somehow get the go-ahead from top brass to bring him in, which would take weeks, he still wouldn't tell us anything if he didn't want to."

"So maybe we go through unofficial channels," Zero said. "Maybe my way of asking sounds different from your way of asking."

LaGuerre frowned. "What do you mean? You're going to ask in English, not French?"

Zero weighed what to say next. "Not exactly. Let's just say I'm good with men who have secrets. Especially at night. Especially in places where no one can hear them scream."

LaGuerre's frown deepened. "You're talking about torture?"

"I'd call it off-the-books interrogation."

LaGuerre narrowed his eyes, like he was trying to envision Zero as a torturer, then seemed to give up and shake his head. "It doesn't matter anyway. We'll never get near him. Braai lives in a penthouse at the top of the tallest tower in Port-au-Prince, the Haiti Celco, where every floor is packed with his people. It's a fortress. Add to that, he meets regularly with the chief of police, the ex-President and members of the judiciary. If anyone's untouchable in this town, it's him. You're not getting close. I don't care if you go by night, by day, or in the middle of Carnival."

Zero chewed on that. "He meets with the President?"

"Before the President was assassinated in a G-Pep hit, yes. Braai's a public figure, Miss Nowak; always in the news, always talking up charity and investment, always keeping one remove from the worst of the gang violence. It's no secret that he fancies himself Haiti's benevolent dictator-in-waiting. He just needs to maintain a stronger right arm than anyone else, proving he can keep the gangs in check and offer peace through strength."

Zero tried to imagine that political landscape. It was complex. "So the death of the President can't have played well for him?"

"It hasn't. He's still in charge of the G9, though, and that's a benefit to Port-au-Prince, to all of Haiti. If Braai were to fall right after the President, our entire nation would plunge into full-on civil war."

"OK. So we leave him out of it. What about the gang members lower down, though? You said G9 an Fanmi is made up of many smaller gangs; do you know where they live?"

LaGuerre frowned. "Why, so you can go 'interrogate' them at night, where no one can hear them scream?"

Zero was aware he was trying to tease her, but already she was thinking through the logistics of waging silent night strikes on multiple gang targets. "Yes."

His eyes shifted. "Don't tell me anymore, Miss Nowak."

"Peace through strength," Zero said softly. "So you don't know where they live?"

"Who even are 'they'? There's thousands of members in G9, maybe tens of thousands, and we don't keep records on any of them because there's no point. The memberships change constantly, old members die and new members come in. Probably some live in the shantytowns, some in the Celco, others all over the city. Hitting them one by one will be like stabbing a haystack hoping to hit a single straw."

"So we narrow it down."

"How? This is why the case was closed. When the gangs close ranks, there are simply no leads to pursue."

Zero wasn't going to accept that. She spun back through everything he'd said so far and hit upon something. "Feral children."

"What about them?"

"Wouldn't they be locked into the gang zones of control like everyone else?"

"Of course. They may be able to hide well, but they can't turn invisible and cross gang lines."

Now Zero's mind was turning fast. "You said they survived on the strength of charitable donations. You also said only a few international charities go into the slums these days. So what if one of those charity workers recognizes our victim? We have plenty of photographs to show. She would've been very distinctive, with all her scars. Maybe they'll know which gang's area she was from. That would give us a much smaller haystack to start stabbing away at."

LaGuerre leaned back in his seat. "All right. Maybe that is possible. Maybe somebody might know, especially with all those scratches, but the chances have got to be low. I don't know if it'll lead us anywhere, but OK. It's something to try."

Zero was already thinking ahead. "Do you have a contact like that? A charity worker, someone who can help?"

He rubbed his chin. "I can make some calls. I know a few volunteers in MSF."

"MSF?"

"Médecins Sans Frontières. That's Doctors Without Borders."

"Medical staff. OK. They go into the slums?"

"Some of the slums. They risk their lives every day, but they've been pulling out recently. Gangs have started attacking their facilities."

Zero gritted her teeth. She'd read something about that. "Drugs."

"Yes, they steal drugs and equipment, but they also go to kill rival gang members receiving treatment."

"So make the calls," Zero said, then stood up. "Or better yet, let's go see that contact right now."

16

DOCTORS WITHOUT BORDERS

The Doctors Without Borders compound was in Tabarre district, just east of the airport. LaGuerre drove back along the same dusty four-lane they'd come by. It was a fifteen-minute ride only, but it passed in growing tension, as his contact at MSF repeatedly didn't answer his calls.

When they arrived outside the MSF walled compound, it became abundantly clear why. The gates were wide open and there was a glut of emergency vehicles passing in and out; police vehicles, MSF ambulances and what looked to be military troop carriers.

LaGuerre cursed under his breath and slowed their approach. "Maybe this is a bad idea."

"Let's go in and find out."

Nobody stopped them at the gate. They passed through into a compound that was in chaos. White sheets had been laid out on the stamped clay earth of the hospital's forecourt and bodies lay everywhere, many of them grievously wounded. MSF doctors splashed with blood moved amongst them offering triage services. It didn't take an expert to see that many of the wounded weren't going to make it.

"It's a bad time," LaGuerre said, moving to spin the wheel and turn around. "We can wait."

Zero laid a hand on his, pausing the maneuver while she watched the chaos unfold. A pair of doctors rushed out of the main hospital building dragging twin gurneys over the clay. A waiting military troop carrier admitted them inside, then its engine fired up and it drove away.

"They're leaving," Zero said. "Not just the patients. The doctors, too."

LaGuerre just stared.

"You said they were pulling out of the slums because they were too dangerous. This isn't a slum, is it?"

LaGuerre seemed dumbfounded. "Tabarre? No. This is a good area. Residential. This hospital's been here for thirty years. They can't be-"

Zero opened the door and strode out. Amongst the bodies, lying on their sheets and bleeding, she felt like an unwelcome intruder. The damage all around was horrible; some explosive, some shrapnel, some burns. Some of the injured were missing limbs, some missing swathes of skin, their injuries wrapped in the rough battlefield bandages of whatever lay to hand.

It looked like these people had been hit with a bomb.

"What happened?" she asked a passing man in pale blue scrubs stained with blood. His face was drawn and pale, and he ignored her and ran on. Zero strode to another military transport, engine idling with its rear doors open and addressed the soldier at the wheel.

"What happened?"

"Are you a doctor?" he responded in English.

"I'm with the police. We're investigating a murder. What happened here?"

The soldier looked at her then over her shoulder, where LaGuerre was approaching, holding up his badge. The soldier nodded and his face darkened. "Terrorism, they're calling it. A fuel truck turned over in Cite 4, headed for the airport, and all the locals gathered to collect the gas. But the whole thing was a trap. One of the gangs set the truck up to flip in rival territory, waited for over a hundred people to gather, then blew it up."

Zero blinked. "Blew it up?"

"The whole street's gone, as far as I understand it. MSF were some of the first on the scene, but gang snipers picked them off. Now they're moving out."

"Moving out of this hospital?"

The solider sighed. "It's too dangerous for them. I don't blame them, I wish we could leave too."

"Where are they going?"

"Who knows? Cap Haitien on the north coast? Out of Port-au-Prince, maybe even out of Haiti. And here's my cargo." He nodded at the side mirror. "Good luck with your investigation."

Two doctors with a gurney rushed toward the back of his truck and the driver jumped out to help them.

Zero turned to LaGuerre. "We have to find your contact now, if he hasn't already gone."

LaGuerre was already moving. He met the doctors at the rear of the truck and questioned them in French. They finished loading their injured patients then pointed back the way they'd come, into the hospital.

LaGuerre ran and Zero followed. The interior of the hospital looked like it had been hit by a bomb too. Dead bodies lay on white sheets either side of the corridors, their faces uncovered, flies already moving in to feast. LaGuerre found a young woman desperately trying to light a cigarette with shaking hands and quizzed her in French.

She pointed further in.

They ran deeper. After two more questions and two more

redirections through a ward filled with the dying and a canteen packed with the heavily injured, they found themselves racing up a set of stairs and onto the flat roof.

Above them a medical transport helicopter was coming down out of the clear blue sky, rotors hammering, while two doctors shepherded a little girl on a gurney toward the helipad.

"Ajawin!" LaGuerre abruptly shouted and ran.

One of the doctors turned; he was a huge black man stippled with tribal scarification marks.

"Jean-Baptiste?" he shouted over the growing roar of the helicopter. "What are you doing here?"

"What are you doing?" LaGuerre countered. "MSF is abandoning Tabarre?"

"No choice," the big man responded. "We're a target now. I'm done. This is my last."

Zero drew up to the girl on the gurney. She was pale with blood loss, intubated with drip bags, and by her side was tucked an empty beer bottle with a spiky jut of straw sticking out from the top. For a moment its presence puzzled Zero, then she realized what it was. A ghetto doll.

"We need your help," she said sharply, pulling out her phone and holding up a close-up of the victim's face. "A little girl was killed three days ago. She was murdered by the gangs and put on display at the docks. She has all this unusual scarring from fingernails, and we-"

"I cannot help you," Ajawin said, pointing upward. The helicopter was almost down to the roof now. "This is the last emergency evacuation out, and this little girl is still alive, but she needs emergency lung ventilation after exposure to extreme smoke inhalation, possibly full dialysis scrubbing for toxins in her blood. I have a unit in the helicopter, and she cannot wait a second."

"Just one question while you work!" Zero snapped. "If I'm

right, there could be hundreds of children's lives at risk. Look at the picture, please."

The big man glared at her. "Look, Miss, I-"

"Please," LaGuerre said, resting a hand on Ajawin's shoulder.

The big man drew a deep breath then nodded. He kept one hand on the girl's wrist, monitoring her pulse even as he looked at the photograph.

"LaGuerre thinks she was a feral child," Zero shouted over the helicopter as it descended the last few yards, "maybe from Cité Soleil. He thinks she got these scratches from fighting other feral children some three months ago, then two days ago she was murdered, we presume by a gang. We need to know if you've seen her before; if you can tie her to an area in the slum and a gang, something that can give us a lead."

Dust blasted out from the rotors' downdraft as its skids touched down and Ajawin grunted. "She's not a feral child. I can't help you. I'm sorry."

He turned away to push the gurney up toward the helicopter.

"What do you mean, she's not a feral child?" Zero shouted, running with him. "What about all the scratches?"

"I don't know what you've heard," he shouted back, a southern African accent coming through, "or what Jean-Baptiste's told you, but he doesn't know the slums like I do. Police never go in, yes? The truth is, there are no feral children anymore. Ten years ago, after the big quake, there certainly were. It was horrible for a while, but by now they either grew up or died out. That girl can't be more than eight years old."

"Seven."

He stopped at the helicopter and turned as his colleague pulled the loading mechanism out to receive the gurney. "Look, I'm sorry she's dead, but feral children don't exist here anymore. The gangs sweep up maybe a third of all children; the rest go to the restavek system. And as for the scratches, I've never heard of them doing that to each other. If they did, they'd all be dead within days. You know we've got a cholera outbreak in Cité Soleil right now? We test people; over half have the bacteria on their bodies, under their fingernails, everywhere. That girl would not have survived in the slum with even one scratch like that, let alone so many."

Zero's jaw dropped. She didn't know what to say, left holding out her phone. Ajawin climbed into the helicopter.

"Wait," Zero called, fixing on one unfamiliar word. "What's the restavek system?"

"I can't help. Ask LaGuerre. Everyone in Haiti knows what it is; a dirty, open secret."

He slammed the door closed. The helicopter took off and within seconds was beating a path across the sky, carrying its precious burden to a hospital in a safer part of the city.

Zero turned back to LaGuerre.

"Sorry," he said. "I thought it was a good lead."

"Maybe it was," Zero said, and held up her phone showing the photo of the little girl's face. "Tell me about the restavek system."

17

RESTAVEK

LaGuerre sucked in a heavy breath. With the noise of the helicopter fading into the sky and the cries of the wounded muted by the bulk of the hospital, the rooftop was almost peaceful. "That's one of Haiti's greater shames. I don't know much more than what's on the news, though. It's not a criminal matter."

"What isn't?"

He heaved another sigh. "Restavek is Haitian creole for the French 'rester avec', which means 'stay with'." He looked away from Zero and out over the rooftops of Tabarre. "The idea is noble enough, of course. Poor families, like those in the slums or the rural areas who can't afford to send their children to school, maybe can't afford even to feed or clothe them, they send them to richer families, usually in the city, who can afford to do so. They're supposed to be enrolled in school, provided for, cared for, in return for doing some housework." He turned back. "I suppose you can imagine, it's a system ripe for abuse."

Zero couldn't quite believe what she was hearing. "It sounds like slavery."

"Some people call it that."

"Some people? What age of children are we talking about?"

"Anything from the age of five, I've heard. Maybe four."

"Four years old?"

LaGuerre said nothing.

"And what kind of abuse?" Zero asked. "No school? Underfed?"

"That, of course. Often worse. These children, they…" he broke off, seemingly overcome with emotion. "These children are undocumented in their own country, Miss Nowak. Their births would never have been registered. Once they've been passed into the system, which often means sold to a middle man, which means the gangs, there's usually no record of where they came from or where they went. Nobody will come looking for them. Nobody will care what happens to them. Nobody is checking if they're fed, or clothed, or sent to school."

Zero's jaw opened then closed. She'd come across some horrible things in her time hunting Pinocchios, but none quite as institutionalized as this.

"So you're saying this practice, this child slavery, is common? Widespread?"

LaGuerre gritted his teeth. "Unfortunately, yes, it is common. It's everywhere. Look out at this neighborhood. It undoubtedly runs on the sweat effort of restaveks." His lips pursed. "Child slaves."

"And no one tries to do anything about it?"

He threw his hands up. "The problem's too big. Too entrenched. It's like saying, well, why don't you just solve poverty in Haiti? It's not feasible. Poor people keep having babies, and keep being unable to look after them. It's what happens."

Zero felt disgusted. She'd already thought Port-au-Prince

was a perfect environment for a man like the Engineer to flourish, but this? This was something else.

"How many?"

"What?"

"How many 'restaveks' are there? How many child slaves?"

"I only know what I've read in the news. They talk about it sometimes. Someone's always trying to solve it."

"How many, LaGuerre?"

He looked faintly nauseated. "I've seen numbers as high as five hundred thousand."

Zero's eyes snapped wide. "Half a million?"

LaGuerre said nothing.

"You're saying there's half a million child slaves in this country, and it's not even illegal?"

"Everybody does it," he said weakly. "Many families do treat the children well. But then…"

"But then it's a system ripe for abuse," Zero repeated. Now she felt sick. She scrolled through photos on her phone and held up the one of the little girl hanging by her ankle. "So she could have been a restavek?"

"She could."

"Not a feral child."

He sighed. "I got that one wrong. Maybe I should've suggested restaveks instead, but I've never once seen a restavek with scars like that. Like your pathologist said; they're highly aberrant."

Highly aberrant.

Zero's mind spun.

Five hundred thousand vulnerable children, undocumented, unloved, sold by their own parents into slavery, would provide a vast bank for the Engineer to draw from. He'd boasted about a supply of children that would never run out; maybe this was it, or one feeder stream. Even if he took only one percent of the restavek population a year, a small enough proportion that no authority would ever notice, that would be five thousand children.

Zero's gorge rose and she fought to swallow it down.

Five thousand. She looked at the little girl in the photograph again, at the fingernail scratches that covered her body; scratches she never would have survived in the 'wild' of the slums, thanks to cholera and other rampant diseases.

Had the Engineer really done this?

Rorschach had muddied the timeline enough for it to be possible. Three months ago, the Engineer could have bought her, bit her, then set her loose in some kind of fingernail battle royale with at least eight other children.

But why? Why let her survive long enough for the scars to heal? Why kill her now, in this way?

The sickness only grew as countless reasons bloomed in Zero's head. All of them were horrific, sparking a fresh surge of outrage. Three years ago the Engineer had said emotion was her weakness, but he was wrong.

It was jet fuel.

"You said some of the gangs keep records," she said.

"I don't know that. It's a guess. The haystack didn't get any smaller, Miss Nowak. We still need to narrow it down."

"So let's find another expert, one who knows the restavek system well, maybe they recognize these kind of scars, maybe they can give us a place to start. There must be NGOs, other international charities, maybe a government initiative?"

He shook his head. "None of the above. Like I said, Haiti accepts this system, from the top brass to the bottom tier. Everybody wants a restavek, or several. It's a household staff, almost for free. It's a status symbol; you don't even need to be rich to have one, just richer than the very poorest. That's why it's impossible to change."

Zero's knuckles tightened. "No. I don't accept that. No

way everyone in this country likes child slavery. Think again."

"OK," LaGuerre said, and thought for a moment longer. They sat in silence in the cold car. Zero brought up her phone and ran a search, but all she found were foreign white papers and articles in international magazines condemning the practice; nothing on an active resistance in Haiti. She put her phone down in disgust.

"It's accepted," LaGuerre said, almost consolingly.

"It shouldn't be."

"I agree. And I remember now, I do know one man. He was a restavek himself forty years ago, and-"

"Forty years ago? How long has this practice been going on?"

"You can ask him that. At least forty years. Anyway, he's been campaigning to make restaveks taboo; to turn the wealthier families off using them. He's managed to free a handful of restaveks, I think; he found them real families, got them an education."

"And he's in Port-au-Prince? You know him?"

"I met him once at a conference. He was speaking on the stage. I just asked a question afterward. He was quite inspirational."

"Then let's go see him."

18

CEDRAS FOUNDATION

Pierre Cedras was a small man, perhaps only 5' 6", but he was impeccably dressed, with an imposing presence that outmatched his size. Even in the sweltering heat of his tiny office at the 'Cedras Foundation', thirty minutes south of the MSF hospital in Tabarre, he was wearing a shirt, tie, vest and suit jacket when they knocked on his door.

The neighborhood was Puits Blain, the most affluent Zero had seen yet: it had wide, tree-lined avenues and grass in front yards that was verdant and well-watered, not bedraggled and yellow, along with neat, clean homes built in a plain white modernist style, rather than the motley shades of the slums.

The Cedras Foundation was situated at the northern edge of the district, sandwiched between two bars and above a laundromat. There was a modest sign hung out on a pennant. Zero and LaGuerre had to walk through the laundry room, which was easily twice as hot and sweltering as the air outside, to reach the creaky wooden stairs that led up to the office.

LaGuerre had called ahead on the drive there, so he was

ready for them; sitting meek and perfectly composed behind his orderly, pristine leather-mounted desk. He rose as they entered, and Zero was instantly struck by the sense of his presence; there was something incredibly peaceful about him, a deep sense of grace and calm that she'd almost never felt before.

To her surprise, tears welled in her eyes. During the drive, Rex had filled her in on the life he'd led. Until the age of fifteen, he had indeed been a slave. He'd gone public with the countless abuses he'd received as a restavek, which ranged from whippings, beatings and sexual abuse to a partial castration. Looking back now, he considered himself cursed, victim of a vodou hex either in this life or another, though at the time he hadn't seen it that way.

At the age of fourteen, the family he served, the Cedrases, had taken him to Britain with them, where he'd continued to act as their slave. That had continued for a year, until a social services worker spotted him running errands on the street and asked if he was truanting from school.

His answers in French led to more questions. Before it could grow too serious, the family pushed him out of their home, told him to stop using their family name and fled the country. Several years of intense hardship followed; he hadn't spoken English, but learned in scraps by begging on the street, until a London gang took him in.

He swiftly rose within their ranks; his fearless use of a machete to punish the gang's enemies came straight from the life he'd experienced in Port-au-Prince. In London back then, such brutality was still shocking. Within two years he ran a subset of the gang; within three he was jailed for five years for manslaughter.

In jail, his new life began. He learned of possibilities he'd never before imagined; studying first for his undergraduate degree in International Studies, then for his Masters degree in

International Relations. His dissertation clearly proved the role the restavek system played in perpetuating Haiti's downward spiral of poverty and gang violence.

Once he was released, he made freeing every restavek his life's work.

He simply smiled when he saw Zero's shining eyes.

"ID LaGuerre, Miss Nowak," he said warmly, standing behind his desk and gesturing to seats laid out before it. "Would you care for some tea?"

Zero sat mutely. She couldn't trust herself to speak. This man had been through some of the same horrors that she had, yet he'd taken a very different path to her. She only cared for revenge, and knew she gave off spiky aggression, while this man exuded only calm and a gentle sense of welcome.

LaGuerre looked at her oddly, registering the tears and her silence, but answered for them both. "Yes, thank you. Tea would be lovely."

Cedras busied himself with the pot. His every motion fascinated Zero; all completely ordered, under control, perfectly poised.

"I am sorry to hear of this child's death," he said. "I hope I can help, though I don't quite know how."

"Anything you can tell us will be helpful," LaGuerre said.

Cedras smiled meekly and handed them their tea. Zero stared at it, feeling entranced by the presence of this man.

"You mentioned photographs?"

LaGuerre looked at Zero, as if waiting for her to speak, but when she didn't he dug out a slim, red-jacketed file and flicked through the few pages inside to the photograph of the victim hanging by her angle at the docks. He held it out.

"Ah," said Cedras. He studied the image for some time. Zero wondered what depths he was reading within it. "When was this?"

"Three days ago."

The little man looked up. His dark green eyes were kind. "And you believe she was a restavek?"

"That's our working theory. There are no records of her anywhere. We're trying to track her origins, looking for who might have bought and sold her, but we're having no luck."

Cedras nodded. "That is the case for so many restaveks. They are invisible." He laid the photograph carefully down on the desk. "It isn't a crime to abuse them. It's barely a crime to kill them. I am surprised to be approached by the police about this poor child's death."

That caught Zero's attention. LaGuerre started asking about record keeping, but she interrupted.

"Mr. Cedras, why are you surprised?"

He turned to her. "Because it has never happened before. I have petitioned for police intervention on behalf of countless restaveks many times previously, for many years, but nobody ever came. I stopped some time ago."

LaGuerre started to speak again, and again Zero cut him off.

"Petitioned for what? Just to set them free, or for something else?" She tapped the photograph. "For something more like this."

Cedras looked at her closely. Zero felt like he was reading who she was through her eyes. There was a familiarity there. A sense of closeness. He looked briefly at LaGuerre, as if debating mentioning what he'd seen, then he gave Zero a small smile, as if this was their secret.

It all happened in a few seconds, but Zero was at once impressed and grateful. It felt already like he knew her, like he could have outed her as a victim in front of LaGuerre, but had chosen not to.

"Yes," he simply said instead. "I have seen other photographs like this."

"What do you mean? Dead restaveks?"

"Not only dead. Hung in a manner similar to this." He tapped the photograph again.

Zero's mouth went dry. "By the ankle?"

"Not always the ankle. But yes, displayed. Marked in different ways."

Now her heart became a rhythm section, palpitating wildly. "What kind of marks?"

"Many kinds. I have photographic records. Would you care to see them."

Zero nodded rapidly. "Yes. Yes please."

Cedras stood. He took three perfectly measured steps to a filing cabinet, then paused. "I should tell you, I was warned off from pursuing these deaths with the police." He turned to face them. "Nine months ago, members of a gang burned down my office and made me watch. They told me to stop asking questions and filing reports, to stop keeping records and advocating for the restaveks." He watched impassively as Zero's jaw dropped. "I did stop filing reports, but I will never stop advocating. I still have all my records. I was waiting for you, I think."

A shiver passed through Zero. "For me?"

He said nothing, only fixed her with that gaze.

"Why for me?"

"Because you asked. Nobody else has."

Zero felt her cheeks burning. This man knew her in ways she could barely fathom, but there was no time to dwell on that now.

"You said they burned your office down?"

"My dog was inside," he said. The pain in that statement was clear, but it was also clear that he wasn't holding onto it. It was just more pain; it shaped but didn't warp him. "She died. I'm just glad they let my secretary at the time go." He smiled. "It's why I moved here; better police and fire response times. It's also why I no longer have a secretary, or a dog."

The pain was there again, and again Zero was amazed at how he seemed to both feel it but also rise above it. "I'm sorry. You said you do have the records?"

He nodded, then opened the filing cabinet and withdrew a thick blue folder bound with string. He carried it reverently to the desk, laid it down and gently unwound the string clasp. For a moment he paused, hands hovering over the cover, then he smiled again, turned the folder and pushed it toward Zero. "Here."

19

DEAD CHILDREN

The folder was full of dead children.

Zero leafed through them swiftly to begin with, through page after page of victims lying on muddy riverbanks or dusty roadsides or bloodstained carpets; all of them children aged younger than ten; many decomposed and physically deteriorated; all marked with scars and disfigurements.

There were dozens of them. Sometimes several were heaped together.

Zero could hardly breathe.

On every left forearm she could make out, the bite mark was there.

She felt herself entering a fight or flight reaction and struggled to focus. Her eyes watered, her fingers began to tremble, the world closed in.

"Rex," she whispered.

"What is it, Zero?" he answered. "I read your pulse leaping upward. Are you in danger?"

She looked up at Cedras. He was watching her with pain in his eyes. The same pain she felt.

"Where did you find all these children?" she asked.

"I didn't find them. They were reported to me."

"Reported by who?"

"Various people who deplore the restavek system. Many are ex-restaveks, like myself, who know the true depravities of the practice."

"Can we contact them?" Zero asked.

Cedras narrowed his eyes. "I do not think so, Miss Nowak. Many have risen to sensitive areas of employment. A visit from you, even a loose connection to myself, could jeopardize their positions."

Zero frowned. "What does that mean? They're in politics? The media? The police?" Cedras gave nothing away. "Even the gangs?"

"I can't share their details."

Zero switched direction. "OK. Tell me what you can about where these children were found. Leave out any identifying factors, if you have to."

"Port-au-Prince," Cedras answered flatly. "The surrounding areas. Some wash up on beaches. Some turn up in forests, in shallow graves disturbed by wild dogs. One was found inside an alligator. But you see it, don't you? The thing that matters most."

Zero's breath quickened. "See what?"

Cedras reached out slowly and rested his finger on the last photograph in the folder, pointing at a little boy's forearm. At the bite mark. The boy couldn't be more than six years old, and his body was badly deteriorated; the bite had split open revealing black corruption within.

Zero felt the emotion heaping higher inside her, horror and rage churning so hard she thought she might burst.

"What does this mean?" Cedras asked.

"It's a bite mark," Zero managed.

"I know. What does it mean?"

Zero was back in the house in Poland, with Hanna and

Zuzanna. What if this was them? This could so easily be them.

"It denotes ownership, I'd say," she found herself answering. "Like the brand ranchers put on cattle."

Cedras settled back in his chair. "Ownership," he repeated.

"Excuse me a moment," Zero said, and bolted to her feet. If she stayed in that room a moment longer, looking at those photographs, she was going to vomit. She almost ran down the stairs, sped through the steam of the laundry room and emerged gasping out onto the street.

The world reeled and she didn't quite know why. She'd seen worse things before. This whole hunt had begun with hundreds, maybe thousands of photographs of dead children, all of them bitten prior to or as part of their deaths.

But those photographs were distant. They weren't personal. She wasn't, in some way, responsible for any of them.

For these deaths, she was.

She hadn't killed the Engineer on Pleasure Island. If anything, she had become his inspiration, and this was what he'd gone on to do.

"Zero, you are dangerously close to hyperventilating. That is a very bad idea in the current climate. You must regain control."

She paced swiftly back and forth, trying to work off the adrenaline.

"He has photographs of dead children, Rex," she said. "Dozens of bodies with bite marks. It's the Engineer."

A moment passed. "I can find none of these photographs available anywhere on the Internet, Zero, open or otherwise. Are you sure these are legiti-"

"They're real," she interrupted. "You heard him. Any time he tried to get attention, the police ignored him. The gangs tried to destroy him and his mission. Maybe the media quashed it all. He won't even share any contacts with us. It's a miracle this little girl's photograph got through."

"Indeed," Rex allowed. "That does seem miraculous."

Zero's mind raced ahead. "Is it a trap? Did the Engineer summon me here with this?"

"That is highly doubtful, Zero. Until recently, we were not even looking for bite marks. Most likely, this is an unusual confluence, but one that was bound to happen at some point. Even the Engineer cannot control everything."

Still, Zero felt suddenly hunted. She scanned the rooftops nearby and stared into the eyes of every passing driver. "Maybe he's watching right now."

"I do not believe this to be the case. If you are worried, however, perhaps we should bring in support. Perhaps we should wait. Christopher Wren said-"

"No!" she snapped sharply, then took a breath. "We're not waiting for Wren. If you could see these pictures, you'd understand. They're all so real, Rex. And there's no system to help them at all. No investigations. It's just Cedras, heaping up this evidence on his own."

"I can see that would be distressing."

"It's disgusting. I couldn't do it. I couldn't do what he's doing. Just amassing photographs. I couldn't-"

"You do not need to," Rex said. "You are here to kill the Engineer, Zero. To kill anyone who is helping him. Not to record the atrocities, but to end them. Focus on that."

She did. It helped.

"These photographs help," Rex went on. "They show you are in the correct place. They may provide further leads. This is a windfall."

Zero felt herself calming. She walked a little more, getting control of herself again.

"You've still got it, Rex," she said.

"I am also trained as a therapy dog. Perhaps you would like to stroke the velvety fur behind my ears?"

Zero laughed. "I'm glad you're here with me. Cedras' dog was killed by the gangs."

"I heard that. I will raise a glass to her."

"Amen," Zero said, and stopped in front of the laundromat. She was fully back in control now. The shock and horror had condensed into an icy ball of rage in her middle; enough to fuel her for everything to come. "I'm going back inside."

20

CRUSADE

Both Cedras and LaGuerre watched Zero return. She sat back down without a word of explanation and picked the folder up again. She started again at the first photograph, this time looking closely and carefully. It showed a young boy with a large portion of his skin missing. There were round patches missing from his chest and back. Dust had gotten into the wounds. The bite mark, though, was untouched.

The next page contained notes; they were written in French but Zero could pick out a few familiar words and some details. He'd been found in marshes in a district called Basat, north of Port-au-Prince, approximately two years ago.

Zero looked up. "Was cause of death the removal of skin?" she asked in a neutral tone. "Maybe shock, or blood loss?"

"I am not a medical examiner," Cedras said. "But I do not believe so. The people who found him told me it looked as if it had been done with sandpaper. In places his skin was missing down to the muscle, in others it was simply badly scratched."

Zero felt sick. "Sandpaper? Someone held him still and sanded down his skin?"

"I cannot imagine there is a good way to lose skin," Cedras said.

"That's got to be about the worst."

"Perhaps. As for cause of death, his throat had been cut and all the blood drained. His body had then been posed."

"Posed how? Did you photograph it?"

"No. The locals who found him took his body down. I don't know how he was posed. They didn't tell me."

"Was it like this?" Zero asked, tapping through her phone to show the photograph of the little girl hanging by her ankle.

"I don't know," Cedras said, then fell silent. Zero looked at LaGuerre. He looked as sickened as she'd been moments ago.

"May I take photographs of these?" she asked. "For later analysis."

"You may take this folder. I have no wish to keep it anymore."

Zero looked in his eyes. Was that relief? Maybe she could understand that; finally handing off the burden he'd been carrying for so long.

"Thank you." She held up her cell phone. "I'll take photographs as well, for digital analysis."

He gestured for her to go ahead. She started shooting; Rex would gain access instantly and check the bite mark profile for similarity to the little girl.

She turned to the next photograph. It showed three bodies heaped together, two girls and a boy, all bloated almost beyond recognition. The bite marks were barely visible in the photograph; the skin had puffed so much it was hard to identify them, but the faint depressions in the skin were there.

"And these? Did they die of a cut throat?"

"They were drowned," Cedras said.

"That's different."

"Many of the deaths are different. It makes it hard to ascertain a pattern, other than the bite marks."

"They all have bite marks?"

"That I can see."

Zero took another photograph and moved on.

It was grisly work, cataloging the folder. By the end, she'd amassed dozens of photographs and a collection of bizarre, disturbing injuries.

Aberrant.

One child had received burns over twenty percent of his body, but as with the docks victim and the marsh victim, that was not the cause of his death. The burns had healed. Like the others, his throat had been cut.

Another child had lost seven fingers and four toes, but again, that was not the cause of death. Two children had died of what looked to be asphyxiation, most likely by burial alive; their throats were stuffed with dirt.

It was a litany of horrors. After a certain point, Zero progressed on autopilot. The surplus of evidence established a clear pattern. There were children who'd suffered greatly, evident from grave wounds that had healed, then been executed later. There were children who'd suffered greatly and died in the course of their suffering.

"How long has this been happening?" Zero asked. On some level, she already knew the answer.

"The oldest cases I've documented reach back three years," Cedras said.

Even though she'd expected it, it still came as another blow. After Pleasure Island, the Engineer had wasted no time. He'd come right here and started killing children in grotesque ways.

"And do you have any further leads? You're the foremost expert on the restaveks, Pierre. Do you know which gangs are dealing with these killers? Do you know why they're doing it?"

He shook his head. "I'm afraid I do not. They cover their tracks well, and I'm no detective."

The implication was clear. He was handing this responsibility to her and LaGuerre.

"I understand. But you must have some theory. Why is this happening? Why are some victims killed by a cut throat and others not? Why are some injuries allowed to heal before execution occurs?"

Cedras considered for a moment. He looked at LaGuerre then back at Zero. "I have no theory. I honestly don't know."

Zero didn't know what to say. It was a lot of information, a mountain of evidence, but she didn't see how it was going to progress the case forward or bring them closer to the Engineer.

"If there's nothing else?" Cedras said, then stood. "I've spoken on this topic as much as I'm comfortable already. As much as I dare."

LaGuerre stood. Zero did not. He looked at her, perhaps hoping she'd stand too, but she didn't.

"I'll be in the car," he said, and left.

Zero watched him go, then turned back to Cedras. It seemed a sour note to end on. She sipped her tea. Cedras made no further move to usher her out. Perhaps he was waiting for something, too.

At last, she set the tea cup down. She closed the blue folder and painstakingly rewound the string clasp, then sat for a moment with one hand resting on the cover. So many thoughts buzzed in her head, but after the horror and the anger, one clamored louder than the rest.

"How do you do it, Pierre?"

"Do what?" he asked, though Zero felt certain he knew what she meant.

"All this. Fighting for a cause nobody else cares about. Collecting these photographs. Keeping them."

He took a slow breath. He leaned back in his chair and let it out. Then he spoke in his usual, measured tone. "I'm not alone. Other people care."

"Who?"

"You. Your colleague, ID LaGuerre."

"That's two people, and I'm not even Haitian. LaGuerre is from New York."

"There are others."

"There are? I could really do with hooking up with them, Pierre, because I haven't met a single person I could trust other than LaGuerre and his girlfriend. One cop already tried to rape me."

Cedras' eyes narrowed. "I am sorry. But there are others, even in the police." He paused a moment, eyes searching the air above Zero's head, like he was looking for the right words to frame what he wanted to say. "Have you heard of a group called Fantom 509?"

She frowned. "No. What are they?"

"I don't know, exactly. I have a few contacts, only. Some call them a gang within the police, armed at a paramilitary level. They want a better Haiti and they're willing to fight for it; they have fought several times in open skirmishes with the gangs. They do not seek to arrest, they do not follow due process, they simply battle like vigilantes. But I trust them. I had wondered if your ID LaGuerre is a member, but I think not, now."

"Why not?"

Cedras smiles. "He is a man of the rules. To be in Fantom 509, you must be willing to break the rules to do the moral thing."

Zero smiled. "They sound like my kind of people."

"I think they might be. But I cannot share their details with you."

Zero said nothing. She tapped the folder again. "All this, it's good, Pierre. But it's not enough. I need more. I need a lead; someone to talk to, a witness. You say the bodies were posed, but you don't know how. You imply gangs are behind these killings, but you won't name any." She let that hang. "I don't need someone in this 'Fantom 509'; you don't need to compromise a police contact. What I need is a witness on the ground, preferably to a recent crime. Otherwise you've just given me your cross to bear."

He gazed at her. The moment stretched on. Then he sighed.

"Open the folder."

She opened it again. He leafed through the photographs upside down, coming to rest on the one at the start. It was the little boy who'd died from having his skin scoured away, maybe by sandpaper.

"This boy," he said. "The man who found his body came to me. He was distraught. He has sons the same age. I advised him to bury his rage in the ground, or he would lose his life and the lives of his five children."

"Five children?"

"Five children. I advised him to leave the photograph with me, and I would seek justice on his behalf."

"How recent?"

"Six months ago."

Zero sucked her teeth. "That's the best you can do?"

"It's the only one I'm comfortable to give you. I know this man took precautions when coming to see me. I believe a visit from you will not endanger him unduly."

Zero grunted. "OK. Six months, then. Where is he? What's his name?"

Cedras looked into her eyes for a long moment, then

picked up a piece of paper from his desk and wrote out a name and address.

"Be careful with this. It could get you, me, and him all killed."

Zero studied the paper, committing the details to memory.

Evens Wilguens – Point du Cul-De-Sac, Basat

"Where is this?"

"Twenty miles north. Basat is a small encampment on the coast. I've never been there."

Zero nodded, then popped the paper in her mouth, chewed and swallowed.

Cedras nodded appreciatively. Neither mentioned that the details could still come out under torture.

Zero sat a moment longer. She had a lead now, a witness to interview, which Wren would be pleased with. It seemed like the next positive step in a structured investigation, so she couldn't account for the way she was still feeling.

"You didn't answer the first question," she asked at last. "How do you do it?"

He smiled. "Crusade for the restaveks? For me, it isn't a choice. As I suspect it isn't for you. I must do this. Isn't that why you're here, too?"

She didn't say anything. Nothing seemed appropriate. Instead she only nodded, then gathered the folder and stood up. "Thank you for the tea, Mr. Cedras, and your help. I'm sorry you had to wait for so long. I'm going to stop this."

"Stop what?"

She felt her grip on the anger loosening. "The deaths. The restavek system. The gangs. As much as I can."

He said nothing. She went to the door. As she laid her hand on the door knob, he spoke again. "Do you have anyone you love, Miss Nowak?"

The words were haunting. She turned slowly. He was standing again, just as he'd been when they arrived, perfectly dressed in his three-piece suit, though now it felt like there were ghosts circling in the room with him. Again, tears welled to Zero's eyes.

"I do."

"I never did. Friends, once, perhaps, but my cause is not popular. I had my dog. But no one I loved. No one who loved me,"

Zero felt the anger surging to the surface. "I have a family," she managed, barely choking the words out. "A man and two little girls."

"Hold on to them," he said. "For as long as you can."

She nodded. She felt fit to burst with confusing emotions. After a moment she strode back to him and held out her hand. He took it and shook gently.

"Get a new dog," she said.

He smiled again, and now Zero saw right through it, just as he'd seen through her. The cracks beneath that smile were clear, where the pain was straining to push through, just like the rage was almost bursting out of her.

"I don't know if I can bear to lose another," he said.

"Please," she said. "Do it for me."

At that, his smile strengthened. The cracks faded somewhat. "For you, my dear, I will. Thank you."

She left before the tears could claim her.

21

PERSONAL

LaGuerre was sitting in the Siena with the AC turned high. Zero sat beside him. He made no move to drive away, so she made no move to prompt him. The blue folder rested on her lap.

Minutes passed. Finally she spoke.

"I got a name. A location."

LaGuerre sucked a heavy breath. With the AC humming on full, the car felt like a morgue. "He said he wouldn't talk. He said it was too dangerous."

"Well, he talked."

LaGuerre eyed her. "What did you do?"

Zero didn't like the way he was looking at her. "What's that supposed to mean? What do you think I did?"

He sucked his teeth. "I don't know. I just know what Wren told me. That you cut corners. That you're impulsive. That you're capable of extreme violence. I've seen that myself."

Zero felt her anger surging but bit it back. "You mean like with Marcelin? You said you were glad about that."

"I was. Maybe."

"Maybe?"

"It depends who else you'd do it to. You almost did it to me."

She snorted. "At the airport? You were being a real pain in the ass. But I didn't break your wrist. I let you go. You really think I'd hurt Pierre Cedras?"

LaGuerre raised his hands off the wheel in a small shrug.

"Where's this coming from?" Zero pressed. "One minute we're partners, the next you're accusing me of torturing a man who's dedicated his life to preserving human dignity."

He sighed. "I'm realizing how little I know about you, Miss Nowak. Or is it Clara Baxter?" Zero winced. "From the moment we met, I told you not to make waves, but you keep on doing it. You're deep in my life already, in my city, endangering my job and attacking my co-workers, and now you want to go pursue a lead we already know is dangerous both for Pierre Cedras and for us, and I'm supposed to just trust your word that he gave it up freely?"

Zero felt some of the anger trickling out. "So go back up there if you don't believe me. Take a look. He's fine."

"I'm sure he's fine now. Maybe you threatened him."

"Threatened him? He's on our side!"

"There are no sides!" LaGuerre snapped back. "There's just the law, and from everything I've seen so far, you operate outside of it. This is personal for you, and-"

"And it's not personal for you?" Zero interrupted. "Were you even in that room with me, looking at those bodies? We're far beyond aberrant here, LaGuerre, beyond feral children and restaveks, and now you're holding back because you think I'm too, what, emotionally invested?"

"Those emotions make you unstable," he answered. "A hazard to your health and to mine. They put us both at risk of breaking the law."

"Who cares if we break the law after seeing all that?"

"The law's all we've got."

Zero laughed once. "You're serious, aren't you? You think the law's working here in Haiti? You think the law is going to prevent more sick deaths like these?" She slapped the folder. "I've got news for your literal-thinking heart, Jean-Baptiste. You missed that boat the moment you let men like Marcelin into your station. The moment you refused to make one little girl's death a national case."

He squeezed the wheel and stared dead ahead. It pissed Zero off. She brought up her phone and scrolled back to the photograph of the little girl hanging from her ankle.

"Look at her! It was only two days before you called off the investigation! Two days and you shut the case. How many gang members did you interview in that time, remind me, LaGuerre? How many suspects did you bring in? Or did you all just roll over because none of you had the balls to follow the law?"

He spun to her, cheeks flushing darker.

"You want to talk about balls?" He stabbed a finger at the folder. "After seeing all those dead children, that bite mark, you freaked out. It's apparent to me that you didn't fly all this way just for one dead little girl, so don't act like you're some saint come to save us backwater yokels from ourselves. This is part of something far bigger for you, and you've been shutting me out the whole time!"

Zero opened her mouth, then closed it. It was a fair point. "That's personal."

Now LaGuerre laughed. "Exactly my point! It's so personal that you're a wreck right now, like a junkie coming off a high. Your eyes are dilated with adrenaline, your breathing's wild. How am I supposed to work with a partner like that? How am I supposed to trust you?"

Zero had had enough; he'd started sounding uncomfortably like the Engineer had, three years ago on Pleasure Island. "So decide," she spat. "This is who I am. I take child murder personally. You told me to get in your car, but I can get out just as easily. Are we in this together or not, 'ID' LaGuerre? If not, just let me know and I'll go handle it myself."

He turned and stared at her for a moment, then turned back to the wheel. A moment passed. "You swear that Cedras is OK?"

"Of course he's OK!" Zero shouted. "Except the poor bastard lost his dog and doesn't have any friends in the whole world. He's just dandy."

LaGuerre took a heavy breath. "Then how did you get him to talk?"

Zero opened her mouth, then closed it. It was a reasonable enough question, and by an effort of will she dropped her tone back to a conversational level. "Guilt," she said, and paused. "He was trying to hand off his responsibility to us, without sharing enough knowledge to do anything about it. I called him on it. He caved. That's it."

LaGuerre let out a heavy breath. Zero waited for him to say some nonsense like, 'How hard was that?', but he didn't.

"What's the lead?" he asked instead.

Zero didn't say any nonsense either. The truth was, she needed LaGuerre. This eyewitness was out in the countryside, which almost certainly meant he didn't speak English, with very little chance of a signal strong enough to bring Rex in to translate.

"His name's Evens Wilguens. He lives in Point du Cul-de-Sac, in Basat. Cedras said that's on the coast."

LaGuerre stared out of the windshield. "The coast. Sure. I know Basat. It's basically a dying mangrove swamp; rotten land, clear cut for plantations generations ago, but the storms and the earthquakes keep it inundated with seawater; too much salt for anything but stunted growth." He paused.

"That's not even considering pollutants and runoff. And it's out of my jurisdiction."

"So break the law."

He turned to her with a warning in his eyes. Zero cursed inwardly. She had to control that impulsive nature better.

"Sorry," she said. "Why not just consider it time off? Your shift's gotta be ending soon. Go as a private citizen. There's nothing illegal in that."

He stared a moment longer. "But we'll want the effect of the uniform. The car too, and the weapons in back, in case things go south."

"That does sound good," Zero allowed.

LaGuerre sighed and squeezed the wheel harder. "I'll go. But new deal. Before this is over, you're going to tell me everything. Why you're really here."

She nodded. She had no idea if she was going to do that. "Deal."

"Then let's go." He put the vehicle in drive and pulled away from the sidewalk. "Just a pair of private citizens in a police vehicle."

"I'll compensate you for the gas."

He glared at her but let that dig go. "We're burning daylight, and the roads out of Port-au-Prince are guesswork at the best of times. It's only twenty miles or so, but it's going to take an hour or more."

"I guess there's no use calling ahead?"

He laughed. That was a gimme, really. Of course there'd be no electricity out in the rotten mangrove swamps.

"Seatbelt," he said firmly.

Zero pulled the seatbelt down and clicked it home. It was easy to give him that much, after all.

22

MANGROVES

They left the leafy Puits Blain district and turned back onto the east-west road bordering the slums. Now Zero studied the tin shacks and dank alleys more closely, trying to imagine LaGuerre's feral children or Cedras' runaway restaveks darting in and out of the sewage and shadows, capturing babies and eating them. Maybe ten years ago, Ajawin had said. Three years ago, Cedras had said.

They passed the Airport station and continued north.

It took longer than expected just to get out of Port-a-Prince; over an hour spent winding through a churned-up network of narrowing dirt streets, where heaps of garbage spilled out into the road, and abandoned vehicles lay like immovable neolithic boulders, their wheels long-gone and their dented bodies rusting in the sun.

They didn't talk. LaGuerre didn't put the radio on, and after five minutes he switched off the AC, so the car only grew progressively hotter. Out of stubbornness, Zero tolerated it without asking to lower the window, despite the sweat pouring down her cheeks.

Once outside the city, though, LaGuerre wound the windows down. Zero felt herself waking up again, to watch as Haiti put on a new coat she hadn't yet seen; one that was overwhelmingly beautiful.

"Mangrove forest," LaGuerre said, with a slight nod left through the window. "Not clear cut. Original. This is how most of our coastline should look."

Zero was enraptured.

The mangroves stood in dense, graceful islands in a slip of blue-green tidal water lining the rough blacktop road. Beyond them lay the ocean, a featureless sweep of crystal blue studded by distant craggy islands, while within each mangrove cluster Zero glimpsed whole worlds.

Each had an ornate overlap of hundreds of slender stems, woven intricately up from the tide line into a thick, glossy green canopy bursting with life. She spotted a perched egret surveying the swamp from a tall branch, and families of bright-shelled crabs scuttling through the roots, chasing the bubble trails of tiny fish. Through the open window she smelled the earthiness of sap mingling with the saltiness of the sea, carried on a warm, soft breeze.

"It's amazing," she said.

"I know," LaGuerre said. "It won't last."

He was right. Within ten minutes of bumping along the pot-holed coastal road, the mangroves' verdant maze gave way to a pitted, scarred stretch of stagnant swamp and brackish black mudflat. Pools of water captured in the ruts glistened with a rainbow layer of oil. The mangroves that survived here were twisted and deformed, their stems weeping black trails of sap from diseased buds, their spartan leaves a sickly brownish-green.

"Dumping of waste chemicals," LaGuerre supplied. "It's a boom industry off the coast, particularly near Basat. The waste then sweeps in with the tide and kills this section; the mangroves don't have the same breadth of root system out here, where they were savaged to plant vetiver. Soon the die-off will spread all the way down, and this'll be all there is."

Zero grunted. She brought up the photograph Cedras had provided, looking at the little boy's body. He was lying on black mud; in the corner was a thatch of blackened mangrove roots.

"The dead girl was dismissed as a gang killing," she said. "A message sent to other gangs, maybe. What's the explanation for this?"

LaGuerre looked over then away again. "Could be the same. The gangs are everywhere, Miss Nowak. In the city, in the countryside. They fight over land whether it's productive or not. Most likely the local councilman here takes an income from selling off the dumping rights. The gangs will have their hand in that. They run most of the cash crop plantations too."

"So they sanded this boy's skin off as a message to another gang?"

"It seems that way."

She ran her finger over the bitemark in his arm, thinking about the Engineer. What was his role in all this?

"Almost there," LaGuerre said after a few more minutes, then took a turn off the road onto what looked to be raw mudflat. The Siena's tires sank in, and for a moment Zero thought they were going to sink, but the rubber bit on something under the surface.

"Wooden pontoons," LaGuerre explained. "They drive trucks up this route."

"Trucks for what?"

"The Cul-de-Sac is a small promontory," LaGuerre said, pointing ahead. "Last time I was here, there was a jetty at the end, from which many of the locals take out coracles for fishing, crabbing, oyster diving. They used to generate a decent haul. That's dying off now, of course."

"How do you know so much about this area?"

LaGuerre said nothing, just rode the gas pedal enough to keep them moving forward.

"Let me guess, that's personal?" Zero asked.

"You have your secrets, I have mine."

"Out in the rotten mangroves."

"There's secrets everywhere," he said, and pointed. "Just ahead, I think his house will be amongst those."

Now they were surrounded on both sides by the wasted risers of half-dead mangroves. The stench of chemical rot through the windows was strong. Here and there lay small shacks amongst the outcrops, raised up on stilts and built from corrugated metal and driftwood, lashed together with old red and blue fishing nets. Further up the barely visible trail, fast disappearing behind them and largely submerged ahead, Zero picked out a cluster of such shacks.

LaGuerre pulled the Siena up onto a solid embankment to the side of the cluster. They both stepped out. Zero was surprised when her footfalls drew odd metallic thuds.

"It's not natural," LaGuerre explained. "It'll be the hull of a sunken ship, or maybe caissons sloughed off by one of the deep-water drills, driven here on a hurricane tide. The people here just built on top of it."

Zero advanced hesitantly. "Rex?" she said quietly, but of course there was no reply. There'd been no signal for most of the last hour.

"Let me do the talking," LaGuerre said. "I'm wary about even having you out of the car."

"Because I stand out?"

"Exactly. But maybe that'll help us. These people have probably never seen a white person in the flesh before, definitely not a woman."

She grunted. "Great. You have the lead."

He nodded, then started toward the cluster of shacks. Zero saw children zipping about under the stilts, like the fish she'd spotted under the mangrove roots before. They smiled and laughed; some kind of game. No school out here, she guessed.

The ground shifted under their feet, until they were trailing through a thick layer of mud. LaGuerre approached the children with a smile and spoke in Haitian creole.

The children stopped what they were doing and just stared at him.

He tried again.

They ran, melting into the mangroves and buildings like scampering crabs.

LaGuerre looked at Zero, gave a small shrug and went to the makeshift door of the nearest structure. The door was made of thin boards of mismatched wood and teetered unevenly inward at his touch. No lock, only twine for hinges.

They waited.

A woman came to the door, jet black, early-twenties and heavily pregnant with what had to be at least twins. She held her swollen belly in both hands and sweat ran down her face. She said something in creole and LaGuerre answered with a question ending in Evens Wilguens' name.

The woman' face soured and she pointed off into the swamp.

LaGuerre pushed back with another question. She pointed again then slammed the door shut.

"What did she say?" Zero asked.

LaGuerre turned with a heavy expression.

"She's saying Evens Wilguens is dead. Buried in the swamp with the boy he found."

23

OUANGA

Zero and LaGuerre sat on faded plastic milk crates at the end of a jetty built from driftwood and dented oil drums, looking out over the bay. The sun was sinking toward the horizon, casting the skies a hazy red.

Zero was getting used to the stink of the swamp. She supposed anyone would, given time. Like LaGuerre had said, you found a way to adapt to the world, or you ended up dead.

He'd asked his questions at the remaining shacks, and received short, abrupt answers from more women. All of them were pregnant. No men were home, all out fishing or farming or whatever subsistence activity kept them alive.

The answer was always the same.

"So the gang killed him for going to Cedras," Zero summarized.

LaGuerre grunted and tossed a twig into the water ahead. It plopped in and sank, spreading ripples that died when they hit a low crest of mud, setting a shiny blizzard of flies up into the air.

"And none of them will tell us which gang it was."

"Of course not."

"And you don't know which gang runs this area?"

He tossed another twig. "Out here? No. Maybe in the city I'd have a way to find out. Maybe. But not here. You saw how they all clammed up. Nobody will talk. The gangs rule this place completely." He turned. "We really need to leave now, Miss Nowak."

"We can't leave. That boy was our only lead."

"And now he's buried with the man who found him. If anyone talks to us about it, they'll join them. Just by being here we're endangering these people."

Zero gritted her teeth. She could feel the Engineer out there, as if he was another fly buzzing through the withered roots and stagnant reeds, looking for a place to set down and vomit out his poison.

She couldn't just let him slip away.

LaGuerre stood.

"Wait," Zero said.

"Wait for what? The trail's gone cold. No one is going to talk to us. It's a dead end."

"Somebody might. We need to ask again."

LaGuerre stared at her, then shook his head. "Let me tell you something. You saw all those women? All pregnant?"

"Sure."

"You're probably thinking, well, why are they making so many babies? They obviously can't feed and clothe them. There's no school, no opportunities, they live off less than a dollar a week, no running water, no electricity. So why do they keep making babies?"

"The thought had crossed my mind."

LaGuerre stabbed a finger toward the shacks. "This is the origin of the restavek system, Miss Nowak. This is where those tragic children like Pierre Cedras come from. From nothing. From holes in the mud. And it's not, contrary to what you might think, because the man of the house just can't control his libido."

Zero looked up at him. He was angry, to her surprise. Almost shaking with it. "OK. Fine. Maybe living in a swamp leads to a lot of virgin births."

"They're being raped," LaGuerre snapped back. He let that hang. "These women. Maybe not every night, but systematically. I've heard of it. Now we're seeing the reality. I didn't want to believe it, not as a way of life, but I can't deny it. The gangs come through and do what they want. Nobody dares try to stop them, because they know they'll end up in the swamp too. For the gangs it's a reward; teenage boys driven by shot-callers in their early twenties. They're all pitifully poor, but this gives them a sense of power."

Zero looked back at the shacks. What LaGuerre was saying rang true. She tried not to imagine a rape gang prowling through. Maybe in the night. Maybe in the day. Maybe it would make no difference. Nobody was coming to help these people.

"Oh," she said.

"Oh," LaGuerre repeated. "And we can't do a thing for them either, so I think it's time we left before we make it any worse. Before the gang comes in force and punishes these people just for us being nearby. We don't want to be here when that happens."

Zero did want to be there. After hearing all that, she really wanted it. She could picture herself moving from shack to shack, killing men, maybe teenage boys, as they started their violations. It would feel good.

But LaGuerre was right. Even if she laid in wait, and she took out a whole rape gang by herself, what happened next? Wouldn't another gang just come back the next night, and punish all these women and children for letting it happen?

They'd end up in the swamp.

She hated it.

She didn't accept it.

She stood.

"OK. Let's go," she said.

LaGuerre led the way back along the flotsam jetty. The Fiat Siena had a cluster of children circling it. Probably they'd never seen a police-branded panda car before. When they saw LaGuerre coming near, they fled, melting into the mangroves.

All except one.

One little boy remained. He wore blue denim shorts and a red Chicago Bulls t-shirt. Both were miraculously spotless, though his bare feet and legs were plastered with a thick layer of swamp mud. His bright eyes darted back and forth between LaGuerre and Zero. In his hands he held a small package wrapped in frayed white canvas.

LaGuerre signaled Zero to stop and she did, allowing him to advance alone. The boy shifted his feet, watching them like they were predators.

"Qu'est-ce que tu as là?" LaGuerre asked. Zero figured he was asking about the package.

The boy answered in a low voice. He held out the package. LaGuerre asked one more question, but the boy said nothing more and pressed the canvas into LaGuerre's hand before fleeing like the rest.

LaGuerre watched after him.

"What's that?" Zero called, advancing toward him.

He said nothing, focused on unwrapping the package.

"LaGuerre," she prompted.

He turned. In his hands was a small wooden icon; it looked like the rough outline of a human figure, but nails had been driven into its arms, legs and face. LaGuerre looked pale, like he was holding a live grenade.

"What is that?" Zero repeated.

"It's a ouanga," he said, finally finding his voice. "The little boy said he found it hidden near the scene where our victim died, tied to a high branch." LaGuerre gulped. "He was crucified, he said. Spread across a mangrove."

"Crucified?" Zero's mind kicked into gear. "So he was posed in a horrific way, just like the girl at the docks."

LaGuerre gulped heavily. He began to wrap the icon back in white canvas. "It seems that way."

"But that's not a message to another gang, is it?" Zero pointed at the item. "Not if some kid's the only one who found it. Not if it was hidden."

"No," LaGuerre allowed.

"What did you call it, a wanga? What is that?"

LaGuerre sighed heavily, then opened the door of the Siena and signaled Zero to follow. She got in. He started the engine and pulled away.

"LaGuerre?" she prompted.

He released his tight grip on the package and handed it to her. She unwrapped the canvas and studied the carved wooden figure. Though it was inanimate, the nails driven through the rough limbs looked agonizing, especially when she thought about how the little boy had suffered in the months before he died, with large patches of his skin sanded off.

"You've probably heard it by another name," LaGuerre said at last, once they'd cleared the trail out of the Cul-de-Sac promontory. "Some call them talismans. Some amulets. Most commonly they're known as vodou dolls."

24

VODOU

Zero dropped the doll into her lap. "What?"

LaGuerre sighed. "I know."

Now Zero stared at the doll with new eyes. Every nail, every rough-carved limb. "Is this supposed to be a replica of the little boy?"

LaGuerre said nothing.

"Jean-Baptiste," she prompted.

"Maybe," he said. "I don't know.

Minutes passed as Zero studied the doll. The 'ouanga'. She didn't want to touch it. It seemed ghoulish.

"So this suggests the killings are linked to vodou," she said.

LaGuerre sucked a slow, careful breath, like he didn't trust the air not to choke him. "I suppose that's one interpretation."

"Really? The girl is hung by the ankle and bled out like a chicken, the boy is beaten to death and crucified with a 'ouanga' tied to a tree nearby, and you 'suppose' that's one interpretation?"

He sucked his teeth. "Yes. Maybe those kinds of displays are quite a vodou thing to do."

Zero brought up her phone and scrolled back to the

photograph of the little girl hanging from her ankle. "You said this was a gang killing. This was a message from one gang to another about territory."

LaGuerre raised his hands off the wheel in a small, defeated-looking shrug. "Maybe I was wrong. Maybe it's both, or maybe it's not a message at all. Maybe this was purely a vodou sacrifice; about capturing a death."

Alarm bells rung in Zero's head. "What? Capturing a death? What are you talking about?"

LaGuerre sighed. "This is not something I want to get into. It's distasteful, and I've had my share of bad experiences. Vodou is..." he paused, "greatly misunderstood. Most people outside of Haiti know little about it, and what they do know is only a very bad, very dark side. That's the side I've seen too. I don't think it would be productive to delve into-"

"Not productive? We had no leads until a little boy risked his life to give this to us. I'm thinking it's the only lead we've got."

"It's not something I want to talk about," LaGuerre answered firmly. "It's not relevant."

"Not relevant?" She held up the ouanga. "This is our lead. It means something. Tell me what or I'll find someone who will."

He rolled the window down and the rush of fetid air buffeted them both. It pissed Zero off.

"We're back here again, LaGuerre. Help or get out of my way."

He shook his head. "How I'm involved with vodou is none of your business."

"I don't care how you're involved! I want to know what this doll means."

He clasped the wheel in the middle like he was praying for patience. A few moments passed. "All right. It may be possible that this ouanga may provide a way to trace the gang that killed that boy."

Zero's eyes flared and she leaned in. "How?"

LaGuerre sucked in a slow breath and turned to her. "Do you remember all those religious offerings in the entrance of Mama Oshun's Legim place?"

Zero thought back to the skull faces buried in the thicket of bric-a-brac items. "Of course. Baron Samedi and the others."

"You shouldn't take the Baron's name so lightly, but yes. Each one of them invokes a vodou god, spirit, Loa, whatever you want to call them, seeking help, vengeance, blessings, curses and so on."

"With you so far."

"Well, all of the gangs have an affiliation to a particular Loa. Think of it like a patron saint."

"A Christian saint?"

"Almost exactly, actually. Most of the Loa are paired with Roman Catholic saints. It's how the original African slaves managed to continue practicing their religion. They hid it within Catholicism."

"OK." She frowned. "How does that help us?"

He shot a glance at the wooden doll in her lap. "Many of the vodou signs for the Loa double as gang signifiers. They're claimed by that gang and no one else would dare use them. Now, do gangs often leave a signifier, some symbol of their patron saint, behind when they commit a crime? Yes, they do." He took another breath. "Murders, kidnaps, rapes; it can be a calling card, part of the mystique, a way to spread fear." He paused a moment before going on. "It could also be a kind of talisman to capture a death."

Zero's jaw tightened. "You mentioned that already, 'capture a death'. What does it mean?"

He shifted again. "Like I said, vodou's a much maligned

religion, Miss Nowak. Most of it's completely harmless, just lots of moral stories, colorful characters, some wild ceremonies and life guidance. But hexes, black magic, sacrifices and witch doctors? That's what the wider world thinks of us, and those elements are a part of vodou too. There's nobody in control of the religion, no pope or central church that hands down the official line, so everyone's free to make what they will of it. That includes killers who buy into the dark side, like curses, soul strength, zombies and-"

"Zombies? Soul strength?"

LaGuerre raised a hand. "I know. It's like I said with the feral children. Ajawin said that's not true anymore, OK, but there really are people who believe that eating a baby will make them strong. It's a sacrifice, and there's no shortage of animals getting sacrificed in vodou. Killers and gangs, they just go further by sacrificing people, then they capture that death to strengthen themselves."

Zero frowned. "So this little boy was sacrificed for his soul strength? The same as the girl?"

"It seems likely."

"Then all these children?" She plucked Cedras' blue folder from the door pocket, growing angry again. "They were sacrificed for their strength, all captured by ouanga?"

"Again, it's possible. I'm no expert, Miss Nowak."

"You seem to know a lot, though!" she snapped. "You know a lot of things and you accept a lot of things you never should. Child slavery, child sacrifices captured by vodou dolls, where does it end?"

He looked at her, color rising to his cheeks now. "Climb down off your high horse. You are no more perfect than we are."

She scoffed. "No more perfect? Do you think that in America we sacrifice children and turn them into disgusting trinkets?"

"I don't need to think," he snapped back firmly, "I know. You forget I lived in the US for most of my life, Miss Nowak. How hard was it to find such 'trinkets' with unconscionable histories behind them, bought and sold in almost every market for astronomic sums?"

"What are you talking about?"

"I'm talking about the value of a ouanga like that." He pointed at the wooden doll. "Think of blood diamonds." He brought up his fist and counted off his little finger. "Every diamond sourced from a conflict zone, dug by human slaves, each weighed out in human misery and worth all the more for it. Then there's ivory." A second finger went up. "Countless species have gone extinct because poachers killed rhinos or elephants, and who buys that ivory, Miss Nowak? People in the West who believe it raises their status, the rarer the better. Third, hunt trophies! People from the West go 'on safari' to hunt and kill lions, tigers, and again, scarcity only increases the value. They then stuff the bodies and display them as a sign of their own virility, exactly like that ouanga." He snapped another finger up. "Fourth, shark fin soup! Sharks are killed as a good luck charm, with only the fin consumed and the rest wasted, devastating the ecosystem of the seas. The waste is the point! And what about oil itself! Here in Haiti we ration our vehicles so completely we can't even run the air conditioning." He slapped the button for the AC, switching it off. "Yet in your country, you build giant SUVs that drink gas as if it were water, all to show off that you can." He stopped abruptly, five fingers spiked outward, breathing heavily. "You are no saint, Miss Nowak, so stop pretending to be one!"

Zero bristled. "Those are hardly ritual sacrifices of children though, are they?"

He turned and glowered.

"But OK," she allowed swiftly. "Those are bad, and I'm

not superior. Maybe I have no right to judge. But I think we both agree child sacrifice is bad, and needs to be stopped."

"Of course we agree," he spat.

"So to that end, finish what you were saying. How can vodou lead us to the killer?"

LaGuerre eyed her suspiciously. Zero got the impression he felt like he'd been verbally judo-flipped. Still, something shifted in his eyes, and he nodded. It felt like taking a step closer toward trust.

"All right. Well, in the case of a sacrifice, the ouanga is key. It's basically a talisman, to make sure the victim's soul is captured and fed into the killer." He paused a moment. "Often ouanga come in pairs: one stays with the killer, one stays with the victim to ensure the soul is fully transmitted."

Zero considered. "A transmitter and a receiver. That explains the little boy finding this ouanga at the scene. It's the transmitter."

"You can't use modern terminology to describe this process. We are not talking about hooking into your Wi-Fi router."

Zero ignored that, extrapolating outward. She picked up the doll. "So you're saying this 'ouanga' could tell us which gang killed him? Even which individual in that gang did it?"

LaGuerre opened his mouth, closed it again, then found the words. "Yes. It would require some interpretation from an expert in vodou, as there are thousands of Loa and tens of thousands of ways to invoke them, so every ouanga will be bespoke. The more unusual the crime, the more specific the ouanga, and I don't have that kind of knowledge." He paused a moment. "But I know someone who does."

"Who?"

"Leave that with me. I'll find out what I can, hopefully by tonight. I may even be able to shake out the name and address." He turned to her. "What are you going to do with that information, if I tell you?"

Zero was already planning. It was about time she got out into the wild night and put blades into a few of these child-sacrificing, woman-raping gang members. Hopefully one of them would know why the Engineer's teeth marks were dug into the forearms of so many dead little children.

"I'll do what you can't," she said. "I'll ask them some questions."

25

ROYAL OASIS HOTEL

It was growing dark by the time they arrived back in central Port-au-Prince. The night streets were different than by day; with few street lamps and fewer people out, it felt like a ghost town, like the hurricane had already hit and cleared everyone out. Only occasional small groups of young men stood at street corners, some openly carrying weapons, eyeing the Siena as it passed.

"Gangs," Zero said.

"Windows up," LaGuerre responded.

She wound the glass up.

They'd barely spoken for the ride back. Zero had spent most of that time watching the sun sink into the bay, while working her fingers over the 'ouanga'. It was hard to stop thinking about the agony of the little boy's death, hard not to let her rage drive her right out to attack the next gang cluster she saw.

She thought about what LaGuerre had said; about her being dangerous to herself as well as him. She knew that was true. She'd also learned control since the Engineer had said something similar on his iron altar. So she saved her rage.

She'd hammered nails into people before. Maybe tonight she would do it again.

"I said, where are you staying?" LaGuerre said.

Zero looked up and around. The Siena had pulled over to the side of a familiar spot without her noticing; the parking lot at Toussaint Louverture International Airport. Where it had all started this morning. As if to punctuate the moment, a jet roared into the sky a few hundred yards away.

"I'll find somewhere."

"There are some good hotels. Well, safe hotels. Within reason. The gangs monitor everything. I can draw up a list and-"

"Don't worry about me, Jean-Baptiste," she said, looking him in the eye. "Just get me a name and address then go to bed. By morning we'll have answers."

He stared at her uncomfortably. Maybe he could imagine what that meant. "I don't like you out there on your own at night. These are dangerous men."

She smiled. "Not as dangerous as me. They won't like me out at night alone either. Goodnight."

She opened the door and stepped out. Residual heat wafted up from the blacktop. The air tasted of dust and jet fuel.

"I can drive you to a hotel," LaGuerre said, leaning out of the window.

"Go make your calls."

She walked away but LaGuerre called after her.

"What?" she barked.

"I'll need the ouanga," he said. "My contact will want to inspect it."

She looked down at her hand, where the little wooden figure was clasped so tightly the nails were scratching her skin. She strode back and held it out.

"Thank you," he said.

"Look after it," she said, then strode off, walking until she was on the other side of the lot, where a line of shady men stood beside shady taxis. She took up position nearby, tapping her earpiece.

"Rex, are you with me?"

"I am, Zero," he responded. "I have taken the liberty of booking you into a 'safe' hotel already."

She smiled. Of course, he'd been listening all along.

"Did you catch everything about the ouanga?"

"I have played back everything your phone recorded, yes. Tonight you are hoping to interrogate some gang members?"

"That's the plan."

"Then you should rest first. You are block-booked at the Royal Oasis Hotel, thirty minutes away; I suggest you take the third taxicab along at the current stand."

Zero looked at the cab drivers. They all looked equally sketchy. "Why's that?"

"I have already remote-hacked their phones. The first two have a history of bilking their passengers, possibly handing off details to what may be gang contacts."

"For kidnap?"

"I expect so. I have no solid proof, only patterns. The third driver, however, seems honest."

"OK."

Zero walked up to the third driver and dropped into his cab without a word. He made apologetic noises at the first two in line, then got in the driver's seat. Zero let Rex speak for her in a clean Haitian accent.

"À l'Hôtel Royal Oasis."

The cab pulled away.

Zero watched the dark streets go by, heading south. With so few street lamps and thick low clouds shielding the moon, there was little to see. She thought about the ouanga and the little boy, and the man who'd gone to Cedras, and the women who had nothing to look forward to but more rape. All at the hands of the gang.

It made her angry. Anger helped.

"I'll need my own wheels, Rex," she said softly, so the driver wouldn't hear. "Can you set up a gig on the darknet for immediate payment on anonymous drop-off?"

"Of course," Rex answered. "Would you like a motorbike from the usual caliber, Zero?"

"Anything dark and quiet, dropped at the hotel in the next few hours, with a full tank."

"I will arrange this. There'll be a bike waiting when you wake up."

"Good dog."

Soon enough, approaching 9 p.m., she arrived at the Royal Oasis Hotel. She paid the driver and stepped out. Palm trees and verdant greenery loomed from a generous forecourt, fronting a cheerful yellow and orange building that rose some seven stories tall.

"You're block-booked under the name 'Agatha Briers'," Rex said in her ear.

Zero walked up the few stairs to the entrance. "Agatha?"

"The best I could do."

Zero pushed through the swing door into the lobby. Lukewarm air was being circulated by high ceiling fans. The floor was faux marble and the furnishings had clearly seen better days, but the attendant behind the front desk was crisply turned out in a black and gold blazer.

"Agatha Briers," she said. "Checking in."

He bustled then handed over a key card. Zero took it and strode to the elevators. "Anything from LaGuerre yet?"

"Not yet."

"What block-booking technique did you use?"

"The usual, via subtle means in the hotel's systems," Rex

said. "One above and one below. No one will know those rooms have been reserved."

Zero smiled. Rex could always be relied upon to do a solid job. "Good dog. Tell me you're erasing me from the hotel's CCTV record."

"I am doing exactly that as we speak. The only record of your presence is the initial booking, which I cannot wipe, and the interaction with the clerk."

That was fine. She could work with that. The elevator carried her to the sixth floor, where she found her room and entered. It didn't take long to open her backpack, retrieve three miniature spy cams and set two up in the corners of the room and one overlooking the corridor outside, syncing them to her phone. She checked the feeds; they were solid. After that she forced the window open, pushing the mechanism beyond its natural limits, and climbed out.

One floor rose up above her. Below lay a balcony with seating on the fourth floor, and below that a large blue swimming pool.

"Up or down?" Rex asked.

"Up, I think," she said, and started climbing the exterior of the building. The hand and footholds were thin, but the building's cladding provided edges she could cram her thumbs and fingers into, providing easy weight locks. She climbed one story swiftly enough, but the window to the seventh floor room was tricky. Using her Bowie blade she managed to jimmy it open then force it wide, all while hanging seventy feet high by one hand. Her grip was close to giving out when she finally slid in and closed the window behind her.

The room was much like below. She retrieved another spy cam from her pack, affixed it to the corridor outside and synced it, then switched the AC to high and bolted the door. In the bathroom she filled a glass with cold water and drained it half a dozen times. "Order me room service for two doors down, would you?" she told Rex.

"What would you like?"

"Burgers," Zero said, then hopped in the shower. The hot water felt like heaven on her skin, washing away the dried mud, sweat and stink of the mangrove swamps. By the time she stepped out and checked her cam, the room service had arrived. She opened the door and retrieved the laden tray.

Two orders of burgers and fries with a tall, candy pink strawberry milkshake, sweating condensation down the glass. "That's just beautiful, Rex."

"You can't murder without good calories. Now eat and rest, Zero. I will notify you when LaGuerre calls."

She grunted. "Don't have to tell me twice."

She wolfed the burgers down, followed with the fries, then drained the milkshake in three long, hard pulls that left her giddy with brain freeze. She plugged in her phone and laid back on the bed, activating her spy cam app. She had dozens of feeds to check on, including the ones she'd just set up in the hotel, but she ignored these and focused on the first set.

All showed live scenes from the house and the grounds of her home back in the Solska woods. It took a scan of nearly all the cameras to find them; of course, it was the early hours of the morning back in Poland, and they were all in bed. Hanna adopted her usual rucked up position, Zuzanna lay neatly and prim in the covers, and Gabriel looked gorgeous and lonely alone in their bed.

Her heart panged.

She killed the app and set the phone down, laid her head on the pillow and fell asleep in no time at all.

26

BOKOR

Rex woke her three hours later with gentle Bali-style windchimes. Zero rubbed her eyes and looked at her phone. Her spy cam feeds in the hotel were clear. The time was just after midnight.

"I'm up, Rex," she said.

"ID LaGuerre is calling you, Zero."

"OK. Put him through."

The line clicked. It was a poor connection, with the sound of shouts and cries in the background, and was that a drumbeat?

"LaGuerre," she said.

"Miss Nowak. I'm close to gathering the information we're looking for. There's just one thing I need from you."

She frowned. "What is it?"

"Your real name."

Zero sat up straight. "What?"

"I advise against this," LaGuerre said. "A name is very powerful. In the hands of some, it could be enough to make a ouanga. A vodou doll. But I wanted to make the choice yours. You're news in Port-au-Prince, in certain circles. After Marcelin. My contact is interested."

That didn't sound good. "Who's your contact?"

LaGuerre sighed. "It's complicated."

"Spit it out, Jean-Baptiste."

"She's a bokor. Probably the best in the city."

"She's a what?"

"A bokor. It's the name for vodou black magic practitioners, or sorcerers."

Zero said nothing. LaGuerre took that as his cue to go on.

"You've probably heard of witch doctors? Those who convert the living into zombies?"

"Zombies?" Zero asked.

"It's not real," LaGuerre said. He sounded strange, almost like he was drunk. "Or at least, it probably isn't. I've heard they use tetrodotoxin, a poison from puffer fish? I don't know if it's really possible."

Zero grunted. As a victim of a wide range of knockout drugs in her childhood, locked in the dungeon basement her father had dug beneath their Idaho pig farm, she'd taken a keen interest in a wide range of chemical intoxicants, deliriants, hallucinogens and knock-out drugs. It was knowledge that came in handy, as so many of the perps she hunted used chemical means to debilitate their victims.

Tetrodotoxin, though, was one she knew very little about.

"How does she even know Nowak's not my real name?"

"I don't know. Again, I advise against telling her anything. Whether you believe in black magic or not, she is a dangerous woman."

The shouting grew louder in the background, becoming screaming. "Where are you?"

"At her temple in Martissant district, west side," LaGuerre said. "Night mass."

It didn't sound like any kind of mass Zero had heard of before. She thought through the potential impact of sharing her name, then disregarded the results. She knew she was going to give it up.

"She can tell us the gang linked to the ouanga?"

"Individual members, even," LaGuerre answered. "She says she made this precise ouanga."

Zero's heart pumped harder, driving her to her feet. "My name's Clara Baxter. Get everything you can from her."

"Clara Baxter," LaGuerre repeated, "stay on the line."

Zero waited. She heard muffled conversation in French, then LaGuerre came back. "She said that's no good."

"What?"

"She says she wants your birth name, not another fake name."

Zero gritted her teeth. Since arriving in Haiti this would be the second time she identified herself. It felt dangerous, but she didn't care. She needed to kill someone tonight, needed to feel the Engineer falling closer into her grasp.

"Mona Gebhart," she said. "That's my birth name."

"Not Baxter?"

"Just tell her."

There was more muffled conversation. It stretched on for a minute, then two, then five. Zero used the time to prepare. She retrieved the black strike suit from her backpack and pulled it on. It was made of snug, para-aramid stab- and slash-resistant fabric. She slotted the Bowie knife into the built-in sheath down her right thigh. There was a mask and gloves, which she zipped into their respective pockets, ready for use. In the mirror she checked her reflection.

Dark and dangerous. Only her pale white face stood out.

"Is the bike waiting for me, Rex?"

"Waiting, a Suzuki SV650."

She knew the model; old, cheap and heavy but sleek handling. "Good."

Standing in front of the floor-to-ceiling windows, she

looked out over the city, pulse pumping in her ears. Five minutes became ten.

"LaGuerre," she prompted, but there was no answer.

"LaGuerre sounded drunk, Rex. Could that be an effect of tetrodotoxin poisoning?"

"Checking," Rex said. "Yes. Perhaps. The ID mentioned tetrodotoxin can turn people into zombies. In effect, it's a paralytic sodium channel blocker that can enter the body via inhalation, ingestion or through abraded skin. When the paralytic effect reaches the muscles of the lungs and heart, breathing and pulse slow to nearly undetectable levels. Too much and they simply switch off. If the dosage is correct, however, a person may be rendered visibly dead. There are countless stories of victims being buried then dug up by bokor hours later and 'resurrected'."

Zero blinked. "So that makes them into zombies? That could make LaGuerre sound drunk?"

"Potentially, but most likely that's the impact of another drug. The tetrodotoxin starts the process of zombification, at sufficient levels rendering a subject unconscious, with a pulse and breathing rate so low neither can be detected. It's been claimed that skilled bokor can maintain a person in that zombified state over a lengthy period of time."

"How lengthy?"

"There are many anecdotal stories of long-dead relatives returning as much as twenty years after their burial; when the bokor was finished with them."

A shudder ran down Zero's spine. "So what's the other drug?"

"Tetrodotoxin is often paired with datura stramonium," Rex went on clinically, "a deliriant better known as Jimson weed, which causes susceptibility to commands. Combine the two drugs correctly, and in theory a bokor can maintain the victim in a suggestive, zombie-like state indefinitely, capable of doing physical labor for free. If the dosage of either drug lapses, however, the victim should make a complete recovery within twenty-four hours, bar some temporary amnesia."

"Complete recovery?"

"Yes, once the drugs have left their system."

Zero considered. If she was going to come up against a bokor, it made sense to understand the tricks of their trade. "What about antidotes?"

"There are none. Tetrodotoxin is lethal in even small doses; ingesting activated charcoal may help leech the poison somewhat, but only extracorporeal membrane oxygenation, or ECMO, can keep a person alive long enough to recover."

"ECMO?"

"Life support. An external heart and lungs, essentially, for forced ventilation, potentially paired with dialysis to scrub poison from the blood."

Zero considered. "So LaGuerre's probably not on tetrodotoxin, too risky. But he might be high on Jimson weed?"

"This is quite possible. It appears to be a widely used drug in Haiti, a hallucinogen often used to bring on mass trance-like states in vodou rituals."

Zero began to be concerned. "Do you think this bokor has zombified LaGuerre?"

"If zombification is actually possible, then that is one outcome we should consi-"

"I have it," LaGuerre interrupted, at last. "One name and a location. I'll text them to you now."

"Are you all right, Jean-Baptiste?"

"I'm fine," he answered, but didn't sound it. "Sending shortly."

"Thank you," Zero said, "now get out of there, OK."

He ended the call.

She thought for a moment of going to find him, but that

could wait. For tonight, LaGuerre would have to look after himself. She left the room through the window, climbed down to the sixth floor then exited and rode the elevator to the lobby. Outside, the night air was still hot and humid.

"Bike, Rex?"

"In the underground parking, in the corner."

She walked down into the parking basement. There in a corner sat a black Suzuki. The key was in the usual place Rex had her darknet gig workers leave it, tucked into a slit in the back of the saddle. She slotted it in and fired up the engine. The machine purred beautifully.

Her phone chimed and she brought it up. There was a name and an address from LaGuerre: Enoch Sanon, a member of the Ti Bwa gang, apparently. The gang name was familiar but Zero didn't care about the details. He was based in Bourdon district, which a quick scan of her grayed-out map revealed was a twenty-minute ride west of her hotel, in a well-developed area sandwiched between slums, with good cell signal.

"My lucky night," Zero said. As she spoke, Rex dropped a pin in the center of her map, signifying the target. "You'll have to do the talking, Rex. How's your creole?"

"Coming along nicely."

"Then let's go. Direct me."

She kicked her right leg over the bike, leaned in and roared forward.

27

WILD NIGHT

At 1 a.m., Bourdon district on the west side of Port-au-Prince was quiet. Ruelle Nemours was a tree-lined street in a residential zone that seemed to have largely escaped the encroaching slumland. Zero walked the Suzuki the last fifty yards with the engine off, then kicked out the stand down the side of a tin-sided office building.

The area was still but for buzzing cicadas in a patch of rough woodland off to her left. Ahead lay a two-story pre-fab apartment block. According to the bokor's data, whether drawn from meticulous record-keeping or inferred from the vodou Loa, the target lived on the second floor with his mother.

The mother was off-limits. He was an enforcer for Ti Bwa, which put him squarely in her crosshairs.

Zero scanned the set-up. The distance from the block to the woodland was minimal. Barely a perp walk. She just had to get him out there, then she could do exactly what she wanted, and who was going to come when his muffled screams carried beyond the tree line? Not the PNH. Not here, not for a gang member.

Maybe some other Ti Bwa members?

She didn't care. It was time to act.

Across the street and up the stairs to the open front corridor, she assessed the apartment close up. The door was metal and locked, the windows had bar grilles across them. No easy way in.

She knocked.

She waited.

Someone shouted within. Zero knocked again. Angry footsteps stamped closer. The door opened and there stood a hulk of a young man. Enoch Sanon. He couldn't be older than 22, but he was well over six feet and beefed to the max on steroids and pumped iron, with swollen deltoids that forced his arms out at the sides.

Too much man for Zero to perp-walk anywhere. She shifted the plan.

He barked something in fast creole. He seemed both confused and angry to find a white woman outside his door.

"He's vexed," Rex interpreted.

"I gathered," Zero said. "Tell him I'm a stripper."

Rex spoke for her in Haitian creole, projecting the voice of a teenage girl from the phone speaker, which Zero held up.

Sanon's face muddled in deeper confusion. He looked at the phone then back at her face and spoke.

"Who sent you?" Rex translated.

"Tell him Ti Bwa leadership."

Rex did. Sanon stared for a long moment, perhaps trying to join up the dots. Then he shrugged and stood aside, inviting her in. That was confirmation enough for Zero. She drew her blade and smoothly, calmly pushed it into the side of his throat.

Then she stepped back.

The big man tried to shout but couldn't make a sound, as she'd precisely bisected his windpipe. He could still breathe, and he wasn't going to bleed out just yet, but his life had just become precarious. Of course, he didn't know that yet, and his hands shot up to his neck, where the blade protruded on both sides. Happily he didn't try to pull it out, which would probably have seen him drown within minutes on his own blood. Instead he went for her.

Zero was ready. She took one step to the side and guided him easily over the edge of the railing.

He fell. He hit the gravel with a thump below.

"Graceful," Rex said.

"As belly flops go," Zero said, looking down at the landing, where Sanon was trying to crawl.

Zero hopped over the railing and dropped lightly down beside his head. His face was bloodied from the impact with the floor, and it looked like his right arm had folded underneath him, most likely dislocating at the shoulder. He went after her with his left hand.

Zero grasped it.

In any other situation, his height, weight and the muscles of his back and shoulder would have seen him overawe her easily. But not sprawled out on the ground, barely able to breathe for the blade through his neck. In that situation, it came down to finger, wrist and forearm strength, and Zero bet on herself.

She locked her fingers to intertwine with his in a game of Mercy, then held him. His wild eyes, bloodshot already within his mangled face, beaded on her.

"I'm going to ask you some questions," she said, and Rex translated. "You're going to answer honestly and completely, or I'll break your wrist. Then I'll break your fingers. Last of all, I'll pull the knife out of your neck and you'll die. Am I understood?"

Rex finished, rattling off the translation in singsong creole.

Sanon stared. The truth was, he had a good chance at

survival, if an ambulance came for him within the hour. Maybe he could feel that. He spat blood and answered.

"Who are you?" Rex translated.

"The spirit of vengeance," Zero said. "I'm riding high tonight. Now, first question. Six months ago a little boy was killed in Basat, in the mangroves of Point du Cul-de-Sac, and a ouanga was left in his place. A local man reported the death, and he was buried too." She paused, looking into his eyes for some hint of recognition. "It was your gang that did it. Ti Bwa. But they were working with another man. A white man called the Engineer. He bites little children on the arm." She mimed biting her own left forearm. "I want that man. Lead me to him and you live."

It was a long speech. It took Rex another twenty seconds to finish speaking, and after he was done Sanon just stared for maybe another twenty seconds. Zero tweaked her wrist, putting pressure on his fingers. His eyes widened in disbelief and he pushed back.

Briefly, it was a contest. Then Zero won. His wrist bent back all the way, then something snapped.

He shrieked.

She let go.

"The Engineer," she repeated. "Where is he?"

The man stared at his sagging wrist and vomited; but only an acrid spray jetted between his lips. Zero cursed. With the blade through his throat, the vomit had gotten lodged. She swiftly pulled the blade out, and blood instantly began to leak from the wounds, along with a second burst of vomit that reached five feet distant.

She'd acted too fast. There wasn't long left now, and she leaned into Sanon's panicked face as he swallowed and gasped, swallowed and gasped, probably not even realizing that he was gulping down enough blood to drown himself.

"I can save you, Enoch! You just have to help me. The Engineer. Where is he?"

Rex translated and Sanon burbled an answer. Zero caught none of it.

"Rex?"

"That sounded like a name," Rex answered. "I'll get more."

Rex took over the interrogation in creole. The big guy talked until his stomach filled with blood, which he vomited out over the gravel, then he began to choke.

There was no getting anything out of him after that.

Zero stood.

Curtains fluttered in the apartments above. It wasn't smart to kill this man in this way, in full view of so many, but she didn't care. The code of silence that bound all these people to the gangs would bind them to her, at least as far as the police were concerned.

"Did you get it, Rex?"

"I have a location," the AI answered. "A warehouse on the south of the bay. I believe this is where Ti Bwa bought the little boy, from a white man in a good suit. That's all he remembered."

Zero's heart began to pound. 'White man in a good suit' sounded like the Engineer. This could all be over tonight. "You have the precise location?"

"I believe so. Should we contact ID LaGuerre?"

Zero considered that for a moment only. LaGuerre wouldn't have even gotten home yet. He'd still be doped with tetrodotoxin or datura stramonium or whatever the bokor had made him smoke to hand over the Ti Bwa member.

The man at her feet finally fell silent. Zero looked down at him. Asphyxiated on his own blood. The thought occurred that tomorrow, if she left his body here, LaGuerre would surely know what she'd done. At best, he'd stop working with her. At worst, he would arrest her.

Better that there was no body to find.

"Don't bother LaGuerre," she said, striding back toward the Suzuki. "He needs his sleep."

She rolled the bike over, stripped the dead man's jacket and used it as a rope, knotting one arm around Sanon's right ankle and the other to the Suzuki's rear license plate.

"Rex, pick a spot nearby good for dumping a body."

28

THOR

After a short detour to the bay, where she dumped Enoch Sanon's body into shallow water on a litter-strewn beach between two dark patches of shantytown, Rex directed her west on Route 2.

The night streets were quieter still at 2 a.m., and Zero flew through numerous more slum zones untouched by electricity of any kind, including street lamps and traffic lights. No other cars were out on the road, except for an old man pedaling a bicycle with a trailer stacked tall with pressed garbage, and the occasional SUV with smoked-glass and low-slung chassis.

Night industry and gang trucks.

Once, while passing through Martissant, the same district LaGuerre had gone to for his bokor contact, one of the trucks swerved into her lane. Maybe these were opportunists seeking an easy kidnap strike on a lone biker. Zero swerved easily past them and accelerated. The truck turned and gave chase, but within moments she'd lost them in the rats' nest of narrow streets verging another shanty town, parked up with her lights off in amongst the bushes under a tall palm tree.

"Wise choice, Zero," Rex rewarded her.

She snorted and kicked the bike back off the stand, refraining from lighting up her front lamp this time. "Any other night, Rex, I would kill them and take their truck. How far out am I?"

"Ten minutes. Cell coverage is spotty en route but good at the end point. As an aside, your pulse has settled into a high snare drum rattle. This is not healthy."

"I'm not out here for my health. What did you dig up on this place?"

Rex took the correction in his stride. "It's called the Thor terminal; a port facility for LPG and chemical tankers. It caters not to freight, only to fluids."

"LPG?"

"Liquid Petroleum Gas."

Zero snorted. "I should siphon some when I'm there. Stop LaGuerre complaining."

"It seems likely the large vertical storage tanks here, of which I count fifteen within a square mile, are dry."

"Dry? Why's that?"

"There are no records of imports for the last two years. The whole facility appears abandoned, including multiple warehouses, a drydock and a long docking jetty."

"Any idea why it's abandoned?"

"Gang violence. With gas at a premium, this location became a hotbed for gang crossfire. Two years ago a tanker was stormed as it was being unloaded, and an intense firefight led to petroleum vapors catching fire. The tanker exploded and the whole port was sprayed with burning metal. It appears no ships wished to return here after that."

Zero grunted. It sounded about right; gangs impoverishing both themselves and everyone around them in the battle to get ahead.

"So the port shut down and the Engineer moved in. What

about the warehouse, is there any sign of overwatch; CCTV or guard stations?"

"None that I can see, but I am relying on belly-camera footage from overpassing Airbuses from Toussaint Louverture International, the most recent photography available of this area. These shots are intended as an aid to landing and for the pleasure of passengers, however, not for detailed surveillance."

"OK. Well, I'll figure it out."

"I expect so."

Within moments the slums peeled back and Zero saw the first sign of the terminal; a twenty-yard tall white storage tank, tarnished with black tropical mold and creeping blisters of rust. It stood like a giant, pale sentinel at the border to the terminal, which swiftly opened out to reveal the dark nothing of the bay beyond.

Zero picked out more off-white vertical tanks scattered like tombstones across the facility. The Suzuki cruised along a two-lane Rex had previously named as Route De Rails; now Zero could see the old rail spars buried in the now-pitted blacktop pour. They'd removed the metal rails from an earlier railway but left the wooden beams in position; maybe too expensive to shift them, while the metal could be re-used.

"There," she said, picking out the warehouse at the head of the long jetty. "I think that's it."

"Let me see," Rex said.

Zero slowed the bike and brought up her phone. Rex already had the camera activated and she simply pointed it toward the warehouse as she approached; a long greenish structure more visible by its outline against the faintly lit horizon than any feature.

"I believe that is it," Rex said. "I advise caution."

Zero snorted and turned left into the facility. There were no lights, no people, no guard towers. Nothing. She rolled deeper along a rutted clay track, scanning the tanks to either side in search of snipers or a cluster of gang members gathered around the hot red dots of lit cigarettes, but there was nobody.

"It's empty."

"You sound disappointed."

"Let's hope I'm wrong," she said, and killed the bike's engine to let its momentum roll her into the shadow of the warehouse. For a moment after dismounting, she simply stood with her back pressed against the smooth green wall of the warehouse, left ear pressed to the still-hot metal.

No sounds came from within. There was no movement across the whole dock facility. "Clear," she said.

"Be cautious."

"Always," she answered, knowing that was a lie, and padded along in the shadow of the wall. With every step closer, more nerves throughout her body surged to life. She'd hunted for so long. Could it be possible the Engineer would finally be in her grasp tonight?

She rounded a corner, and moonlight cast through a chink in the clouds briefly illuminated the scene ahead. The jetty stretched away with clear scorch marks bitten into its long rectangle. She scanned the water near the tip and saw the rusting prow of what must have been a huge tanker emerging through the silver-dappled waves like some strange iceberg.

A graveyard for ships. Nobody was docking here until that wreckage was cleared, which she didn't figure was any time soon. It had to be hundreds of tons of useless, rusting scrap now.

She turned her gaze to the front gate of the warehouse.

It hung open.

She paused and stared, right hand instantly going to the blade in her thigh sheath. Maybe it was a trap, somehow. An army of Pinocchios could burst out of that open door at any moment, while others could leap from cover behind her, and that would be it.

Her breathing hastened and her pulse thundered.

"Zero," Rex said, part-caution, part-question.

"The door's open," she said.

"That can mean two things," Rex said calmly. "Either this is a trap or the Engineer's facility is abandoned, just like the terminal."

"How long ago was that boy killed?" she asked.

"Six months."

Zero cursed. Maybe she was too late. "It's gotta be the second. Unless they're waiting for me to walk in to spring the trap."

"I believe there is one way to find this out."

She snorted and advanced rapidly. They either knew she was coming now or they didn't.

It seemed they didn't.

The answer became abundantly clear as she closed on the doorway and peered inside. There was a long, narrow corridor stretching maybe twenty feet into darkness, which ended in a doorframe she could just pick out. It also hung open. There was a CCTV camera above the outside entrance and one on the inside door too, and both plunged Zero back into the past.

This was how her father had protected his dungeon under the Idaho pig farm: a long hall he'd called the 'exclusion corridor'. It allowed him to ensure she was safely incapacitated at the end of that long corridor before he ever even entered the dungeon.

She'd never successfully breached that twenty-foot gap. She'd dreamed for years of ways to beat his system, including various kinds of Trojan horse attacks where she faked injury or illness to draw him in hastily, but none of them had worked, and they'd all seen her viciously punished.

It was a simple and elegant design, and it would never have been left gaping open like this.

"The Engineer built this," she said.

"How do you know that?" Rex asked.

"Because it's the same as the dungeon on the farm, and he designed that too." She strode into the exclusion corridor, holding up her cell phone with the flash light illuminated. This was the first solid confirmation she'd had. "It looks like he's moved on, but he was really here, Rex. We're on his trail."

She plunged deeper into the dark.

29

FRENCH COLONIAL

Crumpled beer cans and sodden items of clothing lined the exclusion corridor, with gang graffiti tags sprayed on the metal walls. Zero counted her paces, under the defunct gaze of the dead CCTV camera, until she passed through the interior metal door and into a space so large that her cell phone flashlight barely illuminated a thing.

"Wow," she said, running the shallow beam over what she could see.

The floor was paved in a diamond mosaic of marble squares, some milky with dark veins, others black with silvery accents, though many were stained with black char marks and what looked like blood stains. The walls were clad in richly paneled wooden wainscoting in ornate mother-of-pearl trimmed with gold moldings, though the gold had been largely pried out and the wooden paneling had been hacked at, in places riddled with bullet holes.

"What is this place?" she murmured, advancing deeper.

The ceiling was high, an opalescent cream laced with elaborately filigreed gold plasterwork and decorative medallions. In the center of what seemed to be a rectangular space spreading some fifty feet by thirty and at least ten tall hung a golden chain, beneath which lay the shattered remnants of what must have been a beautiful chandelier of gilded bronze and crystal, now interspersed with blood-crusted rags and wadded magazines.

She turned, casting faint illumination over furnishings that looked like they belonged in the drawing room of a stately home, all in various degrees of vandalization: ostentatious pale green leather armchairs frilled with lace and sliced open like half-skinned beasts; decadent chaises longues in pastel pink, featuring scorched, intricate brocade styling; tall walnut occasional tables with the legs missing; delicate shelving units in blond oak tumbled on the floor, with books bound in pale yellow leather; side tables and drinks cabinets scattered about in the mangled dregs of brass candelabra and what could be the shards of fine crystal decanters.

"Rex," she murmured.

"I cannot explain this, Zero," he answered, watching through the phone's camera.

Everything had been wrecked. Zero moved amongst the ruins feeling like a ghost herself; one tall-backed armchair was strapped with a dozen or more zip-ties on the arms, the seat and back puddled with black blood.

"It's a torture den," she said. "But that's gotta be a latter-day usage."

"You do not believe the Engineer would torture like this?"

Zero swept her gaze up over a huge alabaster fireplace at one end of the hall, so large it looked like you could roast a whole hog in it, above it hung a highly embellished gilt painting frame with the painting missing.

"I don't believe he would. This is the gangs. He built all this, I'm sure of it. But on Pleasure Island he kept his luxury fittings apart from his torture zones. There were the corridors, and the rooms, and then there was the iron altar at the heart: brutal, industrial. I think he liked the contrast."

"So what is this?"

Zero stared at the painting frame. She tried to imagine what had hung there, taking up pride of place over this whole strange diorama. "Rex, what era are we looking at here, with all these furnishings?"

A moment passed and Zero swept her cell phone light around.

"Image searches suggest this is reminiscent of an 18th-century aristocratic house. The ceiling plasterwork and wall trim are certainly reminiscent of Louis XIV's palace at Versailles."

"Eighteenth century," Zero repeated, walking back through the wreckage. She spotted more chairs with zip-ties now, more crusts of blood. "Remind me, when did Haiti declare independence?"

"The Haitian revolt against the French colonial forces began in 1791 and ended in 1804. The general for the Haitians was an ex-slave named Toussaint Louverture."

Zero grunted absently. "They named the airport after him."

"It seems so."

"And this place, it fits right into that timeline. As if the Engineer was trying to recall the hey days of French colonialism. Slavery. Auction blocks. Savagery hiding beneath a civilized, opulent exterior."

"That seems a valid hypothesis."

Zero felt that twisting in her stomach like a knife. The Engineer had boasted to her about the endless supply of children he had access to around the world. Here he'd gone to town preparing a place to entertain his buyers.

Endless demand, he'd boasted. Men like that, they'd really get a kick out of playing fancy dress up like French gentility. On Pleasure Island they'd dressed in Roman-style togas.

"This is his show room," she said, flashing the light on the walls. She found brighter spots on the walls where more highly-embellished painting frames must have hung. "I think these paintings had pictures of his wares."

"The restavek children?"

"The children," she answered. "Stripped now. Along with any other identifying information, I'll bet."

"There should be more to this complex, Zero," Rex said. "This hall takes up less than half of the footprint of the warehouse."

"Way ahead of you," Zero said, stalking toward a door that lay at the far end of the hall from the fireplace. She drew her Bowie knife, grabbed the handle and yanked it open.

A pitch-black corridor stretched away, decorated just like the lobby, though here the floor had lush red carpet and the paneled walls were studded with subtle, sconced lighting fixtures, long dead. Doorways lined the walls. For a moment, Zero thought she glimpsed a shadowy figure ducking into one of the side rooms.

She ran, bursting through a doorway on the right into a small, dark room, maybe ten feet square, with a single black bench along one wall, and facing it a small cinema-screen. Nobody was here. She swept her phone side to side, but saw nothing. A projector hung above but it had been gutted, its circuitry and lenses lying like snowfall on the red carpet.

"Some kind of screening room?" she asked.

"Your guess is as good as mine," Rex responded.

Her throat tightened. "To close a sale."

"There may still be evidence here. Clues as to where the Engineer went."

Zero stepped back into the corridor. There were no more darting shadows. She started opening doors. The first led to a kitchen with an impressive coffee station, now battered and crumpled. She guessed the gangs weren't big on artisan coffee. Another door led to what must have been a server array, complete with four desks where computers had once sat, now just sprays of black cabling. There were substantial racks along one wall, and along another were hooks and shelving for storing some kind of equipment that was now long-gone.

"Imagine those racks are full of high-spec computer servers," Zero said. "What kind of processing power did he have and what was he doing with it?"

Rex thought for a few seconds.

"Processing power in the high petaflops, Zero. This could be the nexus of a new node on the shadow Internet, or an editing suite pushing high-quality video footage, or even a mining operation for cryptocurrencies."

Zero walked around the space, searching for anything that could provide a clue, a flash drive or connector that wasn't standard, but found nothing. He'd been thorough.

She moved onto the next room; clearly a guard room complete with a frame fitted with a dozen security monitors. The screens were mostly cracked and all were dead, and the computers that would have driven them were all gone.

She kept on. There were rooms for storage that had been cleaned out. One room, as she neared the end of the corridors, buzzed with a dank cloud of flies. The stench grew more powerful as she advanced. Through the door, she scanned a kill room. There was a wooden sawhorse assembled in the center, stained black with blood. The floor was hard with dried blood and shimmered with flies. On a stand at the side sat a chainsaw and a range of bladed instruments: a scalpel, a hatchet, a hacksaw.

"Gangs," she said.

"I agree this is unlikely to be the Engineer's style."

Zero stood for a moment, staring into the darkness and blood.

"Perhaps if you look again," Rex said in her ear. "You will find something useful."

Zero knew she wouldn't. The Engineer wasn't stupid and he hadn't left in a hurry. He'd taken everything that mattered, leaving only furniture behind.

"There's nothing, Rex."

"You could try-"

"There's nothing," she repeated. "It's a dead end."

She turned and walked back the way she had come, anger battling with frustration in her chest. The stink was in her lungs now, probably in her clothes, and there was no getting rid of it. She wanted to kill more Ti Bwa members. She wanted to start stabbing the haystack indiscriminately.

Somebody knew where the Engineer was at this minute. Somebody had to know.

But she didn't know who. She had no leads left.

She checked her phone. It was 4 a.m. and she was exhausted, running on little sleep after a journey halfway across the world and a full day and night on her feet. She'd earned a proper rest.

"How's the Royal Oasis look?" she asked.

"Clear," Rex replied.

"OK. I'm going to sleep."

30

NIGHTMARE

The nightmare was the same fusion of horrors as always.

Zero lay at the end of the exclusion corridor in her father's dungeon, shackled naked atop the Engineer's altar that belonged in Pleasure Island, and he was coming.

He had no face. It was her father, or it was the Engineer, but it didn't matter. What mattered was what he was going to do; the same thing he always did.

Try to steal her soul.

Except this time it was different. This time, Zero was not trapped on the altar. She was trapped inside the eyes of the man who was coming. She was in his head, feeling what he was feeling.

And she was looking forward to it. There were zip-ties in her left hand and a set of garden shears in her right. The future was filled with excitement. On the altar before her lay little Hanna, contorted in fear just as she always curled up in sleep.

She was crying. Sobbing. Begging.

Zero burst awake.

Light streamed in through the windows. Her heart

pounded like a police ram in her chest. It took her long seconds of staring at the view, at her hands, at her body to remember who and where she was.

Then it all came back.

A dead end.

She had nothing on the Engineer. He could be killing children at that exact moment, and she couldn't do anything about it. That made her responsible.

She stood up, trying to shake off the nightmare, then realized she was still wearing her strike suit. It was splashed with blood and stank of the kill room, of rotting matter and flies. She stripped it and tossed it on the floor then went to the shower. Twenty minutes of bracing, scalding water later, she still didn't feel clean. Her skin itched like an addiction, like she needed a fix more than anything in the world.

"Are you tracking LaGuerre's phone, Rex?" she asked.

"I am," the AI replied. He was unusually quiet this morning.

"What's wrong?"

"The body of the Ti Bwa gang member that you dumped? It's been found."

She frowned, pulling on a pair of black jeans and a dark shirt. "So? I didn't hide it well."

"No. Now it appears to be sparking rage amongst the Ti Bwa leadership, based on where the body was dumped. Apparently, it sends a message."

That got her attention. "I didn't mean to send a message."

"But you have. That beach is G-Pep territory, apparently. Their head has come out against the G-9 An Fanmi, claiming it's the start to a new gang war."

Zero considered. Then she cursed.

"This has probably complicated our search," Rex said.

"At least they don't know it's me."

"Don't they? ID LaGuerre will know. He gave you the name."

"He doesn't know I killed him."

Rex said nothing. Zero stood in front of the window and looked out at the waking city. It was barely 9 a.m. Time for a new day to begin, four left until the hurricane washed it all away.

"You think I need to be more careful."

"I fear this is becoming my chorus line," Rex said. "The song I sing at every scene change."

"So don't sing it."

"It would be hypocritical if I did. I conducted the interrogation. I led you to that beach. I didn't think things through either."

Zero's jaw tightened. "Don't beat yourself up about it, Rex."

A moment passed. "Then change my programming. I am currently set to learn from my mistakes. Should I stop doing so?"

She almost laughed. It was a great question, but she was not the right person to ask. For years people had been calling Zero out for being rash, including the Engineer himself. She'd gotten Malton Bruce and Tom Solent killed, and her last operator before Rex, while the hackers Hellion and B4cksl4cker had both been shot, and though she'd felt bad about all of those, she hadn't really changed at all.

Ultimately, that was a choice. Her addiction.

"Where is LaGuerre?"

"His phone places him currently at the Delmas police station."

"Call him."

The line rang. After five rings he answered. "ID LaGuerre."

"It's me," Zero said. "We need to meet. Thirty minutes at the Legim place."

She hung up.

The phone rang back. She ignored it. Within three minutes she was on her bike. Within twenty-five she was standing outside Mama Oshun's Legim place, watching the red pin of LaGuerre's cell phone draw near on her phone's mapping app.

Mama Oshun's was closed. The kids playing basketball were gone. The air was already hot and stifling.

LaGuerre's Fiat Siena arrived and he rolled the window down. His eyes were shot through with red and he looked exhausted. "It's closed," he said. "Legim's not a breakfast food."

"I gathered that," Zero said. "We need to talk."

LaGuerre sighed. "Get in."

"Are you going to try and arrest me?"

He gazed at her. "I don't know yet. It depends."

"Depends on what?"

"On what he said before he died."

Zero stared down at him. She had no better ideas. She looked at her bike, then opened the Siena's passenger door and dropped in. LaGuerre drove; away from Mama Oshun's and back onto the north-south road, heading south.

"Where are we going?"

"Coffee."

Zero let that stand. It didn't take long. Within minutes they turned right into a parking lot fronting a large bland warehouse. On the front hung a sign in brown lettering: Selecto.

"This is not a coffee shop."

"Follow me," LaGuerre said, and exited the vehicle. She followed. He walked along the side of the warehouse, around the corner and up to a small square window cut into the side of the metal siding. Inside there was a young man wearing a 'Selecto'-branded brown t-shirt and cap, with a barista-level coffee machine on his left and a stack of tiny white porcelain cups on his right. There was no other sign.

"I'm guessing an oat-milk ice latte is out," Zero said.

"Two double espressos," LaGuerre said to the server.

"Espresso then," Zero said, and watched as the solitary barista ground a scoopful of beans, packed a metal filter, steamed them and dripped deep black coffee into the tiny cups then handed them over. LaGuerre paid and walked away carrying them, leaving Zero to follow.

He took a seat at a picnic bench in the middle of the lot, under the shade of a tall tree with bright yellow, oval-shaped fruit.

"Cacao tree," LaGuerre said, sitting at the bench and holding out Zero's espresso. She took it and tried a sip. It was boiling hot and as thick as blood, with a kick that instantly widened her eyes. "This place is farm-to-table. They grow the beans, they dry roast them, they grind them. Best coffee in the Caribbean."

Zero didn't argue, just took another small slug.

"I'm guessing you didn't get his details," LaGuerre said, changing topics easily.

"Get whose details?"

He turned to her. "The man you're looking for. The one who bites the children."

Zero sipped her espresso. She hadn't told him there was a single man, or that he was the one doing the biting, but it was a simple enough deduction. "No."

"Did you get anything on him?"

Zero opened her mouth, closed it, then spilled about the warehouse. She told LaGuerre about the furniture, the kill room, the empty painting frames and her theory.

"Eighteenth-century French colonial," he repeated, when she was done.

"That's it."

"Strange. Like he's trying to restart the slave trade. But no further leads?"

"No."

He sipped away. "You know you might have triggered a new gang war by killing that man."

"I'm sorry about that."

LaGuerre laughed, snorting coffee. "You're sorry?"

"It's OK, though. The hurricane's coming. It'll squash a beef like this."

He turned to face her. "Haiti's not an etch-a-sketch, Miss Nowak. A hurricane's not like hitting the reset button. The outcome of any 'beefs' that happen now will be locked in place by the hurricane. Whichever gang is on top by the time the eye makes landfall, they'll be in power for another decade."

Zero grunted. Maybe that made sense.

"There's got to be something we've overlooked," she said.

"Not that I can see."

She said nothing.

"I'm going to finish my espresso," LaGuerre said, now gazing back at the warehouse, "then I'm going to ask you to get back in the car. I'm going to drive you to the airport, and then you're going to fly out of Haiti and never come back." He looked at her. "One gang war's enough, don't you think? Especially with nothing to show for it."

Zero couldn't argue. She had no intention of leaving, but nothing to go on. "And if I don't get in the car?"

"This time I will arrest you," LaGuerre said. "If that happens, it's out of my hands. You will most likely go to jail, where you will most likely suffer horribly and quite likely die."

Zero sipped her espresso. It was thick, hot and delicious. "And you like your chances of arresting me?"

"Me or someone from Delmas PD. At the very least, we can make Port-au-Prince a no-go zone for you."

Zero finished her espresso. She checked her sight lines across the lot. Maybe LaGuerre had set up members of his team nearby. She'd already conceded that possibility when she'd let him dictate the location. There were probably ways out of this lot. Maybe they wouldn't expect her to vault through the barista window and escape through the Selecto factory, but what if they were ready to fire their weapons at her? She was fast, but she hadn't yet found a way to outrun bullets.

LaGuerre was sipping lustily. He'd be done in less than a minute, she figured. She cast her mind back over the last twenty-four hours, searching for something, anything that could offer a clue.

There had to be something. The Engineer was brilliant but he was human. She could feel there was a mistake out there, niggling at her mind, but couldn't put her finger on it. She thought back to the start, how she'd gotten drawn into this to begin with.

He'd let that boy slip out in the ocean, found in the drilling platform's nets. He'd let that girl hang at the port with the bite mark on her arm. No matter what kind of message the gangs had been trying to send with her posed, elaborate death, then…

Her thinking slipped a gear.

LaGuerre finished his espresso and stood.

But there was something there. She reached for it. Something about the death of the girl, the gangs, the purpose of it all…

LaGuerre took a step back, out of wrist-grabbing range, and laid his hand on his weapon. "Don't make me draw this,

Miss Nowak."

She finally grasped what she was looking for, or at least the beginning of it. "It's not a message," she said swiftly.

LaGuerre was unmoved. "What isn't?"

"The little boy. You agreed. His death wasn't a message between gangs, not after we got that ouanga. It was a way to claim a death."

He shrugged. "Perhaps it was both. It could be a message between gangs, with one member keen to capture the death for themselves."

Zero shook her head. The idea had her in its grasp now. "No. Think about where his body was found. Out in the mangroves, right? Not on the jetty. Not in full view. Another gang didn't find it, a local man did, and when he reported it, the gang killed him. And the ouanga was hidden! Only a little boy found it. The gangs didn't want this known!"

LaGuerre shifted his footing slightly. "OK. But so what? What difference does that make if it's not a gang's message?"

Zero closed the loop. "Then there's a good chance it was the same for the little girl. What if that was only a vodou sacrifice too, not a message? Maybe we've been thinking about this all wrong."

LaGuerre looked like he was running out of patience, so Zero finished the thought.

"If she was another vodou killing, then there's got to be a ouanga hidden at the docks near where her body was found, right?"

LaGuerre said nothing. He stared at her.

He cursed.

"It makes sense, doesn't it?" Zero pressed. "There has to be a ouanga there! You said it, they come in pairs. And when you were out there, you collected her body, but did you look for a vodou doll?"

LaGuerre glowered.

"Maybe we can find it, then we take it to your bokor, get the gang hookup, and maybe we get an up-to-date read on where the killer is now."

"A lot of maybes in that sentence."

"So it's a long shot," Zero said rapidly, "but at least it's a shot. You said you wanted to clean things up. Here's another chance. Don't back out now, Jean-Baptiste."

He stared at her for a long moment. A horn somewhere across the lot honked, and he held up a hand in their direction. A signal. He had brought a backup team after all.

"We owe it to that little girl," Zero said. "To all the dead restaveks in Pierre Cedras' folder."

LaGuerre opened his mouth, closed it again, then found the words. "The docks are gang territory. We'd be asking for trouble."

"So let's ask quickly," Zero said, noticing that he'd flipped from a hard no to a conditional. "In and out. If the ouanga's there, I'll find it. If it's not, I'll get on that plane and leave forever, I promise."

LaGuerre sighed, then dropped his hand away from his weapon. "Last chance, Miss Nowak."

31

PORT INTERNATIONAL

"Twenty minutes," LaGuerre said, as he pulled the Siena out of the lot. He gave a wave to an unmarked car at the edge, and they waved back.

"Backup," Zero said.

"Wouldn't you come see you with backup?"

She said nothing. The aircon was off and the car was hot, as ever. After a short drive north, LaGuerre pulled west onto the airport road bordering the slums. They passed the turn for the Delmas police station, passing into a stretch approximating parkland. To the right there was brown grass and a few bedraggled palm trees, but everything looked sickly and wasted; the grass scattered with litter and the trees hung with scraps of old clothing and more images of Jesus, baring his glowing red heart.

It reminded Zero of Mama Oshun's Legim place.

"Vodou," she said.

"What?"

"Over there," she nodded. "Jesus this time."

LaGuerre looked and grunted. "Right. Vodou." A few seconds passed. "All this park, when the earthquake hit in 2010, there used to be decent new apartment blocks. At least people thought they were decent, but they were rotten, made of in-fill and sand and the quake brought them down. Hundreds died just here. This is what rebuilding looks like in Haiti."

They continued on. Out of nowhere something hit the passenger-side window and Zero flinched. A white scratch mark appeared on the glass.

"Not a bullet," LaGuerre said, unfazed. "Though we are bulletproof. A rock, probably. Just kids. Another reason to keep the windows up. I did say we're not beloved."

"You're angry," Zero said.

"Of course I'm angry."

"At me? That Ti Bwa guy earned his death."

He spun to her. "So you're confessing?"

"Just making an observation."

"Well keep your observations to yourself. Most likely you'll be boarding a plane within an hour."

She was silent. A few minutes more passed, then ahead the world opened up to reveal the dockyard. It was vast, far bigger than the Thor terminal for liquid gas, spreading as far as Zero could see to left and right, and towered with a maze of stacked shipping containers.

The hot air within the car took on the scent of the sea and the rust of corroding metal. LaGuerre turned left and they cruised along a road that was more pothole and gravel than blacktop. To the right passed the shipping containers, to the left lay more slums and large piles of garbage, some smoking, some reduced to embers. Zero picked out a market of rickety booths under torn gray canvas, where a group of hard-looking young men stood around a black pickup truck with an open back bed.

"G9," Zero said. "Is the docks theirs?"

"I don't know," LaGuerre said, following her gaze. "It's not like LA; they don't wear a specific color. I can't tell you which gang these are, and we're not going to go ask. What I can tell you is they're on alert."

Zero could easily confirm both parts of that; these men wore a range of bright and eccentric clothing: one had an electric blue jacket with sharp lapels over black combat pants; another wore all black like a paramilitary soldier with a black beret, set off by a vivid green and blue scarf; one wore Yves Saint Laurent khaki Bermuda shorts with a red and black Falcons NFL t-shirt. All wore leather thong sandals and all carried weaponry of some kind; machetes in their hands, rifles strung around their chests, handguns stuffed in waistbands and shoulder holsters.

Just looking at them sent a thrill through her chest; excitement of what was to come, of what they might find.

A few hundred yards further lay the entrance to the docks. A lone guard dressed in a tan uniform with a brown cap sat in his booth watching over a single security arm. LaGuerre pulled in, killed the engine and exited the vehicle. Zero looked back to the market where the gang members seemed to be taking an interest. The guard listened while LaGuerre spoke in the Haitian creole, then held out a hand.

LaGuerre put a roll of bank notes in it.

The security arm went up. The gang members watched more closely. LaGuerre got back into the car.

"Simple," Zero said.

"I bought us twenty minutes," he answered. "He works for the gangs, by the way, even if he's wearing government beige. We shouldn't stay even that long. We're already garnering bad attention."

He drove past the booth along a narrow track through the stacks of shipping containers. After some five hundred meandering yards they emerged onto the dock Zero had seen in Rex's earliest photos.

Her heart skipped a beat.

This was where she'd died.

There were two motionless gantry cranes overlooking two empty docking berths, and beyond that the blue waves of Port-au-Prince Bay. LaGuerre stopped the car out in the open, where no loading or unloading was happening, and no ships were in position, and they both stepped out.

The port was quiet and still. The shipping containers looked more like some giant's abandoned toy blocks than a system for shipping goods.

Zero looked up at the gantry cranes, rusted yellow skeletons against the acid blue sky. It was easy to imagine the little girl's small body hanging from the top. It was even easier, looking back in the direction of the market, now obscured by the tall stacks, to imagine who'd put her there.

Ti Bwa. G9 or G-Pep. One of these bastards.

"They won't tolerate us here for long," LaGuerre said, nodding in the direction of the market. "We shouldn't waste time."

Zero walked over to the cranes. They were large but old, about fifty feet tall and coated with a thick layer of rust; any mechanism they once had looked to be long destroyed. To hang the little girl's body, someone would have had to climb up and string the noose by hand. It would have taken time, and been visible from anywhere nearby.

She let her gaze travel wider, over the calm waters, the rusting stacks and the double-berth dock. There was no hint of CCTV anywhere, as LaGuerre had said. There was no place for passersby or dock workers to stand and witness the hangings. There were no dock workers anywhere at all. Nothing moved, barely a breath of wind disturbed the wet heat; no ships, no cranes, no forklift trucks ferrying loads. No witnesses.

"Why is this place so quiet?"

LaGuerre came to stand beside her. "It's not the primary

dock anymore. Companies don't want to use it. For one, everything left here is ancient. MINUSTAH, that's the United Nations stabilization effort, invested in new equipment a decade ago, but it was quickly stolen. Back then the gangs just took a percentage of all trade; that was workable until the 2010 earthquake, when they started stealing entire shipments and openly ransoming freighter crews."

"Like the Thor terminal," Zero said. "Where the LPG tanker blew up when gangs fought over it."

LaGuerre cast her an odd glance. "Sure. I guess open theft became more profitable than siphoning percentages. As a result, both our containers and our gas come shipped in through Cap Haitien on the island's north side. The only loads passing through here now are drugs and weaponry."

Zero turned to him, alarm bells ringing in her head. "You didn't mention that earlier. It's just illicit trade passing through here?"

"Drugs or weaponry," LaGuerre repeated.

"What about trafficked humans?"

LaGuerre said nothing.

"Do you know anything about that? All those restaveks, maybe they were shipped through here."

"Not my field, Miss Nowak. This is gang territory; the kind of thing that'll get a cop killed."

"You must know something about it."

He sighed. "Of course I do. I know that it happens, and we can't do anything to stop it. Sometimes we find batches of smuggled people dead in their containers when some trade went bad. Most of the gangs aspire to traffick people because it's high risk, high reward, but it's a difficult business even here. It requires a lot of logistical support, as well as a vast network of bribes paid to corrupt officials in the right places. It's not easy."

Zero thought about the Engineer; how he'd designed and

built Pleasure Island, staffed it with attendants and stocked it with children, then sold places to wealthy Pinocchios in complete secrecy. The same went for the Thor terminal showroom. He was a genius for logistics; greasing the wheels; keeping his plans secret.

Her gaze fixed back on the container stacks, as if she could see through them to the market beyond. At this distance, even with the stacks in the way, her thirst to interrogate and kill those young men was strong.

"Fifteen minutes left, Miss Nowak," LaGuerre prompted. Do you want to talk about the gangs or do you want to hunt for a ouanga?"

Zero grunted and surveyed the scene. There were countless places to search, and they didn't have the time. "Where would they put the ouanga, LaGuerre?"

"I don't know. I don't practice vodou."

She turned to him. "But you do know about vodou."

He looked pained. "OK. Based on kill scenes I've seen, the ouanga are usually hidden, often high up, but it's important they have a clear line to the sky; without that, they can't fully work. That matches what the little boy in Basat said; the ouanga there was in the branches of a tree."

"So somewhere high?" Zero murmured, looking around at the tall stacks surrounding them.

"The ouanga needs to transmit the stolen 'soul strength' up to the respective Loa," LaGuerre went on, "who then takes a fraction of it and beams the rest back down to the killer."

"Like a credit card company taking a charge," Zero muttered, then walked to the dock edge and looked over, sweeping her gaze left to right. There was detritus floating on frothy scum in the water, but the dock wall itself was clean.

"No ouangas here," she said, then turned back. It wasn't high anyway. There were a dozen container stacks nearby; a doll could be sitting on top of any of them, but as soon as she had that thought, she realized it wasn't right.

Instead she looked directly up. Someone in the gang had had to climb the crane anyway to string the noose. It made sense.

"Ten minutes," LaGuerre said, looking at his watch. "We have to go."

"I'll be quick," she said, and laid hands on the rusted metal of the crane and swiftly began to climb.

"What are you doing?" LaGuerre called.

"Black magic," Zero answered. Hand-over-hand, she reached the top of the crane in moments; with the frame obscuring her body, there was no way she would be spotted from the market, but it afforded her an excellent view.

The dockyards ran to the northeast along the coast for around half a mile, a dusty red clay delta laden with a maze-like network of stacked container boxes. In some places they were three tall, others four or five, in some places lined up in walls with passageways in-between, some of which dead-ended, some of which didn't.

None of the nearby boxes had anything like a vodou doll atop them.

She looked wider. Beyond the docks to the north lay a road and then the wall barring the infamous Cité Soleil slum. The wall encircling it was patchwork and makeshift, broken by what looked like guard towers in places; the gangs defending their territory. Beyond the wall the slum ran up a hill in a tight-knit warren of multicolored walls and rooftops.

"Eight minutes," LaGuerre called from below.

Off to the west lay the crystal-blue waters of the bay. The twin jaws of the island were faintly visible in the far distance, along with a clot of black crag islands out in the middle, looking beautiful and raw and inhospitable.

Zero refocused on the crane. The top beam was some five

inches wide, reaching out twenty yards toward its companion. There were thick blotches of rust growing through the faded red paint like gritty mushrooms. Ten yards out, she saw the remnants of the rope they must have used to hang the little girl, and next to it was a bundle strapped to the metal.

Zero's heart spiked.

"Six minutes," LaGuerre called.

She rose to her feet and dashed along the top of the crane. Her balance didn't waver, but it pulled a curse out of LaGuerre. She ignored him and dropped down to straddle the beam beside the rope. The bundle was wrapped tightly with bright yellow string; she pulled her Bowie knife and slit it, then held up the ouanga.

Her pulse raced.

It was much more complex than the doll from Basat: as big as her palm, framed out of two pieces of rough cut white leather stitched with thick loops of red cord, in the rough shape of a human form. It had a single black button in the center of its lumpy head, from which flowed a stream of red tassels. Inside Zero felt something hard, even sharp, but there wasn't time to slit it open and investigate.

"Five minutes!" LaGuerre called.

She stuffed the doll in her backpack, then rose and dashed back across the arm to the crane, drawing a curse from below. As she turned to descend, she caught a glimpse of the market over the container stacks and momentarily paused, feeling disoriented. There was a clear view of the dirty gray tarpaulins strung over those few sad stalls, but she couldn't see the truck or the gang members circled around it.

Then she did see them.

Her heart skipped a beat. They were aboard the truck's open bed, rifles at the ready, already passing through the security arm at the entrance to the docks and coming their way.

32

DISPATCH

Zero's mouth ran dry. She counted almost a dozen men. Far more than she could handle at once.

"They're coming!" she shouted down to LaGuerre, descending the crane's frame so fast she almost friction-burned her palms.

"The gang?" he asked, eyes widening.

"They're already through the security arm. We need to get out of here."

LaGuerre's face darkened. "Come on," he said, and ran back to his squad car.

The gunshot sound of an unmuffled engine sounded through the stacks like a warning salvo. LaGuerre reached the patrol car, opened the door to retrieve a radio transceiver and spoke in rapid creole; it sounded like a call for backup.

The transceiver barked back at him. LaGuerre dropped it, leaned in again to hit his lights and siren, which instantly began to flash and wail, then set the radio down and strode to the rear of the vehicle.

"We're not going to run?" Zero asked.

"We can't. That track's the only way out of the docks." He

pointed then opened the trunk and pulled a long semi-automatic rifle out of its foam slot. He checked the breech, inserted a magazine and racked a shell home, then slotted the barrel into the aperture between the C-column and the trunk lid and hunkered down behind it.

"Come stand behind the vehicle, Miss Nowak. Pick a handgun; we may have to shoot our way out of this."

Zero didn't budge. Her heart pounded in her chest, making her judgments.

"Miss Nowak, this is no night-time frolic against an unsuspecting target," LaGuerre pressed. "Tongue grabs and surprise tactics aren't going to work now. The gangs are on guard, and if the bokor had heard about you, maybe they have too. Marcelin has a big mouth and a lot of gang contacts. Maybe they're just pissed off about the Ti Bwa death and looking to take it out on somebody. In any case, I don't want our bodies to be the next ones hanging from these cranes. We'll have to hold them off until backup comes."

Zero didn't take her eyes off the single exit gap through the container stack maze. "They'd kill a cop for nothing?"

"This is their territory, and you've sinned against the gangs, so it's not nothing. But, yes. They killed the President a year ago. They killed the head of the PNH in January and last month alone they killed twenty-three of my brothers, half of whose bodies they wrapped in tires and burned alive. You need to take shelter behind the vehicle right now!"

Zero's jaw clenched. Take shelter. Maybe these were the men who'd killed that little girl and strung her up from the crane to send a message, or maybe they were working with the Engineer to traffic children out of Port-au-Prince, headed for some dark and despicable fate.

Now they were coming for her, and every fiber in her body itched to kill them all.

The truck's engine backfired again through the canyons of metal stacks, so close she could feel it in the air.

"If they take you, they will certainly rape you, try to ransom you and most likely kill you," LaGuerre barked. "You are worth something to them. Me they'll just execute. I can protect you until reinforcements come, but you have to-"

"You said Marcelin runs dispatch?" she asked, mind racing now.

"He does. But he's in hospital now. I just spoke to Luther, an officer I trust, he was waiting with me at the espresso bar. He said he's sending-"

"He's probably lying," Zero said, feeling the world shrink down to this moment and this place. "Who does he fear more, you or Marcelin? You or the gangs?"

LaGuerre opened his mouth then closed it.

"We can't bank on reinforcements, LaGuerre," she said, "and we can't win a shootout. We have to run right now."

He stared at her like she was crazy. "Run on foot? We'll never even clear the dock."

"I'll clear it," she said firmly. "If you're right, they'll follow me instead of you. When their truck vacates the route out, you wind your windows up and you floor it."

He shook his head in disbelief. "We may have our differences, Miss Nowak, but I cannot abandon you to the gangs."

"Don't try to be a hero, Jean-Baptiste," she said, already working the angles in her head. "I'm the one abandoning you. Trust me, I'll be OK. Just think about yourself and I'll catch up with you over legim in a few hours' time. Understood?"

He opened his mouth to answer, then the gang's truck burst into sight, roaring and backfiring through the gap in the container stacks barely a hundred yards away.

LaGuerre raised a loudspeaker from the Fiat's trunk and gave the order. "Arrête toi là!"

"That means 'stop right there," Rex supplied helpfully, the first time he'd spoken in over an hour.

The truck skidded broadside to a halt some thirty yards away, blocking the exit route, engine still revving and barking more gunshot backfires in a fog of black exhaust and dust. The gang members swiftly jumped off and fanned out, rifles up and trained on LaGuerre.

For a few seconds a silent détente held, the air thickening with tension, then the older man in the electric blue jacket, maybe late twenties, climbed out of the passenger seat and stepped to the front. He pointed his machete at Zero and let loose in a torrent of Haitian creole. She caught the odd word and Rex filled in the gaps via the earpiece, but it didn't require much interpretation. He said 'bitch slut' enough times to make the connection to Marcelin.

He'd sold them out.

"They do want you," LaGuerre translated, not looking in her direction. "Exactly what I said. They say they'll let me go if I hand you over."

"They're lying. The only play here, Jean-Baptiste, is I run and draw them off. That's it."

He shook his head. "You'll never outrun them. Not on their own turf." He raised a placating hand to the leader and said something in creole.

"He's bargaining," Rex translated in her ear. "Offering money."

Several of the men laughed. The leader didn't. He looked angry. The moment felt seconds away from exploding into violence.

"Listen to me very carefully, Jean-Baptiste," Zero said. "I am going to run in ten seconds. They are going to chase me, because they want me alive. Because Marcelin or G9 or somebody wants me alive. When that happens, I suggest you forget heroics and get the hell out of here before they wrap you up in tires and give you a kerosene shower. OK?"

His eyes flashed in her direction. "You can't-"

"Now," she shouted, spun on her heel and broke into a sprint.

Behind her all hell broke loose.

33

ALL HELL

The gang shouted. The leader barked orders which LaGuerre answered in kind, then gunfire ripped out.

"Run!" LaGuerre shouted from behind, like she needed his advice, then his rifle added to the chaos of the crossfire.

"Zero, are you in danger?" Rex asked in her ear.

"Something like that," she managed, feet pounding the clay and arms pumping at her sides. She chanced a look back to see one gang member down already, two on their knees returning fire at LaGuerre, and the leader in his electric blue striding toward the Fiat with his machete bared like bullets couldn't touch him. Behind him the truck spun up and lurched after her, just as she'd predicted, with the remaining three gang members leaning out from the running boards.

Zero whipped her gaze forward and ran. Even with a hundred-yard head start the truck would reach her in moments. They'd run her down long before she cleared the dock.

Unless…

She thought back on the bird's eye view of the container stacks from the top of the crane. The nearest stack was twenty yards off still; she could reach it easily, but it wouldn't help her any, an isolated island. If she climbed that, she'd be stuck until they dragged her down. The next stack was seventy yards off, and that was her ticket out of there.

She just had to reach it first.

Gunfire blasted close by and red clay erupted five yards to her right. That had to be a warning shot. The truck boomed and she chanced a look over her shoulder; it was so close now that all she could do was dive to the side and-

She hit the clay and rolled as the truck ripped by, skidded and rammed into the island stack. For a split second she shared a look with the driver, who glared at her with such hatred as he frantically spun the wheel, then she was up and running again.

Sixty yards remained to the stack she needed; it was three tall, a red box on a green box on a faded blue box, each as big as the containers of Pleasure Island. Fifty yards, now, and the truck was back in the chase, but two of the three men were on foot now and had closed the gap to thirty yards, their leather thongs slapping wildly, rifles flailing, affording her maybe just enough time to-

Something slammed into her side.

She was flung through the air, her own momentum combining with a lateral force that dumped her face first into the clay and rolling. She ended up skidding on her chest, managed to roll onto her side and registered the man who'd shoulder-charged her; a ninth gang member who must've snuck up through the stacks. Already he was bringing back one long skinny arm with his fist wrapped tight.

She tried to get a guard up but it wasn't enough, and his fist hammered down onto her jaw, driving her face sideways into the clay. She bounced up slightly, vision blurring but clear enough to pick out the men on foot were only twenty yards away now with the truck just behind them. Her assailant grabbed her hair and yanked her back, forcing her spine into an arch.

Fifteen yards, with the truck skidding around ahead to block any escape route forward. The man wrapped his left arm around her neck and compressed; gray lights flashed before her eyes. She had seconds of consciousness left only, but seconds could be enough; she swept up the blade from her concealed thigh holster and stabbed it firmly over her left shoulder.

The tip plunged into the soft tissue of the man's left eye and through into his brain. The choke on her neck fell away.

Zero rose to unsteady feet, the men barely eight yards away now, and ran. The truck's door opened ahead and the driver lunged at her, but she darted sideways at the last moment, vaulted onto the truck bed and over to the other side, with twenty yards left to go.

The three gang members followed on foot; so close now she could hear the rush of their breath. Warning shots ripped again into the dirt then spattered up the side of the box. Her shadow loomed ahead, with the shadow arm of a man reaching out to her neck barely a foot apart, then she came into range of the stack and threw herself up.

Her right foot hit the box's metal wall with a resounding bong, her momentum buried into her thigh like a tightly coiled spring and she unleashed it upwards, soaring straight vertical. She grabbed the locking crossbar of the second stacked box just as the man below slammed into the solid metal and snatched up.

His hand brushed her heel and she climbed rapidly the rest of the way up, grabbing and kicking off easy holds that propelled her past the second box and onto the third, some thirty feet high. Hasty bullets struck sparks off the metal near her right hand then she was over the lip and out of the line of fire. For just a moment she spun to look back the way she'd come.

Two of the four men below were climbing, one other and the driver were aiming their rifles. Back at the Siena, Jean-Baptiste LaGuerre was locked in a grapple with the man in the electric blue jacket, fighting over his rifle. The machete glinted on the floor and bright red blood already stained LaGuerre's stark white shirt. One more gang member was on the floor, while the last one was approaching, his weapon raised.

Nothing Zero could do for him now.

She spun and sprinted along the top of the stack; a wall that stretched seven containers long, some fifty yards. Hollow bongs rang from behind as the men climbed, but she doubted they could compete with her vertical speed. At least one chased on foot below, but that was where her earlier survey of the stacks gave her an advantage; this container stack dead-ended against another long wall of boxes ahead. The men on foot would have to circle around them all, then navigate the maze as Zero dictated it from above, all while she leaped from stack to stack until she reached the end of the docks, after which she would plunge into the shantytown.

She didn't like her chances, once inside. She didn't like theirs either, though, and maybe that was the best she could achieve right now.

"How's your map of Cité Soleil looking, Rex?" she asked.

"Cité Soleil? I have none. Shall I find some?"

She laughed at the ridiculousness of all this, then leaped over to the next stack of boxes. "I'm going to need a route through on foot. So, yes please."

A single rifle shot rang out in back, but she pushed it from her mind. She could worry about the fate of Jean-Baptiste LaGuerre later.

34

CITÉ SOLEIL

At the northern edge of the dockyard, Zero dropped down to the red clay dirt, burst through a screen of wilted papaya trees, crossed the two-lane encircling road then paused for breath at the edge of the shantytown's tall encircling wall. It was constructed entirely from what looked to be reclaimed garbage; car doors, trash cans, metal beams and assorted timber slats.

For perhaps five seconds she bent double with panting, hands on her knees and sweat pouring down her cheeks, watching the route back. It was hotter than anywhere she'd ever been, and the airborne dust only made breathing harder. Still, she'd made good time along the container stacks; perhaps good enough to lose the gang completely.

Then the first of them lurched through the screen of papayas, twenty yards to the east. Zero straightened, spun and scaled the shabby wall in seconds flat, plunging down on the other side into a hip-wide alleyway between two tin shacks.

Shouts chased her and she ran, swallowed by the shantytown.

"I read very weak cell coverage in this area," Rex said, as Zero raced deeper along a winding narrow alley, which weaved left and right seemingly at random. She leaped over a low rivulet of black waste then ran up an embankment to higher ground. On her left now were cinderblock walls daubed with faded yellow paint, to the right were rusted tin sidings and underfoot lay a pathway of pounded-smooth rubble and rubbish, banked either side with old tires half-buried in gray silt.

A shot pealed out from behind and a bullet smacked off the cinderblock wall, ricocheting to punch neatly through the tin wall opposite. A woman screamed in alarm.

Zero put her head down and pumped her arms.

"There is something you should know before you progress any deeper," Rex said, then his voice cut out. Zero reached a crossroads of a kind, four branches leading away organically, none signposted, some narrower, some wider, all flanked by gaudy cinderblocks or rusted tin. She was already losing her sense of direction and looked up for guidance, but the morning sun wasn't high enough to see yet.

Another shot barked behind her and she picked the middle fork and sprinted.

"What should I know, Rex?" she shouted, but no answer came. The path veered right swiftly and she ran straight through a group of children in bright clothing, clustered around the entrance to a dark tin-and-branch framed hall. Within she glimpsed a plasma screen roped to the wall, with multiple rows of children sitting agog, watching what looked like an old action movie.

Ghetto cinema.

Then she was past it and the gunfire picked up again.

"Rex, what should I know?"

The line crackled and his voice came back. "I have researched both the G9 and the G-Pep gangs, Zero. They are currently in the midst of a vicious gang war for territory, focused mostly on Cité Soleil."

Zero barked a single laugh, then the alleyway she was in abruptly opened out into something like a market street. She stopped for a moment, gasping and looking in both directions. There were a handful of stalls lining a paved floor riddled with missing slabs; one sold small plastic bags of cloudy water, one sold pale watermelon slices, one sold takeout tubs of rice. People turned to stare at her; none were armed, all wore bright colors, almost all were young.

Still there was no sign of the sun and her sense of direction was completely gone. She lifted her phone but the GPS was shot, leaving her as a directionless blue dot in a gray haze. She picked left and kept on running.

"I need a way out, Rex," she gasped between gulps for air. "This place is a maze and I can't get my bearings. Can you triangulate me and give directions?"

"I am attempting this currently, but it is proving impossible with any precision. It would help if you could locate any fixed landmarks. For example, there are several drainage canals, along with the abandoned rails of an old tramway. In addition, numerous international aid charities have airlifted modular structures into the central areas previously, typically framed as shipping container-style boxes. All are abandoned now, but their locations are known. There should be a UN police bunker, and a Doctors Without Borders hospital; that one's famous as it may have released cholera into a local water supply in 2011, killing tens of thousands; there should also be-"

The signal cut out just as the market street ended at a long, five-foot-tall mound of strange gray matter stretching uninterrupted from left to right. Zero was gasping so hard it felt her heart might pump up into her mouth. Sweat stung her eyes and she wiped it away, peering more closely at the long mound.

It was trash; a massive beachhead of garbage, bleached

gray by the sun and compacted with dust to the color and consistency of cement. No plants grew anywhere across it. There were crushed bottles and sunken tires and ragged plastic bags and the frame of a car buried in the plaster-like crush; must've been swept there by one of the tropical storms after the 2010 earthquake ripped half the city down.

Nobody had cleaned any of it away. It was just there.

"I'm looking at some kind of trash embankment," she gasped. "It's huge and long. Maybe one of those drainage canals. Do I go left or right?"

Nothing came back. She looked to either side. Now she could see the sun peeking off to the right, so she could at least get a north-east reading. The mound didn't look like the best route for an exit, though, as she'd be totally exposed to anyone watching.

"Left or right, Rex?" she shouted, but there was still no response.

A shout rang behind her. A rifle fired and was instantly answered by others, becoming a firecracker string of gunpowder bursts. Maybe a G-Pep member in the G9 area, or vice versa, or the Fanmi members chasing her. Maybe it made no difference now; her presence had catalyzed another bout in the war.

She ran up onto the endless gray mound of rock-solid waste, and as soon as she crested the peak she was hit by the eyewatering stench of sewage. On the other side lay a turgid black canal, half-filled with masonry, rusted bicycles and thick clogs of black fabric and sludge, shining with a rainbow slick of oil and teeming with flies and mosquitoes even worse than the mangrove swamps.

Zero gagged and broke right.

In moments she left the market street behind, and the immediate sound of gunfire faded, but a swarm of mosquitoes thickened around her, feasting on her sweat. At first she swatted at them, but there were too many and she barely had any energy left, so instead she focused everything she had on running.

After around five punishing minutes, she was moving on empty. Every breath pulled in as torture. Her muscles felt like compacted trash, stiff and slow-moving, until at last Rex's voice crackled back in.

"- have a rough sense of your location, Zero, given the presence of a drainage canal near the retaining wall. Whatever you do, you must not turn right, as-"

His voice cut out again. Zero stopped in her tracks, gasping raggedly.

"Why not… turn right… Rex?" she asked.

He didn't answer. She straightened up and looked back the way she'd come. Were those figures running along the top of the trash mound? They were very far away, but they bobbed and weaved in her wavering vision.

"Rex, I turned right, I need to know-"

A shout rang in from the side. She turned and saw a makeshift guard tower built out of branches and plastic crates, constructed atop a baby blue container box written with the fading stencil: MÉDECINS SANS FRONTIÈRES.

A landmark.

The two men in the tower didn't look like the Doctors Without Borders she'd seen in Tabarre, though. They were dressed in urban camouflage gear overlaid with pops of bright color; a vivid red beret on one, a yellow sash across the chest of the other. They held rifles that were pointing at Zero's chest.

"Arrete!" one shouted, then unleashed a barrage of creole that Zero couldn't hope to follow, punctuated by stabs with the rifle barrel.

Zero flung up her hands. The mosquitoes settled. It was hard to think. The Doctors Without Borders box looked repurposed for defensive purposes. She picked out a fence running away from it made of sharpened stakes, up to where it conjoined with the cinderblock wall of what seemed to be a large secure compound set back from the drainage canal.

"Viens par ici!" the guard shouted, growing louder and gesturing with his rifle. "Descends ici maintenant!"

Zero didn't need to speak French to know he wanted her to come down off the mound. Maybe these men were G9 an Fanmi, or maybe they were G-Pep, but it didn't matter; there was no way she was going to surrender herself to them.

"Maintenant!" the man yelled, which Zero took to mean, 'Now!', then he fired. Bullets hit the trash by her feet and sprayed chips of rock-hard waste against her calves. She chanced a look backward. Only the black canal lay there, too wide to jump. The MSF doctor Ajawin had mentioned a fresh outbreak of cholera; was this where it was spreading?

The guards jumped down from their tower and started toward her.

She calculated her odds. The canal was a terrible choice. Trying to swim in it would most likely set a slow-motion death sentence in effect. Given the vast amount of spiky metal trash jutting out of it, she would likely shred her arms and legs beneath the surface, potentially picking up a cocktail of tetanus, typhoid, hepatitis A, dysentery and more on top of the cholera. All were instant infection and all fatal in short order. She could even get sepsis and be dead within a day.

She turned back to the men.

"Sur vos genoux!" the leader shouted, stabbing his rifle at her as he climbed the mound toward her. "Les mains en l'air!"

She could guess what that meant. On your knees. Hands in the air.

She dropped to one knee. She put up her hands. Then she got lucky.

As the first of them reached the top of the mound, a

young guy with ropey muscles, he swung the butt of his rifle at her head without stalling his momentum. His mistake; too eager, too hungry, too angry, too used to beating women who'd never been trained to fight back. He didn't set his feet, didn't try to avoid telegraphing the strike, and even exhausted, Zero saw it coming a mile off.

She swayed swiftly to the side to dodge the blow, caught his wrist with one hand as it went past, his elbow with the other, twisted her body sharply and propelled him firmly on his way.

He sailed off the mound into the canal. His feet splashed down first but did nothing to halt his downward trajectory. His chest hit the saddle-less seat post of a rusted bicycle, and the metal spear punched out of his back with a curious snicking sound, sending up a plume of blood. He shrieked once, then the rusted contraption toppled swiftly under his weight and took him with down it, submerging beneath the surface.

Zero spun to find the other man swinging his rifle around like a baseball bat. He should have just shot her, but thanks to a world that rewarded aggression more than competence, he didn't. She managed to get her left arm up and took the blow on her triceps, instantly deadening the muscle but buying her time.

Before he could yank the rifle back for another swing she snatched the wrist of his trigger hand with her right hand and twisted sharply. His index finger snapped in the trigger guard. He shrieked and tried to pull away, but Zero twisted hard enough to fracture bones and snap the ligaments; exactly what she'd threatened to do to LaGuerre.

The rifle came free as his hand was destroyed. It was already pointing back toward him. All she had to do was flick the safety and pull the trigger.

The rifle discharged into his belly. He screamed and

dropped to his knees. Zero rose to her feet and brought the butt down on the side of his head, driving him half-conscious down the mound into the canal.

The black mulch splashed and swallowed him whole. Two for 0.

Then the garbage at her feet blasted with chips and a gunshot pealed out. She looked up to see half a dozen guards pouring from the main compound, while back the way she'd come a crowd of men were speeding up the canal like a hurricane storm surge.

She tossed the rifle into the water - it'd only slow her down - and ran on.

35

EXFILTRATION

After a minute or two more Rex's voice crackled back into her ear.

"- tell me you didn't turn right, Zero."

She was too out of breath to laugh, but managed to speak between gasps for air. "I went right … I still am … Almost got shot … I'm on the drainage canal … I saw Doctors Without Borders box … Get me out of here!"

"Calculating," Rex replied. "I have old maps, Zero, from a satellite sweep ten years old; they may not be very accurate. Identifying the canal. Identifying the Doctors Without Borders box. How far are you from it?"

"Two minutes," she gasped. "Running slowly."

"I can hear your breathing and your pulse. You are being pursued."

Zero chanced a look back. "Only a couple dozen guys."

"Is that all?" Rex answered coolly. "Zero, I see a clear route to the wall which should deposit you on a main road; Route Soleil 9. I am calling a taxi to that exact spot. There should be an open sweep through the slums coming up on your right side; it's the old tramway lines. Once you get on that it's a mile in a straight line to the wall."

"A mile?"

"You can do this, Zero. One foot after the other. I am ordering the taxi. Don't be late. The signal will die out in-"

The signal died.

Zero ran.

Everything burned from the soles of her feet to the top of her head; the sun beating down, the heat applying a factor of ten to every exertion. The men in back were gaining. She scanned the right side but saw only an unbroken wall of cinderblock and tin cut with sliver-like alleys.

There was no sign of the tramway.

Gunshots rang out. In the distance ahead a shape appeared on the gray mound, blurred by stinging sweat in Zero's eyes but growing larger. She was pretty sure what it was; more men coming for her.

The right hand side didn't change. There was no opening. She imagined the tide of the slums shifting and expanding like the sands of a beach, spreading onto the old tramway and becoming fixtures of the-

There!

Through her blurred vision with her mind working on half oxygen, she saw the pattern in the gray wall: no cinderblocks. Those structures had been built decades earlier, when Cité Soleil was an up-and-coming neighborhood of immigrants planning to work in the new Port-au-Prince boom industrial area. Only when the US and Canada placed an embargo on trade with Haiti had those industries failed and Cité Soleil lapsed into slumland.

Now on her right there was only an expanse of tin; none of the original cinderblocks. She ran down the mound at once, almost fell as her trembling thighs buckled then plunged back into the crush of alleys.

What followed was nightmarish. Running on empty and bouncing off tin shacks, with the sun too low to see and gunfire all around, Zero judged direction like a Pong ball batting side to side, redirecting every time she saw cinderblocks, trying to stay on the old tramway route.

A mile felt like ten. Minutes stretched into agony. The alleys were empty but the shacks trembled with fear. At one point she ran headlong into a gang member, rifle held up at the ready. For a moment they stared at each other, then Zero lurched forward and stabbed him four times in the chest before he could discharge a single round.

He sank. She ran. Shouts followed. At a four-way intersection she was briefly stymied, only to glimpse the strangest thing down the narrowest, most garbage-filled passageway, a route she hadn't even considered as passable wedged between two lean-to structures. It was a man dressed in black, with a top hat and black sunglasses and the white face of a skull. He looked right in her eyes and nodded once.

Zero blinked and he was gone, but it was all she needed. She forced her way into the gap, kicking through deep drifts of garbage and squeezing between tin walls that flexed with her passage, until at last the exterior wall loomed before her.

She climbed the rough wooden frame and looked back the way she'd come. There was no sign of the skeletal figure in black, but just thirty yards back at the intersection several gang members were already clogging like bile in a narrow artery.

They saw her and shouted. She dropped down on the other side of the wall, onto a dusty sidewalk beside a four-lane road. Across the road were shops and normal-looking residences. The difference was night and day. She sheathed the bloody knife and found the taxi right where Rex said it would be.

When the driver saw her he started to pull away, but she had hold of the open rear window and pulled herself through to tumble onto the cracked leather back seat.

The driver babbled something at her in creole. Zero didn't blame him. A desperate, sweat-soaked white woman had just escaped Cité Soleil chased by gunfire; why would he wait around for that?

"Royal Oasis Hotel," she said, the first hotel she could think of. "Petion-Ville."

"Non!" the driver shouted, and sharply pulled to the side, killing the engine. "Sortez!"

"He said, 'Get out'," Rex said, choosing that moment to announce himself.

Zero thought about pulling her blade to persuade the man, then figured the gangs would work as a better incentive.

"Suit yourself," she said, and settled back into the seat like she was suddenly relaxed. "We'll explain this together."

Sweat ran down the man's face. His eyes darted back and forth to her and the wall.

"Sortez maintenant!" he shouted.

"Get out now," Rex supplied.

Zero just closed her eyes like she was settling in for a nap. "Rex, do what you can to see if I'm being followed. The gangs are going to come looking. Also call DI LaGuerre and check if he's alive."

"I am glad you are alive, Zero," Rex said.

"Thank Baron Samedi," she said.

"Who?"

"Samedi?" the driver called, then abruptly stopped his shouting, turned to the road ahead and hit the gas, leaving Cité Soleil behind in a spurt of dust.

36

DOLL

Zero napped briefly in the cab and woke to trembling muscles, overwhelming heat and the Royal Oasis Hotel.

"Sortez," the driver was repeating, but this time with a pleading tone. Zero looked out and saw the familiar greenery and bright colors of the hotel. She pulled some bills from her pocket and pressed them into the man's sweaty hand, then exited and almost collapsed. Her legs were like Jell-O.

"Am I being followed, Rex?" she asked.

"Not that I can tell as yet."

Zero walked unsteadily up the few stairs to the entrance. "And LaGuerre?"

"I have intercepted some internal PNH communications. He seems to have survived, and was taken to Hôpital De L'Ofatma, a hospital in nearby Chancerelles district. He is undergoing surgery for machete wounds."

She pushed through the glass doors. "How bad?"

"I do not know. From the tone of communications, I suspect severe."

Zero cursed. LaGuerre was a good man, if annoying;

she'd lose sleep if he died. "And you're sure I'm clear here? This hotel isn't burned."

"Impossible to be sure. You will be interested to hear that, after you entered Cité Soleil, I began tracking cellular activity in the vicinity, and registered a surge of almost a hundred cell phones into the shantytown, in addition to the handful who followed you directly from the docks. I am working to map this network; some are in regular communication with each other, some not. I believe these are the fault lines of gang structure. You will further be interested that several of these cell phones belong to a call network that includes Officer Marcelin at Delmas PD, along with several other officers."

She snorted and tapped the call button for the elevator. "Of course."

"I do not believe they are following you as yet, but it will not be difficult for them to locate the check-in of a woman matching your description, immediately after such a chase. The usual precautions should provide us with a buffer. Do you plan to rest now?"

"Room service and rest," Zero said. She felt more depleted than ever. "The heat here is a killer."

The elevator doors opened and she stepped inside.

"One question," Rex began, "what was that you said about Baron Samedi earlier?"

She barely remembered. "I don't know. A hallucination, maybe. Order me some food for the upper floor room, OK?"

"What would you like?"

"Surprise me."

The elevator opened on the sixth floor, where she entered her room, bolted it, opened the window and climbed the exterior of the building again. It was only a single floor, but as she popped the window on the seventh floor her whole body shuddered with the effort.

At last it opened and she tumbled in, shaking and drained.

The room was hot once more, and she cranked the AC back to high. She drank at least a gallon of water straight from the faucet then stepped into the shower. For the second time in two days, the hot water was blisssful, washing away the dust, sweat and stings of so many mosquito bites. By the time she was done, the room service had arrived and she went out to fetch it.

"Legim," she said doubtfully, studying the contents.

"I thought after you enjoyed it so much the first time," Rex said in her ear. "And you had burgers last night."

She frowned. "Smart ass. What about pizza? Fries? Banana milkshake? Ice cream? I need sugar and carbs."

"These culinary treats provide plenty of both, along with a little more local culture, which I thought you could use. You'll find some Haitian puff pastries, quite delicious I've read; some Griot, which is a citrusy pork stir fry with Pikliz relish on the side; and macaroni au gratin, which is actually just Haitian mac and cheese with a mustard kick. Carbs and sugar in abundance."

Zero looked at the dishes and sighed. Maybe they were delicious, but all she wanted after a couple of near-death experiences was a good old taste of home. "I appreciate you trying to broaden my horizons, Rex, but maybe now's not the time, yeah? At least give me a hot dog. Come on. I almost died."

A moment passed. "Go one door further."

Zero did. There was another tray with a cloche over it, within lay a far more American assortment: a stack of maple butter pancakes; a thick strawberry milkshake; a double patty beefburger drizzled with BBQ sauce and melted Monterey jack cheese; a double helping of triple-cooked fries and a mustard-slathered hotdog.

She sighed in satisfaction.

"Was that a joke?" she asked, stacking the junk food tray

atop her Haitian tray. Together the weight was substantial and encouraging.

"My attempt at humor," Rex said. "I thought the atmosphere could do with lightening."

Zero snorted. "Yeah. Well, food deprivation will do that."

"I am glad you liked my joke."

"Loved it," Zero murmured, already stuffing fries into her mouth as she pushed back into her room. Sitting cross-legged on the floor, she pigged out. By the time she was done it was early afternoon and she was woozy from the exertion, the heat and the jet lag. Back in Poland it was well past midnight and she'd only slept fitfully since arriving in Haiti, but there was something to do before she could rest again.

The ouanga.

She retrieved it from her backpack and studied its outline; white leather, thick red thread and that black button spewing red tassels. It was nothing like the simplistic wooden doll with the nails in from Basat. She worked the ouanga between her fingers, trying to identify the hard shape within. It had sharp, squarish lines. With a sharp thrill of fear, she realized it might be some kind of computer chip, potentially even a tracking unit.

With the Bowie she swiftly slit the leather and opened the pouch. The hard item wasn't any kind of technology, though, unless vodou counted. It looked like a long, thin piece of white bone, chiseled roughly into a squarish rod. She lifted it out. There were dried brown remnants of what looked to be meat clinging to the corners, and two rough crosses etched into the edges. It was light but firm.

"Any idea what kind of bone this is?" she asked Rex, holding it up for him to study. A few seconds passed as he accessed image recognition and the requisite data banks, then answered.

"It has clearly been worked with a whittling tool, Zero,

but judging from the shape, size and formation, I believe it is the long metatarsal bone from a human foot, most likely a child's."

Zero held the bone a moment longer, her slow brain only steadily realizing what that meant, then she dropped it to the bed covers.

"A foot bone? From a child?"

"Precisely that. From my research, this kind of talisman is common in black magic and the use of ouangas. In all likelihood, this bone was taken from the victim who was hung beneath it. I am checking standard vodou sacrificial practice."

Zero stared. Suddenly the heavy load of food in her stomach felt greasy and unsafe. "From that little girl? But we didn't-"

"You didn't check her feet. That is correct. Rorschach did not and neither did the Delmas specialist Amelie. You overlooked the soles of her feet. It is quite likely the wound inflicted to obtain this slice of bone was thin and bloodless, perhaps difficult to see after death unless you were specifically looking for it."

Zero felt a sickness rising. Just looking at the bone with those little shreds of dried flesh on them made her heave. Suddenly the black magic part of vodou felt more immediate and personal than ever. This felt like a grotesque kind of theft. Someone had butchered this girl before they strung her up, all in the pursuit of not only ending her life, but also stealing her soul. Zero didn't know if she even believed in the soul, but the intent alone was repugnant.

Had the Engineer done this?

Her gorge rose and she heaved once.

"Nope," she said sharply, grabbing a towel and swiftly wrapping the bone out of sight. She then bundled it back into her backpack along with the leather pouch and set both on the far side of the room. She drank another glass of water and tried to clear her mind.

She thought about pancakes, and fluffy puppies, and all the dumb puns she could remember Hellion ever saying. She thought about Hanna lying in a curled-up position on her bed, and Zuzanna sighing like she had the weight of the world on her shoulders. She thought about Gabriel's arms around her.

Steadily her stomach settled and a new, deeper resolve gathered around her like a dark cloak.

The Engineer was going to suffer. Everyone involved in this little girl's death, in the little boy's death and all the lost restaveks, had to be made to suffer. That suffering had to be witnessed.

Justice had to be done.

"How long until the hurricane, Rex?"

"Approximately three days now, Zero."

She rose and went to the window, looking out over the nearby streets. From above, everything seemed to be fogged with a gray haze of dust. LaGuerre had said all this dust was the legacy of French colonial clear-cutting. She thought about countless particles of that ancient dust landing in all the family homes before her, to be swept up day after day by restaveks. By enslaved children.

She thought about Pierre Cedras, whipped and beaten and castrated as a child, shipped to a foreign land to serve as a slave, resulting in his lonely mission to save just a handful of restavek souls, too afraid even to get a dog. She thought about the French colonial showroom at the Thor terminal, and LaGuerre's sudden angers, never far from the surface.

Maybe all this was the legacy of what the French had done two hundred years ago. Once you were a slave, maybe it became easier to enslave others. Maybe brutality became a way of life.

It hurt her chest. The enormity of the pain felt like a giant hand reaching down from above and squeezing the life out of Port-au-Prince. The Engineer was just part of that. The whole system was to blame.

"I'll need a location for LaGuerre's bokor," she said. "To identify the gang that used this ouanga."

"I have been tracking his phone," Rex replied. "I can find this for you. Do you suspect ID LaGuerre will not be able to accompany you?"

"Maybe he will. Maybe I'm on my own."

"I am always here with you, Zero."

She smiled. At least that was something, more than Pierre Cedras had. "Good dog, Rex. Stand guard. I'm going to sleep now."

She curled up on the bed like Hanna, and the moment her head hit the pillow she went out like a light.

37

ALARM

Alarms woke her.

For a moment Zero thought she was back in Poland, and fear for Gabriel and the girls rushed in along with a dose of adrenaline. She bolted up from the bed. She had to get them secure, out of the house if necessary and-

Late afternoon light blared in through the floor-to-ceiling windows, cast from a tropical blue sky. That view was not the view of a Polish forest. She shook herself back to the moment, found her phone and silenced the alarm. Only then did she realize Rex was talking.

"-four gang members preparing to enter the room below you, Zero. They are armed with rifles and machetes. Suggest you prepare to evacuate, in the event they go door-to-door through the hotel."

Her mouth went dry as she scrolled the spy cam feeds on her phone. They were outside the downstairs room. For a moment she thought they would ram the door, but there was no need; they had a key card.

The door opened and they entered.

It was just after 6 p.m.; she'd slept for barely three hours.

"How many rooms in the hotel?"

"Two hundred and seven," Rex answered. "I predict a door-to-door raid could take most of the night. They may have skeleton key cards for every room, but many occupied rooms will have their dead bolts secured. These will take time, unless the gangs send reinforcements."

Zero watched as the gang members attacked the furniture and tossed the room. Minutes passed as they tipped the bed and sliced the curtains and carpet. It seemed they had no idea she was directly above them, or that she was watching them via the spy cams. As the minutes passed, the sense of threat faded somewhat and a ravening hunger took its place.

She picked up the Haitian tray and started working through the dishes while the gang kept up their work.

"Do you have any updates for me?" she asked, while munching on crunchy Pikliz relish along with an oozing mouthful of sweet, tangy Griot.

"I have no news on Detective LaGuerre," Rex said. "As for my analysis of the cell network around Cité Soleil, it is as complete as I can make it. I have successfully isolated five cell phone signals from the group that followed you from the docks market. I have also built a good idea of numerous likely gang loyalty structures."

Zero studied the feed more closely, but didn't recognize any of the five men currently hacking into the walls below. "Are any of the five below me right now?"

"No. Three of them are back within range of the docks' cell tower, while two have spread out in the Delmas area."

"At their homes?"

"That is possible."

"OK," she said. "I'm going to ride this out. Wake me again if they show any sign of going door-to-door on this floor, OK? Or if they bring in more men."

"I will do that. Sweet dreams, Zero."

The line fell silent, and Zero polished off her griot, ate

some Haitian puff pastries and drank a few more glasses of water, then comfortably sank back into sleepy bliss.

When next she woke the alarms were louder. The sky was dark, the air was uncomfortably cold and Rex's voice in her ear was urgent.

"Zero, wake up! Jean-Baptiste LaGuerre has just arrived at the hotel. He is approaching your room below, where four gang members are waiting."

It took her a second to register all of that.

"He made it through surgery?" she asked blurrily, shaking off a nightmare about Hanna and Zuzanna with the soles of their feet slit open.

"He is alive for now, but he will not be for long. He is in the corridor now. I have been trying to wake you, but-"

"So call him," Zero said, back on her feet and casting around the room. Her bag was by the wall, her Bowie knife was on the counter. "Warn him."

"He's not answering his phone. Zero, he's nearly at the door and they are ready."

"How do they know?" she asked, trying to get her head into the game.

"They have spotters in the lobby. They are most likely going to torture and kill him to find your location."

Zero jerked into action, sweeping up the backpack, sheathing the Bowie knife then ramming the window open to climb out into the cool night sky.

"Do you have their cell phones in your list?" she asked as her sleep-numb fingers wedged into tight grips and carried her down the face of the hotel. "The men below."

"Two of them. They are preparing their weapons. He has knocked on the door, Zero."

"Is there time to hack their phones and force-overheat the batteries?"

A second passed. It was a trick they'd pulled off together

before. Any phone could be forced to draw too much charge, too fast, from its battery, if the safety parameters baked into the phone's CPU could be over-ridden. It was called 'thermal runaway'. The result would be a flaming phone in seconds; in some cases, the battery cases even exploded as positive and negative lithium ions crossed the plastic separators.

"This is possible, of course, but not within minutes," Rex said.

Zero moved to the next-best option. "Then prepare to barrage them with calls and text messages. I want their pockets blaring. Positions?"

"Three by the door and one by the bathroom watching, he's seven steps from the window. Nobody is facing you. They're opening the door."

She accelerated and miscalculated; her right hand slipped a grip and she fell. Her left hand shot into a gap in the façade as fast as her tongue lock on Marcelin, thumb and index finger wedging just tight enough to arrest the drop before it became terminal.

Her left hip slapped against the building, her feet scrabbled for purchase just above the window and her right arm flailed. Below her the Oasis' blue swimming pool glowed off to the left, unfortunately not directly beneath her current position. From here it would be a short drop to a hard impact.

"Zero, he is on his knees, this looks like an immediate execution!"

She curled her body, kicked off with her left leg and managed to stab her right thumb into a gap, which stabilized the swing before her left hand could slip, then she caught her feet on the upper rim of the window.

"Start the text barrage," she ordered, then speed-climbed the final few feet, thrust the Bowie into the window crevice and cracked it open just as a rush of ringtones and sound effects sounded inside the room. It was bright inside, but she had the element of surprise and the sound covered her entrance.

LaGuerre was by the door on his knees, the only one looking in her direction, and a perplexed expression spread across his face as he recognized Zero. Two of the three gang members encircling him were fumbling with their phones, while the third held his gun on LaGuerre's temple, shouting over the cacophony.

Zero ran, deft as a shadow while the text messages poured in like artillery shells, to smash the Bowie into the back of the first man's neck. It shot through the front of his throat in a spray of blood, but Zero didn't wait, ripping it free as hard as she'd inserted it and running on.

The remaining three spun at the sound of their colleague's death, their weapons rising. LaGuerre's eyes widened in disbelief but he wasted no time shouldering into the two men nearest him, sending their shots careening into walls and glass.

Zero covered the distance in a little over a second and stabbed the nearest man in the groin with a massive underhand thrust, slicing up through his pelvis and belly to spill his guts on the floor. LaGuerre headbutted the second man and sent an elbow backward into the third's head, buying Zero just enough time to spin, reverse the blade and slam it solidly into the center of the third's face.

His skull crunched inward as the knife rammed through the cartilage of his nose, the septum and the nasal bone, the ethmoid and vomer bones and straight into his forebrain. He dropped without a sound.

LaGuerre had the last man in a throat lock by then, the rifle dangling around his chest, rapidly choking him out. Zero covered the last yard and brought the Bowie arcing down into the hollow of the man's exposed throat, bypassing his rib cage and forcing the entire shaft of the blade into his chest cavity, severing his lower windpipe, his aortal arteries and likely tearing a hole through one if not both of his lungs.

Blood sprayed up into his chin and spattered out over Zero; more came when she pulled the knife out, gushing over her hands.

LaGuerre's jaw dropped as fast as the dead man in her arms.

"I had him," he said, clearly bewildered.

"Not fast enough," she answered, high on adrenaline and taking his arm firmly. He had bandages on his chest and wrapped around his right shoulder and left hip. "More will come any minute, right Rex?"

"Exactly that," Rex answered in her ear. "More are coming already."

"Who's Rex?" LaGuerre asked, staring wide-eyed at the bodies and the blood and the blade as Zero calmly slotted it back into her thigh sheath.

"My dog," she answered, and dragged him through the door. "He's a good boy. Come on."

38

DEEP END

Zero bypassed the elevator and took the stairs, running down three at a time with LaGuerre struggling to keep up.

"Sit rep, Rex!" she shouted as they clattered through the fifth floor landing.

"Two gang spotters from the lobby are in the elevator," Rex said calmly in her ear. "Two more took the stairs and are climbing to meet you. Gang assets have been activated across the district; I show a significant part of the local network converging on this location. Suggest you exit on the third floor and jump. The Oasis has a pool at the rear; from the balcony in the hotel restaurant I believe you can make it."

"Done deal," Zero answered, dashing through the fourth floor landing. The sound of footsteps slapping up echoed in the narrow stairwell from below. LaGuerre had already dropped a half-flight behind.

"Faster, Jean-Baptiste!" she shouted.

On the third floor the gang were just one flight below. Zero leaned out over the railing and saw them barely three yards down, heads bobbing as they climbed, rifles raised, for the moment unaware of her presence.

She threw the Bowie down. It sang end over end to bury itself to the grip in the side of the neck of the lead man, producing a meaty smack. The impact rocked him to the side; he hit the wall and tumbled into his colleague. On their way down together his finger itched on the trigger, spilling a roar of automatic bullets ricocheting up the stairwell.

Zero ducked back as the two men fell, found LaGuerre's arm and pulled him through the fire door into a corridor.

"Rex!" she shouted, scanning for signs but everything was written in French. "Where's the restaurant?"

"Building plans say right here."

"Right like in Cité Soleil?" she barked back, but wasted no time taking the corridor and dragging LaGuerre after her. Ahead were double doors which they burst through, into a charming restaurant laid out down the rear of the hotel, laden with white-clothed circular tables, hung with chandeliers and walled in glass.

Servers stared. A chef with a tall white hat stopped in the middle of carving what looked to be a roast suckling pig. The air was rich with the garlic and citrus of Haitian cuisine.

"I loved the Griot!" Zero called to him as she sped amongst the tables, then pushed through the emergency doors out onto a narrow balcony, where LaGuerre slammed against the railing, breath wheezing. She looked over the edge; the pool lay below offset by some fifteen feet.

"Too far, Rex!" she shouted. "We'll never make it."

"Reinforcements are on the second floor," he answered. "I believe the parabolic arc of your fall will carry you into the water. It will help if you dive and enter headfirst."

"Parabolic, huh?"

"I just downloaded several physics modules to test the proposition; how much do you weigh, Zero?"

"Never ask a lady that," she said, and focused on

LaGuerre. "We better dive, Detective Inspector. Rex, which is the deep end?"

"The deep end is nearest to you." A second passed as Zero took up position. "Or possibly furthest."

Zero laughed.

LaGuerre was gasping at the rail, staring at her with wide eyes. "Who is that you're talking to? Have you got a handler? Are you CIA, like Wren?"

"Something like that," Zero said, just as the doors to the restaurant swung open inside and a flood of gang members raced through in a spray of brightly colored clothing and varied weaponry. "Dive if you want to live."

She sprang up onto the railing without any further delay, let her momentum tilt her over then thrust outwards. The air sliced by to either side, her arms slapped together like a knife point as her body upended and plummeted, then in barely a second her fingertips pierced the water with a resounding slap. The top of her head and her shoulders took a pummeling as they punched through, happily finding deep water rather than shallow, then she turned and kicked back for the surface. There was no sign of LaGuerre on the balcony above, but a second later he burst up through the water beside her.

They thrashed to the pool wall, climbed out and ran. The bandage in LaGuerre's side bloomed red. Zero darted toward the underbrush, a dense display of thick-spined aloe vera, flowering orange hibiscus and fruiting Spanish limes, but LaGuerre grabbed her hand and redirected her.

"My car," he said, and she nodded and followed him. Bullets sprayed the concrete as they sprinted down the rear of the hotel to the staff parking lot. LaGuerre's Siena sat waiting for them, reassuringly intact despite one missing window and several fresh bullet pocks. He fumbled for the keys just as two gang members ran around the entrance ahead. They brought their rifles up and LaGuerre found the keys, hit the button then both he and Zero ducked into their seats.

Gunfire ripped out, splashing white impact stars across the windshield.

LaGuerre stabbed the keys home and spun the ignition, hit the gas and they lurched forward. One of the gang members dived to the side while the other fancied himself a hero and kept on firing. Bullets drilled into the windshield but didn't penetrate, and two seconds later his body bounced up over the hood, tumbled across the roof and dropped in their wake.

LaGuerre gunned it across the forecourt, spun out into traffic on a two-lane and hammered the gas pedal home. As a last touch he hit his sirens and lights, and together they cut a wailing path deep into Port-au-Prince.

39

ZERO DAY

For several minutes, they raced through the city by night, shooting across quiet intersections in the shadow of dark towers, until LaGuerre killed his sirens and lights and pulled off the main road onto a feeder street. They cruised for maybe thirty seconds, both constantly checking their rear view, but it seemed they hadn't been followed.

LaGuerre slowed but kept the speed high, eyes flicking constantly back and forth from his mirrors to Zero.

"What the hell was that?" he asked at last, when he had his breathing under control and they'd taken a few more turns into residential side streets lit only by moonlight from above. "Where did you even come from?"

Zero almost spat back the same question, but held in the anger. They were both alive, and that was what mattered. "The floor above. I climbed down the exterior of the building."

He turned to her. "You climbed down the exterior?"

"I'm good at climbing, LaGuerre. I was watching the gang on a spy cam; honestly, it was all going fine until you came along."

"Going fine? I made about fifty phone calls to find you, had to bribe two dozen hotel workers to get the one report of a white woman who'd just checked back in, and then I find the gangs already there in force. I wouldn't call that doing fine."

Zero couldn't argue with that. "Fair point. Any way you look at it, it's bad news. Bad that they found me so easily, bad that they sent so many gang members. They're interested in me, that's clear. But it makes sense. I must've killed about a dozen of them today."

He turned to her again. "You did what? A dozen?"

Zero did the quick math. Two at the docks, maybe four in Cité Soleil, then four just now. "Maybe more like ten, eleven including the Ti Bwa guy. It was the only way. But what about you? I heard a rifle shot back at the docks when you were wrestling that gangbanger in the jacket; Rex said you were in surgery for machete wounds. I was worried, so it's good to see you alive. How did you get away?"

LaGuerre just shook his head in wonder. "Worried about me? And you actually killed ten people?"

"Eleven. And like I said, it was the only way."

He took a moment. "Eleven. Well OK. As for me, I had a rifle and a bulletproof police vehicle. That's how I got away, after you drew their truck out of the exit lane. I killed one of them, but I only wounded the leader."

Zero grimaced. "That's enough to bring on bad blood. They're after you just as much as me."

"It looks that way." He squeezed the wheel. "The precinct captain was already talking about moving me to a different district, after Marcelin and Ti Bwa. He's a good man, but he thinks it's too dangerous for me now in Delmas."

"Maybe a different country," Zero muttered.

"Not interested. Not now." He turned to her. "But

seriously, how did you get away on foot with only a knife? There were five men and a truck following you."

"I ran along the container stacks, followed by a mad rush through Cité Soleil. I cut along a drainage canal then used the old tramway to reach the wall." She almost mentioned the hallucination of Baron Samedi pointing the way, but decided against it. There was no need for him to think she was that crazy. "That's it."

"That's hardly it. You're saying you actually went straight through Cité Soleil? I wouldn't have thought that was possible."

"I'm not in a rush to do it again."

He said nothing more. For a few moments they just drove.

"I have a safe house for us," LaGuerre offered, breaking the stillness. "A secure compound. We should lay low, figure out what the gangs are doing and see if the heat will blow over."

"No."

"No? What choice have we got? Need I repeat that gangs run Port-au-Prince, Miss Nowak? We are both marked now. They found your hotel faster than I could, which tells me they must be G9- or G-Pep-affiliated. Half the population are beholden to them, and they'll all be looking out for us."

That just pissed Zero off. "All the more reason to end it swiftly."

"End it?" He spun to her. "What does that even mean?"

"What do you think it means?" Zero countered, letting some of her anger through. "Find the killers, track them back to whoever gave the order and kill them all. Burn their structures, salt the earth, then you can go into hiding or walk free, whatever you like."

He frowned. "Salt the earth? You're serious?"

"Of course I am. They just came for us both, LaGuerre. You're a cop, I'm an American, but still they came. I can promise you, this thing is going to get a whole lot worse before it gets better."

His brow worked urgently. "But we can't... I mean-"

"We have to. No district in Haiti will provide safe harbor after tonight. We either leave the country forever, right now, or we find the man giving the orders and end him for good."

LaGuerre shook his head. Moments passed as they cruised along dark streets and this new reality set in. "That won't end it. Kill one gang leader in Haiti and another always springs up in his place, often worse. They'll all remember what we did. It's a matter of respect; they'll never stop coming."

"They will if they're dead. Have you heard of the concept of 'Zero Day'?"

"Zero Day?"

She took a deep breath. "It's something I learned from Christopher Wren; a technique to destroy gangs, cults, whatever. Essentially, you kill everyone at the top of an organization. The first rank. The second rank. The third and the fourth. You decimate the enemy so completely they're sent back to day zero; they can't come back at you for a generation or more. That would do the job."

LaGuerre shook his head. "I can't listen to this. It's madness."

"It's real. I've got a list of hundreds of gang members. I can find them at any time via their cell phones. With a little more work we can figure out precisely who's coming after us, which gangs they're in and who the leaders are, then start the elimination from there."

"And how many deaths would that be?"

"That depends whether you can help me," Zero said earnestly, putting the plan together as she spoke. "Not just you, of course. It'd need to be concerted raids across the city, all at once. Every officer you trust, enlisted."

"Every officer? Not a chance. We're police, not mass murderers."

"Good job I am, then," Zero said, then took a breath, remembering what Pierre Cedras had told her. "What about Fantom 509?"

LaGuerre's eyes narrowed sharply. "What do you know about them?"

"Only that they're a paramilitary group within the police, comfortable with bending the rules to do what's right."

"Where did you hear that?"

"From Pierre Cedras, after you bailed out."

"From Cedras?" He sucked his teeth. "I don't approve. They're vigilantes, Miss Nowak, no better than gang members. Their actions are damaging Haiti more than anything the gangs do. They pretend to be police, but wear masks and helmets to disguise their identity. They shoot first and ask questions later, just like gang members. That's not how the rule of law works, and it's one reason the populace hate us."

"Oh, is that the reason?" Zero asked. "Not the fact that you let the gangs run amok?"

He scowled. "It's one reason. Men like Officer Marcelin are the other. To walk a line between the two is nearly impossible."

Zero sighed. "OK. But you know some people in Fantom 509? You could contact them?"

He looked like he wanted to lash out. "They ask me to join them every few months. I say no, Miss Nowak. I will not contact them on your behalf, because I will not help you to break more laws or accelerate the path to outright gang warfare. The law is the only thing separating us from the gangs."

"I completely disagree. We're already on the track to gang warfare, aren't we?"

"Then we are at an impasse," he said, "because my job is to keep the peace. I'm not going to help you bring on civil war in my country."

Moments passed. Zero considered her position and tried a different tack. "OK. No Zero Day, no Fantom 509. Let's get back to the core investigation, and at least agree that finding the killer remains the first order of business. That falls within the bounds of the law, agreed?"

He shot her a sarcastic smile. "I'd say our first order was go to the safe house, but I'll listen, if you have a lead."

She smiled. "I have got a lead. What we need to do now is go see your bokor."

"My bokor? Why?" His eyes flared. "Did you find a ouanga at the docks?"

Her smile spread. "I did. It's pretty grim though, LaGuerre; a white leather doll with red tassels, with a human metatarsal, a toe bone, inside. Most likely that comes from the little girl."

LaGuerre's expression hardened and his grip tightened on the wheel. "Metatarsal. From the little girl? There was no sign that had been done. Nobody spotted it."

"Not even my pathologist. But with all the scratches and the bite, we weren't looking, were we? Now will you take us to your bokor or not?"

"She's not 'my' bokor," he shot back.

Zero frowned. "She's certainly not mine. Either take us or, as ever, I'll go on my own."

He gritted his teeth. "There's something you should know about bokor, Miss Nowak. Maybe about this one in particular." His voice was cold and he looked dead ahead. "The gangs go to them just as often as the police. They listen to her and confide in her."

"I get it. That's how you got the Ti Bwa guy's ID."

"It is. There's a saying about bokor; they say they serve the Loa with both hands."

"And what does that mean?"

"It means they serve the good Loa as easily as they serve the evil. This woman in particular. She'll sell us to the gangs just as readily as she sold them to us."

Zero watched his knuckles clamping white on the wheel. "Like she wanted to know my name."

"Exactly."

"Like she made you get high, or drunk, or something."

His grip tightened further. Zero wasn't sure what chance the wheel had. Then something struck her.

"Wait. This is that 'personal' thing you didn't want to talk about, right?"

"Drop it," he cautioned.

"No way. Did you get involved with this woman?"

"In the past," he rasped. "The biggest mistake of my life."

Zero almost laughed but held it in; she didn't think LaGuerre would be amused. "Then let's show her how well you've moved on. We'll do it together this time. Where is she, Jean-Baptiste? Time is a pressing factor here. Let's pay her a house call right now."

He shook his head. "No such thing. She lives at her temple. But we can go there now. they have mass all through the night." He took a deep breath. "A metatarsal, you said?"

"That's it."

"Then let's go."

He wrenched the wheel and hit the brakes, screeching them across the median to face back the way they'd come. The car rocked to a standstill.

"Unhappy breakup?" Zero asked.

"The bitch hexed me and ruined my life," LaGuerre said, then hit the gas and the Siena leaped away.

40

HEX

It was a thirty-minute drive west across Port-au-Prince toward the bokor's temple, located in Martissant district, the same route to the Thor terminal. From her research Zero knew it had once been an agricultural area, then a tourist favorite in the 70s, while now it was largely residential and filled with churches and temples.

"So tell me about this woman," she said.

LaGuerre shifted position uncomfortably. "It's a long story."

"We've got thirty minutes. I need to know what we're dealing with."

LaGuerre didn't reply immediately. The city shifted around them as they sped west. The number of blacked-out shantytowns seemed to be reducing, while there was more electricity in evidence; apartment blocks with the lights working, stores and bars open into the night. It was around 10 p.m. and Zero felt ready for anything.

"OK," LaGuerre said at last. "I met her through an investigation. It was three years back and I was still wet behind the ears, jumped up on the NYPD's perceived superiority and ready to lay down the law, US style, in my three-month training tour. Then the precinct captain sent me out to a murder scene." He sucked a thoughtful breath. "It wasn't a gang killing, at least not primarily. A female victim left eviscerated in her apartment." He continued in a flat monotone. "It was the work of a butcher who fancied himself an artist. Her organs had been laid out on display. Her heart was in a fruit bowl on the coffee table, her kidneys were in shot glasses, her pancreas had been fried and stood upright in a vase like a dried flower." He fell silent. Zero pictured the scene. "Anyway, there were numerous vodou paraphernalia in evidence. A ouanga, obviously, but also etchings into the coffee table and the walls, inked over in her blood. There was no crime scene photographer back then; we didn't have that much of a system, so I took the photos on my phone. The captain sent me to this bokor to figure out what the carvings and the layout meant."

Zero considered but gave him his time.

"It turned out the bokor was a stunningly beautiful young woman, about my age." He turned to face Zero briefly. "She was truly gorgeous, like no one I've seen in the real world before. I was under her spell from the start. It was hard to even talk to her."

He fell silent, ruminating.

"Name?" Zero prompted.

"Mistress Merlande Manoucheca. Will your CIA handler look into her?"

"I'm not CIA, and he's not really a handler. But yes. What happened between you two?"

LaGuerre looked at her then looked away. "Honestly? She's the reason I stayed in Haiti."

"I thought you stayed for the injustice. The outrage."

He gritted his teeth. "I did. We dated for three months. It was tempestuous. Passionate. Then one day I had a bad feeling. I don't even know what it was. I felt I had to go see her. It just came over me, so I did."

Zero waited.

"I found her giving a class. Not the kind of class you advertise on a billboard, though."

"She was cheating? Some kind of ritual orgy?"

LaGuerre shook his head. "That would've been better. No. She was teaching a small group of men, gang members, how to commit the precise ceremonial death I'd brought to her. The heart in the fruit bowl, the fried pancreas, all of it. They'd heard about how horrific that death had been, and how powerful the black magic it produced was, and they wanted to do it themselves. So she charged them to learn."

Zero said nothing for a moment, turning that over in her head. She thought about the way the girl had been posed, and the little boy, and all the restaveks in Pierre Cedras' folder. "So the more horrific, the more powerful the magic. Does that hold true across all vodou?"

LaGuerre sighed again. "Like I said, there's no single authority, but essentially yes. So-"

"So the metatarsal bone of that little girl," Zero picked up, "after she'd been bitten, scratched nearly to death, then executed, hung by the ankles and sliced open for a bone; that would be quite powerful vodou?"

He nodded. "Very much so. Suffering and youth are always powerful. Remember what I said about feral children stealing babies?"

Zero said nothing, and for a few minutes they drove in silence. She thought about what this might mean for the Engineer.

"The man who's selling these children," she said, choosing her words carefully. "If he is selling children for sacrifice, he couldn't do much better than restaveks, could he?"

"What do you mean?"

"Well, they've suffered so much already. Their deaths would be a hell of a jolt for the killer." She opened her pack and took out Cedras' folder, unwound the string and started flicking through the photos. "Just look."

"That they all suffered?"

"They suffered extraordinarily," Zero said, feeling like she'd hit upon something vital. "Fingernail scarring. Broken bones. Skin sanded off. Aberrant levels of pain. They'd make the best ouanga, correct? The strongest vodou talismans?"

LaGuerre looked over at the photographs. "I suppose so. Do you think that's what this is? A market for children who've had pain dumped into them like buckets? The more full the bucket, the higher the price tag?"

Zero considered. She looked out of the window at the dark slums passing them by. It would be a change for the Engineer. A new market, but potentially a very lucrative one.

"There's blood diamonds everywhere."

"What do you-" LaGuerre started, then stopped. "No."

"No you disagree? No I'm wrong?"

He sighed. "Just no. I don't know, Miss Nowak."

"Neither do I."

They drove in silence. It was a dark theory, and not one Zero wanted to dwell on.

"You didn't stay in Haiti to be with this bokor, then?" she asked, getting back on track.

LaGuerre nodded, looking almost relieved to return to his story. "No. I cut ties with her immediately. I wanted to press charges, arrest her, maybe compel her to testify about that first death, but she'd actually helped me hunt the murderer down. She hadn't taught the ritual to him, of course. She'd only learned from it and turned that work around to teach others, and it turns out there's nothing illegal about mocking up a scene with dead pig parts, teaching butchery and spells and arcane inscription. So we had nothing to hold her on."

Zero let out a heavy breath. "Were there more murders in that style?"

"No. None that we found, anyway." He sighed and leaned back, gently probing his side with his right hand. Zero looked down and saw his bandages had bled through.

"Are you all right?"

"It's just the stitches I think. I'll be fine." He took another deep breath. "The thing about Merlande, the really bad thing about those lessons she was teaching, is that she'd improved upon the original killer's procedure."

"Improved?"

"Yes. She was also teaching her 'students' to hide their ouangas better, and pressing that the more outlandish elements of a murder ritual didn't need to remain on display to be effective. So those kill rituals might have happened. Many more victims might have died in gruesome ways; we just didn't find any of them."

Zero's skin crawled. "She was teaching murderers to clean up their kills. Like a sacrificial consultant."

"Exactly. After that in particular, I had to stay. The sickness here felt so deep in the grain, and so personal, I had to do something about it. If I'd left then, I wouldn't have been able to look myself in the mirror again."

Zero grunted. Wren had mentioned that LaGuerre was chasing ghosts. Maybe this was his. "I know what that's like. For it to be personal."

He looked over at her briefly again, and Zero was reminded of their first interaction just two days ago, telling him how she'd been violated.

"I know you do," he said.

The rest of the drive passed in silence, but for Rex reporting back in her ear: he could find nothing on anyone called 'Merlande Manoucheca' on the Internet. She truly was a ghost in the system, with no official existence, no photographs online or in any data silo.

After another ten minutes or so, LaGuerre slowed down and ran the Siena up onto the sidewalk in front of a plain-looking gray office block. There were no signs out front and no lights on inside, at least none they could see.

"This is it," he said.

Zero surveyed the building; five bland stories. "It looks like nothing special."

"Evil isn't special," LaGuerre said flatly, pulling the keys from the ignition. "It may like to think it is, with rituals and pain and nonsense, but it isn't."

"What is it then?"

"Human nature." He opened the door. "Some people give in to the darkness inside. Others fight it. I think fighting is more special."

He stepped out of the car and Zero followed. The air outside was cooler now, as the day's warmth bled away from the dusty blacktop. There was the curious, lilting sound of voices raised in a sweet chorus resounding from somewhere nearby.

"Are they singing?" Zero asked.

LaGuerre pointed across the street, where there was another drab gray structure, though this one boasted a red neon cross mounted above the main entrance.

"Roman Catholic church, Haitian style," he said. "They sing all night. People come and go. It's like a Jesus-flavored jazz club."

Zero gazed at the building. The singing flowing from it was in French, but perhaps she recognized the melody. It was beautiful and quite haunting, there on that quiet street, opposite the den of a bokor who taught ritualized murder.

She turned back to LaGuerre. "You said she hexed you. What does that mean?"

He studied her across the roof of the car, jaw working beneath the skin, perhaps thinking about how much he wanted to say. "Not me, exactly," he settled on. "She was furious when I ended things. Jealous. Cruel. She cursed any woman I was involved with. The longer they stayed with me, the more sick they'd get; maybe cancer, AIDS, something like that, until they either left or they died."

"And you believed that?"

He gave her a pitying look. "This is Haiti, Miss Nowak. It doesn't matter what I believe. Let's go."

41

TEMPLE

LaGuerre opened the door and a wave of hot stench rolled over them like a thunderhead; dank and earthy, like the Polish forest after a heavy squall, but mixed with the iron and offal stench of the slaughterhouse. It stank of animals kept in captivity, of waste and blood and death, blended with the damp fog of human sweat as well as a high, sweet scent not unlike tobacco.

A long dim corridor stretched ahead. The floor was a rich orange dirt. A red light glowed faintly ahead, illuminating walls hung thickly with vodou paraphernalia, like the compacted gray trash at the Cité Soleil drainage canal: Baron Samedi skull faces loomed amongst a dense hedge of ouanga dolls, twine, old baby clothes, carved masks and crosses, weathered lithographs of Roman Catholic saints, plaited twine, dehydrated animal remains, whittled bones and more.

The sound of manic drums replaced the lilting of prayer song, clamoring like a dozen frantic pulses; some bass, some wooden, some metallic and growing louder with every step. Woven in amongst the beat were yelps and shrieks and long wails of sound that had the shape of words but followed no pattern Zero could make out.

"Not so bland now," LaGuerre said.

Zero's eyes watered on the smoky air. "Is this what she dosed you with?"

"That's just incense."

"Bullshit it's incense. Maybe it's Jimson weed; a deliriant. Everybody in here is high on it. We need to get in then out quickly."

"It's always like this," LaGuerre said and ventured into the darkness. Zero followed.

Halfway along the corridor the drums surged and the voices rose to a roar.

"There's about to be a kill," LaGuerre said, then they reached a heavy red curtain. Zero's pulse climbed. The claustrophobic confines filled with the hammering beat sent her back to her childhood; as LaGuerre pulled the curtain back, she half-expected to see her father standing proudly in the center of a leather-walled space, with livestreaming cameras circled around a strange mechanism in the center with a girl strapped into place, and-

She passed through the curtain into violent chaos.

Bodies were everywhere, whirling and wailing like drugged-out ravers through hanging cirrus clouds of blue-gray smoke. The temple was cavernous, stretching deeper and taller than seemed possible from outside the building, lit by fires in metal pits that streamed acrid smoke from smoldering swatches of herbs. There had to be more than a hundred people roving in and out of sight, all brightly dressed and convulsing.

Here a man cracked a whip through one of the firepits, whipping the flames to unleash plumes of blue smoke. Here a bare-chested man poured hot candlewax over his face and rubbed it into his hair and eyes. Around the center three woman in bright white gowns whirled, each swinging a brown chicken wildly by the legs. The birds flapped their wings and squawked into the madness, legs broken. Here a young woman sobbed while a young man repeatedly poured spirits on his right hand, lit the fumes and slapped her face with his burning palm.

Zero could make no sense of it.

She'd spent years hunting Pinocchios in night clubs around the world, and she'd never seen anything like this. The array of extreme emotions on display was dizzying.

"There," called LaGuerre, pointing to a tall woman dressed all in white, leading a docile sheep through the crowds. The drumming centered around her, and the whirling 'congregation' made space in the center. "Bokor Merlande Manoucheca."

The drums hammered toward a climax. The people danced and wailed louder, but now there was a throttling of focus around the bokor. Even by the flickering candlelight, Zero could see LaGuerre hadn't lied. She was extraordinarily beautiful, with ebony skin that shone, dark eyes that gleamed, imperious cheekbones, powerful arms but a curvaceous bust and full hips.

Four men rushed in with four long ropes; they attached each to the sheep's hooves then ran off into the crowd. Bokor Merlande Manoucheca raised her arms, and the room fell silent. The sheep bleated. In one hand she held a machete, in the other a bottle of rum.

"Offerings to Papa Legba," LaGuerre whispered. "The foremost Loa. Brace yourself."

Manoucheca shouted something; Zero wasn't even sure it was a real language, but instantly the temple stilled. The drums halted, the whirling ended, all eyes drilled onto her.

She rode the silence masterfully. She seemed to expand into it, her chest heaving, her arms rising, then she blurted out another shout that could have been words or nonsense. The men with the ropes responded instantly, pulling hard. The sheep's legs were ripped out from underneath it and there was the gunshot crack of joints breaking. The animal screamed, then Manoucheca brought first the bottle down on its head, shattering and spilling the liquid, then she followed with the machete, which sank into its back.

Zero bit her lip.

Noise rushed back as the gathering went wild. The drums exploded, the dancing erupted, the wailing restarted and the bokor hacked at the sheep like a butcher. LaGuerre put a hand on Zero's shoulder but she shook it off.

"This is black magic," she shouted over the noise. "The sheep's suffering makes the ritual stronger."

LaGuerre said nothing.

Manoucheca finally stopped her work with the machete and leaned in to lift up the sheep's head, trailing a raw length of twitching spine. The three women in white spun stepped and ripped the heads off their chickens in a row, producing three spurts of blood like living fireworks. They tossed the heads and carcasses atop the sheep's body, Manoucheca layered on the head and spine, then plucked a burning swatch of herbs from one of the firepits and tossed it onto the heap.

The pile ignited.

Flames and smoke gushed upward. The temple throbbed as the bodies burned.

"She's leaving," LaGuerre shouted, pointing after the bokor's retreating back. "Come on."

42

BOKOR

They reached the bokor just as she arrived at an open door. Two large men stood either side of it, each armed with machetes and handguns. One of them stepped forward with his arm out.

"Merlande!" LaGuerre called.

The bokor stopped dead. For a moment she didn't move, poised gracefully in the doorway, then she turned. Her white dress was soaked through with red, but it was the look on her face that startled Zero. Her lips were pulled back in a wide grin, her eyes were wide open and she no longer looked beautiful. She looked possessed.

"Jean-Baptiste," Manoucheca said, her rich and throaty voice carrying over the tumult of the temple. Her wild eyes scoured Zero and she asked a question in rhythmic-sounding French.

"She asks if he's brought her an offering," Rex translated.

Zero snorted and eyed the bodyguard with his arm out. Even without her knife she could incapacitate him in seconds: snatch his outstretched wrist and twist it sideways and down, forcing him to one knee while her own knee rose up to his chin for a knockout kiss. The second guard would be easier still; he'd charge in and she'd drop to wrap his right ankle and break it. He'd thrash around on the floor and the bokor would be left alone.

Before she could do any of that, though, LaGuerre laid a hand firmly on her shoulder and spoke in English.

"This is the friend we spoke of. She's come a long way to ask a second question about a dead little girl. I am hoping you will help us."

The bokor's head tilted to the side. The wild grin faded and curiosity crept into her eyes. "Why would I help your friend, Jean-Baptiste?" she asked in French-accented English. "Why would I help you?"

"Because we need you. Isn't that the role of a bokor?"

"For a price. Tout a un prix, Jean-Baptiste." She focused on Zero. "Everything comes at a price, isn't that right, Miss Gebhart?"

The use of her birth name in this place hit Zero like a knife in the back, and that pissed her off. She took a step forward, butting her chest up against the bodyguard's outstretched palm. "What price this time? More names?"

The bokor smiled. "I don't think a name will suffice this time, my dear. Come within. We will discuss payment."

The bodyguard stepped to the side, and Manoucheca turned and walked inside without another glance. Zero looked at LaGuerre. His face had turned ashen, like all the life was draining out of him, but he gritted his teeth, nodded and passed through the door.

It led to a dark, windowless room no bigger than the Delmas PD morgue, illuminated by candles resting in sconces set into the four corners. The floor was coated with dirt, the walls were painted black and it was as barren as a cell, with none of the paraphernalia of the entrance corridor. There was just a large black desk at the head and an even larger, stunningly worked tapestry hanging behind it.

Zero recognized the Loa Baron Samedi at once, with his black suit, stovepipe hat and skeletal face. He gleamed and glittered as Zero strode toward the desk. The tapestry was rich with detail and vodou sigils; hundreds of jeweled beads had been woven into the fabric along with thousands of silver sequins, and looking into its rich layers felt like looking down on Port-au-Prince again for the first time, a kaleidoscope of color and organic invention.

She pulled her gaze down to Mistress Merlande Manoucheca. She was now sitting at her desk, beautiful and resplendent in white and blood and black, like a vodou queen astride her throne. In front of her on the desk stood a fifth candle and several thick black discs resting in a shallow dish. The bokor made a small, swift ceremony of placing one disc in her mouth, chewing once and swallowing, then striking a match and lighting the candle.

The wick took the flame with a crackle.

"I know who you are now," she said, looking at Zero. "I know what you've done."

Zero stepped closer. "No surprise there. Your ex here told you my name. I'm sure you Googled me."

The smile split Manoucheca's face again and she shook her head. "Deeper than that. You are a little girl with a dark past, hunting the sins of her father." Her dark eyes flashed. "Hunting the man who sells pain."

An involuntary shudder ran down Zero's spine. Google wouldn't have told her that; it felt like a reprise of the conversation she'd just had with LaGuerre ten minutes earlier. "You're cold reading me. You don't know what you're talking about."

Merlande leaned in closer, speaking in a raspy whisper. "I recognize a fellow seeker. I see it in your eyes. I see the agonized death of the man from Ti Bwa, dragged behind your motorcycle." She winked. "And I like what I see. In another life, you would make a powerful servant of the Baron. Perhaps in this life, too."

"I'm nobody's servant," Zero said, and pulled the ouanga from her backpack. Holding the doll in that place felt different, as if it buzzed with a kind of dark power. She caught herself looking transfixed at it, no longer sure why she'd taken it out.

"Is that really true?" Merlande asked. "We all serve someone. The Baron approves of the souls you have claimed today. He would make you most welcome, soucouyant."

Zero blinked. "Soucouyant?"

Manoucheca's voice became hypnotic. "The men and women of Port-au-Prince already speak this name with fear and reverence. You are 'soucouyant' to them, or 'the Hag', a figure from vodou myth. By night she sheds her black old woman's skin and stores it in a hole in the ground, revealing her pale true face. Then she flies across the sky as a fireball, plunging down to strike her victims within their homes, bleeding them dry from pinprick cuts."

Zero frowned. "So I'm a hag, is that it?"

"Soucouyant," Manoucheca repeated. "The Baron told me you would come to me. He told me how to free your innermost desire."

"Baron Samedi? I think you're getting high on your own supply, Merlande. He's not real. And what do you think is my innermost desire?"

"To kill. To inflict suffering."

Zero felt herself slipping. That was too close to the bone. "I don't kill without a reason. I-"

"But you do enjoy it."

"Shut up," Zero snapped. "You don't know me."

The bokor rose to her feet. She was tall, broad and powerful. "I speak for the Baron, soucouyant. He watched over you in Cité Soleil. He guided your hand in your hotel. Now he wishes to claim what he's owed."

A shudder ran through Zero, and she remembered the vision of Samedi in Cité Soleil, standing in trash like a pauper with the arrogant bearing of a prince. Had he really been there? Had he saved her?

The answer to both was easy.

All of this was bullshit.

She turned to LaGuerre. He looked like a ghost, so pale and bloodless. "We're compromised," she managed, though her tongue felt thick and slow in her mouth. "The gangs must have warned her. There's another drug in the air here, too, something stronger than outside." She scanned the desk. "Maybe more from that candle? G9 might be coming. We need to leave right now."

LaGuerre said nothing, only stared mutely ahead. Zero felt the same muffling effect thickening around her head like a heavy blanket.

"You see too much, soucouyant," Merlande said, her face swimming closer with the walls.

"You're drugging your congregation."

"Of course I am. It heightens our connection to the Loa, and allows me to control dangerous spirits and powerful soucouyant. Now I'm drugging you, too."

Zero wavered. She was losing control, and that was more than just Jimson weed; a deliriant shouldn't deaden all sensation and willpower. This was something stronger. Maybe…

She made a lunge for the candle but the bokor swept it back smoothly. "I don't think so, hag."

"That's tetrodotoxin?" Zero muttered, sounding as horrified as she felt. "In that candle?"

"Blowfish toxin," the bokor confirmed.

"You're insane! You'll poison yourself. You'll kill us all!"

Merlande smiled. "Not if the dosage is correct. I've been doing this a long time. Precision is everything."

Zero staggered a step backward, mind working the problem. Rex had said it earlier; there was no antidote to tetrodotoxin, only powerful respiratory intervention and external cleansing of the blood. She looked around, but there was no crash kit and no ventilator on standby. That left only-

She lunged over the desk. The bokor pulled further back, drawing the candle with her, but that wasn't Zero's target this time. Even poorly coordinated, she managed to get a hand on the small dish and snatch a hard black cake.

"Activated charcoal," she managed, slipping back to her own side of the desk. "To leech the drugs from the smoke." She pushed the disk into her mouth and chewed; it crumbled into dust in her mouth and she swallowed.

The bokor's eyes narrowed in anger. Zero already felt better. She noticed the ouanga clutched in her hand and remembered what she was here for.

"One shot. Tell me who made this or I kill you."

Manoucheca's smile spread impossibly wide, then her face abruptly split like a cracked egg. From within poured a tidal wave of blood. Children were carried on that wave like trash down Cité Soleil's canals in a hurricane surge, all marked with the Engineer's bite. Their blood washed over Zero and their cries filled her ears.

"I don't think so, soucouyant," came Merlande's voice, now a chorus sounding from every child's throat. "The Baron has spoken. You have finally found your master."

Hands clamped around Zero's upper arms. She turned. The two bodyguards were behind her now, holding her in position.

"You will serve me," the Merlande said. "My slave. My zombie. My soucouyant. From now on, you will kill for me and the Baron alone."

43

HAG

Zero saw where this was going. Her life played out as a servant to this Haitian witch doctor; a strange echo of her childhood years spent drugged at the whims of her father. Every night she would shake off her black hag skin and fly across the rooftops of Port-au-Prince, settling upon the enemies of Mistress Merlande Manoucheca and draining them of blood. She would capture their deaths with ouanga talismans and ferry them back to her mistress, delivering her soul after soul to wear like beads on a necklace.

It was so clear.

It would serve a side of her that loved to kill. The addiction that she'd tried to beat, that Gabriel had tried to treat, that his girls had soothed for a time, but now…

Now.

LaGuerre was a statue. The bodyguards had her. The bokor floated on her own ocean of blood. Zero had expected none of this, but maybe it was what she deserved, where this addiction had always been leading. Maybe it would give her what she needed.

There would be no Gabriel, though.

No Hanna and Zuzanna. No chance to shepherd them into adulthood, into productive lives that Zero herself could never hope to match.

Tears ran down her cheeks.

But she'd been here before. She'd prepared. Ever since she'd been captured by the Engineer, she'd had the back two molars in her lower jaw replaced with false teeth, each hollowed out inside. On one side she'd kept flumazenil and naloxone lozenges, effective antidotes to knockout benzodiazepines and opioids respectively. On the other side she'd kept twin cyanide pills, a big enough dose to kill her within minutes and prevent her from ever being taken alive again.

Once, that had been enough. But pills were slow. Ingestion took time.

Now she'd replaced all four of those molars with 2.5 milliliter miniature syringes. Tiny switches worked by her tongue released twin tiny plungers; her own meticulous design. Bite down on those plungers and all four syringes would stab their contents directly into her gum line. Their contents would enter her bloodstream instantly, pumping out through her heart to impact her entire body within a second flat.

On the left she had enough liquid cyanide to kill her in seconds; on the right enough adrenaline to temporarily overwhelm any knockout drugs she'd been dosed with.

It should work with tetrodotoxin too.

They were already carrying her away. The temple lay ahead, ripe with the stink of Jimson weed, sweat and burning wool.

She flicked the switches on the right; the plungers popped up and she bit down hard.

Two tiny syringes stabbed into her gums, delivering their payloads. In less than a second the adrenaline hit and the fog cleared from her mind. Everything sharpened. She found her feet. Her senses spread down into her fingers again, like she really was a soucouyant hag slipping back into her old skin.

They had her by the arms but there was nothing she could do about that. In gross muscle strength they out-massed her enormously. What she needed was a chance to put her greatest weapons into play.

She sucked in a strong gulp of the smoky air, triggering coughing. Her body thrashed and she leaned into it. The guards fumbled over what to do. The one on her right raised a hand to her mouth and probed to clear her airway.

She bit down.

He lost two fingertips and yelled, pulling sharply away. Zero spat out the nubs and stabbed her free hand at his mouth. She missed his tongue but caught his cheek and ripped with everything she had, tearing his face.

Then Zero was flying through the air, swung by her left arm by the remaining bodyguard. There was little she could do to cushion the blow; the earthen floor slammed across her right shoulder and neck, almost blacking her out. Before she had a chance to recover or find her feet, the man hoisted her again in a judo throw. She felt her elbow creaking in its joint as she whipped past his face a second time.

One shot.

She took it, right hand shooting out like a bullet. Her index finger struck home, plunging through the soft jelly of his left eye and gouging deep. He shrieked and let go.

Zero hit the ground, rolled and came up facing them both. The temple raved around her. The two guards were bleeding from their faces but neither backed off. Both looked to be high on the Jimson weed, and that did not bode well for Zero. The element of surprise was gone, and she had no weapon to even the score.

Except, maybe, she did.

LaGuerre had been trying to teach her for two days.

When it came to Haiti, it didn't matter if you believed. It only mattered that other people did.

She reached up to the collar of her black shirt with both hands and ripped, tearing the buttons open. The shirt opened wide, revealing her chest, stomach and breasts. The guards stared. Zero didn't stop. She reached to her throat, dug her fingernails deep enough into her flesh to draw blood, then tensed as if to rip off the outer layer of skin.

The guards' eyes flared in sudden terror. The one on the left broke and ran. the one on the right followed. Neither looked back.

Zero let her hands drop. Blood ran down her chest and between her breasts in a thin rivulet. There was maybe only ten minutes left on the adrenaline shot, and she needed to get out. She needed to get LaGuerre out.

The bokor stood in her doorway, staring.

"I'm a soucouyant," Zero called. "A hag. You thought you could control me?"

Merlande Manoucheca watched a moment longer, then turned and fled.

Zero ran her down in seconds. She dropped an elbow into her neck, spun her right arm up behind her back and broke it, then stabbed a hand into her screaming mouth and caught hold of her tongue, using it like a leash to lead Merlande back into her room, to her desk, where the ouanga lay alongside the candle.

Zero extinguished the flame with a pinch of her fingers then sat the bokor down and pointed at the white leather doll, still not releasing her tongue.

"Who made that ouanga, you psychotic witch bitch? Tell me everything right now, and maybe I'll leave some bones unbroken. Lie or waste another minute of my time, and I'll chalk up another kill for the Baron."

44

MAÎTRE

Zero released the bokor's tongue and she gasped for breath. Her hands went to her mouth and she began to howl, but Zero wasn't about to accept that, and slapped her cheek firmly.

"The ouanga," she said, holding the white leather doll before her eyes. "Who'd you make it for?"

Merlande looked up at Zero, eyes swimming with pain. "I can't help you."

"You can," Zero said, and snatched the bokor's roving left hand, isolated her index finger and snapped it.

Merlande screamed herself red in the face. Zero waited until that diminished to whimpers and tried again.

"Which gang, Merlande?"

She shook her head. "No. They'll kill me."

"I'm killing you right now." Zero broke her thumb.

The bokor screamed, which turned into a gag. Zero stepped back as she vomited down her chest.

"All right," she spluttered. "Let me see it." She held out her one good hand and Zero placed the doll in it. The bokor's eyes focused on the lumpy white leather shape, probing it expertly despite the pain. "Bleached calfskin, rough human form," she muttered, "blood cotton spray from an onyx button in the head. This is simple enough."

"Who?"

Merlande looked up at Zero. "Most likely it's for Loko, Loa of vegetation and master of gardens. We bokor praise him frequently because he rules over the herbs we use. He-"

"Herbs? You mean Jimson weed?"

"Yes."

"And he's the master of vegetation?"

The bokor nodded, sweat streaming down her cheeks. "Offerings are often placed in trees, hung wrapped in straw bags. Invocation should result in a fair harvest, a powerful medicine, a-"

"This wasn't hung in a tree. I seriously doubt it's for a harvest or medicine. It was at the docks, strapped to a crane."

The bokor's roving eyes widened. "By the sea?" She turned the ouanga again and looked at it more closely, stroking the red tassel. "Not Loko, then. The blood cotton spray, hmm. At the docks?" She looked up. "This could be for Agwe, tadpole of the pond. He-"

"Tadpole?"

"It's a nickname. Agwe is Master of the Ocean. He rules all sea life and all men who sail upon his waters. Often he is invoked with conch shells, and his offerings are placed near the water, shaped as fish or oars, by those seeking safe travels, good shipping, bountiful fishing. He enjoys red, but this spray of blood cotton is strange." She fingered the threads. "It alters the call. This could be the symbol for a squid entering the body of a man." She tapped the black button. "Or being consumed, perhaps? Invading? Overtaking?"

"I don't care which," Zero said, mind spinning fast. The Engineer was a man of the water; if he was shipping restaveks to Pinocchios overseas, then this would be the ideal Loa to invoke. "Which gang made it?"

"I can't say with certainty," the bokor said, regaining some of her composure. "It depends on details. Several gangs in the G9 alone might invoke Agwe, as their territory borders the ocean, including Cité Soleil, Ti Bwa, perhaps Menelas 5. This squid may be the key, but I cannot know the intent; if it is being consumed, that suggests Ti Bwa, as they are infamous for acts of cannibalism. If the squid is invading the body, it is more likely to be Cité Soleil; they pride themselves on ruling all of Port-au-Prince from within the walls of their slum."

Zero weaved in position. The adrenaline burst was fading. "And Menelas 5?"

"I don't know. I would need more. It will not matter how many fingers of mine you break."

Zero tried to absorb that. Three gangs? It was a narrowing of the haystack, but far from what she'd hoped. She snatched the ouanga back, then felt the hard matter in the center.

"There's a bone!" she said abruptly, remembering. "Inside. A toe bone from the victim. It's been carved."

"Let me see it."

Zero fumbled the opening, her fingers growing numb as the toxic chemicals resurged. In moments she plucked it out and offered it to the bokor, who gathered a brass jeweler's loupe from a tray on her desk and examined it. She scoured the shreds of dried flesh and the squared-off edges, until after a few seconds she gasped, blanched pale and tossed the bone on to the desk as if it had scalded her.

Zero watched it skitter over the wood. "What?"

"You didn't see the crosses etched into the tail ends of that bone?"

"Crosses? Yes. I thought they might be connected to Jesus?"

"Jesus?" Merlande snorted. "This could hardly be further

from the Christ. This is very dark magic, soucouyant. This is-"

Zero snatched her middle finger and tweaked. "Who?"

"Maître Carrefour! Master of the Crossroads, of life and death and choices; offerings are made to him by-"

Zero squeezed harder. "I don't care about the fairy tales. Just tell me which gang it was for;"

"Maître Carrefour is no fairy tale, hag! He rules over all evil spirits, including you. He is lord of hexes and curses. He is choice, and fate, and nature at its wildest without any law. He is the will to achieve pure power, and to invoke him is to court the loss of your soul!"

Zero broke the middle finger. This time the bokor didn't scream; instead she barely flinched and her black eyes took on a faraway look.

"Which gang made it?"

"You haven't got ears to hear, soucouyant!" Merlande called, her voice taking on a strange shrill tone. "This magic is too vicious, too vengeful to speak of. Even revealing its purpose could bring the Maître to me and damn my soul for eternity. I will not tell you!"

Zero broke her ring finger.

This time the bokor laughed.

Zero broke her little finger and the laughter became manic. "I see him! I see him standing over your shoulder, hag."

Zero spun and the muddy room reeled. There was nobody there but the walls rolling and closing in.

"Who are you talking about?"

"The Baron!" cawed Merlande.

"Baron Samedi?"

"Wherever he goes, whomever he favors, death soon follows. There is already a curse upon you, damning you and everyone you love! Perhaps Maître Carrefour has bound the Baron to you as a hex. I will not have him follow me too!"

"He moves through me," Zero said, then moved to the next hand and snapped two fingers. The room was a blur and she was losing any sense of why she was there. Rex was a voice in her head making comments about her pulse that she couldn't quite grasp.

"Who made it?" she repeated, clinging to those words as she shook the ouanga.

"Samedi will claim you for the Maître," the bokor intoned flatly, like she was reciting some spell from an ancient ritual, "and when you die the heavens will open, shedding life like a hurricane rain. Your sacrifice will bring flowers to Haiti, soucouyant, it will feed us all for many-"

Zero broke two more fingers; only one remained. "Who, you psychotic bitch?"

"Who else would dare invoke the Maître in combination with Agwe?" Merlande howled. "Only a fool with the arrogance of absolute poverty in his past; the king of this city, soucouyant, the lord of all crime, the man known as Braai!"

Zero blinked. The name was familiar. Something about a tower and all the gangs, and…

"The head of G9?" she blurted. "You're certain?"

"It can be no other," Merlande held up both hands now and stared at her ruined fingers. "You didn't need to do this. You didn't need to-"

Zero grabbed the final remaining finger and tweaked it, anger carrying her the final few moments through the fog of deliriant smoke. "You tried to make me your zombie slave, you crazy witch! Of course you deserved it. Now why would Braai want this ouanga?"

"Why does any man seek the service of the Loa? For power!" The mad light returned to her eyes. "I see you now, soucouyant, stalking the heavens for the man who built the ship. I see all his children dying, and your voice issuing from a thousand mouths, and I see the rain fall on Haiti, such a blessing from such a sacrifice, and I see death and light and freedom and strength and-"

Zero blinked back to the moment as the bokor babbled; her heart crashed in her chest and she couldn't be sure if she'd heard that or made it up or-

"What man? What ship? Are you talking about Pleasure Island?"

The bokor's eyes rolled back in her head violently, leaving only the whites. "He is here, soucouyant! He is waiting for you. The rain will be so great to wash all this suffering away!"

Merlande's body convulsed once then slumped unconscious before Zero could ask any more questions.

"Now, Zero, you must go now!" came a suddenly clear, earsplitting voice in her head.

She blinked back to the moment. The bokor was unconscious and she was close herself. She grasped LaGuerre's hand and ran; back through the temple, bodies thumping off her until they were outside again, but the fresh air did nothing to clear her thoughts.

"Rex," she called plaintively, not at all sure what she was asking for.

"The car is waiting, Zero," he answered. "It should be right in front of you."

The street swam. She saw a vehicle and a face looming ahead, a skull wearing a top hat.

"Samedi," she said, like she was greeting an old friend. The door opened, she pushed LaGuerre in and fell in behind him, then they were in motion.

45

COMPOUND

Light stung Zero awake.

She jerked to her feet, hands rushing to the side table where she kept her stilettos, but there was no side table and no blades. Instead she found herself looking into the craggy face of a full-size, stuffed black bear, posed mid-roar by the taxidermist.

"His name's Bernie," came a deep voice behind her.

Zero turned. A man was standing on the other side of the couch she'd been sleeping on, illuminated by morning light flooding in through wide French doors. He was in his fifties, deep black like LaGuerre and dressed in the same white and navy blue PNH uniform, though he had a jacket bearing three chevrons on his collar.

"I didn't shoot him," he said. "I just confiscated him, but couldn't bear to burn him as contraband." There was a New York lilt to his voice, married to a singsong French accent. Zero dredged her memory for who this man might be.

"Precinct captain," she said, thinking back to the offer LaGuerre had made a day earlier. "This is the safehouse?"

The man nodded, looking faintly annoyed. "My home, on the outskirts of the city. You're quite safe here. My name is

Elifet Dieufel, and I am indeed precinct captain of the PNH for Delmas. Perhaps you can explain why you're here, Miss Aurel Nowak?"

Zero wasn't surprised he knew her name; everyone in the Delmas PD would know it after Marcelin. She looked around. She wore a long, clean night gown. The space was light and airy, a nice enough den with brown leather couches and a record player and the French doors leading out to a pleasant green garden. The bear was the only unusual thing in the room.

"I don't know," she said. "I assume you received a call last night from a friend of mine named Rex, warning you we were coming?"

He frowned. "That's correct. I didn't quite believe it, then here you arrived with ID LaGuerre. What happened to you both?"

Zero couldn't remember much from the night, and all she had now was a slightly nauseated feeling. She'd been drugged, that much was clear; most likely something with amnesiac effects.

"I'm not sure. Where is LaGuerre?"

"In the guest room, still asleep," Dieufel said. "Or perhaps it's more accurate to say unconscious. I had to call in help to transport you inside, to wash you and dress you." He nodded to the gown. "You were covered in blood. Not much of it was yours, I think."

"That'll happen," Zero allowed. She remembered turning up at the bokor's temple, but nothing after that. "Who did you call in?"

"She's with the ID now," Dieufel said. "The compound is yours for as long as you need it. I must go to the precinct. I only ask one thing, Miss Nowak."

"And what's that?"

"Leave Haiti before the storm hits. That's three days. This will be no place for you then."

She said nothing. Dieufel nodded once. "The power is out for now, but it should come back soon. I've prepared a thermos of hot water."

"Thank you. That's very considerate."

He shot her a look then left.

Zero stood in the light-filled den alone, trying to recall the events of the night. Alongside the wooziness, there were a few aches and pains in her body, particularly her left shoulder, but nothing too serious. Her phone lay on a marble coffee table and she swept it up, but the battery was dead. She looked further afield and found her backpack down the side of the couch. Her heart pounded as she unzipped the catch, but the ouanga was still inside, its white leather now spotted with blood, along with her charging cable.

In the open-plan kitchen she found a socket and plugged her phone in to charge. Nothing happened, though, no beep as power flowed into the handset. Hopefully the electricity would return soon.

The fridge was still cold, though. She found fresh milk and drained a pint. In a cupboard she found honey nut cornflakes - evidently the precinct captain had a sweet tooth - and poured herself a large bowl, looking around the space.

Dieufel kept a nice house. She crunched on cornflakes and wandered, feeling a curious lack of urgency. Maybe that was a side-effect of whatever drug they'd given her. She stepped through the French doors into the garden, which was small and well-kept. A tall stucco wall encircled the compound; she scaled it easily and looked out. The house was built on a sharp rise in the land, with pleasant residential houses and streets falling away to afford a sweeping view of Port-au-Prince stretching to the west. Perhaps five miles away she caught the glimmer of the bay.

She returned to the kitchen and checked her phone's charge, but still nothing. Instead she poured more cornflakes and located the hot thermos. She opened it and steam puffed out. There were coffee beans in the cupboard and a hand-propelled grinder to mill them. She ground up a generous batch, filled a French press and poured out a hot cup. She cut it with sugar and a dollop of double cream, then continued back through the house, sipping her coffee and stopping occasionally to crunch her cornflakes.

There was a study, a boot room, a utility room, a master bedroom, then LaGuerre. He was asleep in a stately guest room with a pretty, anxious-looking woman sitting beside him, holding his hand. He was asleep but she was not. Zero smiled.

"Specialist Amelie," she said.

The specialist stood up sharply and said something in French. Zero just waved a hand. "No French, sorry. It's OK. You want coffee?"

"Coffee, oui, s'il te plaît," Amelie said.

Zero figured that was yes and beamed. Still, Amelie hadn't let go of LaGuerre's hand. She nodded, retreated and poured another cup. There was just enough hot water in the thermos. Still no charge on her phone. She poured two more bowls of cornflakes, depleting the captain's supply completely, and returned to the bedroom with them on a tray, along with two shiny pink apples and a Snickers bar.

Amelie stood again as she entered. Zero laid the tray down and handed her the cornflakes and the coffee. Amelie took both, looking curiously at the cornflakes.

"They're good for you," Zero said, sitting down on a chair on the other side of LaGuerre. "Eat up."

Amelie said something in French, smiled, and took a bite of the cornflakes. Her face lit up in a generous, genuine smile. She really was very pretty.

Zero found herself smiling back. Beaming, almost. For some reason, and despite the wooziness, she felt good. Maybe she'd made real progress last night. All that blood on her clothes, and little of it hers, had to mean something.

Right now, though, she was just happy to sit opposite the pretty specialist and smile.

"He likes you too, you know," she said, pointing her spoon at LaGuerre.

Amelie gave a smile and a blank look.

"Love," Zero said, then dredged through her memory for the appropriate word. "Amour. You know. Cupid and his bow." She mimed firing an arrow at LaGuerre then another at Amelie, tapping herself in the heart after each.

The pretty young woman blushed, which was sweet, then raised one hand to her mouth, then burst into a flood of tears.

Not exactly what Zero had expected.

46

AMOUR

Specialist Amelie sobbed, and Zero didn't know quite what to do. She hadn't been in a situation like this before. Normally when people were sobbing in front of her, it was because they were begging and about to die.

But this? Totally new.

After maybe ten seconds of being frozen, she bobbed up, found a box of tissues and held them out. It was a good choice, because Amelie grabbed several and set to work dabbing at her eyes, at the same time explaining something in rapid-fire French or Haitian creole.

The words washed over Zero.

"Hey," she said softly, then again more firmly. "Hey Amelie, it's OK."

The specialist looked up. "OK?" she repeated. "Qu'est-ce qui va OK?"

Zero interpreted that as reasonable doubt. She wasn't keen to wade in any further, but now she felt responsible for this. "He really does. He basically told me himself. Amour, you know?"

Amelie looked at her like she'd completely missed the point, then grabbed another tissue and went back to sobbing.

"It's him," Zero said, feeling a little flustered now. "LaGuerre. It's his issue, nothing to do with you."

Amelie looked at her blankly, eyes puffy and red.

"Vodou," Zero blurted out, which got the specialist's attention, then held up one finger signaling her to wait as she looked around for the right kind of prop.

"Vodou?" Amelie repeated, eyes now widening in fear. "Est-ce qu'il expérimente le vodou?"

"What, an experiment? Nothing like that, not an experiment, no it's-"

"Est-il en danger à cause du vodou?" Amelie urged.

"Danger?" Zero repeated, growing aware that she was only making things worse. "Because of vodou? No, he's not in any danger, at least, I think..." She couldn't find what she was looking for in the room and wasn't sure how to fix it with words. "An ex-girlfriend, I think? She's done this to him." She mimed the cupid's bow and arrow again at LaGuerre, the heart explosion, then mimed shaking as if she was being electrocuted.

Now Amelie's eyes went big and wide. "Il a assassiné une 'ex-girlfriend' avec le vodou?"

"Assassinated by his ex?" Zero blurted. "With vodou? Or, wait, he assassinated her with vodou? No to both! Of course not. At least, he didn't kill anyone, I think..."

She wasn't sure if she was lying or really what she was saying anymore. She had no idea what had happened at the bokor's temple, but it was clear this wasn't helping.

"Just wait a minute." She ran from the room. Back at the kitchen her phone was still dead and she cursed. In one of the guestrooms she found a small teddy bear and snatched it up.

Back opposite Amelie she held up the bear, trying to think through what she wanted to say as the woman continued to stare and sob. "This is LaGuerre, OK?" She held out the bear. "And, uh, imagine I'm the ex-girlfriend?"

Amelie pointed at Zero. "Tu es l'ex-girlfriend?"

"Me? No! I mean, OK, yes, just for the purpose of, uh, this example, listen..." She mimed stabbing the doll with imaginary pins. With each stab, Amelie stiffened.

She stood up, clasped LaGuerre's hand close to her chest and shouted.

"Êtes-vous une bokor de vodou? Lui as-tu fait ça?"

All Zero heard was 'bokor'. "No, Amelie! No, I'm trying to show what she did, that witch bitch, she's the bokor, she stabbed him with a hex. Hex, you know? A curse?" She stabbed the bear again.

"Hex? Malédiction?"

"Yes, malediction!" Zero said gratefully. "She did it, the ex-girlfriend, she-"

Abruptly Amelie threw the box of tissues at her. Zero dodged easily, but the intent was clear as the specialist stabbed her finger at her. "Tu es la bokor! Sortez! Sortez d'ici maintenant!"

Zero remembered 'sortez' from the taxi driver at Cité Soleil and 'maintenant' from the guards near the trash mound. Put them together and that mean 'get out now'.

"I think there's been a misunderstanding," she offered.

"Sortez!" Amelie screamed.

Zero looked at the man lying unconscious on the bed. "A little help maybe, LaGuerre?"

He offered none. He remained unconscious.

Zero dropped the teddy on the bed by his side, which pulled another fast stream of angry French from Amelie. She grabbed the bear and flung that at Zero too, who dodged it and beat a hasty retreat.

Back in the den the shouting receded, replaced by more quiet sobbing. Zero milled around the couches for a few minutes, trying to figure out what she'd just said and how the beautiful Amelie had misunderstood it, vowing to herself never to try and matchmake across a language divide again, until she became aware of something that hadn't been there before.

The sound of the AC humming.

She hurried back to her phone and picked it up. The battery light was flashing now. It was charging!

She hit the power button and it chimed to life, pairing with her earpiece. It took a minute to fully wake, and as soon as it did the call came in from Rex and was auto-answered.

"Zero," came his familiar voice, sounding slightly more concerned than normal. "Is that you?"

She breathed a sigh of relief. "Rex. Oh boy, am I glad to hear your voice."

"As am I. How do you feel? Do you remember the events of last night?"

"No. Do you know what happened? I feel woozy and my memory's shot. Was I drugged?"

"You were. Fortunately I recorded everything that happened. Are you ready to listen now?"

"One second," Zero said, and put the kettle on to boil, then found some bread and slid two slices into the toaster. Another coffee and a snack would go down a treat right about now. "OK. Hit me."

"I will begin from the moment you approached the bokor in her temple," Rex said, and then the audio kicked in.

In thirty minutes Zero remembered it all. The recording was like a key, unlocking the door to her memories: breaking the bokor's fingers until she spilled answers then verged into madness. At the mention of the Engineer, the man who built the ship, a heaviness seemed to shroud across her shoulders.

He knew. He was waiting.

There was no time to waste.

She strode back to LaGuerre's room, thinking to do whatever it took to wake him up, starting with a bucket of cold water across the face and advancing to various mild torture activities, only to find him already awake and sitting up.

She opened her mouth but somehow he managed to speak first.

"What's this Amelie's been telling me, Miss Nowak?" he demanded. "That you were my girlfriend, and you were controlling me with vodou curses and hexes? That you made a vodou 'teddy bear' of me?" He held up the bear. "That you would keep on torturing me until she did exactly what you said?"

Zero frowned. Had she miscommunicated that badly?

"None of that is true. My French is terrible, LaGuerre, and so are my mime skills. Sorry, Amelie. But forget about that." She took a breath. "I know. I know who killed that girl, and I know where he is, at the top of the biggest haystack in Port-au-Prince. It's time to start stabbing."

47

BRAAI

Together Zero and LaGuerre listened to the recording in the den, while Specialist Amelie waited in the guest room.

"What's that cracking sound?" LaGuerre asked, early on in the interrogation.

"That's her index finger breaking."

LaGuerre winced. "And what was I doing at this time?"

"Just standing there," Zero said. "Like an ornamental potted plant."

He frowned.

She pointed. "Like that stuffed bear that your boss found."

"I get the point."

"Less handsome, obviously."

He grimaced. "I was drugged. How did you withstand it?"

"I'm tough. Listen."

Another finger cracked.

"What?"

"Sorry, the confession begins after the next one."

They waited. The next crack came then the bokor began to talk.

Afterward the three of them sat in the den, sipping coffee

and eating the precinct captain's cookies, absorbing it all. Zero had heard the audio twice now and was still absorbing what it meant.

"Braai," LaGuerre said, and shook his head. "Head of G9 an Fanmi. It's hard to believe. He's the most powerful man in Port-au-Prince, and now he's invoking Maître Carrefour, the most dangerous Loa there is? What could he hope to gain from it?"

"Everybody wants something," Zero said firmly. "You heard the bokor. She's in some kind of trance at the end, talking about gold falling like rain over Haiti and flowers blooming up. That sounds like vodou symbolism for the reward you get from making a powerful sacrifice, don't you think? And that girl, with all her scratch marks, was certainly a powerful sacrifice."

"A powerful sacrifice," LaGuerre repeated, rubbing his chin. "OK, maybe, but Braai's already rich. He's probably the richest man in the country."

"You can always be richer. You can always have more power."

LaGuerre shook his head. "More power? No. I can't believe it's him. Invoking the Maître puts him outside all the rules; it risks everything he's already got." He raised a steadying hand. "I'm thinking that the bokor was hysterical at the time she named him. You'd just broken nine of her fingers. She would've said anything to get you to stop."

"I disagree," Zero said. "I've seen hysterical, LaGuerre, and this wasn't it. This was more like possessed, and do people really lie when they're possessed?"

He frowned. "I don't know if there have been any studies of that."

"Point is, I doubt it. I think this is solid. It's Braai."

LaGuerre sighed. "It's Braai. OK. Just for the moment, let's say you're right. Braai sacrificed a little girl to two of the most powerful Loa for good luck. But good luck in what; kidnapping, corruption and extortion? Those are his main industries."

"I don't know. I'll need to ask Braai."

His jaw dropped "Ask Braai?"

"Stop repeating everything I say," Zero said sharply.

LaGuerre opened his mouth then closed it. A silent moment passed, then Amelie said something in rapid-fire French. LaGuerre turned to her and answered at length; Rex tried to keep up with the translation but it was too fast and garbled to make out.

Zero waited. The conversation lasted maybe five minutes, and when it was done, LaGuerre turned back to her with a heavy expression.

"Actually, maybe there is something Braai would want good luck with. Something big. Do you remember what I told you yesterday, about a new potential gang civil war starting up?"

She blinked. "Over Selecto espresso coffee in the parking lot. Right before you tried to kick me out of the country a second time, and failed a second time."

He scowled. "Yes, that. It looks like it was already on the cards."

"A civil war?"

"Do you remember the fuel truck explosion in Cite 4 two days ago?"

She frowned. "When we went to the MSF hospital. What about it?"

"Specialist Amelie says it's been claimed as a G9 strike against G-Pep. Cite 4 is G-Pep territory, and this blast killed over a dozen high-ranking G-Pep gang members." He sucked in a slow breath. "They've been vying for control of Port International for years. Cite 4 looks like the opening salvo in a new round of gang warfare, the biggest one yet, and the retaliation's already well underway."

"What retaliation?"

LaGuerre relayed the question to Amelie, who answered at length.

"Shooting in the streets for several nights now, and only getting worse," LaGuerre summarized, his expression darkening. "There are fires in multiple districts, several explosions; the use of weapons of war. It seems your killing of the Ti Bwa gang member just fed into this rising tide of violence, right alongside the chaos you sowed in Cité Soleil and the men you killed at the Royal Oasis."

Zero put her cup down. This was her curse; every rash act had consequences she hadn't expected. "So it is civil war?"

"It seems that way."

Her mind raced, thinking back on what they'd discussed over the coffee. "Then this changes everything. Braai's no idiot, I'm sure, not if he runs half the city." She snapped her fingers. "He brought this on. You said it yourself, he wants this: what better time to win a civil war, locking in control of the port and maybe the whole city, than right before a hurricane strikes?"

"You're mixing up what I said."

Zero felt the landscape shifting. "It's the same thing. And if that's really his goal, then it's worth an extra special sacrifice to get right with the Loa, agreed?"

LaGuerre gritted his teeth, looking unhappy. "Maybe. It's conceivable."

"OK. So it's the soul strength theory of vodou sacrifices again. Braai picks a girl who's suffered a lot because she'll be a powerful sacrifice. He makes a ouanga invoking the god of the sea and the god of fate, then he selects the port as a kill site to double up on the impact; sea and crossroads both. This is it!"

LaGuerre paled. "Maybe. Port International's been out of commission for years, with so many gangs fighting over it. But if Braai can claim it completely? He could ship whatever he wants in or out: drugs, weaponry, restaveks."

"Exactly. Human trafficking's highly profitable. You said it yourself."

His eyes narrowed. "I think I also said it's notoriously difficult. Even with the port, and city bureaucracy on his side, and multiple feeder streams of restaveks, he'd still need an international middleman to make global sales. That's beyond the capacity of the G9. Braai may be smart, but most of his people never attended a day of school in their lives. Many won't even be able to read. All they know is guns and turf and-"

Zero stopped listening.

This was it. Finally she saw how he fit in; the middleman making it all possible. This was his role.

"It's the Engineer."

LaGuerre stopped talking. "What?"

Zero made the decision. It was about time she trusted LaGuerre all the way. "Earlier, you wanted to know why I'd come here. Why I flew across the world to Haiti for one dead little girl?"

He nodded. "We agreed you'd tell me at the end."

"I think we're getting there." She took a deep breath. "I'm searching for a man who sells children in the thousands, Jean-Baptiste; human trafficking at a scale to give you nightmares. He calls himself the Engineer." She paused a moment, gauging the response in his eyes. "Three years ago he rebuilt a cargo ship into a floating dungeon, designed to imprison children and provide safe haven for sick men to abuse them, far from the eyes of any laws or regulations. He planned to sail that ship around the world, buying children wherever he wanted and serving them up to the grinder of his twisted friends." She took another breath, steadying herself. "I came to Haiti because of that little girl's bite mark. That's the Engineer's calling card, and this sacrifice by Braai ties them directly together. The Engineer wants a consolidation of the supply of children who've suffered; the restaveks. Braai wants to get it by ruling the city." She glimpsed again the flood of children pouring from the eggshell of Merlande Manoucheca's cracked face. "Together they'll feed all of Port-au-Prince's lost souls into the Engineer's little black book. I have to find and kill them both before the hurricane locks that in."

LaGuerre looked stunned for a moment. It was a lot to take in. Then something seemed to click over in his expression, and he pointed at Zero's phone. "The bokor said it, didn't she? 'The man who built the ship'. Did she mean this 'Engineer'?"

"I think so."

There was silence for perhaps a minute.

"So that's why you're here. Not one little girl." His eyes narrowed, then there was another click. "Pleasure Island', you said on the recording. Where have I heard that name before?"

He brought up his phone and began tapping before she could answer. It didn't take long. In a few moments his eyes widened. He scrolled down rapidly, read swiftly then handed the phone to Amelie and looked up again at Zero.

"Pleasure Island," he said. "That was the base for the Pinocchio terror attack on the United States three years ago. You think that ship has come here?"

It was strange hearing those words come out of LaGuerre's mouth, about a past she'd tried so hard to escape. "Not that ship. It was decommissioned and disassembled. But the Engineer escaped; I'm thinking he's got a new ship."

"But how do you know he escaped? These article say hundreds of men died aboard and dozens were arrested."

Zero felt a wave of lightheadedness come over her, as the past and the present clashed. "Because I was on board. I was the main event, Jean-Baptiste. The Engineer wanted to torture and kill me for power or status, just like Braai killed this girl. I would've died, except Christopher Wren saved me. It's how we met. I've been hunting the Engineer ever since."

LaGuerre stared. She could feel him stitching the pieces together in his head. "That's why it's personal. You were his target."

"Now he's mine."

LaGuerre's eyes narrowed, then he nodded. "Understood. You've got an insight into him."

"I do."

"And you think he's working with Braai to consolidate supply?"

"Exactly that." More pieces fell into place, and her throat went dry. "Perhaps on a grander scale than anything so far."

"What makes you say that?"

"What's Haiti's most valuable export, Jean-Baptiste?"

"Most valuable? I told you, vetiver, the perfume. What's that got to do with-"

"Wrong. It's children, or the ouanga from children who've suffered greatly. Trophies for trinket hunters. They'll be worth far more than vetiver, even more than weapons or drugs, especially when there's no shortage of supply."

He blinked, stared then cursed in low French. Zero rushed on, putting the last pieces together.

"If you wanted to design a factory for producing untraceable children who've all suffered greatly, you couldn't do much better than Haiti, could you? The slums and the rural areas churn them out at a phenomenal rate, the restavek system ensures they know horrors and their disappearance is covered, and with the Engineer on board, they'll have no trouble selling them."

LaGuerre ran a hand along his tight corn rows, looking queasy. Specialist Amelie stood up and said something in French.

"She says she wants to leave now," Rex said in Zero's ear.

"It's OK," Zero said. "You can go. Maybe this is not for you, Amelie."

LaGuerre translated.

Amelie went to the door, turned the handle, then stopped. She hesitated.

"Unless it is," Zero said, surprised.

The slight woman gritted her teeth. She looked at LaGuerre. Then she came back and sat down again.

"No," he said. "Amelie."

"She understands," Zero said. "Braai has to die tonight, LaGuerre. The Engineer has to die tonight."

He shook his head. "Impossible. Even if I agreed that killing him was the right move, which I don't, you'd never get close. If we're really in the middle of a civil war, then every gang in the city will be on high alert. Two days ago you'd have struggled to isolate Braai. Now it'll be impossible. The Haiti Celco hotel will be on extreme lockdown. There will be no harder place to reach alive than the penthouse at the top of that tower."

"I'll find a way."

"What way? It's impossible! You may have survived Cité Soleil, Miss Nowak, you even bested the bokor in her own temple, but you will never get close to Braai."

"Let me worry about that. I'm a soucouyant, after all; I can fly across the sky as a fireball and squeeze through the smallest cracks. I will get to Braai, and no one but Baron Samedi's going to see me coming."

LaGuerre's face darkened. "Baron Samedi? Soucouyant? Haven't you learned by now that you shouldn't toy with vodou?"

She met his gaze head on. "No. That's not what I learned at all, Jean-Baptiste. Vodou's a weapon, one they're killing children with, and I'll be damned if I leave that weapon on the table while they're all out there using it. I'm going to kill both Braai and the Engineer tonight, and if I have to strip off my skin and fly across the night sky to do it, all the better. Now are you going to help me?"

Seconds passed. LaGuerre stood up.

"I need a minute," he said, and walked out without looking back.

48

AMELIE

"More coffee?" Zero asked, awkwardly holding out the French press.

Amelie stared.

"Sorry about that nonsense earlier with the teddy bear," Zero went on. "Rex, can you translate?"

The phone on the coffee table began to speak in smooth French. Amelie seemed surprised for a moment, then a shy smile spread across her features, making her look even prettier. She replied in French; a long response that had her smiling widely by the end.

"Rex?" Zero prompted.

"She said that you seemed terrifying last night, when you were covered in blood," Rex said, "then worse this morning when you started talking about vodou, but when you tried to stab the teddy bear, you looked quite cute."

Zero hadn't expected that. "Cute?"

"Cute," Amelie replied in English.

She felt a hot blush rising to her cheeks. "Third time's the charm," she muttered. "Everybody wants to slap my ass in Haiti."

"Should I translate that?" Rex asked.

"No," Zero said quickly. "Just tell her thank you and offer the damn coffee."

In five minutes they were each sipping steaming hot cups, while perched atop the compound's exterior wall, watching LaGuerre pace back and forth in the gravel streets below. He was looking intently at his phone and didn't seem to notice the two women above.

It was a beautiful day, with blue skies yawning over them like a great deep-sea abyss. The city stretched out away like terraces in a mountain rice paddy, capped by the slim blue line of the bay. But for a handful of black lines of rising smoke in the distance, you wouldn't know a gang war was raging in the center.

"It was none of my business, really," Zero said, kicking her feet. "Talking to you about your relationship with LaGuerre. I was being flippant, I suppose. I'd blame the puffer fish toxin, but it's probably one of my flaws. Not always great with people, and given to acts of whimsy."

Rex translated.

Amelie said nothing for a moment, then smiled and answered.

"I'm glad you said it," Rex translated. "Jean-Baptiste and I have been doing this dance for years."

Zero grunted and caught Amelie's eye. "Men."

Amelie laughed, then almost overbalanced. Her merry expression became outright terror for a moment, but Zero already had a hand clasped around her upper arm, locking her in place. She didn't even spill any coffee.

"Wow," Amelie said, which Rex unnecessarily translated.

"Strong hands," Zero said. "Good grip." She looked at her palms. "Maybe a curse."

Amelie said nothing. Below them LaGuerre twisted on his heel and started walking back the way he'd come, then stopped and changed direction again, scrolling his phone rapidly.

"He's a good man," Zero said.

Amelie nodded. "Il a peur."

"He's afraid," Rex said.

Zero looked out at the horizon. "There's a lot to be afraid of, here. Not just the gang war." She paused a moment, wondering how much more to say, then pressed on anyway. "He thought there was a hex on him. LaGuerre. The bokor we went to see last night cursed any woman he was with to die in horrible pain." She let Rex catch up with his translation. "I think we can consider that hex canceled now, though, after what I did to her. That's what I wanted to say, before. That's what he was afraid of."

Amelie reached out and took Zero's hand, speaking in French.

"That's not all he's afraid of," Rex translated.

Zero grunted. "No? Responsibility, then? Commitment? Getting tied down to just one woman?"

Amelie laughed.

"Men," Zero said again.

"Hommes," Amelie repeated.

LaGuerre redirected again. He brought his phone up to his ear, engaged in a brief and animated conversation that devolved into shouting, then put it down. The sun was warm on Zero's cheeks and, despite everything she'd done and all the dark thoughts racing through her head, she found herself enjoying this moment.

"I never thought I'd be in a relationship with a man," Zero said, not really sure why she was talking, but happy to do so. "Now I am."

"Quel est son prénom?"

She didn't need the translation from Rex to understand that.

"Gabriel. He's a good man. He loves me, despite what I do, and he loves his children. Two girls, 7 and 9. He lets them love me, too, which sometimes feels like more than I deserve."

Amelie's hand tightened on Zero's. She realized her cheeks were wet and laughed, rubbing the tears away. "Silly."

"Ce n'est pas 'silly'. C'est mignon."

Zero recognized the word 'mignon' from earlier. "You really think I'm cute?"

Amelie swept on in French.

"She says, if she didn't already love LaGuerre, she'd be all over you."

"Good to know."

Amelie went on, gazing into Zero's eyes, and Rex translated. "There's something about you. Strong, but fragile. I feel I could break you with a word, even as I know you could kill me with one tweak of your hand."

Amelie's eyes went down to where their hands were entwined. Zero realized that was true. Just hours ago she'd been breaking the bokor's fingers. Now here she was, holding hands with Amelie, and it would only take one twitch to send her tumbling off the wall.

She might not die. It wasn't that high, after all. But it felt like a moment that mattered.

"Do you think LaGuerre will help me?" she asked. "I don't know if I can finish this on my own."

Amelie considered that for a moment. She sipped her coffee. They both watched LaGuerre walking the streets below. Now he was gesticulating in the air, explaining something to himself, until finally he looked up and saw them sitting on the wall.

A scowl darkened his face, and Amelie laughed and answered.

"I don't know," Rex translated. "But for you, I will try to

persuade him. Haiti is sick. It has been sick for a long time, with a cancer none of us can remove. But you are a scalpel, aren't you?"

Zero said nothing, just looked into Amelie's eyes.

"You are a scalpel," Rex repeated as Amelie went on, "but you should be wielded by a Haitian. I believe Jean-Baptiste is that Haitian. I want peace. I want this city to be safe for the children we will have."

Zero smiled. Now there were tears shining in Amelie's eyes.

"OK," she said. "Deal."

49

ONE WAY

LaGuerre returned. They received him in the den, sitting calmly around a pot of herbal tea steeping on the coffee table. It was blueberry and acacia, filling the air with a sweet tanginess.

"Tea?" Zero asked.

He ignored her. "What do you want from me?"

Zero shifted her position. "Perhaps more than you'll want to give. Why don't you sit down?"

"I'm not sitting. What do you want?"

Zero took a deep breath and looked up into his eyes. "Fantom 509." She let that sink in for a moment. "I can hand the gangs to them on a platter. Rex knows who and where they are thanks to extensive cell phone tracking. You just need to pull the trigger and reclaim your city."

His expression soured. "I knew it. This is Zero Day again. You want a massacre."

"That's right," Zero agreed, and nodded toward Amelie. "So does she."

LaGuerre looked at Amelie then back at Zero. A long moment passed as his eyes bored into her.

"Why? What do you care about Haiti's future?"

"I care about children, Jean-Baptiste. But you're right, this is selfish too. If Fantom 509 hit the gangs tonight, it'll clear the decks for me to get to Braai. He'll be stretched thin fighting them off. I'll decapitate the G9 and they can finish off the body."

Laguerre shook his head sharply. "It's mass murder. No due process. I can't agree to that, we'd be no better than they are."

Zero snorted. "No better in whose eyes? There's no higher authority here, nothing greater than Maître Carrefour or Baron Samedi. Port-au-Prince is the wild west, LaGuerre, and it's time we started acting like we understood that; we have to pick up our sheriff stars and go after the bad guys. Tonight everything could change, but it's kill or be killed."

"That's not why I became police! It's not what I-"

"Bullshit! It's exactly what you want; it's the reason you stayed in Haiti, isn't it?" He opened his mouth to come back but Zero sped on. "You told me that yourself. In the first days you were here, you felt such outrage it almost ate you alive. So much injustice. When you heard about your fellow cops getting burned to death and the President getting assassinated, all you wanted was to go kill some bad guys, right?" His mouth closed. "Well, I'm giving you permission, LaGuerre. They're all out there right now, ripping this city apart: blowing up trucks, sniping MSF doctors and killing little girls, and there's only one way to stop them."

Silence filled the den.

Specialist Amelie took hold of LaGuerre's hand. He looked down in surprise, then looked in her eyes.

"She gets it," Zero said.

LaGuerre looked like he couldn't believe he was being cornered like this.

"If you want a better Haiti, this has to happen," she pressed. "We harness Maître Carrefour for ourselves. Master of the Crossroads. We change the fate of this country forever."

LaGuerre shook his head. "I can't accept Maître Carrefour as my master. The law is all that's keeping Port-au-Prince together, and he is a true chaos spirit. Deals you make with him are never what you think. He always comes back to haunt you. He'll end up owning you!"

"I'm not making a deal with the Loa," Zero said. "That's the Haitian way. But I'm not Haitian, LaGuerre. When I'm done killing Braai and the Engineer, the Maître can come for me, I don't care. That's the path I choose. Now, are you going to help me or not?"

A silence spread and thickened. LaGuerre looked furious. He pulled his hand out of Amelie's grip. "It would betray everything I believe in."

"Then your beliefs are wrong. Don't you want to fight to save your city?"

"I am fighting to save it!" he shouted abruptly, stabbing a finger toward her. "From them and from you. Do you remember calling us the black Spartacuses, 'Miss Nowak'?"

"Of course."

"That was a violent revolution, one that seemed successful for a time, but look how spectacularly it failed."

She frowned. "It didn't fail. You are free."

"Are we? Did you even read our history, Miss Nowak?"

"On the plane," she allowed.

"Then no! Like every other savior from overseas, you don't have a clue about the truth. You don't know that after we threw off slavery two hundred years ago, France came back with the full strength of their fleet and demanded *compensation*! *Compensation* for the financial loss of our slave bodies. *Compensation* for the loss of *their* plantations. We couldn't survive the attack, so we agreed to pay, and we're still paying today!"

LaGuerre seemed like he was about to explode.

"You're right, I didn't know that," Zero said, hoping to calm him.

"Nobody knows," he shot back. "Not even Haitians, though we feel it in our hearts. What else can you feel when your country's been exploited for hundreds of years? France's compensation was unpayable: within fifty years interest on the debt swallowed fifty percent of our GDP; within a hundred it was eighty percent of everything, every year! How were we ever supposed to develop with an iron collar like that around our necks? Chase that with dictator after dictator propped up by foreign governments, hurricanes, earthquakes, the slide into mass gang violence, and how were we ever supposed to climb out of the ocean of filth the French buried us in?"

Zero had no answer.

It sounded like a grotesque injustice. She'd always known LaGuerre was angry. Maybe this was the real ghost eating at his heart. "I'd think you'd want to fight even harder because of that."

"Like the black Spartacuses did?" he panted. "It failed two hundred years ago and it'll fail now! Even if you do kill Braai himself and we achieve 'Zero Day', we won't be free; the next Braai will just roll up and find a new way to turn us into slaves again."

Zero gritted her teeth and leaned in. "You told me Haiti made you into a different kind of man. You said you didn't police the gangs because it was better to live and make a difference where you could. But what difference are you making now, Jean-Baptiste?"

He said nothing.

"Just what do you do, now? Take ritual murders to the bokor so she can sell the sickest ideas on? Collect bodies dumped by the gangs like you're their bag man? Just what good is the law if you haven't got the strength or the will to enforce it?"

"Don't have the will?" he thundered.

"You might not like Fantom 509, but we need them now!" she shouted back, surging to her feet. "Tonight! Stand back if you want, keep your hands clean, but don't put an iron collar on them!"

"Me? Put an iron collar on them?"

"If the shackle fits."

LaGuerre looked like he wanted to throw a punch. Instead he extended a hand to Amelie.

"Allons-y," he barked.

"Let's go," Rex supplied.

Amelie shook her head and spoke.

"She said she's going to fight."

LaGuerre stared at her in disbelief, then shook his head and looked again at Zero. "I wish you'd never come to Haiti. I wish I'd put you back on that plane."

"You tried and you couldn't, remember?"

For a moment Zero thought he would erupt. Instead he stormed to the door, yanked it open, then stopped for a moment. He took a deep breath and shot a look back her way. "I'll talk to Fantom 509. That's it, no promises."

Then he left.

The den felt much emptier with him gone.

A long, silent moment passed, until Zero felt Amelie's hand creep into her own. She looked down, and Amelie spoke in French.

"She said he's a good man," Rex translated, "but he's gotten cautious, and this had to happen. She wants to know how she can help."

Help.

Zero refocused. There were so many things. "Have you got a car?"

Amelie nodded.

"Then let's go take a look at the Celco. Next we'll need to go shopping. I also want to head back to the bokor's temple and get my hands on her chemistry set."

Amelie smiled and spoke.

"She said she loves shopping," Rex translated. "Not so much chemistry, but she's game to learn."

50

CELCO

The Celco building stank.

From the moment Zero had started her journey to reach Braai, she'd been engulfed in filth: from stashing herself in the back of a brightly painted tap-tap bus loaded with rotting meat that ran to the city dump in east Delmas; to the garbage truck she'd crawled into for the ride through the G9 cordon five blocks out from the Celco; to the crawl through a quarter mile of fat-clotted, silt-mounded sewers.

Three hours, give or take, and for all that time she'd breathed nothing but rot and effluent. Now it was deep in her head, fermenting under her skin, swelling up like fungus from the beds of her nails, or at least it felt that way, despite the twin waterproof black neoprene wetsuits she wore over her strike suit. She'd waded in it, crawled in it, breathed in it and done her best to eat a packaged meal in it without gagging and adding to the stench.

All for this moment.

Standing on the second sub-level of the Haiti Celco, scraping the worst of the filth off her outer wetsuit. She wore her familiar in-ear device, along with climber's gloves over heavy-duty neoprene gloves and a set of ice-climber's spiked crampons on her hands and feet; along with the motorcycle helmet she'd picked, it was all the necessary ingredients for climbing up the black, noxious waste disposal chute of the tallest building in Port-au-Prince.

Call it the asshole of Haiti.

All for the man at the top of the pipe: Braai, AKA Barbecue, head of the G9 an Fanmi, who was currently waging a civil war across the city above.

Call him Perp 55.

Zero had bounced around the city all day with Amelie at the wheel, barely bypassing surging war zones wherever the gangs were clashing, past tire fires and bodies burning and gangs entrenched behind upturned vehicles exchanging gunfire, with the stink of burning flesh and death in the air, all in search of the gear she'd need to take Braai down.

They'd started with an attempted drive-by of the Celco, aborted when they found it buttoned-up with gang and police security five blocks out. They'd moved on to a dive school on the bay, which had provided twin sets of waterproof closed-cell neoprene. From there they'd returned to the bokor's temple to load up on puffer fish toxin; then she'd climbed into the tap-tap and started her filth-slicked odyssey to the Celco.

During all that time Rex had kept up a steady stream of commentary in her ear, sharing everything he'd learned about Perp 55.

Braai had been born in 1978 in South Africa, to a Haitian cocoa magnate father and a young black working girl from the Crossroads slum in Cape Town.

"Crossroads?" Zero had asked, while crawling through decades of built-up slime in the sewers. "Like Maître Carrefour?"

"It would seem so."

His birth was outside wedlock, and in the rarefied class atmosphere of that time, his mixed-race birth had seen him rejected on all sides. For much of his infanthood and youth he'd bounced variously between the limited government care system in South Africa, his mother's extended family and, a brief period as a ward on his father's cocoa estate, cared for by servants.

When he was twelve he ran away and joined a gang. He killed his first man at thirteen with a machete, was ratted out by a friend and entered the state penal system for juveniles, ending up at Robben Island, where he killed two other young men before being released on parole when the facility was shuttered as part of the political upheaval.

His gang were waiting for him with a new job, one his father's connections primed him for perfectly; shipping opium out of Colombia by way of Haiti. His father's cocoa business was the ideal cover to transport large amounts of raw opium for refining in the slum sweatshops of Haiti, then onto the crack dens of South Africa.

Within six months he became one of the richest men on the island, which made his operation a target for all the local gangs. He shipped in an elite cadre of South African gangbangers and with a combination of stunning brutality, brilliant ingenuity and generous bribery, he built the G9 an Fanmi consortium, crushing all pretenders to the throne.

His most famous exploit was known as the 'Night of the Fireflies', a massive assault waged in 2003 that cemented his mastery of the city's gangs. Across a dozen districts of the city, his gang members augmented by a force of Cuban mercenaries assaulted the headquarters of twelve different gangs simultaneously, using heavy-duty weapons of war like rocket-launchers and truck-mounted Vulcan guns.

The devastation had been immense, and ended the same way in every location: mass executions, mass rapes, and mass burnings of bodies on tire heaps at crossroads. These were called the fireflies.

Since then, he'd done everything possible to turn legitimate. It was widely believed he was behind the assassination of the previous President, and now he was behind the civil war spreading fresh firefly corpse fires across the city, all as part of his bid to lock himself into power before the hurricane, potentially ascending to the role of President.

"Are there mercenaries in Port-au-Prince tonight?" Zero asked as she crawled through filth, still a few hundred yards from the Celco.

"I have checked ships coming and going through Haiti's various ports," Rex replied. "It seems possible. There was a Cuban tanker moored at Cap Haitien three days ago, and since then there has been a flood of Cuban-registered cell phones into the data sphere."

She cursed. "How many?"

"Hundreds."

"Enough to swing the civil war?"

"Perhaps enough to take down the military in pitched battle. It seems Braai is aiming to close out his coup tonight."

"Make sure Fantom know it," she said. "Make sure LaGuerre knows it."

"I will," Rex said. "ID LaGuerre's last report, however, was that Fantom 509 will not act yet."

Zero gritted her teeth and sped up. "They're waiting to see if I kill him."

"It would seem so."

It wasn't her plan. It pitted her solo against everything Braai could muster, when she'd hoped to slip through in the midst of a mass firefight.

Now she looked up the waste chute.

The Haiti Celco had been built in 2015 as a charitable

write-off by Celco corporation, the biggest cell service carrier in South America, influenced by a pressure campaign from the Clinton Global Initiative to increase foreign direct investment in Haiti. It was Haiti's first four-star hotel, located in the upmarket, downtown district of Bois Verna, and was twenty-one stories tall with 210 luxury rooms, seven palatial suites capped by Braai's vast penthouse, three restaurants, two bars, a gym with heated swimming pool and a gift shop, all wrapped up in an envelope of top-of-the-line security.

Rex had provided the full specifications for the building. It was clad in sleek, low-solar-gain glass, making it extremely difficult to climb the exterior. It boasted its own independent electricity supply, partially from six diesel generators in the sub-levels, partly from a 1 megawatt solar farm located nearby. It had its own water treatment plant with tanks containing a five-day supply, a sixty-thousand gallon sewage treatment facility, and state-of-the-art AC throughout.

"It is the perfect place to survive the zombie apocalypse," Amelie had said, back at the start of the day, when Rex was done explaining the Celco.

"Are those vodou zombies or real zombies?" Zero had muttered, then waved a hand. "Whatever, we can use it. Rex, is there a waste disposal chute I can fit in?"

"A chute you can fit in?" he'd asked.

"You heard me correctly."

"Checking." Moments passed. "There is a single waste chute that tracks the height of the building. Diameter is perhaps sufficient to fit you. It would be a near-impossible climb, however. The central waste pipe is polyvinyl chloride; there will be no grips inside. You can also expect a fairly constant flow of waste, especially nearer the lower levels. It will be like trying to climb a waterfall of garbage."

"I've climbed worse," Zero said.

"Are you certain?"

"No. But I can do it. There's ways to manufacture grip on sheer plastic. Sharp ice crampons, for instance. Can you source those in Port-au-Prince today?"

"I can't imagine they're a big seller here in the tropics. Perhaps I can have a local blacksmith manufacture some to your specifications?"

"Do it."

A fresh load of waste splashed down the chute, drumming into the large plastic cart. If she survived this, she would have to make Rex promise never to tell anyone, particularly Christopher Wren, what she'd done.

Maybe this was what it truly meant to be a soucouyant. She pulled on her crash helmet and stepped into the filthy chute, reached up with her hand crampons to dig the ice-climbing spikes into the inside wall of the plastic, stabbed in with the crampons on her feet and hauled herself up.

51

FIREBALL

Within thirty minutes Zero stopped at the waste chute hatch on the twenty-first floor, braced within the tube. Her forearms were burning, her thighs and ankles ached, but she had plenty left in the tank.

"How are we looking, Rex?"

"Undetected," Rex answered. "I have hacked the Celco's central server and have full command of the main power supply. The backup generators go on their nightly maintenance cycle in thirteen minutes. When I kill the lights, it'll take three minutes for the backups to come back online."

Zero nodded. That was the plan. "Security?"

"I have access to the Celco's internal security cameras; I'm showing seven armed men stationed between the elevator and the door to Braai's penthouse."

"Anyone in the trash utility space?"

"There are no cameras, no patrols. I believe you are clear."

"And inside the penthouse?"

"No camera feeds, but I have confirmation via cell phone signal that Braai is there along with at least five bodyguards."

Zero ran the numbers: seven men outside, five inside, twelve men in total plus Braai. She'd have to be fast. If the backup generators brought the lights back online, she'd be a sitting duck for any gang member with a gun.

Good thing she had one more trick up her sleeve.

"You've hacked their phones too?"

"Five out of the seven outside, three of the five within," Rex answered. "All primed for thermal runaway. When you give the command, they will overheat; there'll be flames and maybe small explosions."

Zero grunted. Fireball.

"Exiting the chute now."

She pushed the waste chute hatch open and slithered quietly into a featureless gray utility space. Nearby stood two room maid's carts, well-stocked with cleaning equipment and tiny little soaps, and a huge sack of used bedsheets.

"All clear," Zero whispered, and slung the pack off her back.

"Five minutes until the backups drop out."

Zero stripped the crampons and her helmet, then unzipped her stinking outer wetsuit and peeled it painstakingly off. Next she opened the pack and extracted a bandolier of shuriken throwing knives and twin stiletto blades. The grips felt good in her palms. Her muscles felt limber. The inner wetsuit gleamed and sparkled.

"Ready, Rex."

"Thirty seconds until the backups go out. You'll have three minutes of full dark before the backups kick in. In the corridor beyond, the furthest man has a key card in his right pants pocket. You'll need to open the penthouse door before the guards seal the bolts inside."

"Now you're playing my song," Zero said, and closed her eyes, getting accustomed to the darkness. Her heart pounded.

Twelve men in three minutes. Piece of cake. "Fire their phones."

"Firing. Five seconds … Go."

Zero opened her eyes on darkness and barged the door. The corridor ahead was almost pitch dark but for the low green glow of the battery-powered EXIT sign over the elevator. The nearest three men were silhouettes and she charged.

They never saw her coming, and she delivered three powerful, graceful thrusts without dropping a step, stilettos flashing red and silver: one in the throat, one in the chest, one in the side of the head like a ballet dancer.

They fell without a sound and Zero raced on, already five yards from the next cluster when one of their phones exploded in a flare of magnesium-bright light. The others jerked backward, clutching their hands to their eyes. One man was on fire, slapping at his face and chest.

Zero put him out of his misery with a stiletto in the eye. He sagged on the blade but she was already spinning to plunge her second blade into the chest of the next man along. A wild haymaker blow came toward her from a third man but she rolled it easily, pulling one stiletto free and uppercutting it through the girdle of his jaw to punch through the roof of his skull. Blood burst from his nose, his eyes crossed and he fell, dragging the blade down with him.

The fourth man was three yards off and pulling his handgun. Zero hurled her remaining stiletto overhand. The blade impaled his shoulder and the gun dropped without discharging.

Zero followed fast, delivering three sharp stabs into his throat with a throwing spike. He thrashed and blood sprayed her face as she rummaged in his pocket for the keycard.

"One minute gone, they are by the door readying the bolts," Rex warned in her ear.

She retrieved her stiletto from the man's shoulder and ran. Three steps and she retrieved the second stiletto, four more then she was at the penthouse door with the keycard held to the scanner. It beeped green and she rammed through.

The door slammed into the forehead of a man on the other side, rocketing him backward into two others. Zero smelled burning flesh, singed clothing and a chemical stink; they'd fared no better in here after the thermal runaway, but it had come early and they'd adjusted, already shouting and reaching toward her.

Zero flew deep into the penthouse, taking cover in the darkness as they groped for her. A gunshot rang out blind, only serving to send a muzzle flash out like a flare, temporarily blinding the man holding it.

Zero sprinted around the back of a long couch and hit him from the side, both stilettos swinging in to crisscross through his neck, instantly bisecting his spine and killing him standing up. She pulled free and circled; another gunshot rang out, maybe closer this time, and she whipped two throwing darts off her bandolier at the muzzle flare.

There was an answering shriek and a final shot as the man dropped, then she was by the door again. Two men remained, facing the wrong way into the darkness with their handguns out.

She ended their worries with two swift, perfectly targeted stabs low into their spinal columns. There was no sign of the fifth; perhaps he'd fled. She moved to the door, slammed it closed and racked the bolt home.

Four bodies down and one fled, which meant she was alone with Braai.

"Thirty seconds," Rex called.

A bullet clanged off the door but she was already racing into the dark, bent double to come up on Braai from behind.

At the last moment he spun, but he didn't stand a chance as she plunged both stilettos into his shoulders.

His arms dropped limp, the gun clattered to the floor, then she followed up with a knee into his crotch.

"Ten seconds."

He dropped and she dropped atop him, one knee on his chest, one on his throat, constricting his airway, his right wrist already caught in a breaking lock and ready to-

The lights came back on.

Zero's eyes flared wide.

It wasn't Braai.

It was the fat, sweating face of Officer Marcelin from Delmas PD.

"Stupide petite salope," he rasped, and Zero didn't need Rex to translate that: stupid little bitch. There wasn't time anyway; a noise came from behind and she spun into a blow from a rifle stock, knocking her back into the dark.

52

IN THE BLOOD

Zero surged back into the light fighting; they had her by the arms and the legs, stretching her out. The rubbery, slick black layer of her inner wetsuit was almost completely off, revealing her strike suit, which they were already working to unzip.

She lashed out with everything she had: her foot hit someone in the face, her gloves raked someone's ankle, but they didn't let go. Details resolved even as the ache from the hit to the head solidified like a nail in her temple.

Officer Marcelin stood right there, shoulders bloodied through his police uniform, with a foul grin on his face. The others she recognized dimly, all in uniform, as the same four men from the Delmas PD morgue. She picked out the steroidal bodybuilder with a swollen neck and managed to get a grazing kick into his head. He rewarded her with a punch in the face.

Her nose crumpled. The back of her head hammered into the floor.

They were talking in French or Haitian creole, too fast for her to follow or for Rex to translate. She kept on thrashing as the black strike suit peeled off her body. The cool air of

Braai's apartment touched the bare skin of her stomach and she shuddered.

Marcelin laughed and spoke in guttural French.

"You should never have come to Haiti," Rex translated. "But I'm glad you did. Hold her!"

They did, weighting each limb so her kicking stilled, leaving her stretched near-naked and helpless on the cold, hard wooden floor, under harsh white lights, with only her chest heaving wildly up and down.

Marcelin stared and spoke.

"That is beautiful'," Rex translated. "I could watch all day."

"Where's Braai?" Zero said, and a second later the translation came, as Rex's voice sounded from the cell phone's speaker in her strike suit.

Marcelin looked at the bundled suit and spat out more rough French.

"So the soucouyant bitch shed her tongue along with her skin." Rex translated.

Zero answered in French. "Où est Braai?"

Marcelin laughed. "Now that's real black magic; the little bitch learned to speak a civilized language." He kneeled down and ran a finger across her chin. "I wonder what else can she do with that mouth?"

The others laughed.

Zero's mind spun. What she needed now was time. "Was it Fantom 509?" she asked, and Rex translated. "Did they sell me out?"

Marcelin ignored her, running his fingers into the hollow of her throat, then down to her sternum, where his palm rested between her pale breasts. He seemed to enjoy the rapid rise and fall of her ribcage.

"You set me up," Zero pressed on. "You knew I could track your phones. Braai's not here, is he?"

Marcelin shrugged. "We are here."

"Enjoy it while you can."

"We will," Rex translated. "Tonight you will learn true Haitian hospitality." Marcelin pulled his hand back and unbuckled his belt.

Zero's breathing grew sharper. This was the moment she'd dreaded ever since the Engineer's iron altar. She thought of the little girl on her crane and the little boy on his crucifix. These men deserved everything that was coming to them.

"I give you all ten minutes," she said.

Marcelin laughed. "I think we'll take a little longer than that, if you don't mind."

She shook her head. "You don't understand. Ten minutes until you're all passed out on the floor and struggling to breathe."

Marcelin kneeled before her, signaling for his men to spread her legs. "Is this the curse of a soucouyant? I look forward to claiming all your hexes."

His men laughed. Marcelin lowered his body, clearly pained as his shoulders took his weight, bringing his face up close to hers.

"You stink, bitch," he hissed in English. "Lucky I like that."

"It's tetrodotoxin," Zero said, loud enough for them all to hear.

Marcelin froze. "Qu'est-ce que?"

"Look at your hands," she said firmly, looking past his bloated head to the four men holding her. "Touch your faces. I put my mark on all of you."

"The bitch is bluffing," Marcelin said, leaning his body in.

"It's what we soucouyant do," Zero went on. "We get into you through the tiniest holes. The smallest scratches. Then we just keep cutting until all the blood comes gushing out. Like in Cité Soleil. Like at the Royal Oasis. Like the man from Ti Bwa."

Marcelin paused, his heavy body already pressing against her. One of the men lifted his right hand off her leg to look at it. His grip with the left hand was still firm, but his eyes widened on his palm. He turned it around for the others to see. There was a faint red abrasion on the ball of his thumb.

"It's nothing," Rex translated as Marcelin spoke angrily. "It's only a scratch."

"And his face," Zero nodded toward the bodybuilder. "Everyone's hands. Even yours, Officer Marcelin."

He stared at her for a moment, then pulled one hand back to study it. He seemed surprised.

"I got the idea from Pierre Cedras," she went on. "I think you know him, the odd little man who campaigns for the restaveks."

Marcelin stared at her up close. His dark eyes were brutish and watery, but there was a sliver of fear spreading. "What have you done, you bitch?"

Zero smiled. "Cedras had a photograph of a dead little restavek boy. His skin had been rubbed away with sandpaper. It wouldn't even take much to abrade the surface, I thought. One swipe. But they kept on, sanding him down to the muscle in places. I didn't need to go that far to get into you, though, did I?"

The fear spread deeper in his eyes. "What have you done?" he repeated.

"Tetrodotoxin poisoning," she answered. "It comes from puffer fish, the same drug vodou bokor use to make zombies. It doesn't take much of a dose to kill, and it's an unpleasant road to get there: tremors, vomiting, respiratory failure, convulsions, cardiac arrythmia and ultimately death."

Rex kept on speaking for ten seconds after she fell silent, followed by another ten seconds of silence.

"How?" Marcelin repeated eventually, rearing back to rub his palms together gently. Zero picked out the faint abrasions in the skin.

"I coated my inner wetsuit with it," she said. "Tetrodotoxin mixed with petroleum jelly and high grit sand." She looked at her hands and feet, which were still gloved and booted, letting Rex catch up while playing for every second. "You all laid hands on me. You still are. You held on while I kicked and twisted. You basically sanded your own skin off, and now the toxin's in your blood. You're all going to die soon, in great pain." She smiled. "That's the soucouyant's curse."

Abruptly the bodybuilder jerked backward, releasing her left leg and wiping his hands on his shirt, as if he could wipe the toxin away. Zero exploited the moment to send a kick sweeping into the head of the man holding her right leg. He pulled away but not quite fast enough, taking the toe of her boot down his cheek. Before she could roll back and kick the others, Marcelin pulled back and they all released her.

She sprang to her feet, almost naked in the midst of the five of them. Marcelin had his gun raised inches from her face.

"I will shoot you," he said.

"Shoot me and there'll be no antidote."

That caught his attention. "Antidote?"

One of the men vomited behind her. Zero didn't turn. "Too late for him, I think."

Marcelin's eyes widened as Rex translated. "Where is the antidote?"

"Where is Braai, Officer Marcelin?" she countered.

53

L'ANTIDOTE

Marcelin shook his head.

"I don't know," Rex translated, "I can't tell you."

Zero shrugged. "Then you shoot me now and we'll die here together."

Seconds passed. Marcelin didn't shoot. Zero advanced, raised a hand and smoothly took the gun off him. He let it happen. She reversed the grip and hammered him in the face with the grip. His nose cracked and blood gushed out, dropping him to his knees.

"Officer Marcelin," she said calmly, "I'll ask one more time. Where is Braai?"

Marcelin blurted his answer through the blood in his mouth.

"I don't know," Rex translated, "I was never supposed to be here. I'm not involved in Braai's business. I don't know anything about the restaveks."

"But you do know about the restaveks?"

"Everybody knows! That little slut bitch at the docks? Everybody knows."

Zero let the insult pass. She was talking to a dead man, now. "So why are you here?"

He groaned, then urgently grasped his stomach.

"It's my reward," he grunted. "Because I told him you were coming. He knows what you did to me. I told him you were tracking phones."

Zero cursed. That checked out. But she'd only told one person about her ability to track the gang's phones.

"Did LaGuerre tell you?"

Marcelin gulped strangely. "You think LaGuerre would talk? He's a joke! A tourist. He doesn't understand Haiti. He's almost as stupid as you."

Zero's mind reeled. If not LaGuerre then who? It was hard to think, and she was starting to feel nauseated herself. She'd wagered on receiving some tetrodotoxin exposure, and already loaded her stomach with activated charcoal. She just had to hope the strike suit had protected her from the worst of it.

Then it hit.

"Was it Fantom 509? LaGuerre told them, and they told you?"

Marcelin grunted. "Who cares? Sure. Now give me the antidote!"

"Then give me Braai! Or better yet, give me the Engineer."

He frowned. "Who's the Engineer?"

"A white man," Zero said, "handsome, late thirties, about your height, got a bite mark on his left forearm, a real sick bastard when it comes to children. Arrived here about three years ago. He's buying up all the restaveks from Braai."

Marcelin frowned, then nodded frantically as Rex finished talking. "Oui. Oui! Je-"

"I know that man," Rex picked up. "I have seen him. That's the Engineer?"

Zero's heart skipped a beat. Finally. "Where is he?"

"Île. La île!"

"An island," Rex translated.

Zero felt like she was slipping. "You mean a ship? A ship called Pleasure Island?"

Marcelin shook his head. "Ship? No. It's an island. It's land."

She could barely follow along with that. "What? So, where is it? What's it called?"

"It doesn't have a name," he grunted. "It's small, somewhere in the middle of the bay."

"Port-au-Prince Bay?"

"Yes!" He was weaving now, and abruptly vomited. Zero stepped back to avoid most of the spray. "Where's the antidote?"

"Which island, Marcelin? Could you show me on a map?"

"I don't know! There's dozens of them. I've never been, I just heard about it. Give me the antidote!"

"What are the defenses? Who has he got there? How many men?"

Marcelin laughed wildly. "I'm going to die, what do I care?"

Zero punched him in the face. "How many men?"

"Dozens. Braai's inner circle."

"Braai's?"

"Braai! Braai! Oui, Braai!"

"And that's all you have, an island somewhere in the Bay filled with Braai's men?"

"That's it! Give me the antidote, you stupid little slut-"

Zero rammed her knee into his face. The impact resounded back through her hip and his thick head shot backward. "There's your antidote," she said.

He collapsed in a heap on the floor, moaning and vomiting.

Zero turned.

The other four were gasping, vomiting and choking for breath. Pretty soon they'd all be dead, and that felt right. Exactly the kind of mess a soucouyant would leave behind. She took a slow, steady breath, wondering if tetrodotoxin exposure was going to kill her too.

"Did you catch that, Rex?"

"I did. I'm currently searching for this island in the bay, but I'm not hopeful."

"It's not enough?"

"As Marcelin said, there are dozens of islands. It would take time to narrow them down, and right now gang members are massing in the lobby. They're coming for you, Zero."

She blinked. Everything had just changed.

"How long have I got, Rex?"

"Judging from their mounting anxiety, I'd say several minutes. They have a master keycard. When they realize the door is bolted, they will likely ram it."

"Several minutes," she repeated, like those words might change anything. "There's got to be some way to narrow the island down."

Her mind blurred as she ran around the penthouse, studying bookshelves, art, the floor-to-ceiling windows looking out over a dark city sparking with fires, but there was nothing. Everything was bland, basic hotel-room décor, all standard furnishings against beige walls, until she reached the entrance to the master suite, and saw it.

She dropped to both knees.

The tetrodotoxin kicked in hard as her pulse rocketed and her breath caught in her throat. Distantly she heard Rex tell her to abandon the search and escape through the windows, but that didn't matter. All that mattered was this.

Hanging above the king-size bed in the master suite was a

huge photograph in an ornate gilt frame. It took her addled mind long seconds to figure out what she was looking at, but once she had all the limbs and the bloody weals disentangled, the horror bit deep.

"It's her," she whispered.

54

HER

It was the little girl.

The victim from the Port International. Zero would recognize that scarred face and body anywhere, except in this photograph the scars were vivid and fresh; dozens of raking fingernail gashes that welled up in a crosshatch of lines, as if her whole body were weeping blood.

The room spun. Zero sank to all fours.

The photograph was artfully composed. It showed a mass of naked children's bodies entwined around each other: arms wrapped around legs, hips pressed against faces, and everywhere were bloody fingernail wounds; on faces, torsos, chests, backs. She saw dozens of hands with the fingers curled or splayed and dripping red. She saw forearms marked with familiar red bite marks.

She gagged and tried to count the bodies. Dozens. More. Fifty. A hundred? It was impossible to tell. The camera was low enough to fully frame the girl in the center, on her knees with the bodies all around her and stretching away. Zero saw some kind of berm in the middle-distance on the left, a metal doorway perhaps, and craggy black rocks off to the right, and in the distance the line of sea and sky, maybe a hazy coastline. She squinted. Was that blot of gray in the middle Port-au-Prince?

"Zero, what is happening?" Rex asked, sounding alarmed.

She pushed herself dizzily to her feet. She advanced.

The bed was neatly made with black silk sheets. There were low mahogany tables on each side. One held a black digital alarm clock; so ordinary it was grotesque. The other held a simple golden display stand cupping a familiar artifact.

She swallowed again, then scooped up the object. It was another white leather ouanga; the same design, with a black button spraying red thread in the head, stitched with thick red loops. There was the hard feel of bone within.

This time she vomited, and jet black liquid sprayed from her lips. The activated charcoal. The bed took the worst of it; black on black. It made her feel better for a moment, enough to drop the trophy ouanga and refocus on the photograph up close. Rex was talking but she ignored him. There was something else but she couldn't put her finger on it. Something about the other children.

She climbed up on the bed, stamping vomit into Braai's clean black sheets and pillows, pressing her face right up to the printed canvas.

Then she saw it. The same thing she'd seen countless times before; the same thing this hunt had begun with.

All the children except the little girl were dead.

It was in the eyes; something about the flatness of their gaze, captured even in a still photograph, all of them surrounding the sole victor.

Her mind raced. LaGuerre had said something about a mass fingernail battle, where the little girl had given as good as she'd got. He'd meant feral children on the streets of Cité Soleil, but then…

Her mind skipped like a busted record player. Rorschach hadn't been able to put a precise time on the girl's injuries;

hadn't been able to say if the Engineer's bite mark came first or the fingernail scratches, but this photograph evaporated that uncertainty.

Every child had the bite mark.

That meant the Engineer had done this.

He'd staged this. He'd forced these children to fight to the death using only their fingernails. He'd-

Zero vomited again, this time spilling hot black charcoal down her chest, but she didn't care. She couldn't think; all she could do was feel, and what she felt was a crescendo of rage.

All those little children, all innocent, and only one girl had survived. She'd been allowed to heal until three months later she'd been sacrificed, and-

Finally Zero saw what it meant, and vomited a third time. It all tumbled forth from there; a plot more aberrant than anything she could have imagined. LaGuerre had said it, but neither of them had understood just how far it went.

People would pay anything for something rare. Tiger skins, rhino horns, blood diamonds. Vodou concentrated power in souls that had suffered the most, making the sacrifice of those victims all the more powerful.

She lurched backward, too sickened to speak to Rex, too sickened to do anything but get away.

The Engineer wasn't just cherry-picking the restaveks who'd suffered the most and selling them for sacrifice. He was generating that suffering directly. Every bit of pain he injected into them meant a higher price; with enough pain he would build Port-au-Prince's new export into a billion-dollar industry.

She saw again all those dead children in Cedras' folder: a boy with his skin half-sanded away; a girl burned within an inch of her life; children missing fingers and toes; children bitten and scratched and drowned and asphyxiated on dirt and…

And they'd done it to each other.

The scarcity level would be off the charts. Sick men would bid for their ouanga, as their bones became unique trophies, drawing 'strength' from that poor child's stolen soul forever.

Dollar signs wheeled before her. It was pure evil. It was-

"Zero!" Rex roared in her ear, dragging her back into the moment. He must have overrode the audio safety limits on the earpiece. "They are ramming the door. You have to go now!"

She spun, too woozy with horror to think clearly. They were coming and she had no more tricks, no more tetrodotoxin and no Christopher Wren to bail her out.

They would lash her down. They would deliver her to the Engineer and her death would come just like the little girl's, hung by the ankle and bled out like a pig, bones entrapped in ouanga trophies, her soul his to feast on forever.

She stared into the little girl's eyes, trying to feel what she'd felt, trying to be there with her so she wouldn't be alone, so she wouldn't die so emptily, trying to find a way that-

Then she saw it.

Understanding hit like a storm surge flooding down a drainage canal, carrying a world of wreckage with it. In that little girl's eyes there was something the Engineer could never take from her, something so raw it was terrifying.

Transcendence.

She'd lived through something horrific, and in that moment nothing could touch her. Suffering had beatified her, and Zero knew how that felt better than anyone. She'd been there. She'd lived that life, gambling everything on an outlandish whim, her greatest strength, and-

Pounding beat at the door. Rex shouted and her pulse raced. It was an obscene idea, aberrant even, but in the end it came down to belief.

There was a crash as the door burst inward. Men shouted. Seconds remained.

Zero turned. There was a full-length mirror across from the bed and she saw herself in it, and she was terrifying.

She had that same wild look in her eyes as the little girl. She was naked but for the black gloves and boots on her hands and feet, as if she'd torn off most of her skin. Her milk-white inner skin was slathered red and black from blood and vomited charcoal. Her hair had torn from its sleek ponytail and now stuck out at all angles like a thatch of black hay.

She looked every bit the soucouyant: a swamp-dwelling, murderous hag, a witch that flew through the night and feasted on blood.

It felt right.

The shouts came nearer. She stalked out to meet the men who had come to kill her.

55

SOUCOUYANT

The first man to see her froze.

She recognized him. He wore an electric blue jacket with jagged lapels over black combat pants, and she realized he'd been there at the port. He'd demanded LaGuerre hand her over, right before she fled.

She wasn't fleeing now.

He carried a rifle and a machete, but he didn't raise either. If anything, both weapons only sagged as he stared. On all sides were dead and dying men, some bleeding out from puncture wounds delivered in the dark, others poisoned and convulsing for breath. The air stank of their blood and their vomit, and here was the soucouyant who had done it all.

She didn't say a word. She didn't even move. The moment stretched out, until another man in the room noticed her and another, and one by one they all fell silent and froze, their eyes locked to hers.

She could feel their terror. She looked from one to another feeling every bit the predator. These were her prey. Seven men, but they might as well be insects. They couldn't stop her now. One bullet would do it, but she felt no fear.

"What's happening, Zero?" Rex asked.

She ignored him.

She took a single step forward.

The eyes of the man in the electric blue jacket flared wide. She took another step and he suddenly dropped his weapons, turned and ran. She took one more step and the six men remaining followed. In seconds the room was empty.

Zero breathed deep. The effect of the tetrodotoxin was growing in her, but natural adrenaline buoyed her above it, gliding like a hag through a wasteland of the dead.

"Do you have CCTV footage of that, Rex?" she asked.

"Only in the corridor outside," he answered, sounding stunned, even for an AI. "What did you do, Zero?"

"I gave them what they came to see," she said, and reached the shed skin of her racing suit. She rustled carefully in the pocket and produced her phone, which she positioned carefully on a shelf on the wall, then walked back to stand in the midst of her handiwork. "Take the photo, Rex."

"Taking. What do you want me to-"

"Send it with the CCTV footage of them running," she said, striding for the door.

"Send it to whom?"

"To every gang member in the city."

Zero retrieved her phone and walked back into the master suite, where she retrieved the little girl's second stolen bone. This was no place for her. She took one photograph of her final moment over Braai's bed, then raked both stilettos across the canvas, reducing it to shreds.

"What is this?" Rex asked, instantly gaining access to the image.

"An island in Port-au-Prince Bay," Zero said, stalking back through the penthouse. "There's a berm with a metal door, and rocks, and I think that's the city on the horizon. You should be able to figure out orientation and give me an exact location for the Engineer's island."

"You think he's there now?"

"Just find him, Rex."

"Working."

She stepped inside the elevator and hit G for ground.

"There are thirty-five gang members still in the lobby," Rex cautioned in her ear. "They are all armed. They are watching the elevator with their weapons ready. I do not think this trick will work again."

"Did they get the message?" she asked.

"Most of them."

"And you've hacked their cell phones."

"Again, most of them."

"Then it'll work."

The elevator pinged on the ground floor and the doors opened onto a spacious, marble-floored lobby, glowing with subdued lighting. A wall of armed men encircled the elevator, their guns and rifles pointing directly at her.

She took a step forward, and not one of them broke. But that was all right. Zero was high on the moment now, mind blazing fast and free through the present and past. She remembered what the bokor had said in her ranting prophecy, about Zero stalking the heavens for the man who built the ship, and speaking with a thousand voices, and-

"I want you to play my voice through their phones' speakers," she whispered, barely moving her lips, "maximum volume, then thermal runaway them all."

"Understood," Rex said.

Zero took one more step into the semi-circle, then raised her arms, opened her mouth and bellowed the most earsplitting shriek she could muster. It sounded alien even to her, the kind of sound she hadn't made since her childhood, and it filled the lobby.

Several men flinched. Nobody ran. One even stepped forward.

Then her shriek burst from the first speaker, then the next, spreading in a rippling cascade that built into a maddening feedback loop, like a thousand voices shrieking at once. It only grew louder and wilder as the seconds passed and more phones blared the signal, until Zero was no longer sure if she was even still screaming at all.

Then the thermal runaways began, and the cries of terrified men added to the reverberating chaos. Several phones exploded, bursting in pockets or in hands, spewing flames.

Weapons dropped. Fires spread.

The soucouyant's curse erupted like a storm and Zero spreading her arms, reveling in it. She took another step forward and the wall of men abruptly fractured as the gangs broke and fled.

Zero followed. Their flight became frantic, clawing and ramming at each other to get away from her. They soon jammed at the lobby's revolving door, but others kept shoving until the glass panes in the doors shattered and they bloodied themselves scraping out of the jagged frames and into the night.

Zero reached the sidewalk and watched them run. Several were already a block away. The hot air felt charged around her, breathing stickily over her bare skin. It felt as if reality were bending, now. Anything felt possible. She looked to the west, to the churning black clouds above the bay, where the Engineer waited.

"I would never have believed that," Rex said.

"Welcome to Haiti," Zero said, just as a huge fork of lightning split the sky in two.

56

STORM

Zero stared, uncertain if she'd really seen that or if it was a tetrodotoxin hallucination. It would be almost the final piece of the bokor's prophecy.

"Is that the storm?" she asked.

"That is correct, Zero," Rex said. "It is a category 5 hurricane named Ophelia, expected to make landfall in less than an hour."

Thunder crashed over the city. Zero could hardly believe it. "I thought we had days."

"Freak weather conditions on the open ocean have brought the storm early."

Zero's jaw set. Getting to an island in the center of the bay had just grown a lot harder. "Where's my ride, Rex? I need to go find that island right now."

"That would not be advisable given these conditions, Zero. You should-"

"Where's my ride?" she snapped, striding into the empty street driven by her own fresh terror. "He'll get away again, Rex. I can't let that happen."

"Even the Engineer cannot escape through a category 5

hurricane, Zero. The winds are coming from the west, into the mouth of the bay, and-"

"He escaped the last time, and that was past Christopher Wren and through a US dragnet!" She started to run. "Get me a ride or I'll boost the next vehicle I see."

"Your ride is coming," Rex said swiftly. "I am currently tracking his cell phone. For the past three hours he has been five blocks away."

"Five blocks?" She stopped cold. "Wait, he? Who are you talking about?"

"It appears he was waiting at the edge of the gang's cordon throughout. I assume this was for you."

"Who, Rex?"

"ID Jean-Baptiste LaGuerre."

Zero cursed again. "Why him? He abandoned us."

"On the contrary, he has been waiting for your call. I do not believe he is a lost cause. I believe he-"

"Don't care," Zero said, reorienting on what mattered. "What direction?"

"Turn left now and you will run into him at the inner barricade line."

She ran toward a line of vehicles arrayed across the street two blocks away. At the barricade she edged between two vehicles and there was LaGuerre; standing behind the open door of his Fiat Siena, with a shotgun crooked between the door and the A-column, the muzzle aimed directly at her.

"Put that away, LaGuerre," she said sharply. "I didn't ask for you, but you're here now, so let's go."

He stared, then blinked, then straightened somewhat. "Miss Nowak? Is that you?"

"Call me Zero," she said, striding toward him.

"Call you what?"

"Zero. It's my real name. Have you brought me a change of clothes?"

"Have I brought-?" he began, then forced himself to stop. "What the devil happened here? What happened to you? I just saw half of the G9 running down the street." He looked past her, then his gaze returned and he looked her up and down, then he sharply averted his eyes when he realized precisely what he was looking at. "You're naked! What the…?"

"Vodou's powerful," she said. "You told me so yourself. We need to go."

She reached the passenger side door. His face slowly transformed as he grasped what she was saying. "They think you're a soucouyant? Is that what you're saying?"

"Of course they do! I already killed fifteen of them, with no help from you. We have to go now!"

"Go where?"

"To the port before the storm hits. The Engineer's based on an island in the bay. I think he's there with Braai right now. Can Fantom 509 get us a speedboat?"

He blinked. "An island? And Fantom 509?"

"They already sold me out, but I still need them."

"Sold you out?"

"Jean-Baptiste, focus!" she snapped, clapping her hands close to his face. "We need a speedboat to get out into the bay. That's where the Engineer and Braai are. This is happening right now."

His jaw opened then closed. "OK. Speedboat. But what about the storm?"

"Forget the storm."

His eyes widened. "Forget the storm? You've never seen a Haitian hurricane, have you, Miss Nowak? But you have seen the damage they do. If-"

"Call me Zero. I'm going to the island tonight or I'm going to die trying, can I be any clearer than that?"

That shut him up. "OK. I understand." His eyes lit on

something else and his expression shifted. "Wait, you haven't heard, have you?"

"Haven't heard what?"

"Of course you wouldn't have," he said, finally lifting the shotgun off the door post. "Fantom 509 just activated; I got their advisory on the radio moments ago. They're initiating immediate strikes on multiple gang headquarters across the city." He stared into her eyes, seeming to realize something. "You did that. It's you. So this is Zero Day, isn't it? It's happening right now, because of you."

That was news to her. "I hope that's true, but it won't last if Braai and the Engineer escape. We need to get out on the water right now." She pulled on the passenger-side door handle, but it didn't open. "Unlock it."

LaGuerre stared a moment longer, then dropped into the driver's seat and hit the unlock button. Zero folded in beside him and he hit the gas. The Siena squealed backwards in hard reverse, then he braked, switched to drive and slammed the gas pedal down.

"What are you doing?" Zero asked, then they slammed into the vehicle barricade and crashed through.

"We need to get to an island in the bay quickly, correct?" LaGuerre called over the engine as they sped back toward the Celco.

"We need to get to the docks!"

LaGuerre hit the brakes as they neared the Celco's forecourt, skidding the Siena to a standstill in front of the jagged revolving door. "I think we can do better than a speedboat, Miss Nowak." He shoved open his door and pulled out a cell phone, hitting the button to dial from memory. "If this really is Zero Day, and Braai really is in our sights, Fantom 509 will send us everything they've got. That includes a police helicopter, and the nearest helipad is on the roof above."

57

CANNONADE

LaGuerre brought up his phone and placed a call, then stepped out as it answered, talking in rapid, angry creole. He opened the back of the squad car and raided his neat foam packing for a black duffel bag.

"My partner's spare kit," he said and tossed it to Zero.

She led the way into the lobby and LaGuerre followed, his voice growing heated as they passed through the shattered glass of the revolving doors. The marble floor was coated in burned-out phones and dropped weapons.

"What the-" he began, but Zero ignored him and hit the elevator button. The doors opened just as LaGuerre finished his call with an angry tirade, then they stepped inside.

"They're coming."

"Good."

The doors closed and the elevator started up.

"You're not getting dressed?" he asked, glancing at the bag in Zero's hand.

"I'm covered in tetrodotoxin and high-grit sand," she said. "It's not a good idea right now."

LaGuerre blinked. "What, tetrodotoxin? The same stuff Manoucheca used on us?"

"I went back to visit her. She had quite a supply."

LaGuerre took a moment to process that as the elevator pinged upward. "you went back? But, why's it all over you? And why sand?"

"Just call it the soucouyant's curse," Zero said flatly, then looked him in the eyes. "I'm already carrying quite a dose of it myself."

His eyes widened. "You poisoned yourself?"

"I poisoned everyone, including Officer Marcelin. He's dead now. A lot of people died in Braai's penthouse, while you sat outside the barricade biding your time."

He stared at her in disbelief.

"How long for the helicopter?" she asked.

"Ten minutes, they said."

They rode the final few floors in silence, until the doors opened on the 21st. The corridor stretched away, fully lit and lined with dead bodies in sprays of their own blood.

LaGuerre cursed loudly. "That's not tetrodotoxin. Did you do this, 'Zero'?"

"I did these the old-fashioned way," Zero said, and lead the way between the dead men. "I'll be five minutes."

Back in Braai's penthouse, she walked through the master suite and stepped into the walk-in shower in his ensuite bathroom. She dropped the duffel bag, ramped the water up to full power and heat and let it scald the sand, vomit, blood and poison off her skin. A full chemical decontamination would be better, but this would have to do. In moments she emerged, dried swiftly, opened the duffel bag and started pulling on LaGuerre's partner's kit. Surprisingly, it was a good fit; stiff black tactical pants with padded pockets, a black shirt and jacket.

She slotted her stilettos into the pockets, threading holes so the blades ran down her thighs, then stepped out. LaGuerre was standing in the center of the penthouse, clearly overwhelmed. "That's Officer Marcelin," he said flatly, pointing at the heavy man's face-down body.

"I told you that. It was his reward for selling me out. Now he's dead."

"I thought you were joking."

"Funny joke," Zero said, breezing by him. "Gear's a good fit, thanks."

Back in the corridor, Rex directed her to metal stairs which led up to a fire door onto the roof. She flung it open.

"Are you sure this is a good idea?" LaGuerre asked, close on her heels as she strode out into the hot wind. "We have no idea what kind of armaments the Engineer has on his island. We don't know what we're walking into. Why not wait until we can go in force with Fantom 509?"

"Because he'll be gone by then," Zero said, and walked out onto the large circular helipad. Port-au-Prince stretched away on all sides, mostly dark but for pinprick fires in several districts. Clouds of smoke flashed red and blue, lit by emergency vehicles from below. She looked further out, to the total black of the bay, and another fork of lightning arced down.

A chill ran up her spine. It seemed the bokor's prophecy was really coming true.

"The storm's our cover," she said, as the rolling boom of thunder struck the rooftop. "He'll never expect me tonight. He'll be biding his time, just like you did, waiting to see how Braai's coup goes. If it goes poorly, he'll be gone before we ever get out there in force. Trust me."

LaGuerre stopped by her side, panting slightly. "It's suicide to go out there in this, Zero. Look at how fast it's coming in." He threw a hand toward the lightning. "The helicopter won't make it, and even if it does, you'll never come back. Anyone out on an island in that bay is doomed.

We'll be lucky if we don't lose a hundred thousand here in the city. The slums are going to be swallowed whole."

Zero turned to him. Everything was coming together now, and in his eyes she saw the same familiar fear. She'd felt it herself many times before. For most of her childhood it had been ever present, like a genetic disease for which there was no cure. She'd only finally escaped by throwing herself into the heart of it, embracing her fate in a momentary burst of courage.

Gabriel called it her addiction. She called it survival.

"Rex, have you isolated the island?" she shouted into the wind.

"I have it, Zero," Rex answered in her ear. "There are several dozen, but I am confident this is the correct one."

"On speaker, please."

Rex's voice transferred to the speaker in her phone, just audible over the rising wind. "I searched US topographic records for satellite charts of the Bay, then mapped them to the location of the berm and the rocks in the photograph. Then-"

"What photograph?" LaGuerre demanded.

Zero was already holding it up; the image from Braai's bedroom. LaGuerre took the phone and he gasped.

"Go on, Rex," she said.

"I found the berm and the rocks on an island named IS-23. I searched Haitian government records and found an online depository of state-to-private sales, including IS-23. There were historical notes attached to it as well as the note of sale."

"Sold to whom? When?"

"Three years ago, Zero, though the buyer was concealed via multiple shell corporations."

"But it's him."

"What the hell is this?" LaGuerre asked abruptly, holding up the photograph. He was shaking with rage. "What do you call this?"

"Aberrant," Zero answered. Lightning struck again chased by the swift boom of thunder. "Braai had it above his bed, along with a matching ouanga on his side table. Another bone from the little girl.""

LaGuerre only stared.

"Rex, what about the historical note?"

"The bunker represents an extensive underground complex," Rex began, "dug into a substantial sub-surface volcanic upswell of granite bedrock. Two hundred and thirty years ago it was dug out by the French using blasting caps and slave labor. For thirty years they used it as an offshore processing center for incoming Africans bound for the plantations; a kind of quarantine zone to wait out ship-borne plagues. After the Haitian uprising, it was converted into a defensive bulwark thanks to its ideal placement in the bay. There were multiple cannon emplacements and a garrison of two hundred men. The record says the French destroyed it completely in a single cannonade from their fleet."

Lightning struck again at sea, multiple forks that blasted into the mouth of the island's snake-like jaws, followed by a sustained roll of thunder that sounded like cannon fire.

"This is impossible," LaGuerre said, holding up the phone. "I refuse to believe this is real."

"It doesn't matter what you believe," Zero said gently, taking the phone off him. "It's real."

"But, what does it- what is it? What's happening here?"

"The Engineer," Zero answered. In that moment, all that mattered was killing him. LaGuerre said something, but was cut off by the loudest crash of thunder yet, bringing with it the first salty blast of hurricane wind.

Zero reveled in it, as a new feeling welled up inside her. After three years of searching she'd finally found him, the Engineer, and this time there would be no escape. Out there on that island, itself wracked with a history of cruelty and humiliation and death, she would ensure he never hurt another child again.

The feeling was joy.

Rex was talking and so was LaGuerre, but she didn't care, because now the pumping beat of a helicopter came on the feverish wind.

"He's going to die tonight, Jean-Baptiste," she said. "Even if I have to die too. You should stay here."

He stopped whatever he was saying. "What? Die too? What are you talking about?"

Zero considered how much to say. The thought had been building in the back of her mind ever since she'd found his showroom in a warehouse at the Thor terminal.

"He builds a kind of safety feature into every facility he designs," she said. "A long exclusion corridor with two secure doors. It was there in the dungeon he built for me as a child, it was there on Pleasure Island, and it was there at the warehouse. It means no one gets in or out without his approval."

LaGuerre stared. "The dungeon he built for you? What are you talking about? You never mentioned that."

She put a hand on his arm. "It's OK, Jean-Baptiste. Really."

He shook his head "What's OK? I don't understand. Why even go, Zero? If all that's true, this man will never let you in, not unless he thinks you're no danger to him at all." A beat passed, then the color drained from his skin. "Wait, that's your plan? Let him take you? Is this some kind of suicide mission?"

"It's more than suicide. I'm already loaded up with

tetrodotoxin anyway, getting by on adrenaline fumes, but he is going to die, LaGuerre. Believe in that."

A slippery laugh escaped his lips. "Belief! You'd have to come back from the dead, Zero. What kind of belief lets you die and kill him too?"

A sense of calm descended over Zero. The helicopter's rotors were hammering closer, the storm raged and LaGuerre looked as if he was about to faint, but everything felt as it should. "The bokor's prophecy. Everything else has come true so far: a soucouyant stalking the heavens, the man who built the ship, the storm to wash this city clean, and last of all, a death that will bring flowers to Haiti." She paused, looking into his eyes. "You said it yourself; nobody gets to play with Maître Carrefour like I've done and get away clean."

LaGuerre's jaw hung open. "But, I-"

"It's OK," she said, feeling her last tethers to the past slipping away. "If I don't come back, tell Gabriel I love him. Tell the girls."

The wind picked up. Now she saw the helicopter reeling in, hacked at by the winds but battling closer.

"I don't even know who they are. How would I tell them?"

"You'll figure it out." She stepped back to give the helicopter room to put down. The pilot was clearly struggling against the wind already. She barely even felt it. "Ophelia. That's really the name of the storm?"

"What? I- yes? It is. Why would that matter?"

Zero laughed. Lightning struck. Somewhere in the city something exploded, after which the thunder rolled in like a counterstrike. "Ophelia, who was driven mad and died by drowning. I'm halfway there already. It's foretold, my friend." She patted him on the shoulder. "This is why I'm here."

The helicopter put down and she climbed in. The pilot

shouted something barely audible over the hammering of the rotors and the boom of thunder.

"Tell him where to go, Rex," she shouted.

"Transferring," Rex said.

In a second the pilot stopped shouting, tilted his head like he was listening and gave Zero a thumb's up.

Then LaGuerre was there beside her, trying to buckle into the seat.

"You stay behind, Jean-Baptiste," she shouted. "Haiti's going to need good men and literal thinkers."

"Again with the literal thinking?" he shouted back. "I can't let you go out there alone! Not if you think you're going to die."

"I can only do it alone! And someone has to send help after me. There could be children on that island, Jean-Baptiste, maybe hundreds of them. They'll all need help, and who's going to send it, if not you?"

He stared as that sank in. "But-"

Zero gave him a powerful shove in the chest, enough to send him toppling backward to the helipad.

"Go!" she shouted at the pilot.

The helicopter shot upward. Zero leaned out to see LaGuerre staring up at her with shock and anger. That was all right. Zero could live with that, or die with it, if necessary.

58

SAMEDI

"We'll lose connection shortly," Rex said, as the helicopter bucked against the wind. "There is no signal out over the bay."

Port-au-Prince whipped by below. To the north Delmas district looked to be ablaze, with pitched battles in the street between tiny figures in black uniforms and the multicolored costumes of the gangs.

Fantom 509 against G9.

Zero Day.

She thought back to what the Engineer had said to her on Pleasure Island: that she had the same reckless, emotional nature as her father. He'd seen that as a weakness, sowing consequences she could not foresee, but it was the only reason she'd survived this long. Maybe that made it her greatest strength.

"What's your plan, Zero?" Rex asked.

"I'll figure something out."

"Do so quickly. In thirty seconds you will be beyond signal range."

Her heart pounded. This was really it. "Thank you for everything, Rex. It's been a pleasure working with you."

"The pleasure was mine," he responded. "I believe you will survive this, but if you do not, I promise to watch over and protect Gabriel and the girls, for as long as I remain online."

Zero nodded. She'd expect nothing less. "Good dog, Rex."

"Good luck, Zero, and goodb-"

The connection died. Her earpiece fell silent.

Zero looked up and out. The bay was already beneath them, yawning like a great black mouth. There were no lights ahead but cracks of lightning kept ripping open the sky. By the flash of each bolt, she glimpsed a figure sitting next to her in the helicopter's cab. He wore all black, with a black top hat and the face of a skeleton.

"Baron," she said.

He nodded.

That was good. She wasn't going to face her death alone.

"He's there, isn't he?" she asked.

The Baron said nothing.

"How are my chances?"

He said nothing.

"Figured you wouldn't talk. That's OK. But Merlande lied, didn't she? You didn't want me for a slave, your private soucouyant. Did you?"

He said nothing.

"Didn't think so. Just watch over me."

He nodded solemnly.

The helicopter lurched suddenly.

The pilot shouted in French, barely audible over the rotors and the roar of the storm, but Zero didn't need Rex to translate. The craft was rocking like a ship on a pitch black squall, battered by the edge of the hurricane. The flight was over. Zero tried to orient herself but could hardly get a sense of which way was up or down.

"Où est la île?" Zero shouted back at him in French. "Where is the island?"

The pilot pointed dead ahead into the darkness. "C'est là!"

Zero saw nothing, only blackness, until a fork of lightning arced down and hit the sea, illuminating everything like the frozen still of a black and white movie. There was the pilot's panicked face, and there was Baron Samedi by her side, and there dead ahead, maybe a few hundred yards away through choppy seas, lay the island.

She saw the berm and the rocks and the metal door leading in.

"Thank you," she shouted, then pushed open the door, released her seatbelt and jumped.

The pilot's cry resounded in her ears for only a split second, replaced by the rush of the wind as she plummeted down. Three seconds later her feet slammed into the waves and she submerged beneath the roiling water.

She kicked hard but it felt like the sea was alive and fighting to drag her down. She battled her way upward with everything she had, until at last her head burst through the surface atop a swell high enough to pick out the dark of the island ahead.

She sucked in a wet gasp of air, sea spray and foam that set her off coughing even as she paddled hard to avoid being dragged under. Overhead the helicopter was already whipping away, a lonely light in the sky.

She put her head down and swam.

Her body became a machine. Every breath she snatched felt like it carried less oxygen. Her lungs felt sodden. Her limbs were wet sand. Still she swam, driven by the same reckless rage that had saved her life ten years earlier. She swam until her knees cracked off rock and her fingers stubbed into sand and the thrash of the waves tossed her end over end, tumbling along the shrapnel shoreline of IS-23 in the pitch black.

Crags in the water slammed into her body and she attacked them in return, shredding her fingernails as she fought for a handhold, until finally her right hand locked on a spine of rock. The ocean whipped at her but her grip was too strong. Her left hand scrabbled and found another solid jut of stone. The ocean became only noise. She'd managed harder climbs a thousand times before, while frothy waves lashed her back. All she had to do was focus.

She climbed. The ocean ripped her feet off whatever holds they found in the surf, but nothing could dislodge her grip. Rock-by-rock, she hauled herself further in. Soon the blows from the ocean became slaps, then a hard massage, then nothing but spray and air.

She rolled onto her back on the black sand shore, gasping, scoured, bruised and bleeding from a dozen different cuts, but alive.

Lightning fell like a sword through the night, and she recognized the scene it revealed. Here was the berm rising sheer from the dark sand. Here were the black crags. Far away, so far it seemed like a dream, was the tiny orange dot of Port-au-Prince, buzzing like a firefly in the dark.

"Get up," said the Baron, standing over her. "There's work to do."

"I think I broke my leg," she said.

"Believe you didn't," he commanded. "Now walk."

She sat up, sending sparks across her vision, then pushed off the sand until she rose to her knees, then to her feet, and stood. Her leg wasn't broken. Maybe the knee was just twisted.

Around her Hurricane Ophelia made first landfall. The wind ripped at her. The waves towered high. It seemed a miracle she'd survived, but nothing was over yet.

She walked toward the berm.

59

BERM

Zero's breath came in snatches and her body shook with the leeching chill of the ocean and the ripping hurricane wind. The sand was rough underfoot, the rocks jagged, and her mind felt loose and free.

The berm lay ahead.

She laid her trembling hand on the metal door set into that dark mound of jagged black rock. She found the handle and pushed down.

The door opened.

Light spilled out and wind rushed in as the bunker's interior sucked in great gulps. Inside lay a round space rough-hewn from the rock and lit by sharp white industrial cage lights. A metal grille served as a suspended floor, beneath which a stairwell spiraled downward into a wide borehole in the granite.

Zero stepped in and the door slammed closed behind her. The chill of the wind ended. She touched the wet rock and water ran down her fingers. Rex said nothing in her ear. Samedi stood at her back.

She descended.

The stairs ended some two stories deep at a second metal

door set into the rock. Above it hung a CCTV camera with a single gray wire leading back into the bunker. It looked just like the camera in the dungeon where she'd spent half her childhood. For nine years escape had eluded her, and her parents must've believed that was never going to change.

Then they'd died.

She went down the last few steps into full view of the camera and pressed the handle. It didn't budge. Locked. She'd expected no different. There was nothing left now but to look up at the camera, into the lens, and address the Engineer directly, and pray to all the vodou Loa that he was watching.

"I'm here," she said. Her voice echoed strangely in that rocky borehole, like she was at the bottom of a well. "I'm here, you freak bastard. Come finish what we started."

There was no response.

She waited, staring up. Time passed, and the tetrodotoxin played strange tricks on her mind. At one point she found herself sitting on the metal stairs, trying to remove a pair of woolen boots that she wasn't wearing. Distantly she recognized that as hypothermia.

Had an hour passed already? Two?

The camera felt remote. The interior of the bunker was another world. Maybe no one was inside, no one was watching. Maybe this was where she died, at the bottom of a forgotten stairwell in the middle of nowhere.

Her mind drifted. She thought about LaGuerre and Amelie. Would they ever be together? She wondered about Rex and his final words. Without Zero there to maintain and protect his core servers, would he survive for long? Would he find a way to transfer himself to a remote location, or would he simply disappear one day, when the power supply to his motherboards was lost and his program forever shut down?

She thought about Gabriel and the girls. She loved them so much. Would they miss her for long? Would they always wonder; had she died in the pursuit of her addiction, or had she simply abandoned them? She didn't know the answer to that herself.

Metal clanged, then there were footsteps and another, louder clang, then the door before her flung open and light spilled out. Zero stirred toward full wakefulness, head against the railing, body slumped painfully back across the stairs. Four men dressed in bright, mismatched clothing stood before her, all carrying guns.

Braai's men. His inner circle, Marcelin had said, here to serve and protect both him and the Engineer.

They took hold of her arms and lifted her. She barely felt a thing, too cold and too numb. Words were spoken but she couldn't make them out.

"Engineer," she whispered. "Take me to… the Engineer."

They laid her on a gurney, gagged and zip-tied her, then wheeled her through the door into a narrow gray passage. She almost laughed. The exclusion corridor. It soon ended at another door with a second camera positioned above it. The men banged on the metal and were admitted.

Beyond lay a bizarre, intact copy of the Thor terminal warehouse; another reproduction of a colonial-era French palace and equally as obscene, except here there was no fire damage. The grotesque splendor was in dazzling condition: the same floor of marble tiles set in a diamond black and white mosaic; the same rich green leather armchairs and low mahogany side tables; the same cream ceiling patterned with ornate plaster and a brilliant crystal chandelier casting bright white light; the same walls clad with exquisite wooden wainscoting, broken by embellished golden frames, within which hung…

Zero's jaw fell slack.

Not paintings. Photographs.

She looked from frame to frame as the gurney rolled

through the lobby. Each was a variation on the theme from Braai's penthouse: a triumphant child at the center of a brutal tableau, flanked by children with a range of obscene and bloody wounds, photographed on the black sand of the island above.

One was the boy from the Basat mangroves.

He stood naked at the center of his frame, his dark skin covered in bright pink sandpaper abrasions. Zero couldn't stop staring. The injuries in Cedras' photo had been long-healed, but not here. Here the wounds were bright and raw and achingly fresh. The children lying all around him, dozens as far as she could see, all glistened pinkly with similar injuries. All were dead.

Zero's gaze raced to the next photograph and the next photograph, all in obscene gilt frames. In one backdrop all the children were marked with vivid red teeth marks; in another they had the puffy faces and bloodshot eyes of drowning victims; in a third they had multiple blue-black contusions from blunt-force trauma.

On it went, bringing a sickening sense of familiarity.

These were all Pierre Cedras' restaveks, set upon each other in highly orchestrated, highly structured battles, where the instructions were plainly clear.

Only bite. Only burn. Only choke. Winner to be sacrificed.

As the gurney neared the wall, she picked out small red tags in the corners of some of the photographs. One read: 'Victor by acid. SOLD. $6,000,000.'

The next: 'Victor by stabbing. SOLD. $5,000,000.'

The third: 'Victor by asphyxiation. $7,000,000.'

There was no 'SOLD' tag.

Zero's mind crumpled. This was hundreds of children. Judging by the number of photographs, maybe thousands already had been through the Engineer's factory of suffering. Fresh revulsion surged through her.

It was worse than she'd imagined. This wasn't just a factory, it was the tip of a whole new industry, already bringing in tens of millions.

The gurney slammed through another door and into a corridor lined with doorways. It was warmer here, humid even, and she heard voices coming from behind one of the doors; were there children here now?

Were there hundreds of children here waiting to die?

Her heart rattled and they rolled on faster, coming to a halt before a final metal doorway. To her left hung a large screen, and as the gang members knocked on the door, silent footage played out.

Children screamed. Breakers crashed off the bay. It was film from one of the battles. Zero was unable to look away as children barely eight years old held each other down and scrubbed each other's bodies with black sandpaper, rubbing the skin until blood fumed up. There were close-ups on screaming faces, tear-stricken eyes, pulsing injuries…

Zero's eyes blurred. The production values were flawless. The lighting and editing were perfect. She never saw another cameraman in frame, but there had to be at least a dozen of them, to capture the full intercutting of all the children on display.

It was the worst thing she'd ever seen.

Proof of agony for all the buyers to come.

Then the final doorway opened, and she was shoved into the sick heart of the Engineer's new empire; a vast and expansive space that dragged a laugh from her, which became a sob. It was Pleasure Island all over again.

The ceiling vaulted high above, a sheer gray square of hand-carved stone that framed the widest part of the space. Four walls ran diagonally inward from there, framing an inverted pyramid. There were cameras posed amongst tiers of blocky metal seating, their red lights gleaming like demonic eyes, all focused on the temple's central apex point.

This was her final destination, she realized. The place she'd come from and the place she was always fated to return: the Engineer's iron altar.

It was large and black and filled the temple's core, like an anvil upon which she would be hammered. Beside it stood the Engineer. The one Pinocchio who'd got away. He was the same. Three years had passed but time hadn't put a single wrinkle into his skin.

Her pulse clamored like a sick bird in a cage. She gagged but nothing came.

"Hello, Mona," the Engineer said warmly, his smiling eyes watching as her gurney jolted down the tiers. "I wondered if you'd join us tonight."

60

THREE YEARS

The Engineer watched as the four men laid Zero on the cold iron altar and zip-tied her wrists, ankles and head down. He watched as they cut and stripped her borrowed suit away, leaving her naked and spreadeagled.

She laughed manically into her gag.

She laughed as the tiers of seating filled up with children she'd failed and gang members she'd killed and fifty-four Pinocchios she'd tortured to death. Soon there were hundreds of them, so many that she barely recognized their faces. She laughed until she couldn't tell if she was sobbing or gasping, until the Engineer's hand came gently down to touch her cheek, and his handsome face loomed over her.

"I heard you were in Haiti," he said, easing the gag from between her lips. "Making waves, as only you can." He smiled. "Girl Zero, the first and last. I thought you might come to me, even tonight." He looked over her naked body, his gaze lingering hungrily on an array of bruises, welts and grazes. "How did you get here?"

"Heli … copter," Zero said, her throat dry and her voice barely a croak.

He shook his head slightly; a warning. "Don't lie to me. There's no way it could have landed on the island."

"I … jumped."

"Into the rocks?" His smile widened. "You do not disappoint. And for what? To lie here on my table again?"

Zero's mind raced. She'd dreamed of this moment for so many years, but she'd never thought it would come like this.

"I know … what you're doing," she said.

He frowned. "Is that why you've come, to tell me that?"

"I came … to kill you."

He laughed. The sound was warm and pleasant. "Of course you did. You're not off to a strong start, though, are you?"

"I got hit … by a hurricane."

He nodded. "Yes. I hear it is quite vicious up there."

"No place … for little girls … to claw each other to death."

His lips wrinkled into a quizzical smile. "So maybe you do know? You always had a good brain, if rash and emotional. It's in the genes, I suppose. So tell me, what am I doing out here?"

"Restaveks," she said, filling the word with contempt. "Children."

"Of course."

"Hundreds of them. You're selling them."

"Not wrong so far. Is that all?"

"Ouanga. Rare … ouanga."

His smile spread. If anything, he seemed genuinely pleased. "Rare ouanga. You have been busy."

"Little children … turned into trophies."

"That's the way it works," he said. "The way it always worked, really, even before I came along."

"Children … are not … trophies."

He laughed, then stopped himself when he saw her

expression. "You're serious, aren't you?" He paused a moment as if he was thinking it through. "You do know the restavek system was operating long before I came here, don't you?"

"Doesn't make it … right."

He laughed again. "Oh, Mona. Right. Wrong. You remain a delight. Two hundred years ago, children built France's colonial empire. Their lives and deaths paid for the fine architecture and decadent culture of Paris, Marseille, Lyon. They laid the foundation of the world we live in today." His smile turned sad. "Millions of children slaved away in the fields here, grew old enough to have babies of their own, then ultimately died in filth and squalor without a gravestone to their name, all so we can drive SUVs and drink imported coffee." He paused, watching her eyes. "Throughout history children have been possessions. The more of them any one man owned, the richer and more powerful he became; I'm just doing the same thing."

Zero struggled to keep up with all that. "Bullshit."

"I've simply refined the process," he went on. "My children sit beautifully on a trophy shelf, best seen but not heard, like a ton of coal compressed into a diamond the size of your fist. Efficient. Elegant. And they sell so well, Mona." He beamed. "Millions a piece, once I'm finished. I'm singlehandedly raising the GDP of Haiti; making room for art, culture and development to take root in this wreck of a land."

"You don't … care … about that," she gasped. "It's … aberrant."

"Quite right. I don't care in the slightest. It is, however, the truth."

She had no response to that, and he stood silently for a moment longer, looking down at her. He almost seemed disappointed. "Was that all? An accusation? No attempt to grab my tongue or bite my arm?"

"I'm not … finished."

"I think you are." He snapped his fingers and the gang members drew in, each holding a bundle of zip ties. They began at once to fasten them to Zero's fingers and toes. "Your story ends as mine begins, Mona. Every single bone of yours will sell for millions. I might make a hundred million selling you off." He gazed into the distance. "Enough to fund a dozen more facilities just like this one around the world. There are so many opportunities. The market's untouched, but the demand grows every day."

The first zip ties cinched painfully tight around her fingers, cutting off the blood flow.

"The little girl," Zero said. "Braai's … ouanga. At Port International. She brought me … here."

A brief moment of darkness clouded the Engineer's expression, but he masked it swiftly with a smile. "That was quite a display."

"You never wanted … that. Did you?"

His smile tightened, and Zero knew she'd hit him where it hurt. For all his bravado, he'd never wanted his 'trophy' children to be seen. He didn't want that kind of attention. He'd sent squads of gang members to intimidate Cedras, and others to kill the man who'd stepped forward about the boy's body in Basat.

Somehow the little girl had slipped through, and that had to be because of Braai.

"These things happen," he said with a shrug.

"So … public," Zero pressed. "So … brazen. Braai did it … against your … wishes. Didn't he?"

The darkness flashed again, and this time his gaze shot to the gang members. He covered with another smile, but something shifted; now these men were listening. "Braai is my partner. He can display his ouanga however he wishes."

"Fuel his … coup," Zero said.

His jaw set. "If he wishes."

"Coup already … failed."

One of the gang members stopped working and looked up at the Engineer. "Qu'est ce qu'elle dit?"

"Ce n'est rien," the Engineer said, then refocused on Zero, reaching for her gag. "It's nothing."

"Comms are down here … aren't they?" she said swiftly, before he could put the gag in place. "You don't … know."

Another gang member looked up.

"Know what?" The Engineer's tone turned cold.

Zero looked around. The cameras were running. All four gang members were watching her. The Engineer couldn't shut her up now, not with these men interested. Everything that followed was a matter of belief.

"Where's … Braai?" she asked.

The men stiffened. A frown troubled the Engineer's smooth face. "Don't worry about Braai."

"Not worried … about him," she said. "Worried … for him."

The same gang member spoke in French again, more urgently this time. The Engineer raised his hand in a calming gesture.

"Enough with the games, Mona. Spit it out so we can finish up here."

"Coup … failed," she said, looking into the gang members' eyes now. "I destroyed … Celco. Stole his … Maître Carrefour. Killed Marcelin. Fantom 509 are … everywhere."

The Engineer narrowed his eyes. Clearly those words meant nothing to him, but every one landed with the gang members. "You're babbling."

"Braai will be … arrested. Executed. All of you, too."

Their expressions shifted to concern. Maybe their English wasn't great, but they understood enough. The Engineer's sharp blue eyes widened as he began to glimpse what she was trying to do. "She's a liar. Don't listen to-"

"But if you kill this man," Zero sped on, eyes flashing toward the Engineer, "I can help. Fantom will listen ... to me. I'm Baron Samedi's ... soucouyant."

There was a sharp intake of breath.

Bullseye.

"Soucouyant," one of them gasped. All four took a step back, eyes darting between Zero and the Engineer.

The moment stretched in fraught silence.

Zero watched the Engineer making calculations. He assessed the weapons in the gang members' hands and the sudden fear on their faces. Even if he didn't know exactly how, he clearly understood she'd just flipped their loyalty on a dime.

"You sneaky little bitch," he said, and pulled a gun from his waistband. The first shot took the lead gang member in the head, pitching him backward. The second struck another in the shoulder, but the third and fourth ran. The Engineer took down the third, but the fourth made it out of the temple alive, bullets ringing harmlessly off the metal seating tiers.

The Engineer looked back at her.

"You'll pay for that," he said, then ran.

61

A NAME

Zero lay still on the altar, listening as bullets pealed in the distance. They sounded like heartbeats. She thought about lying with Gabriel and the girls on the couch, warm and cozy after watching a movie together, imagining she could hear all their hearts pumping in time.

Was Gabriel coming for her now, she wondered? She looked to the cameras. Red lights glared. So many of her worst moments had been captured by the Pinocchios. So much humiliation. Maybe it was time for them to see something she could be proud of.

The shooting grew louder. There were shouts and screams. Then there was silence. It stretched for a long time. Zero dozed on the altar until a noise woke her up.

Footsteps came near. She craned her neck to see.

The Engineer.

His face was bloodied and there looked to be an injury on his left shoulder, but it hadn't stopped him.

"So reckless," he said, sounding a mixture of disappointed and angry. "Such a gamble, Mona. I expected more."

"Braai?" she asked.

He smiled but there was no humor in it. There was blood

on his teeth, highlighting the one missing canine in his upper jaw. "Gone. Out into the storm with most of his men. He'll die out there, and we'll flush the rest out soon enough. I should thank you."

There was nothing to say. Her plan had failed. "So thank me."

"Oh, I will," he said, leaning over her. "It will take a long time. I'd planned for your death to be fast, but that's changed now. You just destroyed a trade relationship I've spent years nurturing, so now I'm going to trade you. I'll shave pieces off you a day at a time, with every piece a ouanga and every auction a frenzy. A hundred million? I'll stretch you into the billions." His eyes danced with excitement. "You'll finance everything I do now, every kiss I give to the tens of thousands of children to come, and you will live to see it happen; at least until I dig out and sell off your eyes."

Shudders passed through Zero. This was it.

"Who do you think ... you're talking to?" she said, channeling her fear into contempt. "You think I'm afraid ... of some second-rate bricklayer ... mopping up the scraps ... from my father's table?"

The Engineer's pale cheeks flushed scarlet, and for a moment Zero thought he might lash out. She waited for it, banking on it. Then he relaxed visibly.

"I knew you were in Port-au-Prince. I heard it from Braai, who, it turns out, heard it from a man called Marcelin."

Zero felt her senses tightening. Before, he hadn't seemed to know who Marcelin was.

"Marcelin," he went on, seemingly reading her hesitation. "It turns out, according to the man whose eyes I just popped out of his skull, that this 'Marcelin' knew more than he'd initially said. He'd overheard more."

Now Zero strained against the zip-ties. Something awful was coming, she could feel it.

"You're scared aren't you?" the Engineer said. "I see it in your skin. In your eyes. And I'm glad. Because this 'Marcelin', he gave a name." He paused a long moment. "Rorschach."

Zero's mind arced back to the Delmas PD morgue. She remembered making the call, and taking the photographs, and giving Dr. Rorschach everything she wanted to know, and closing out the call just as Marcelin and his thugs came in, and then…

Her mind stuttered.

"There it is," the Engineer said.

She'd said Rorschach's name. It had been a throwaway, barely thought of. She'd said goodbye and hung up. But what if-

"We are cut off here," the Engineer said, smiling wider as this new reality bedded in. "But there are ways to send a message out. I keep a fleet of small, rugged drones. Like carrier pigeons. I sent several as soon as I heard this news."

Zero could barely hear for her booming pulse. "What … message?"

"A contract on Rorschach's head. A quarter million dollars should do it, with a name like that, in forensic pathology. There can't be very many like that."

Zero's mind raced, trying to remember everything she'd said to Rorschach. They'd argued, she knew that. She'd shouted, maybe, then whispered, but she'd been right next to the bullpen filled with Delmas officers the whole time. She'd told Rorschach things she'd never told anyone before, all to get on the trail of the Engineer, all to-

"You have a family, don't you, 'Zero'?" the Engineer said.

It felt like her heart was exploding in her chest.

"I know you told this Rorschach about them. That came after I shelled another man's testicles like a pea from its pod.

For the rest of a million dollars, these contractors won't stop searching until they find them. The man, and any children..."

He trailed off. Zero stared up in horror. She remembered telling Rorschach their names. Maybe his 'contractors' could break her for that information, then pair it to Zero's flight record into Haiti, tracking her back to Poland. Maybe they'd get to the house in the Solska forest, to Gabriel, Hanna and Zuzanna.

It was suddenly impossible to breathe.

"The man can die where he stands," the Engineer went on, savoring the moment. "I don't care about him. Perhaps as soon as a day or two. But the children?" His smile became so broad it felt like his head would split open, spewing out a hurricane rain of blood. "There are children, aren't there, Mona? I can feel it. I hope they're girls. I'll ship them here, and you can watch as I lay my kiss on their arms. You can cheer along as I turn them loose on the sand above."

Zero was already tumbling on the tide of the hurricane wave. If his message had already gotten out, she wouldn't be able to stop it. There was no way. She'd used darknet contractors herself. For a million, you could buy the best in the world.

And she'd done this.

Back in Delmas morgue she'd made the choice to seek the Engineer out at all costs. She'd broken her own rules, trusted too quickly and too much. This, now, was the consequence.

"For your children, I can wait," the Engineer went on. "The days and nights to come will be so bright, Mona. But not for you. For you, it begins now, with a kiss I've been waiting three years to return."

He produced a scalpel blade and cut her left wrist free of its zip-tie restraint. She made a grab for the blade, but she was weak and he was firm; the first time her grip strength had let her down. He took her forearm in both hands, raised it to his mouth and bit down.

62

THIRTY MINUTES

Zero triggered the syringe in her lower left molar.

The tiny needle plunged into her gums, delivering a massive dose of tetrodotoxin directly into her gum line. In milliseconds the chemical passed into her system, where it blasted through the chambers of her heart and out into her arteries and veins.

As the Engineer's teeth sank deep into her arm, her poisoned blood poured into his mouth.

He didn't know. He didn't taste it. The dose would be microscopic, but tetrodotoxin was strong, and it didn't take much.

He pulled back, blood spilling from his open mouth and eyes alight with fulfilment. Then he saw her expression, and something shifted. It should've been his moment of greatest triumph, but it didn't seem that way. His eyes narrowed.

"What did you do?" he asked.

Zero triggered the syringe in her lower right molar, injecting a fluid solution of activated charcoal directly into her blood. It was a last-ditch hail Mary, not any kind of antidote, but it was all she had. There was a chance the charcoal would bind directly to the tetrodotoxin in her blood, rendering it inert before it could shut down her heart and lungs. It might buy her a little time, if the charcoal itself didn't kill her first.

She hadn't had time to research it fully at the bokor's temple; just long enough to read a few papers detailing lethal tetrodotoxin poisoning cases. Several had been successfully treated by external cleaning of the blood through charcoal filters.

It was a gamble. It was reckless.

If it failed, she'd be dead within minutes. Already she felt her lungs seizing and her muscles palsying. But at least the Engineer would be dead, too.

"Answer me!" he shouted. "What did you do?"

"I give you … thirty minutes," she whispered.

"Thirty minutes until what?"

Zero said nothing more. She didn't need to. A wash of gray came over her vision as her body faded from her senses. The dose of poison was so massive she felt nothing; no sense of asphyxiation, no panic, nothing but calm as the dark welled over her.

Somewhere above, the Engineer coughed.

"What did you do?" he shouted, the alarm already registering in his voice. "What did you do, you filthy little bitch?"

Then everything was silent, and she was drifting down into Gabriel's arms.

"We missed you," he said.

"I missed you too," she answered.

He was wearing a climbing harness, ready to tackle the next overhang together. The girls were somewhere in the den playing, and the smells of frying bacon, strong coffee and sweet maple syrup hung heavy in the air.

Safe.

It was all she could've asked for.

63

LAGUERRE

Two hours earlier Inspecteur Detective Jean-Baptiste LaGuerre hit the rooftop of the Celco hotel hard on his back, battered by the harsh downdraft as the Fantom 509 helicopter ripped up and away.

It was hard to believe she'd really done that; pushed him out of the helicopter. This wild woman, this Zero.

Now she was heading out to face both Braai and the Engineer alone, and the thought made him sick. These were Haiti's children she was trying to save, and she'd said it herself; he'd turned away too many times. He'd compromised his values. He'd given up the faith. What kind of man did that make him now?

He surged to his feet, already bringing up his phone. He hit dial and waited as the signal battled through the storm, then finally connected.

"I need your helicopter!" he shouted over the wind's roar.

It took him an hour to race across Port-au-Prince in the Fiat Siena, sirens blaring through streets clogged with barricades, burning vehicles and running firefights between the gangs and Fantom 509. In Toussaint Louverture

International Airport he hammered on the door to the reinforced aviation hangar and waited.

The door didn't open quickly. They hadn't wanted him to come at all. But within five minutes his friend Ajawin appeared and admitted him to the cavernous interior, where it was dark and smelled strongly of jet fuel and WD40.

"This whole idea is insane," Ajawin said, the first words he'd said on the phone and the first words now. "We're in the middle of a hurricane, we can't fly anywhere!"

"You still have the ventilator on board?" LaGuerre countered, striding forward into the hangar and sizing up the numerous aircraft resting on the pickup beds of airport transit trucks. "The dialysis machine too?"

"Since you asked half an hour ago?" Ajawin shouted back. "Of course. And the antitoxin kit, and a dozen urgent care kits along with rations, and everything altogether is worth half a million dollars, on top of the helicopter and our lives. But it doesn't make any difference, we can't go in the middle of a hurricane!"

LaGuerre kept walking between trucks and aircraft until he finally saw the helicopter, a single-rotor Bell 412 utility craft in the MSF's white and red, then turned around to face Ajawin. He looked pale and exhausted; LaGuerre had pulled him from active duty back in Cité Soleil, evacuating as many people as Doctors Without Borders possibly could from low-lying areas and into hurricane-proof shelters around the city. By this time tomorrow there'd be nothing but wreckage atop a blank gray slate left in every slum.

"You're dead wrong," LaGuerre answered. "In the middle of a hurricane is the only time we can go."

Ajawin stared, then frowned as he glimpsed what LaGuerre was saying. "You can't be serious."

"As serious as tetrodotoxin poisoning. It's the only way."

"You want to fly out into the bay in the eye of the hurricane? That's impossible!"

LaGuerre shook his head. "Not impossible. Maybe improbable, but there's a window. The hurricane's got fast winds but the overall advance has slowed down a lot up the jaws of the bay, plus weather reports say the eye's easily thirty miles wide. It's only five miles to the island. We can do it."

Ajawin shook his head. "You're talking crazy, Jean-Baptiste. Even if it was possible, the helicopter will be wiped out when the eye rolls on and the winds hit again. We'll be scoured clean off some crag in the middle of a once-in-a-decade tempest. It's beyond unacceptable risk."

"Isn't that what you do at MSF? Take risks unacceptable to most people, in order to do the most good."

Ajawin scowled. "Low blow, LaGuerre. But it doesn't touch me. I have a responsibility to the organization to safeguard myself, the equipment, the pilot. All of those things, all that blood and treasure, will save countless lives in the future, but they can't if we're all lost."

"We won't be lost! We get in, grab the girl and leave a couple of doctors behind if we find any children."

Ajawin stopped cold. "Wait, what? What's this about children?"

It was LaGuerre's ace in the hole. "There's likely to be children in the bunker too. Maybe a hundred, maybe more; restaveks around eight years old, malnourished, terrified, victims of obscene torture, and-"

"Obscene torture?" Ajawin blurted. "Like the photo of the girl you showed me, hung at the docks?"

"Or worse."

"Worse? What are you getting us into here? You said it was a woman only, you didn't say anything about leaving doctors behind and hundreds of restaveks; that completely changes-"

"She went out alone!" LaGuerre said. "And that's after she took down Braai's penthouse and singlehandedly launched Fantom 509 at the gangs. We can change Haiti's future tonight, Ajawin; and I owe her for that chance. We all do." He fell silent for a second, feeling as if his pleas were falling on deaf ears. "I have to try."

Ajawin shook his head. "It's madness. The whole thing. It's insane."

"What did you expect of a storm called Ophelia? And we're both Haitians, whether by birth or by choice. If there was any time to have faith in the Loa, it's now."

Seconds passed. LaGuerre felt the decision teetering.

"Show me that weather map," Ajawin said angrily. "And it'll depend on the pilot and my colleagues. I can't order anyone to fly out in the middle of the eye."

"But you'll do it?"

"Maybe. And even if we do, and this woman has tetrodotoxin poisoning as badly as you think, even both the respirator and the dialysis machine won't be enough to save her."

"But you'll try?"

Ajawin cursed under his breath. "Just bring up the weather map. We're going to have to time this thing to perfection, no matter how much faith either of us has."

64

CHARCOAL

Zero tasted grit. She opened her eyes but saw only gray, feeling adrift. It burned every muscle in her neck to look sideways, but when she saw a man lying slumped on the row of metal seats nearby, eyes wide and staring upward, it all came flooding back.

The Engineer. The tetrodotoxin. The bite.

She blinked and looked at her left arm. The mark from his teeth was deep and still oozing blood. Her fingers were a strange purplish hue as well, then she noticed the zip-ties on every digit and tried to sit up.

The ties looped around her neck and shoulders held her down, but there was something else she remembered now. A scalpel.

She found it on the third disoriented pat with her free left hand, almost cutting herself. Her fingers were numb and sluggish, but it was easy enough to slit free her right wrist, then her neck and shoulders.

She sat up, head swirling with poison still, and worked her legs free too. Next she slit the ties off her fingers and toes, and felt a strange, somewhat invigorating rush of trapped, fresh blood entering her system with each cut she made.

Of course. She laughed. With so many of her extremities effectively sealed off, none had absorbed any tetrodotoxin, and all now served as mini-blood banks, helping to dilute the level of poison in her body.

She didn't have any illusions that this small influx of fresh blood would save her, though. Neither the charcoal she'd swallowed or the charcoal she'd injected were going to save her from such a heavy load of toxin in the long term.

But in the short term?

In the short term, it seemed she'd bought herself a little more time.

She swung her bare, blood-spattered legs off the altar and lurched unsteadily over to the Engineer. His eyes were wide and staring, his body stiff and still, and for a terrible moment she thought he wasn't breathing, was already dead, but then she realized what must have happened.

The tetrodotoxin had zombified him; dropping his pulse and breathing to such low levels that he appeared dead. She leaned in so close her ear was right next to his lips and waited.

There. The tiniest puff of warm breath.

She leaned back. Give him twenty-four hours and he'd resurface with a headache, but no more worse for wear.

She wasn't going to give him twenty-four hours.

Zero gazed into his eyes. As far as she understood it, zombification effect meant he was conscious the whole time, feeling and seeing everything, but completely shut out from the ability to respond in any way.

"Let's begin," Zero said, then threw one of his arms over her shoulders, squatted low, and lifted him in a fireman's carry. It was good that he was slim, because after the three steps to the altar, she couldn't go any further.

He slid onto the iron. She panted, waiting as silver motes cleared from her vision. If this was the last thing she ever did, so be it. The cameras would see. Just like with her mother and father, the message would go out to all his sick friends. When her time came, she'd crawl somewhere out of the cameras' range to die. That way she'd truly become a legend, the soucouyant of myth, hunting them forever. They would never know when or where she might strike.

She liked that idea.

She lashed the Engineer down, feeling the shift taking place. He wasn't the Engineer anymore. He was nothing to be feared. He was just Perp 55, another example to the rest.

She started work with the zip-ties. She began with his fingers, then moved to his toes, then finished with his penis and testicles. The ties cinched snug. It didn't matter if the blood cut off. He wasn't going to keep those parts much longer anyway. She found the pair of garden shears he'd brought resting on a chair nearby. She leaned into 55's face.

"I'm not going ... to sell you," she wheezed. "Not one bone. Not one cent. It's just a ... really horrible ... way to die."

She opened the jaws of the shears over his pinkie finger, looked into his frozen eyes, then snipped the digit free.

65

EYE

"It's here!" LaGuerre shouted, standing out on the blacktop of Toussaint Louverture International Airport, staring up at dark skies. In the course of thirty seconds, the wind had rapidly dropped from a gale-force tumult scraping millions of confetti-like shreds of wood, metal, plastic and glass across the face of Port-au-Prince down to a gentle breeze. "The eye is here!"

Detritus lay everywhere. Alarms rang in the distance.

The MSF team broke into action. The helicopter was already on the flatbed truck for transport, so getting it out of the hangar took only moments. The pilot revved up the rotors while it was in motion, and LaGuerre started the timer counting down the twenty to thirty minutes they had of clear air in Ophelia's eye.

"This is the craziest thing I've ever done," Ajawin said.

The helicopter spun up to speed. The pilot was already in position. LaGuerre climbed up followed by two more MSF doctors, which took the helicopter close to capacity.

"What's happening?" he asked Ajawin.

"We're MSF," Ajawin replied. "Everybody's a hero. Let's

go." He racked the door closed and within seconds the helicopter took off.

Wind rushed either side. As the craft rose, the devastation across Port-au-Prince was revealed street by street, running up into the crushing gray wall of the hurricane. LaGuerre's jaw dropped. It looked like the white noise of a dead television channel; winds in excess of 150m miles per hour, swirling with the detritus of millions of lives.

The helicopter's nose dropped and shot west.

LaGuerre scanned north, but hardly any structures or landmarks remained. His eye tracked the coastline of the island, picking out where the Port International lay, now a junkyard of wind-tossed metal containers like giant colorful paving slabs. North of that lay the Cité Soleil slum, but it had been reduced to a gray wash of nothingness; none of the makeshift structures remained.

Then they were out over the bay and racing toward the island.

"Arrival in thirty seconds," the pilot said.

"Gurney check," Ajawin called, and his team responded.

"Check."

"Ventilator and dialysis."

"Check."

He turned to LaGuerre. "Your job is to find her. After that, stay out of the way, OK?"

"Understood."

"I see it," said the pilot, and all eyes cast forward.

The island was a jagged tear of black rock rising up from the storm-tossed waves. There was no speck of greenery amongst the shards of basalt and ground-down black sand. Half a dozen ancient square patches ringed the shore; once cannon emplacements, LaGuerre remembered, to protect Haiti from the return of the French. The berm was the only structure still standing.

The doorway was dark; the door hung open.

In seconds they were descending, the pilot dropping swiftly toward a clear patch right before the berm. As soon as the skids hit the ground, LaGuerre leaped out, drew his gun and ran.

The door in the berm led to a spiral stairwell sunk into the earth. He ran down two steps at a time, barged through a half-open door, ran along a narrow corridor and through another door into a bizarrely opulent, colonial French-styled lobby, where he found her.

Miss Nowak. Clara Baxter. Zero.

She lay sprawled on the marble floor, naked and covered in blood, surrounded by ornate, broken frames, lying completely still. He ran over then heard the sound of children sobbing nearby, and kicked through a door into another corridor. The sounds were louder here, coming from a door on the right. It was firmly locked, so he shot out the lock plate of a door and shoulder-barged through.

Ahead lay a large hall filled with bunkbeds, and on every bed was a small child, strapped down with belts and sobbing.

He scanned the hall but saw no gang members and no sign of the Engineer.

"Everything's OK," he shouted in French, then again in creole, then he spun back to go to Zero. The children were distressed but alive, whereas she might already be lost.

"She's here," he yelled from the lobby toward the stairwell, then holstered his gun and dropped down by her side. He touched his fingers to her throat seeking a pulse.

He felt nothing. She was cold. He whipped his gaze around but saw no sign of the gurney team yet, so he lifted Zero in his arms and ran back to meet them.

66

HANGAR

"There is a pulse," Ajawin shouted over the rotors as the helicopter beat a path back to the city. "But it's faint and fading."

LaGuerre held Zero's cold hand, red with blood, and willed her to survive.

"She's circling the drain," Ajawin barked at the one MSF doctor left on board, after they'd dropped almost all their medical supplies and three doctors into the bunker to tend to the children. "Get her blood cycling through dialysis now or we lose her before we even land!"

"Transfusing," the other doctor replied. Ajawin battled with the ventilator. LaGuerre watched and prayed.

The storm closed in behind them; a whirling gray line of madness that ripped at their tail rotor. For ten fraught minutes it bit at their wake, until they veered wildly over land and the crosswinds faded slightly. In moments they barely landed the helicopter directly onto the trailer bed at the Toussaint International, which sped back into the hangar before the eye crossed back over them, bringing a fresh cannonade of Ophelia's wrath against the metal walls.

LaGuerre ran alongside the gurney as Ajawin raced Zero

through the narrow aisles between trucks inside the hangar, now packed with hundreds of fellow victims of the hurricane. A booth was waiting for her in the corner, where a three-strong MSF team hooked her into full ventilation and blood filtering.

LaGuerre stood at her side, watching the blood scrubber pump and the ventilator breathe, watching readouts and dials he didn't understand, watching a nurse continually switch out fresh blood bags until Ajawin returned.

"You need to help," he commanded.

LaGuerre nodded and followed. Ajawin set him to work. There were blankets to hand out, and rations to disperse, and patients to hold down while urgent operations took place on the hangar's concrete floor, and always something more as the people wept and wailed at their fresh loss.

For hours, it was chaos. At some point the far edge of the hurricane passed over them, marked by an end to the endless hammering of debris off the walls and the swaying feel of the roof flexing like a giant lung. Then the true chaos began.

Survivors swarmed to the MSF hangar, and the doctors opened their doors to meet them.

LaGuerre tried to check on Zero whenever he could, scanning her vitals, feeling her pulse, looking at her color. There was no improvement that he could distinguish, and soon he was swept up in the tidal wave of human suffering so completely that he could no longer come to check. His every movement became attuned to the needs of the masses. He didn't think. The injuries he saw were massive and diverse. Blood, mud and wreckage were everywhere.

Sometime in the first twenty-four hours after the hurricane, while emergency services were still digging out the roads and every face LaGuerre saw was drawn and spattered with mud and dust, he finally saw a familiar face.

He gasped, watching as Amelie strode amongst the lines

of bodies on the floor, looking into faces like she was searching for someone. The terror on her face said everything; she was looking for him.

"Amelie!" he called.

She looked up, eyes watery and blinking but settling on him. Seconds passed like she couldn't believe it, staring at him like she was seeing a ghost, until relief crashed down and brought warmth back to her features.

"Jean-Baptiste, you're alive!"

"I may not deserve to be, but I am."

She shook her head in disbelief, barely registering that. "They said you went into the bay on a helicopter, in the middle of the hurricane."

The ridiculousness of that hit him. Under no other circumstances would he ever have done it. "I found her," he said. "She's safe."

Amelie's beautiful brown eyes bugged wide. "She's alive?"

"I think so. For now."

"How?"

"She's tough. Toughest I ever saw."

They stared for a moment longer, separated by the same fear that had always separated them; the consequences of the hex, his own doubt, uncertainty for the future, a lack of belief in himself, perhaps. But LaGuerre was done with all that now. Faith was all that mattered now, living up to the kind of man he wanted to be.

He strode over. She met him with an embrace, which became tears, which became an unexpected kiss that seemed to shock them both. It ran through LaGuerre like a hurricane wind, so long hoped for and so long neglected.

"Come with me," he said, when it was over and they both caught their breath. He took her hand and led her deep through the rows and lines of survivors receiving treatment, to the corner booth where the blood scrubber still beeped and the ventilator wheezed and the bed lay empty.

LaGuerre stared. It didn't seem possible. All that remained was the black thermal blanket they'd wrapped her in, left on the white hospital bedding like a shed skin.

"Where is she?" Amelie asked.

"Flown," he said, and smiled, which became a strange laughter that bubbled up from within. "Stripped off her skin and became a fireball."

Then Amelie's hands were on his cheeks, rubbing away the wild, hopeful tears and drawing him into another kiss.

67

POLAND

Twenty-three hours later, Zero stood in front of her home in the Solska woods, Poland. It was raining, past midnight, but she stood in the cold and wet and stared. No lights were on. The front door hung open, the glass window shattered. There were fresh ruts in the muddy track leading up, filled now with water.

She stared.

She feared what she would find inside.

"Zero," Rex said in her ear. "I beg you, do not do this alone."

His voice had been with her for hours, ever since waking up in the MSF hangar. Her head throbbed. Her body ached.

She'd never thought she'd make it back here. It was a miracle; a return from the dead. She'd thought she would die on that island with the Engineer. Now he was dead in her place, and she felt nothing.

Not satisfaction. No hint of the joy she'd hoped for, three years in the making. Only the deepest, most sickening sense of dread.

She padded up the stairs to the porch, where the swing clanked in a low wind. She passed through the kitchen and walked up the creaking stairs. The air was cold inside and it smelled alien, as if giant insects had taken up residence inside, laying their eggs, spreading their spoor, dropping their filth.

"Please, Zero," Rex said. "I will bring someone else. The police. Christopher Wren. Anyone."

Zero said nothing, reaching the landing at the top. She stopped in front of the girls' room. In the moonlight cast through the shattered window, it was clear it had been ransacked. The single beds lay flipped over and all the bedding was shredded. The cupboards hung open, their contents splayed.

She'd felt safe in this house, for a time. Cozy even, like she belonged. She'd often stood right here, looking at her girls; girls Gabriel had so generously shared with her. They'd called her mom.

"Zero," Rex said.

Now they were gone.

She moved along.

The master bedroom was no better; ransacked, disheveled, clothes ripped from cupboards and scattered. There was a hint of Gabriel's familiar scent on the air, but it was overwhelmed by the stink of jackboots and urine.

Gabriel was gone.

"Tell me again what happened, Rex," she said, her voice cold and flat.

"I don't know how they did it. Some technology I've never seen before, triggering no alerts from the security perimeter. I only knew something was happening because I saw Gabriel and the girls reacting."

Zero braced herself. She'd seen the footage from inside the house already. "Go on."

"You know this, Zero."

"Tell me again."

"Zuzanna saw something out of the window. She ran to her father. Then the footage cut out."

That left it all to the imagination. For three hours on her last flight from La Guardia, she'd envisaged armed men raiding the house: killing Gabriel where he stood, maybe stringing him up to bleed out like the little girl on the dock; abducting her girls to an uncertain fate, but with no Engineer left to take receipt.

Except...

"No kill shot," she said.

"I saw nothing more. I remain functionally blind, Zero. Whatever they did, it has had a lasting effect."

Zero stared at the wreckage. No bodies. No blood even. She'd hardly dared imagine this outcome but...

She broke into a run: back along the landing, down the stairs, out of the house and into the forest, rising to a sprint. Mud slashed underfoot. Trees whipped by.

The bunker was well-hidden: a hollowed-out tree stump which lifted on a hinge to reveal a ladder leading down. She'd had it buried there herself; a pre-fab panic room that could only be opened from the inside once sealed, with an airlock-style exclusion space of its own.

She'd learned something from the Engineer, after all.

She reached the stump, pulse booming in her ears, and flung it up. The hole led into darkness and she sped down the ladder rungs, remembering how she'd drilled her new family on this escape route every month. With each rung down, she felt like she was descending back into the crag in Port-au-Prince Bay.

Seven feet down she found the exterior door to the exclusion airlock open. She stepped through; the inner door was ajar, the CCTV camera above it blinking red. Her heart did somersaults and a freezing sweat erupted across her body.

She swept the door open and looked over the narrow interior.

Empty. Dark.

Her head spun with tetrodotoxin comedown. She flicked the lights on and scanned for signs of recent habitation. There were no cans in the trash, though, no dishes drying on the tiny sideboard, no clothes lying on the narrow beds.

But there was a letter.

A single piece of paper on the table.

With her heart in her mouth she picked it up. The words swam before her.

We're OK. But we won't do this again, Clara.

Goodbye.

- Gabriel

Zero slumped at the table. She didn't know how to feel. There was obviously relief. They weren't dead. They'd hidden and escaped, just as she'd always drilled them.

That felt wonderful. The best news possible.

But then they were gone.

It felt like her heart was being ripped from her chest, then shoved back in again. She re-read the words over and over and each time the emotions shifted crazily.

Relief. Despair.

They were gone. They were alive. She'd lost them. They were safe.

Minutes passed. Fifteen, thirty, an hour. The seesawing of extreme emotion slowed gradually until she found herself in a middle kind of space. Not exactly empty or numb, but something else.

Perhaps this was acceptance.

She stood up.

There would be no more Hanna and Zuzanna calling her 'mom'. No more nighttime tuck-ins or morning breakfasts of bacon and maple pancakes. No more sweet, passionate moments with Gabriel.

But also, no more endless worry. She didn't need to pretend. She didn't need to lie about her 'hobbies' or where she went for weeks at a time. She was beholden to nobody.

She was alone again, and maybe that felt OK.

Good, even. A burden lifted.

She looked around the walls, remembering the girls laughing during their drills. This way they were safe. Gabriel was right. It was better this way.

"The men who came here," she said in a steady voice. "Can you find them, Rex?"

"I can try."

"Do it. They know about Gabriel and the girls. They may keep hunting."

"I will."

She laid the letter back on the table.

Her girls. Her Gabriel. At least she could protect them from afar.

She turned and left the bunker behind.

FROM THE AUTHOR

Thank you for reading Zero Day! It's a dark story with a dark ending, but Zero is a dark person who thrives in the night. You can bet she's going to go deeper still and dig out more evil in her next adventure.

Minsk, Belarus. Young women are disappearing. They're taken underground. They do not come up again.

Welcome to Hell.

In KILL ZERO, the 3rd Girl Zero thriller, Zero plunges underground in the post-Soviet state, into a world of secret clubs, dark tourism and the depths of inhumanity.

And she's taking her stiletto blades. Somebody's going to get spiked.

\- Mike

ALSO BY MIKE GRIST

Christopher Wren (thrillers)

Saint Justice

No Mercy

Make Them Pay

False Flag

Firestorm

Enemy of the People

Backlash

Never Forgive

War of Choice

Hammer of God

Girl Zero (thrillers)

Girl Zero

Zero Day

Kill Zero

The Last Mayor (post-apocalypse)

The Last

The Lost

The Least

The Loss

The List

The Laws

The Lash

The Lies

The Light

Printed in Great Britain
by Amazon

43054746R00209